Praise for Heather Neff's *Blackgammon*

"An impressive debut novel chronicling the lives of two fiercely independent soul sisters who break all the rules to live out their dreams."

—*Essence*

"An epic adventure . . . A journey that is real and mythical, joyful and soul-wrenching, classic and modern . . . The story is powerful enough to leave an impression long after you've put the book down to rest."

—*Black Issues Book Review*

"A lustrous meditation on race, love, sisterhood, success, and life . . . I fell headlong into its exotic world from the moment I began reading it. If you've ever lived outside of the United States—or wondered what it might be like—then *Blackgammon* is a must-read."

—TANANARIVE DUE
Author of *The Black Rose*

Also by Heather Neff

Blackgammon

WISDOM

HEATHER NEFF

ONE WORLD

BALLANTINE BOOKS · NEW YORK

A One World Book
Published by The Random House Ballantine Publishing Group

Copyright © 2002 by Heather Neff

www.ballantinebooks.com/one/

Library of Congress Control Number: 2003090355

ISBN 0-345-44744-1

Cover design by Dreu Pennington-McNeil
Cover painting by Heather Neff

Manufactured in the United States of America

First Hardcover Edition: July 2002
First Trade Paperback Edition: May 2003

10 9 8 7 6 5 4 3 2 1

For Aviva Helena, my Crucian princess
In memory of Bobby Gragg

ACKNOWLEDGMENTS

I had the good fortune to live on St. Croix, the easternmost of the United States Virgin Islands, from 1990 to 1992. Deeply moved by the beauty and history of the island, I painted a portrait of a slave sitting on a boulder high above the Caribbean, staring pensively out to sea. This woman seems to be looking into her ancestral past, born in the waters plied by the ships of the Middle Passage. Yet she is also contemplating a future in which her body, mind, and spirit will be free.

This painting provided me with the imaginative seed that grew into Wisdom. The characters in this novel are purely fictional. I drew background materials and ideas for names from many primary sources, including Neville A. T. Hall's *Slave Society in the Danish West Indies*, and William W. Boyer's *America's Virgin Islands: A History of Human Rights and Wrongs*. The patois phrases spoken by some of the characters were taken from Mary W. Toynbee's *A Visitor's Guide to St. Lucien Patois*.

Many thanks go out to my agent James Wolf, and to my editor at One World, Anita Diggs. I deeply appreciate the assistance of Eastern Michigan University, which granted me a Spring-Summer Leave in order to prepare this manuscript for publication.

I also want to give special recognition to my family: Alma Mayson, Michael Mayson, Marcel and Aviva Neff, who continue to provide me with patient and loving support in my literary endeavors.

Finally, I must extend my deepest gratitude to Tanisha Makeba Bailey, whose love and respect for her home offered me many important insights into the people and culture of St. Croix.

TWENTY-ONE DAYS

Severin roared up out of the sea, his hair a thatched mass of bleached ringlets, his skin broiling as salt met parched flesh. Seagulls screamed overhead, drowning out the voice ripped raw from decades of nicotine and rum. Stretching, reaching desperately toward some lost pocket of lung, he found himself bending double to retch out the last vestiges of meaning in his life, knowing now with absolute certainty that the only thing left to face was his death.

Turning his back to the noon, his craggy face, furrowed with drink and sun and salty wind, looked like that of a long-forgotten hermit. Purple bags of swollen flesh made it impossible to guess the color of his eyes, and his crud-thickened hair, bleached by repeated bathings in the salty sea, had lost any semblance of its natural texture and color.

"Ah, shit," he muttered. "Shit, shit shit shit."

His puckered, lardy brown flesh exuded the ripe undertone of caramel-sweetened alcohol, and when he tried to wade through the surf a knifing pain tore more deeply than ever before into his aching bowels. It would have been difficult for anyone to believe that he was barely thirty-five. That he had once been young, and handsome, and considered intelligent. Even brilliant. Now it seemed clear that his doctor was right. He was going to die.

Far up on a powdery dune lay Tina, watching lazily from beneath a wind-bowed palm tree. Her onyx eyes reflected nothing of the equatorial sun; her left hand brought an overripe star fruit to her unsmiling lips. Shifting heavily, she pressed her hips more deeply into the sand and exhaled in slow impatience. Her gaze fell to her feet, once fine and rosy despite a childhood spent in barefoot abandon, but now swollen white with her own alcoholic dissipation.

"Come, Seven!" she called out, her voice slicing through the battering surf.

Severin turned at her bidding, even as his thoughts swept seaward with the undertow. His eyes searched the horizon, momentarily blinded by the searing meridian light, then finally settled on the figure swathed in a billowing robe.

"Seven," she shrilled, "come now!"

He took a step forward and felt the wet sand suck eagerly at his soles as the waves again claimed his thighs.

Tina began chanting in a soft voice; the atonal notes wafted toward Severin between the swells of the surf.

> *Sweet John him cook the one-legged turkey,*
> *John him eat the one-legged turkey,*
> *Massa ask why the one-legged turkey,*
> *John say so it be . . .*

"Hey, you!" he rasped. "You, Tina—you hear me?"
Her chanting voice swelled louder:

> *John him say the one-legged turkey*
> *He born that way the one-legged turkey*
> *Massa say no one-legged turkey, but—*

"Tina, Tina! You! Singing up there! Come help me, woman!"

She ignored him, her voice lilting defiantly above the sting of the surf.

"I calling you, *Theresa!*" he shouted, using the baptism name that few on the island knew and no one had called her since her father, witnessing a fist-fight she'd had with her brother Carlson, had affectionately begun calling her his "Tiny Tiger." Instantly she had become "Tina," and no one had since dared to use her Christian name.

The song stopped abruptly. He heard a long, sullen whistle as she sucked her teeth. Then her voice began again.

Slowly, painfully, Severin waded out of the water. His torn jeans wedded to his hips, he pulled his hands up along the ballooning flesh of his belly and sloughed the water from his matted chest. Tina looked away in disgust.

"Woman—come help me get me up that hill!"

Severin waited, panting heavily while Tina hoisted herself elegantly to her feet. The two stood facing one another while the woman's robe blew lazily around her ample body. Her buttery brown skin fell loose over the high cheeks that bore witness to the mix of French and African blood she bore from her native St. Lucia. She was still remarkably beautiful.

"You coming to help me?" His rasp had an undercurrent of real desperation.

Tina's hand came up to her hip and she snorted out a laugh. "Get your pasty white self out the water, Seven! I'm gone, *meson!*" Slowly she turned, making her way to the top of the dune. Severin watched her with dismay, feeling the keen struggle for power that had always brought them back together, even when other lovers lured them away. Gathering up his breath, he staggered forward, his body little more than driftwood in the undertow.

Minutes later he found Tina lounging on the front seat of his rusting pickup truck, her leopard-print caftan pulled back to reveal a perfect leg propped up in the frame of the open window. He leaned against the blazing hood, his head moving like an aging dog as he drew in slow and shallow breaths. Slowly and involuntarily his gaze rose up to Wisdom.

The open grave of the ruined house leaped out at him from behind the untended hedges and wild forests of grape trees. The elegant, French-styled double windows that opened to cool, deep rooms were now shuttered with warped, broken jalousies. The patched slate roof sank between skeletal beams that barely held the house together, and even the great stone drive that had once welcomed the governor of the Virgin Islands and the vice president of the United States was now overgrown with stiff weeds. Gaping holes at the window frames welcomed lizards, spiders, and centipedes. The hand-carved woodwork that gracefully latticed the gables was now honeycombed with worms.

He sighed, pulling his trembling gaze away.

"So what game you playing?" Tina asked impatiently as he pulled himself behind the wheel. His stained shirt was encrusted with salt from his skin and hair.

"No game, baby."

"What the doctor tell you, Seven? You acting like he say something new."

"He did," Severin managed as he wrestled with the truck in the deep sand.

"You lying!" she laughed. "Doctor say no more rum and Coke?"

Severin grunted, his face empty as the wheels spun helplessly.

"And he tell you no more pussy!"

"No need for that," he said under his breath, his feet working the useless pedals.

"Don't believe it!" she snorted, digging deep into her caftan for the thin cigars she had smoked since her childhood. "I know you, Seven. You never been long without pussy!"

He grimaced and reached across the seat for the cigar, taking it from Tina's ripe lips and shoving it into his thin mouth. He knew that she was willfully refusing to understand his miserable, aching impotence, and he loved her deeply for it.

"Where you want to go?" he asked her and she rolled her eyes toward the house.

"No food up there?"

He shook his head, lowering his throbbing temple to the scalloped edge of the wheel. She looked away. "Thirsty?"

He barely nodded, finding himself awash in dizziness.

"Well," she announced, "then drive to Christiansted. Don't want nobody from Fredriksted to see you right now."

Gratefully he propelled the truck down the rocky path to Centerline Road, forcing his mind to be one with the vehicle. Tina moved her hips back and forth, as if making the seat conform to her hard buttocks. She found another cigar and lit it with expert ease as the hot wind whirled through the soiled cabin.

Severin had dealt with pain before; dealt with it for many years of his life. This pain was not new—what was new were the words of his doctor, the Canadian doctor who had sent his tests to Miami rather than Puerto Rico for conclusive results. *Severin, I have some very serious news.* It was those words that sent him headlong into the noontime surf, cutting the strength from his softening flesh. *The tests confirm that the cancer has metastasized to other parts of your body.* The words made him seek to drown the remnants of himself in the uncaring waves. *You'll have to refrain from alcohol and cigarettes and other chemical substances.* And now he was glad to force his legs and arms and neck and head into the rusting pickup truck. *I'll give you something to help with the pain, but Severin, I strongly recommend surgery, as soon as possible. . . .*

Liver cancer.

He was glad to have someplace—anyplace—to go. He was glad to comply with Tina's whims. Yes, he would drive her all the way to Christiansted. He would drive her all the way to Point Udall—the easternmost point of the island—if she so desired. At that moment he would have driven this woman to the other end of the world if she had so much as lifted the tip of her smallest finger. Anything to vanquish the doctor's *as soon as possible . . .*

Tina's favorite bar on the East End of the island was located on the poolside patio of a tiny hotel tucked between the main street of the town and the sea. Patrons could sit at one of the wrought-iron tables on the deck facing the water, or choose a barstool at the long counter shaded by an aluminum awning. Most of the hotel rooms were rented by the hour to local residents; few real tourists found their way there. The bar survived, therefore, on the goodwill and regular patronage of

Christiansted's permanent inhabitants. No one ever used the pool, but each and every drinker on the deck watched the sun trace its evening path across the sky and drop into the cobalt Caribbean. This was the famous ritual of Brandy's Bar: waiting for the mythic green flash at the moment when the day became night.

"*Bôzu, sésé*—Hello, sister!" Brandy called out affectionately in St. Lucian patois as Tina made her way through the labyrinth of wrought-iron tables circling the pool.

"Hey, *meson*! Had to drag Seven out the water—he needs his *special* real bad!"

Brandy winked at her friend and ignored Severin's crippled walk toward the counter. "Let's see: Grenadine and pineapple juice with a bit of banana on iced Cruzian Rum," she recited, her graceful arms lifting and lowering the bottles. "And of course, the secret ingredient—" she splashed a squirt of Angostura into the mix.

Nodding, Tina settled on a barstool and took a palm full of peanuts from the glass dish. "*Mwê swèf!* Rum and Coke for me," she said as Severin's tall glass swirled from red to golden to yellow to silvery cool.

"And what you got to say for yourself, Seven?" The barmaid's voice was a warm purr in the afternoon heat.

Severin forced a smile, allowing Brandy's face to filter into his aching consciousness. She was a handsome woman—beautiful in a different way from his longtime lover. Her cinnamon face was peppered with freckles and her narrow Asian eyes looked out from beneath a crown of thick winding braids. Many years earlier both Brandy and Tina's mothers had arrived from St. Lucia with their infant daughters, seeking work and fleeing men who were brutally disinterested in what became of them. They ended up in the workers' shacks built on the edge of the Wisdom estate, harvesting cane while their daughters ran wild, chattering in patois and sharing everything from johnnycakes to centipede stings. They had, at times, even shared lovers.

"I'm hanging, sweetheart," he muttered, turning toward Tina with an automatic gesture. She placed a cigar in his open palm and he slid it into his mouth, unlit.

"Why you so sticky?" the barmaid remarked as her gaze rolled distastefully over his damp clothes.

He looked into Brandy's warm brown eyes. "Salt," he said hoarsely.

She glanced toward Tina, sensing that something was seriously wrong.

"Ki-sa ki wivé i?" she asked her friend, who was staring at Severin's reflection in the mirror behind the bar.

"I se malad."

"Don't start that patois crap!" Severin barked in exasperation. "If you two gonna talk about me, do it in English!"

The women smiled briefly at one another, acknowledging their feelings for this man whom they had both touched, sometimes in love, other times in despair.

"So what he say, the Canadian doctor?" Brandy asked him gently.

"I'm dying," he answered.

"Go on, liar!" Brandy laughed, reaching for a cloth to wipe down the steel counter.

"No lie, Brandy," Severin said, bringing his lips gingerly to the tall glass of juiced rum.

"Dying? As in *dead*?" She looked in wonder from Severin to Tina, whose eyes had never left Severin.

"He lying," Tina asserted firmly. "Doctor want to make him scared, that's all."

Severin opened his mouth then closed it, aware of the women's staring eyes.

"Hey, man—you serious?" Brandy asked again, ignoring Tina. When her question was met with silence she leaned over the bar, her face coming close to Severin's.

For a fleeting moment he looked into her, remembering the nights she had closed the bar early and come with him into one of the hotel rooms. Brandy was clever and passionate by nature, but abandoned by too many of the white men who came to the island and never stayed, she sometimes simply needed someone to hold her. She wanted no more than that; the sex came on the side. Severin had taken her despite knowing the real nature of her need. He believed it was part of the punishment she deserved for crossing that unspoken barrier and entering those same rooms with those men from Stateside. And Severin knew that having sex with him was often the closest thing she could get to a *real* white man, because he was white too—although he was the kind of white produced by a world of abandoned slave plantations on a Caribbean island.

"Seven," she now said in her lover's voice, and he was surprised that Tina pulled herself up from the stool next to his and strolled slowly away. "Seven, you not seriously thinking about going away from us?"

He drank in her troubled gaze, amazed that anyone would really care whether he went on living or not. "Seems I got no choice," he whispered, and he felt her hand as she reached forward and touched his arm. Her warm fingers seemed to galvanize him, and he wished that she would hold him there, safe on that chair, forever.

There was movement beside them. A herd of tourists emerged from the narrow pathway bordering the rooms and stopped on the patio beside the pool, cooing and giggling at the placid scene. They trundled to the wrought-iron tables waiting patiently beneath open patio umbrellas.

Brandy stood straight up, fixing her face into a mask of Caribbean hospitality. Severin swung away from the guests, closing his eyes to avoid his reflection in the mirror behind the counter. He heard the barmaid walk forward; heard the swishing of the lacy Mexican dress she liked to wear. He smelled her perfume of frangipani. He heard her speak to the guests and return shortly with a small sigh. The tourists' voices became a low murmur.

"Have you visited Buck Island?" Brandy called out in a loud voice.

For a moment there was no answer. The tourists hadn't expected any more than the perfunctory servant-customer relationship from the tall black woman in lemon crinoline.

"Ah, no," someone replied. "You can snorkel over there, right?"

A white voice, Severin thought through his pain. Young; maybe late twenties. Secretary. Saved three years for five days in the Caribbean Paradise. Looking for an island lover. A big black lover. Or, failing that, a white West Indian lover. She'd probably have to get pretty drunk, first. Easy enough: rum punch or iced mimosas. Then she'd be very nervous. She'd be wearing some kind of bright satin underthing with wires and lace. She'd want him to tear it off of her. And then she'd be very noisy—and a long time coming. Well, it was too late. He was out of service for such things, now.

"Oh, yes," he heard Brandy say in perfect American. "Wonderful snorkeling on Buck Island. You take the boat over there. Look! The one with the tall masts—" Brandy had assumed the voice of a tour guide, mimicking their bland accent with practiced ease.

"My God, what a beautiful ship!" the secretary exclaimed. From behind his closed lids Severin could imagine her already lifting her camera and trying to focus on the Seajammer from her safe haven beneath the wide umbrella.

"Darn!" he heard her mutter. "I can't quite get it from here. I'll be back, okay?"

He knew that she would walk to the end of the deck, where she'd get a panoramic view of the boat and the sea. Of course, she'd stop just short of Tina, who would be standing like a statue with her back to the bar, obstinately waiting for the whites to leave.

Brandy swooshed past him, taking her heavily laden tray to the table. She unloaded the Mexican beers (for they invariably wanted beer) and returned to her counter.

"How about some peanuts?" Brandy asked the other tourists.

Grumbled answers. She reached beneath the counter, muttering, "Peanuts too good for these American swine," and then stood, raising her voice brightly. "Corn chips? Nachos?"

"Actually," a confident voice said, "I'd like some juice. Passion fruit."

Severin's eyes opened. Not because of the voice, but because of the request. A Statesider who liked passion fruit? Who expected to find it at a poolside bar? He felt Brandy's surprise, too. For of course she had passion fruit in the small refrigerator beneath her counter. It was a staple of Crucian life. But its tart taste and bloody tint meant that tourists never, *ever* asked for it. At least, not more than once.

"Passion fruit?" the barmaid repeated politely.

"If you've got it."

Severin lifted his eyes to the mirror behind the counter. They came to rest on a pair of bronzed legs crossed casually at the ankle. Because of the tilt of the large patio umbrella, the rest of the woman's body was hidden from view.

Brandy raised her brows. Provocatively she leaned forward, projecting her voice toward the metal tables. "You've been here before, miss?"

"Definitely, in a past life," the tourist joked. Her voice was cool, not unfriendly.

"So you know something of our island?"

"Not much. But I like what I see." The iron chair scraped the deck as the woman pushed back from the table and stood. Circling the umbrella, she crossed the invisible barrier between islanders and outsiders by joining Severin and Brandy at the counter. Surprised, the barmaid straightened her back. Severin turned away, gripped by a grinding cramp from deep in his belly.

"This is my first visit to St. Croix," the American said, leaning comfortably against the counter. "But everything smells and tastes and feels so—so familiar. When I stepped off the plane it seemed like I was coming home."

"Coming *home*?" the barmaid asked in the subtly ironic tone she reserved for yet another Statesider who believed the island existed for her pleasure alone. "I don't think I've ever heard that from a visitor before."

"And I don't think I've ever felt this way before."

Brandy's mocking smile deepened as she brought out the flask of passion fruit. "What do you call yourself?"

"Maia."

"So tell me, Maia: Our weather's not too hot for you?"

"Hell, no. I nearly freeze to death all year up in Michigan." Clearly at ease, the American watched as the barmaid took a glass from a rack overhead and filled it with the thick red liquid.

"It must snow a lot in Michigan."

She grunted. "Rain in the fall, snow in the winter, fog in the spring, and then only a couple of weeks of suffocating summer."

"I see." Dropping several ice cubes into the glass, Brandy watched her bring it to her lips. The woman drank slowly and closed her eyes, savoring the taste.

"You staying in Christiansted?"

"Cay St. Croix."

"Excellent hotel," Brandy commented, looking briefly toward the shimmering white building, which was built on a small island across the bay.

"It is beautiful," the woman answered, "but sometimes I feel like a castaway."

"The ferry only takes a minute."

"True. But there's nobody out there but tourists, and I didn't exactly come here for that."

"You're not with a group?"

"A group? Oh, no," she responded, glancing toward the other Americans. "I just met those folks at the hotel."

"I see." Brandy appraised the other woman. "So you like our island food?"

"Everything I've tried."

"You need to taste some fungi and saltfish."

"Just point me to the kitchen."

"There's Junie's Place just around the corner on King's Alley—"

"I ate there last night. It was wonderful."

"You have the swordfish?" Brandy asked, aware that the restaurant offered several unspiced dishes prepared especially for the American palate.

"No, I had conch."

"Baked potato?"

"Fried plantain."

"Key lime pie?"

"Soursop ice cream."

Brandy's left eyebrow inched higher. "I know you've tasted Cruzian Rum. All our visitors love it."

The other woman raised her palms apologetically. "I'm not much of a drinker, I'm afraid."

"Have you heard any of our music?"

"I've got everything Roderick Davison has ever done. I love his *Island Songs*."

Brandy swallowed her surprise. The typical tourist didn't know the difference between reggae, calypso, and cha-cha, much less the name of any real Virgin Island performers.

"And what do you think of the way the Crucians talk?"

"It's beautiful. I only wish I could speak it."

Brandy was momentarily silenced by the woman's respectful answer. Most Statesiders complained that the islanders were too lazy to speak a "real" language.

"I guess that even the mosquitoes don't bother you?"

"Actually—" there was a polite silence, followed by a dry chuckle. Brandy joined in, nodding her head in agreement.

"Yes, even we who live here could do without the mosquitoes. And I hope you never meet one of our centipedes." She threw a quick glance at Severin, who was staring hard into space. The tourist went on talking, as if encouraged by their easy rapport.

"What do you call those trees with the orange flowers?"

"Those would be flamboyants, of course. And I don't suppose you have bougainvillea in Michigan."

"Not a chance," she chuckled.

"Hibiscus?" Brandy asked.

The tourist shook her head. "No, everything here is pretty overwhelming. The colors of the sky and the sea and the flowers are so intense that I feel like I've walked into a fantasy. And I've never seen so many birds in my life!"

"Yes, but sometimes the birds keep you from sleeping."

"Then you're awake to do other things."

"First you got to find someone worth doing them with."

"That's why I'm drinking this juice!"

The two women burst into laughter, and if Severin had been paying attention, he would have been surprised by Brandy's genuine warmth toward the stranger. But perched crookedly on his barstool, he was struggling to swallow back his pain by keeping his eyes fixed on the terrazzo floor.

"Have you been to any beaches?" the barmaid was saying.

"Only the beach by my hotel," the American replied, gesturing toward the little island.

"You must go out to Sandy Point. The dolphins come up and swim right beside you!"

"I was hoping I could learn to sail while I'm here."

"There's a fellow over at the dock—the one near your ferry landing—who'll take you anywhere you want to go."

"He's got his own boat?"

"Just ask for Juan."

Severin managed to raise his aching head high enough to see the square set of the tourist's shoulders. He could also see that she was balancing her weight on her elbows, as if to relieve her legs of that duty. As if, perhaps, she, too, might have been in some sort of pain.

"You've got a really nice place," she was saying to Brandy.

"Oh, I don't know about that. Sometimes I feel like switching names with one of you tourists and seeing the world from a different perspective."

"You can spend your whole life looking at the world and never find the place where you really belong."

"But at least you have the chance to try."

"Yes," the American agreed with just a trace of sadness. "I suppose I am pretty lucky."

Brandy eyed her carefully. "So how long will you be staying on St. Croix?"

The woman slowly lifted her glass. "I've got three weeks."

"That's a long vacation. Most tourists only stay for six or seven days."

"If I could," she said as she sipped the passion fruit, "I'd never leave."

"Then you've fallen in love with our island?"

"Already planning the wedding."

"After the wedding always divorce," Brandy replied wryly, and reaching for a cloth, she began wiping off the counter with long, rhythmic strokes.

"I just hope I have time to find what I'm looking for," the tourist murmured before finishing the scarlet juice.

Severin slowly lifted his head. The woman was standing so close that he could smell the clean scent of her lotion. His gaze traveled from the slender feet encased in leather sandals up the strong brown legs to full thighs in khaki shorts. Above her waist the swell of her breasts vanished beneath her arms. He was in too much pain to really look into the mirror and see her face.

"You with the FBI?" Brandy quipped.

"More like the ancestry police," the American answered softly.

"You a professor or something?"

"No, it's just for me." For the first time she glanced at Severin's reflection in the mirror behind the counter. She smiled. Her lips parted over good teeth and her dark caramel skin was smooth and clear. Their gazes locked, and something deep inside him began to stir when he met her eyes, which were wide-set and piercing, with thick, heavy lashes. For a moment they stared at each other, trying to understand why they both felt as if they'd met somewhere before.

"What exactly do you want to know?" Brandy asked, interrupting the stare. "Maybe I can help you."

The tourist pulled her eyes away from Severin, returning her attention to the barmaid. "Actually, I'm looking for some trace of my family. My great-grandfather lived here a long time ago."

"So that's really why you came to the island!"

The woman closed her eyes. She took a deep breath, then shook her head loosely. "I feel like I had to come. Almost as if I've been called."

Brandy's arm stopped moving. "Called?"

Severin started to tremble, the drink vibrating gently in his hand. His other hand closed over the plastic bottle in his damp pocket, his thumbnail flicking nervously at the lid. Brandy's voice deepened. "Your great-grandfather left here and moved to America?"

"First to Panama, then on to the States. But he loved this island. He never stopped talking about it."

The bottle lid popped open and Severin felt two capsules tumble into his sweating palm.

"Then he was born on St. Croix?" Brandy asked.

"Yes, he was."

"When did he leave?"

"I don't know the date. But he used to say that a sunken ship won't stop another's sailing! He made my father promise that one day he'd come back, but—" She paused, her gaze focusing inward for a few seconds. "—But my dad never made it."

Severin reached up and pushed the pain tablets into his mouth as Brandy leaned toward the tourist. "Do you know which estate he came from?"

"Yes. But it's not on any of the maps."

"That's strange," Brandy said softly. "What's the name of this mysterious plantation?"

Severin looked up just as the tourist answered: "He called it Wisdom. Estate Wisdom."

Severin didn't remember much after that. The rum and pineapple juice and grenadine, banana and Angostura began a mad salsa with the pills and his pain vanished and he released himself to Tina's able hands. He was led away from Brandy's Bar to the grill at Chenay Bay, where they continued to drink. After dark they drove the length of the island, all the way back to Fredriksted, and got much drunker in a darkened billiards hall frequented only by black people. Finally someone had driven them home.

When he awakened the following morning, only the pool of bloody vomit beside the bed assured him that he was at home and still alive. The crippling pain in his gut had returned and the bottle in his pocket was empty. The weight of the dank morning air pressed against him like a smothering blanket. He stumbled to the double-doored windows of his room and threw open the ancient wooden jalousies, making it out to the edge of the balcony before retching again.

When he managed to stand, his eyes focused out on the distant blue-black sea, calm and still beyond the cascading hibiscus and stalky palms. A yellow bird flitted by, screeching to an unseen mate in the thick canopy of trees below. He could hear the trickle of water from the overflow of the cistern. It must have rained the night before. Leaning forward, he balanced on the railing of rotting wood and peed into the bushes, breathing precariously as the richly scented earth sent up clouds of wet steam in the emerging equatorial sun.

He needed to bathe. He needed to shave off his filthy hair and he needed to sleep. Sleep for a month. A year. Sleep forever. He needed to eat, but it had been months, perhaps even years, since he'd really consumed anything of substance. Unless you could count the mountains of cigarettes and oceans of rum. With pineapple juice, of course. He'd always gotten his vitamins from the juice.

"I'm not like you, Pete," he muttered to the memory of his brother, who was sitting calmly on the railing of the deck a few feet away. "Now, don't you look at me that way. I never once wanted to swim all the way around this stinking island. Never wanted to be in the Olympics or go to Yale or become the governor." The memory shook its head slowly and Severin croaked out a laugh. "You wanted to be a good boy and marry a nice white girl and make some more Johanssens. And see what it got you? You're fucking dead!"

The memory faded and Severin dragged himself toward the doorway and halted crookedly on the rotting planks, holding his breath against the swelling pain. "I'm the last," he muttered, clenching his fist as the words bubbled through his teeth. "You see, Pete? I'm the very last one." He managed to laugh again, then growled out a mouthful of bloody spit, sending it thick toward the grape leaves below.

His eyes wandered up to the abandoned mill, the sentinel built on the highest point of the estate. In daylight and moonlight the mill was always there, reminding him of Solomon Johanssen—founder of Wisdom—his mythic, Danish forefather. Turning, he caught the sight of a decaying man reflected in a mirror that had hung in the room since the house was built nearly two hundred years before. Skin yellowed and hair crusted, he looked like something the blacks had conjured up with their mumbo jumbo.

Jesus! He needed a drink. But there was no rum in the house. Lurching inside, he searched. The drawers were emptied out, echoing in warped hollowness as he jerked them loose from their fittings. He pitched between the kitchen cabinets, then the wardrobes and laundry boxes, as if he were on a rolling ship. His groping fingers startled sleeping centipedes and a black spider the size of his palm that disappeared more deeply into the recesses of the floorboards as he stretched out his arms beneath the bed.

Bent almost double, he dug into the dusty bathtub, found a relatively clean shirt, and pulled it over his matted chest. A straw hat near the door was enough to hide his locked hair. He moved like a crab out of the house and scuttled down the circular drive to the truck, realizing only after he was behind the wheel that he had no keys. Realizing that he would have to drag himself back up the hill to the house, tears filled his squints of eyes. He blinked through the saltwater and resisted the urge to look up at Wisdom.

"Morning, Mr. Seven."

It was Mimi, the old woman who cleaned the house. He raised his head from the hardness of the steering wheel. The ancient woman gazed impassively through the truck window, her bag of cleaning articles poised delicately on her narrow back.

"Mimi, love, could you—"

"Harm come for you, Mr. Seven?" she asked, the traces of her long-ago childhood during the time when Denmark owned the island still evident in her dialect.

"Death coming, but he don't take me yet," Severin muttered and she sucked her teeth shrilly.

"You'll be needing keys to drive," she remarked.

"Next to the door, on the floor," his voice stumbled and fell.

The old woman trundled away, her white hair fading in and out as she passed through the shadows of the palms. When she returned he nodded in thanks and pulled together his remaining strength, knowing that it was time to surrender, whether or not his mind was actually ready. The Canadian doctor was right. His flesh would wait no more.

NINETEEN DAYS

Maia leaned back on the crisp edge of the smooth bow and marveled at the way the boat responded to her weight as it sliced through the turquoise water. Juan pulled the ropes controlling the sails, sending the craft along the ribbon of water as if the small sailboat and waves were one. His corded brown arms moved automatically, effortlessly, and he watched her even as he worked the swift mating of his vessel and the sea.

It was a perfect day, made even more perfect by the handsome woman on the prow of his fantasies. They cleared the point around Fredriksted, courting the inside of the reef and blasting along the rising pull of the undertow as they approached the deep harbor. The water changed color, growing violet, then almost black as they shot past the deepwater dock used by the cruise ships that anchored at Fredriksted. Maia lifted her binoculars, scouring the shore as if eager to discern something hidden in the thick foliage, but she shouted "No!" when he gestured toward the harbor.

Juan already knew that Maia liked to sail for hours at a time. She had rented out his boat and services as a sailor for two whole days, repeatedly skimming the north face of the island. When she first appeared at the dock, she'd explained that she'd never spent any time on a boat before. That Brandy had sent her. That she wanted to give sailing a try. And he was still amazed that she'd taken to the water with such eagerness and wonder.

Not that she was a novice swimmer. Both days he'd ferried her up and down the island and out to the palm-shaded cays that lined St. Croix's fertile reef. Then he'd waited in the cool of the fronds while she snorkeled along the golden beaches, discovering pearly nautilus shells or ivory chunks of coral. He'd wondered why she always wanted to go around the north coast, and why she stared so intently at the tree-hidden shore as they tore by, soaring past on the hot trade winds.

He watched patiently as she swam in the shallow coves, her skin toasting a fuller, deeper brown, her rubber fins gently breaking the surface of the clear water. Each day she swam for a very long time, then suddenly strolled out of the surf, the water beading like diamonds on her glowing brown skin while the salt formed rivulets between her breasts. Arms loaded with conch shells and bits of coral, she'd slip her slender feet out of the fins and mount the white sandy bank with a private smile. Wordlessly she'd place the shells on the sand, then sit down beside him, opening her woven bag and taking out warm fruit, small flasks of juice, and a tin filled with pills that she swallowed as she studied her sea treasures.

The problem was that she didn't study anything else. Juan had been sailing tourists around the island for years, and in every group there was always one woman who was looking for more than a pretty day at sea. Always one woman whose fantasies were whetted by the sight of his muscular arms, slender torso, and taut brown skin. Who loved his dark eyes, thick curling hair, and white teeth. Who, while the rest of the group was guzzling Cruzian Rum to the midnight purr of steel drums, arranged to let him sail his boat into her harbor. Always. Except for this one.

And it hurt. At thirty-two, Juan was the last of the Cardenas brothers not to have taken a wife. He was already uncle to seventeen nieces and nephews and had two children of his own on the island. Women succumbed to his melodic, broken English, mixed with Puerto Rican expressions and sudden, helpless silences. Where his scripts failed, his heavily lashed, orphan-brown eyes succeeded, and very few women had ever escaped after watching his meringue pelvis on the dance floor.

But Maia only looked at her shells, her gaze hidden behind sunglasses as Juan measured her carefully.

"Hey—excuse me, Miss Maia!"

She looked toward him and her dark gaze sent him struggling for something to say.

"You gonna get a burn sitting out here in the sun."

"You think so?" She laughed coolly.

Maia's simple bathing suit did little to hide a nicely proportioned, youthful body. Juan guessed that she was in her late thirties, probably childless, and was perhaps on the island to forget a relationship gone wrong. That might explain why she ignored his tension as he lay beside her on the sand. Legs stretched forward, lacquered toenails hidden in the white crystals, she examined the shells as he ached to lie in the cusp of her long-boned ankles, her hips like soft melons in his rope-burned palms. She stared toward the shore as his gaze flickered over the tight curls of her scalp where the short springy locks that she usually hid beneath hats, began. He imagined himself nestling her head against his upper arms and pressing his lips into the rough fields of her hair, gently testing the wet coils as his tongue savored the salty tang of the sea. He could feel the tickling of her nipples against his ridged chest, her full belly against his seaman's hips, and those thighs wrapped lusciously around his back. . . .

"Yes," he croaked. "Yes, I do think so."

How could she be ignoring the fact that she was here, on a deserted beach, with a male who was swollen and brawny and fascinated by her? Either she didn't like men, or was trying to prove that she was too good for him. Juan moved nervously, rolling over and walking into a patch of grape trees to relieve himself. When he came back he found her still lying back on an elbow, chewing an overripe carambola and staring intently at the sea.

There was something strange about her intensity: distant and defiant, she was like a wife trying to figure out where her husband hid his money. Or a woman wondering who her man had slept with the night before. He'd seen it lots of times with his own sisters and his brothers' wives.

"Hey, Maia? You thinking about a man?" He kept his voice light and playful.

"A man?" She snorted and looked his way. "God, no!"

"What? You don't like men?"

"Like them?" She laughed and sat up with a grunt. "When did liking them ever get me anywhere? No, Juan, I've been sitting here trying to figure out how to get to a place that doesn't seem to exist."

"What do you mean?"

"Well, I've heard about a beautiful estate that's not on any of the maps. It's called Wisdom."

Juan burst into laughter. "Wisdom's not on the maps because it don't need to be. Everybody know where it is!"

She looked at him in surprise. "That's funny. When I asked Brandy she said she doesn't know."

"She don't tell you because you're a Statesider," he said, lowering his voice. "Wisdom is no place for tourists."

"Why not?"

"Well—" He paused, his eyes turning crafty. "Like every place else on the island, Wisdom has its secrets."

"For example?"

"You come to Club Pan with me tonight and I'll tell you."

"Club Pan?"

"The disco. You'll love it. American music, Puerto Rican music, salsa, reggae, meringue—"

Feeling his eyes on her thighs she looked away quickly, as if disturbed by his all-too-apparent attempt at seduction. "Well, Juan, let me think about it."

Without another word she began gathering up the scraps of her food, wrapping them carefully in plastic and returning them to her bag. He had never seen a tourist who didn't merely throw the leftovers into the bushes, assuming that some animal would appreciate the unwanted human feast. She then gently tossed most of the shells she'd found back into the water. Picking up her snorkel and fins, she found the towel she had hung up to dry on a low-growing tree, and turned to him without speaking.

"Hey—" His eyes were still on her long ankles. "Why your momma call you Maia?"

"She didn't."

"What she call you?"

"Marie Amanda, believe it or not," she laughed as she pushed her belongings into her shoulder bag.

"It's a good name," he said. "You don't like it?"

"I'll stick with Maia," she answered, her chestnut eyes really meeting his for one short moment.

Soon Juan was maneuvering the sailboat back to Christiansted, watching her as she wrapped a batiked sarong around her full thighs, against the rising wind. The wind dried her hair and whitened her limbs with a powdery sheen of salt. Soon they landed at the harbor, pulling up to the listing boardwalk beside a handful of small boats and two shiny yachts. Juan's brother Rico came out of the harbormaster's office and smiled into her breasts as he hoisted her up to the dock. Swiftly Juan tied up his small vessel, intent on not leaving Maia with his older brother for too long.

"We go out tonight," he demanded, pointing to Club Pan, a peeling building a half block away. "You need to discover the island way to party!"

She looked toward her hotel, nesting behind a fringe of palms across the bay. "I don't know, Juan."

"You come, Maia. You sit for one hour and have a drink and maybe dance a little."

"One hour?" she repeated.

"Sure. Then maybe we go someplace better—"

"No, Juan—"

"Why not, Maia? There are very nice places I can show you."

"Not tonight."

"Then you come dance for maybe one hour," he acquiesced with a smile, "and I'll tell you how to get to Wisdom."

She hesitated for a long moment, staring angrily into his lupine eyes. She didn't want to go out with Juan. She didn't want him thinking that their relationship was anything more than business. And she certainly didn't want to barter her affections for knowledge about Wisdom. But everyone she had asked merely shrugged at her questions, and the tourist maps she found in the airport and hotel made no mention of the estate.

Juan was still waiting, a look of silent triumph in his eyes. Aware that she had lost the negotiation, she slowly nodded. "What time?"

"Nine o'clock at Brandy's. We'll have a drink before dancing."

Hoisting up her bag, she set off to the ferry landing to catch the small tug over to her island hotel. Juan watched her hips moving away beneath the colorful fabric. He sucked his teeth loudly.

"No es posible, Juan." He heard his brother's voice. "You'll never get your hands on that."

"La vida es loca," Juan said under his breath. "And crazier things have happened."

As she walked away Maia knotted her sarong more tightly against the brothers' measuring gazes. "Talk about a sunburn?" she whispered angrily. "I must have had a sunstroke to get tangled up with some madness like Juan."

She paused as she reached the end of the boardwalk and gazed around her, still speaking softly to herself. "For thirty years I listened to Grandpa's stories about this place. Thirty years of tales about my great-granddaddy's childhood. About this island—" Her eyes took in the handsome yellow-and-pink buildings that dated back to the years of Danish colonization. "And about the famous, mysterious plantation," she added, staring at the buildings whose brilliant colors hid the fact that they'd been constructed by slaves.

"And now here I am, playing games with clowns like Juan just so I can find out how to get to the phantom estate where my family spent their lives in chains! Well, as Grandpa used to say," she added ruefully, "the poorer you are, the more the dogs will rip your rags!"

She paused and looked around self-consciously, realizing that she was still standing at the end of the boardwalk, in plain view of the brothers. A short distance away the small ferry that would take her back to the hotel bobbed gently in the water, but she was suddenly very tired, and very thirsty from the long afternoon on the sea. Taking a deep breath, she turned away from the waterfront and headed back toward the bustling town.

Christiansted harbor spread out in a maze of pastel-painted eighteenth-century buildings rising around narrow, cobblestoned streets. Slate sidewalks passed under the cool arches, and the open doorways of tourist shops gave it the air of a quaint, half-forgotten colonial village. The islanders rainbowed in color from blond Statesiders to brown East Indians to veiled Palestinians to the black descendants of Africans.

Bored merchants were splashing buckets of bleach-water along the sidewalks outside their tourist-filled shops while their daughters watched soberly from the cash registers. A blue-suited mailman wove his way lazily along the dusty storefronts. A pair of stray dogs wandered out of an alley and several men with dreadlocks pedaled by on rusting bicycles.

Maia paused on a corner, the hot sun causing beads of sweat to form on her salty forehead. She had never known heat like this—punishing, unrepentant—and yet her body seemed at peace with it right away. She had quickly learned to breathe more slowly, to clothe herself in thin, billowing wraps and to nap during the hottest hours of the day. She also realized that surrendering to the heat, rather than complaining about it, was why even the islanders who were forced to wear constricting uniforms appeared cool and comfortable. Every man she met smelled of bay rum. And the women bore a sweet wafting scent of talc.

Maia slowly approached a row of storefronts where curling-edged postcards yellowed beside straw figurines of the stilt-walking Moko Jumbies that thrilled the islanders during Carnival. The sea-palled humidity of the late summer—the height of the hurricane season—caused the racks of T-shirts to stand stiffly in the weighted air, while a saleswoman waved at herself with a paper fan. Now away from the cooling breezes of the harbor, the heat grew solid and smothering.

Up ahead, through a fog of car exhaust and humidity, Maia could see that the entrance to the pharmacy was boiling over with milling, glue-shirted tourists. For a moment she was consumed by irritation, actually forgetting that only three days earlier she'd been one of them. She pushed through the mass of shorts and white gym shoes, working her way slowly by the displays of Cruzian Rum and sunscreen and tabloid magazines to a cooler of juice. Then she struggled back through the paunchy cruise-shippers to reach the broiling street.

Cursing softly, Maia walked away from the chaos and back along the cracked sidewalks toward the island's old stone courthouse, a tall building that bordered the harbor. Taking care not to trip over the broken cement, she stayed close to the high wall, savoring the bit of shade it provided. She was surprised when a blast of cool, perfumed air seemed to blurt out from some unseen source. Pausing, Maia lifted her eyes to the pockmarked walls and small barred windows of the courthouse. Suddenly she caught sight of a long, narrow passage carved into the heavy stones. She slipped into the tunnel and emerged seconds later into the center of a large, palm-shaded private courtyard.

A row of cannons stood sentry at the entrance to the garden, their cannonballs stacked neatly beside the hollow, dusty orifices. Maia mounted a brick staircase and gasped as she stared into an almost violent stillness. Painstakingly trimmed bushes exploded in profusions of blood- and fuchsia-toned bougainvillea. Palm-sized hibiscus flowers in yellow and soft pink leaned invitingly over a shining slate walkway. A block of scarlet cement stood at the top of the courtyard, sheltered by flamboyant trees. The inner windows of the building were flung open, their indolent curtains leaning over the sills. The air was cooled by the swaying palms, but above all, the noise of the broiling, congested streets had vanished.

Dropping heavily onto a mossy bench shaded by a fringe of shaggy leaves, Maia lifted the bottle of juice to her lips and savored the luxurious dryness of ice-cold cranberry. She sat very still, grateful for the breeze that tickled the hairs at the edges of her scalp.

Drawing her shoulders together, her gaze absently followed a flock of gulls sweeping back and forth between the palm trees in the courtyard. Instantly her thoughts flew back to the riddle of Wisdom.

Maia had nearly concluded that either the plantation was a figment of her grandfather's imagination, or simply no longer existed. It was supposedly buried on the edge of the rain forest, high up on the northwestern tip of the island. The land, her grandfather explained, had been chosen by its Danish owners precisely because of its location. It was private, fertile, and protected by a natural bay that had never been hit by a hurricane. The house was supposedly raised on a hill, its rear terrace looking down a steep green drop to a private, sheltered beach. The stables were built on another rise, and the servants' quarters were tucked down in a valley a short distance away. And then there was a tower—some kind of mill used to grind sugarcane during the slave days—that offered a pirate's view of the sea. Wisdom had been the pride of the island during the Danish times. It was, in a sense, the "perfect" plantation.

"That's why it was called Wisdom, Marie Amanda. There was an elegant Great House, with two wide wings—one to the east and the other to the west. It had a French-style veranda built all the way around the rear, overlooking the sea. That's because the first mistress, Marie-Paule, wanted Wisdom to look like her home on Martinique. She loved the house with its breeze-cooled rooms and sun-sweetened fields. But most of all, she loved the great stone mill built up high on the cliffs. You bear her name, Marie Amanda, and you must promise me to go back to Wisdom one day. You see, little girl, Wisdom is your Source. It's where your blood was born . . ."

Maia had never understood how her grandfather could feel such pride in the place where his family had been held as slaves. He had never mentioned anything about the white people who lived there. The people who had owned his grandparents. The Europeans who had guiltlessly kept his ancestors in bondage. Maia found her grandfather's stories strangely chilling, because beneath his claims of the beauty of Wisdom lay something dark and brutal and menacing—the reality of slavery, and what it had meant to her black kinsmen.

So even now, after traveling so far, she felt a wavering uncertainty about visiting the estate. As if she might be met by restless, vengeful spirits. Traces of her people, who would want her to hate the place her family had so mythologized. It was for this reason that she had taken her time, sailing day after day with Juan and staring long at the roiling green shore. Lying on the beach, she'd searched inside herself for the courage to face whatever she might find. It had taken three whole days for her to convince herself that there was nothing to be afraid of. To

convince herself that certainly no one would care. To convinc
that Wisdom really was her home, after all. She had Wisdom
She belonged on the island. Surely—

"You down for vacation?"

The voice was deep, cool, and powerful. Startled, Maia looked up
at a lean mahogany man standing beside the bench. A soft mustache
played over curved lips and his hair curled away from his broad forehead in closely clipped waves. Fine brows swept toward a strongly
defined nose, and his confident smile almost masked the tension of a
man who liked to be in control.

She felt him studying her carefully, the eyes behind the dark sunglasses examining her salty skin, damp sarong, and sea-washed hair.
Her hands rose self-consciously to her face, which was swollen from
exposure to the sun and wind. And although every man on the island,
from the gardeners to the hotel managers looked at her appraisingly,
there was something different in this man's steady gaze. He wasn't just
looking to appreciate. He was looking to know.

She smiled pleasantly. "Just visiting."

"Too bad."

"Now, why's that?"

He came a step closer and removed his dark glasses. Clad in a silk
shirt that swept over his firm triceps, his carefully pressed dark trousers
grew tight around heavy, athletic thighs. He angled his hip casually to
reveal the leather briefcase tucked under his left arm. Glancing away
from her, he picked a flaming pink hibiscus from a nearby bush and
brought it up to his full mouth. She followed the path of the flower with
her eyes, finding herself staring into a somber, intelligent gaze. "We
Crucians," he said lazily, "love to convince *some* visitors to stay."

Maia's curiosity was aroused by the hint of an east-coast accent
hiding beneath the lilt of the islands. Yet troubled by his air of confidence, she kept her voice cool. "If you stay, you pay. And St. Croix is
far from inexpensive."

"Depends on who you know," he answered smoothly. "My mother,
for example, rents out rooms in Fredriksted at a very reasonable rate."

"Fredriksted?"

He laughed lightly. "The black end of the island."

"The black end?" Maia asked, surprised at his candor. "Is there a 'white end' on St. Croix too?"

"Of course," he said. "Just like in the States. And the problem is that too many people think that things are supposed to be that way."

"And what do you think?"

"I think," he answered, "that we Crucians should eat, work, and live wherever we want. But you shouldn't be troubled with St. Croix's struggles while you're on vacation."

He had opened and closed the subject in one abrupt statement. Maia sat still for a moment, wondering whether he was more interested in seducing a tourist—or in lecturing her on the realities of Virgin Island life.

"So tell me more about your mother's hotel."

"Tourists love it, and it's not too close to the water."

"What—the Crucians don't like the water?"

He shook his head. "You won't see many black homes near a beach. We've survived too many hurricanes for that. All those retirement condos and tourist hotels get blown away each time there's a storm—"

"So you just let the Statesiders live in them."

"Well, I was offering you a room with us locals. Believe me: If you stay with us, you'll stay alive."

"Alive?" she laughed. "I didn't realize a vacation could be a matter of life and death."

"There are many things about St. Croix that visitors don't realize." He extended the hibiscus to her. "For example, these days you really can't be too careful. After all, this is our stormy season."

Maia hesitated before taking the flower, then accepted it, strangely relieved to be released from his intense gaze.

"I'm Noah."

"I'm Maia."

He raised one foot to the edge of her bench and leaned toward her. "So tell me, Maia. Are you interested in seeing those rooms?"

"Right now I'm just interested in taking a shower," she said, rising to her feet.

"And later?"

"I'm pretty comfortable out on the cay."

"Now, how will you get to know St. Croix if you're stranded on an island?"

"I'm sure you'd be willing to teach me all about it."

"That's very true." He threw back his head and laughed deeply. The sound ricocheted around the courtyard, scattering the seagulls. He moved a little closer and let his accent come home to the island. "Have dinner with me tonight and we'll start the lessons."

"Students shouldn't date their teachers."

"Think of me as a tutor."

"I'm an independent learner."

"But we could compare notes."

"That would be cheating."

"Sometimes," he purred, "it's good to break the rules."

"But then things fall apart."

"So that new things can be built."

The wind picked up and they paused, silenced by the brittle rustling of the palm fronds. Maia studied the ruffled edges of the flower. "Do you enroll all the tourists in your classes?"

"Good heavens, no. Only the lovely ladies who find their way out of the hotel zone and into my courtyard."

"*Your* courtyard?"

"Yes. You see, Maia—" he stood up straight and again became serious. "My ancestors slaved to build this edifice. My grandfather landscaped and painted it. My father went to night school and worked well past retirement to be certain that his son would have an office in it."

"Well, what do you do in this courtyard?"

"I practice law."

"Then you definitely shouldn't break any rules."

Noah snorted softly. "I had to rewrite a whole bunch of them to get here." Glancing toward the windows on the upper floors of the court-house he added, "But it was worth it. Now I have the chance to pay my ancestors back for their labor."

"Your father must be very proud."

"He's no longer living. But he taught me to think of this building, and all of this island for that matter, as my flesh and blood."

"Flesh and blood?" Maia repeated skeptically.

"The travel brochures didn't lie to you. The beaches are beautiful here. The water is warm and the air is sweet. But I'm fighting for something more." He squinted as two middle-aged white men in golf shorts passed through the courtyard, talking quietly. "We get a lot of wealthy Statesiders who come down for vacation and decide to stay," he explained. "They think of our island as their playground. They invest their money in golf courses and casinos. In restaurants and glass houses with private pools and views of the sea." He looked back into her eyes. "They do nothing to improve life for black people. Without decent schools and opportunities for employment we remain trapped as their gardeners and maids."

Noah gestured toward the small cement platform at the end of the courtyard. "Here we stand, just a few feet away from the block where my ancestors were bought and sold. Too little has changed, Maia. Too many people are still living here without any real security. I'm just trying to make things better."

She paused, strangely moved. "You're a courageous man, Noah."

"Courageous? Not really. It's my responsibility."

"I'm sure you take your responsibilities to heart," she replied.

"Actually Maia, there's room in my heart for a great many things. It's just that—" For the first time he hesitated. "—Well, very few people understand why I've taken on this mission."

Noah's intonation played musical chairs with the words, and his timbre had fallen off to a low throttle. "And the only other thing," he added, "is that I don't have much time for fun."

"So you just stay on the lookout for the tourists who happen to wander into your lair?"

"Yes," he laughed. "And then I move very fast. So how about dinner?"

"I've got plans tonight," she answered, clenching her teeth against the thought of Juan's leering grin.

"How about meeting me for a drink?"

"I'm sorry," she responded, her fingers automatically stroking the blossom's velvety flesh. "I've been out sailing all day and I need some time to rest. What about tomorrow evening?"

"I'm flying up to Miami in the morning," Noah said regretfully. "However, I should be back by the weekend." He brought an embossed card from his pocket and pressed it into her hand, his fingers brushing her open palm. "I'll call your hotel when I get back."

He took several steps backward, still smiling. "Don't go and find yourself another tutor. All right?"

Severin's hand came up. It was strangely burdened by a plethora of tubes that vanished beneath a bandage at his wrist. Sensing that he was being watched, he looked slowly to the left and found his dead brother Peter sitting beside the bed, his eyes gentle and full of concern.

Ah, shit! I don't want you to see me like this.

You shouldn't be messing yourself up, Sev.

What I'm supposed to do? I'm too old to change, man.

Mother and Father would be disappointed in you, brother.

They never gave a shit about me.

Don't say that, Severin.

They only cared about you. The athlete. The college boy. The heir.

You know that's not true.

They drank themselves to death after your plane hit the water.

Wisdom is the only thing that matters. I'm dead, so now it's up to you.

Why?

Because you're the last Johanssen.

Maybe it's better that way—

The bed shook and Severin's mind snapped forward in a mixture of irritation and relief. His body was corpsed with a white sheet, his shoulders braced to the narrow gurney with thin leather straps. From somewhere a cool breeze was wandering down the hospital corridor, and his newly shaved head made him feel naked and vulnerable. He wanted to cry.

"You're awake, Mr. Severin." Of course: the Canadian doctor. Black, and ready to assure Severin that his diploma from McGill meant business.

"You're doing much better, I see."

"So this is your fault?" Severin's voice crawled out of his dream.

"Would you have preferred the alternative?"

"You've got me strapped to this table so I don't even know what you cut off."

"Don't worry: Your machinery is still attached."

"Will it work?"

"If you'll quit your rum-and-tobacco therapy."

"Too much to ask." Severin tried to laugh, but nothing came out.

The doctor cleared his throat. "Well," he said slowly, "I could always use you for anatomy lessons at the university."

"I'm already your guinea pig."

"You haven't seen anything, yet," the doctor replied tartly. He sat down beside his patient. "Mr. Johanssen, that's all finished. Do you understand? No more alcohol." The doctor laid his wrist across Severin's bloated belly. "You know, you've lost fifteen pounds in two days. Most of it was water, of course, but there's still a lot of waste in your system. You're too young a man to destroy your body like this."

Severin pressed his eyes together tightly, hoping to return to his conversation with his brother.

"Seriously, Mr. Johanssen, I'd like to see my good work keep you alive another twenty years or so. But that's entirely up to you. You need to think it over. It's going to be very painful if you ignore my warning and again substitute alcohol for food—"

"Maybe I don't want to stay alive," Severin croaked. The doctor signaled as the head nurse, whom Severin had known since their childhood, entered the room. She picked up a loaded syringe and attached it to the tubes entering his wrist.

"Well, we'll just make sure that we give you that choice."

"I only want one thing, Doctor: Make sure you don't let anyone from my family in here."

"If you like. Anything else?"

"Rum," Severin whispered as he slipped back into his sweet vacuum of unconsciousness.

* * *

Maia knew she wouldn't be able to stand the deafening bass for very long, but she followed a freshly pressed Juan into Club Pan that night. Just nearing ten, it was still too early for the little tables arranged around the too-narrow dance floor to be occupied. A few young people—most likely high school students, scuttled across the tiles to hip-hop music she might have heard in any bar in Michigan. They were dressed in the island's best finery: loudly patterned skirts and shirts and both the boys and girls had on expensive athletic shoes.

Juan led her to a table near the center of the room, his large hand cupped so that the tips of his fingers met at the small of her bare back. He had shed his cutoff pants and sea-dyed T-shirt, appearing at Brandy's in a white polo and jeans so tight that there was little left to be imagined. He'd smiled hard when Maia arrived in a turquoise halter dress, his eyes resting briefly on the imprint of her breasts against the light fabric. He then insisted on ordering her a rum and Coke, despite her patient explanation that she didn't drink alcohol.

Now, in the blinking lights of the disco, Maia absorbed Juan's tempura smile, appreciating his beauty without realizing that every woman in the room had frozen as they entered. Until that very moment, she had found that Juan's presence offered her the most precious gift she could imagine—meaningless chatter—and she had neither looked, nor seen any other use, for him.

Her eyes moved from the boatman to the panorama of the bar and she realized that she had entered a microcosm of island society. And even though she might never come to that room again, Maia instantly understood that most of the guests believed that Club Pan constituted the greatest source of intrigue and romantic melodrama in the world—or at least the greatest portion they would ever know.

It began when a simpering waitress managed to swing her long hair against Juan's chest when she leaned forward to take their order. The woman then moved to the neighboring table and began clearing away the empty glasses while pressing her scarlet buttocks against his shoulder. Maia was amazed to see Juan rub his back gently against the proffered flesh, and speak loudly to her in Spanish. The woman glanced over her shoulder, throwing back her wall of horse hair, and gave a sarcastic reply. Two or three chortling men propped up against the wall joined in the exchange, and Spanish reverberated like tennis balls.

Rising wordlessly, Maia extricated herself from their assaulting gazes and began to stroll slowly through the club, casually observing the other guests. People of various ages and skin colors were beginning to fill up the tables and dance floor. The tourists were immediately recognizable by their seersuckers and white socks; Puerto Ricans seemed to wear a lot of gold jewelry. Natives to the island—both black and brown—were the least conspicuous and most confident of the customers. The Crucian men and women, mostly clad in black, danced like a low murmur, as if determined not to waste a single drop of sweat. They moved as if of one body, while the purple velvet walls, plastic palm trees, and a single spinning mirrored globe seemed to weld them together within the fanatically pounding beat.

Someone spoke to Maia and she recognized Bradley, an employee from her hotel. She let him lead her to the dance floor and take her lightly into his arms as the music faded into a slow love song.

She liked the clean scent of the Crucian men. She enjoyed the teasing cadence of their voices when they flirted with her. Brad, who spent his days patiently serving the white guests without a trace of impoliteness or disrespect, had morphed into an entirely different being. His grasp on her waist was firm, and his eyes were filled with the mocking self-assurance of a man who thought he'd deciphered her secret codes. After four minutes of pretending not to feel his pelvis crushed against hers, his face fixed in an innocent smile, she pulled herself free and politely moved on.

"Where you from, sister?"

Maia glanced up into the face of a brown skeleton whose skull peeped out from between the strands of his stiff, gel-glued curls. "Stateside," she whispered, momentarily fascinated by the sight of mascara-blackened eyes. "And you?"

The mannequin smiled, perfect teeth glistening in the weird lights, and when he turned his head she saw that he wore small hoops in his nose and eyebrow. His head snapped back.

"New York," he said. "Chelsea." He gave her a swift, evaluative glance. "Touristing?"

"Do I look like the tourists?"

"No," he replied above the flaring trumpets of a rollicking salsa. "But you've got way too much class to be a local."

"Thank you," she laughed, taking note of his maple-tanned chest and fine-boned, narrow pelvis. "You've got a beautiful tan," she remarked, returning the compliment.

"Danke schön, meine Schwester," he answered in crisp German as he pumped his hips restlessly. Unlike the other dancers, he was clad in loose-fitting jeans and a button-down shirt, his feet thrust into suede Swedish sandals.

"Aren't you American?" she asked, squinting at him through the flashing lights.

"Afro-European," he replied, his eyes darting quickly toward a man Maia recognized as the taxi driver who'd brought her in from the airport. "German mother and black father. Adopted by African Americans. Raised in Indiana and liberated in New York."

"That's quite a journey," she said over the music.

"Especially the Indiana to New York part," he confirmed, smiling wryly.

"Well, god bless the Big Apple," she said.

"God bless *Chelsea*," he replied with an ironic wink. "In fact—"

A piercing electronic riff sent a tremor through the crowd. Although Maia didn't recognize the piece, it was obvious that everyone else on St. Croix did. Men and women of all races flooded the dance floor and Chelsea Man leaped by her, clambering to the center of the wooden stage, where he positioned himself below the spinning light. He began moving sensuously to the beat, his hands weaving arabesques around his head and hips. The Crucians snorted and turned away, opening up a wide circle around him. Maia leaned against a pillar and watched in fascination as Chelsea Man danced on, eyes screwed shut, in a hauntingly ecstatic solo.

Surrendering to the smoke and sweat and duty-free perfumes, she was soon awash in the island Esperanto of Spanish, English, Crucian, and Creole. She moved back into the darkness and took her place along the wall, letting her thoughts slip away to another time, another place—Maia was at Linda Harlen's house party, and she was sixteen again and gorgeous, fine curly-haired Dyson Greene was going to unglue himself from the opposite wall and cross the sweating basement and ask her to dance. He would smell of his daddy's Aramis and be so tall that her head fit into the crux of his collarbone, and his hands on her hips and the thickening in his pants would leave her dizzy with desire for the back seat of a car—

She opened her eyes and Juan seemed to appear from nowhere just as a fast merengue began. He grasped her arms firmly and brought her out onto the little dance floor and into the dance. She good-naturedly matched both his rhythm and step, keeping her upper body relaxed and steady while her hips and buttocks went to work. And to her surprise, it felt good.

Juan looked into her eyes and she smiled back. Pleased that Club Pan was watching, he added an extra dip to his step and she followed. He varied the rhythm and she came right along with it. He raised his hard palms and her hands formed the other half of the steeple. They worked so naturally and beautifully together that he risked it all by pulling her tightly into his arms and sweeping her backward. And she dipped her head nearly to the floor, letting him rock her from the left to the right. There was a smattering of applause and he spun her around, stepping away so that her turquoise skirt stood out from her body to reveal her full brown thighs. The men began to shout.

Maia felt something shake free, and stepping outside herself, she watched the brown-skinned woman moving with precision and grace beside a man who might have been her lover. She was infused with a soul-quickening sense of liberation. And she felt her skin, muscles, hair come alive in the blaring horns and pulsing Latin beat.

Juan moved closer, instinctively aware of her surrender to the music. He knew—like any hunter closing in on its prey—that the end of the chase began not with the speed, but with the rhythm. Mating was always about rhythm, from the way hands explored, to the way breathing changed, to the stroking of tongues and the meeting of flesh and the mounting quest toward explosion.

This time, when their eyes met there were no horizons between them. Taking in Juan's gleaming eyes, blue-black mane and swollen lips, Maia suddenly understood that she had been very alone in very isolated places with this . . . *male.*

For the first time she really *saw* the small diamond stud in his earlobe. The packed arms emerging from the damp polo shirt. The improbably slender waist. The gliding, pumping thighs.

She also sensed the jealous eyes of the other women, and began to comprehend that even as they were using this salsa as the prelude to an unabashed mating ritual, she was transforming her own position on the island. The Crucian people who were witnessing this rhythmic, sensuous exchange, would see a Statesider stealing Juan's gaze from the women of his world. And those women would resent her. This realization plunged Maia into a sudden, profound loneliness.

At that instant Juan reached out, placing his hands on her shoulders. His fingers slipped down along her collarbone, then in perfect time with the music, touched her nipples through her dress. She stepped back from him and he grasped her waist, pulling her close. Her arms came up to push him away and he slid his palms to her buttocks, grinning triumphantly into her eyes.

Maia wrenched herself free and the music ended as abruptly. They stood staring at each other, chests rising and falling. "I'm leaving, now," she shouted. Juan's incredulous expression followed her as she turned toward the tables.

"You cannot go now!"

"I'm tired."

"So you sit, have a drink, watch the others."

"I'm sorry," she said, her voice rising tersely above the music.

"Ah," he replied quickly. "You want to go to bed?"

She responded by pushing her way down the crowded corridor to the door, wondering nervously whether the boatman would be somewhere near the ferry that crossed the bay to her hotel. She could feel Juan's heat just behind her, following in her wake.

"Why you rushing?" he said in a low voice, grasping her arm as she reached the door. "Too dangerous for a woman alone!"

"I'll risk it," she said, trying to pull away.

"No—" He tightened his grip. "I come, too!"

"Not tonight, Juan."

"Why not, tonight? You go in my boat to Buck Island every day. You spend many hours alone with me. You know I'm a good man."

"I'm not looking for a man."

"What's this bullshit?" he cried. "Every woman looking for a man!"

His assertion elicited laughter from the gauntlet of men lining the entrance.

"Let me go," she insisted in a level voice.

"Why?" he responded, his voice steely.

"Because," a male voice announced firmly, "she's with *me*." Chelsea Man appeared beside her, his thin, glistening chest rising and falling beneath his open cambray shirt. He eyed Juan, his lashes brushing his cheeks as his gaze moved from Juan's thick black hair to the powerful arms to the swollen groin. His lips twisted into a simper. "Although I would really rather leave with *you*—" he began, "I already promised this lady that we'd catch up on old times."

"What's this old times bullshit?" Juan snarled. The men ringing the door laughed again.

"When we used to go dancing at the Roxy," Chelsea Man replied. "Or was it the Limelight, sister?" The mascara-ringed eyes fixed hers, and she smiled despite her pounding heart.

"It was the Garage, of course. Don't tell me you've forgotten!"

"Oh, no sweetheart—I'll never forget that groove!"

There was a tense silence as Juan measured his elegant opponent. The island men watched with weighted stares.

"*La puta*," Juan whispered to Maia. "You like this *aunty*-man?"

She nodded, taking a step closer to her new-found friend.

"Well, one thing's for sure," he spat, nodding toward the other men for approval. "*He* won't be able to make a woman out of you."

Maia and her escort pushed their way past mocking howls and out into the balmy night and were met by a blossom-bearing breeze that almost stunned her in its sweetness. Young people lining the stairs to the disco parted reluctantly to let them through, and she saw someone nod at her companion and whisper, "That one strange, man!" as they passed. Maia knew Juan might still follow them, and she was mildly afraid. The cracked, uneven sidewalk passed beneath a series of dark, vaulted stone archways before opening into a nearly deserted parking lot alongside the pier where the little boat to her hotel was waiting.

They walked quickly, without speaking, and stopped only when they reached the ferry landing. The little skiff was moored not far from Juan's small vessel, its hurricane lamp swimming with mosquitoes. She turned to her companion.

"Thanks for fronting for me."

Chelsea Man laughed. "Your friend really wants some."

"He's no friend," she responded, peering at the fragile figure beside her. "And you really shouldn't go back in there."

"No problem. That's the type I always end up with."

She shook her head. "I hope you know what you're doing."

He snorted. "That's what's so funny about it. Down here, they make so much noise with all that macho crap, but you can hardly beat them off after dark."

"Do you live here?"

"I came down on vacation, got a job managing a very expensive restaurant, and decided to stay the winter."

"Living in a hotel?"

"My boss's guesthouse. She travels a lot and needs someone to look after the estate." He grinned. "Wanna come swimming? I'll turn on the pool lights."

"Thanks, but not tonight." She paused. "I'm Maia. I don't even know your name."

"Damian Roberts." He squinted at her in the darkness. "Are you gonna be all right?"

Maia's eyes wandered out over the oily water. The lights from the hotel across the bay were too faint to welcome her, and for a moment she felt a long way from home. Damian reached up and grasped her shoulder. "Hey—I could use a whiskey sour. Is the bar open at your hotel?"

Soon the two climbed out of the gently rocking boat and tipped the silent ferryman. They walked up the sloping flagstone path toward the modern hotel, hidden behind rows of palm and grape trees flanked by pastel floodlights.

"A good bar is hard to find," Damian remarked.

"That hasn't decreased the number of drunks on this island."

"True," he said good-naturedly. "But it's not our fault, Maia. We drinkers keep trying out all these Puerto Rican bodegas and white folks' tennis clubs and the tourists' heavy metal bars and Crucian steel-drum shacks and—" He sighed. "By the end of the night, we're completely drunk from all that research."

"It's too hot for that," Maia laughed.

"There's nothing else to do but fuck," Damian remarked. "And since my lovers only show up in the darkest hours of the night, I have to drink to pass the time. Besides, with rum costing less than a cola, there's no incentive to stay sober."

The two entered the hotel bar, only to find the bartender locking the steel grill over the shelves of bottles.

"It's not even midnight and you're closed?" Damian wailed, his hands on his hips.

"Sorry," the man answered without turning his head. "Too slow tonight. Everybody over at Club Pan."

"Everybody *important* is here!"

The man glanced at Damian, sucked his teeth musically and shook his head. Then he moved toward the hotel lobby, the cash box under his arm.

"*Scheiss!* Isn't that about some shit!" the New Yorker called loudly.

Maia laughed again. "Relax. All the whiskey you want is back at Club Pan, just a five-minute ferry ride away."

Damian glanced at her. "Well, since I'm here, why don't we at least make up some old times to talk about?"

"Sounds good to me."

They strolled along the hotel's white beach, just across the bay from Christiansted harbor. Music from the disco wafted over the sailboats arranged along the pier, and lights from the many restaurants made silky patterns in the warm, midnight waves. The air was cool and sweet with the scent of night-blooming jasmine.

"So where're you from?" he asked, listening intently as he swept his slender feet through the moonlit sand.

"A small city about an hour north of Detroit. Nothing much going on there, but I've spent a lot of time in your town. I was in love with this guy. A drummer. He went off to New York to make it big in the recording industry, so I'd fly over as often as I could." She paused, then laughed wryly. "He was broke most of the time, so we almost never left his bedroom."

"What finally happened?"

"After three years he met a singer and followed her out to L.A. and I never saw him again."

Damian sighed dramatically. "I'm sure your mama told you never to fall for a musician, Maia."

She laughed. "That's true. No musicians, no actors, and—"

"No island men with little boats and great big dicks!"

They burst into laughter and Maia shook her head, amazed at how comfortable she felt with Damian. He caught her eyes and raised one corner of his mouth ironically.

"Yeah—I see it: There's some major craziness hiding beneath all that Detroit *cool*."

"You think so?" She grinned.

"I know so, woman. And I know something else: This is more than just a vacation for you. Right?"

Maia shot her companion a surprised glance, but the details of his face were lost in the image of the town's shimmering reflection. She refrained from answering as they wandered up to a pair of two-man catamarans that were chained together and pulled high up on the beach. Maia sat on one of the missilelike floats and leaned forward, drawing the toe of her sandal back and forth in the silvery crystals. Damian's silence was soothing against the patient whisper of the sea, and she found herself wondering at the deep cold of the sand, so swift and profound, even after the blazing equatorial sun had tortured the world throughout the day.

"So what is it, sister?" Damian suddenly inquired, lacing an arm through her own looped elbow.

"*It?*"

"Don't try to psych me out. It's all over you, Maia."

She didn't answer, but her body stiffened. She dropped her head, staring at her feet.

"Eighteen days," she said in a voice like burlap. "I've only got eighteen days to take everything apart and put it back together again."

"You mean, to take control of your life?" he asked, a hint of sarcasm in the words.

"My past, my present, and maybe even my future," she answered.

"Eighteen days, huh?" He moved his shoulders restlessly. "That can be a long time, Maia."

"You think so?"

"It depends on whether the clock is ticking—"

"It is," she said simply. Now he looked at her, becoming very still. Slowly she raised her head and met his gaze. A current of understanding passed between them and he blinked slowly, carefully, almost luxuriantly.

"I know all about ticking clocks," he said. "What kind is yours?"

"A tumor in the tubes," she admitted, aware that she had never, ever discussed her condition with anyone but her doctors.

"And you've got?"

"A few months. Maybe a couple of years if I let them cut and burn."

"Sounds amusing."

"Sounds pathetic."

"So you're giving up?"

"My mother had the same thing. I watched her fight and I watched her lose."

"No other family to see you through?"

"My dad's in a home. Alzheimer's. Last time I saw him he didn't even recognize me."

"Friends? Buddies? Acquaintances?"

"A few. But they've got plenty of problems, too."

"Life's worth fighting for—"

"That," she said softly, "is something I came here to think about."

Damian laughed, his voice hollow. "Well, I've got a tick-tock, too. But I've just decided to ignore it."

"In the blood?" she asked.

"Very good sex with a very wrong lover," he answered crisply.

She opened her mouth to speak, then hesitated. He looked at her, then glanced away. "It's all about power, Maia. I could let them cut and burn, too. But I know the Reaper's coming for me and I won't give the clock that kind of power over my life."

"There are new drugs—"

"Of course," he said. "But look at it like this: We could be at home right now, letting the clock decide what we should be thinking and doing. Instead we came here to enjoy our lives. When everything is said and done, we'll face the future with the knowledge that we controlled time, rather than letting it control us."

She sighed and closed her eyes. Damian rose up, taking three leaping steps across the midnight. "Check this out, baby!" he chanted, his voice a brittle reed.

Tiny sand crabs scuttled into their holes and the moon painted a descant over his lean shoulders as his slender feet etched hieroglyphs into the sand. Maia watched him twist and twirl, his body looping to the music warping eerily over the bay. He seemed to mock his earlier solo, exaggerating his gestures until his body moved like a cartoonist's pencil over the dark, moonlit sketchpad.

Finally he dropped, panting and glistening, as the music from Club Pan drifted into a slow reggae. "God—I dance so much better on this side of the bay!"

Maia knelt down in the sand beside him, drawing her knees up beneath her chin. He looked across at her and settled back, folding his arms beneath his head to gaze up at the stars.

"Lonely, aren't you?"

"Yes," she answered.

"All the time?"

She nodded.

"Nobody understood you at home and you kinda hoped that things might be different, here?" He watched as her gaze fell, and sitting up slowly, he looped his arm around her shoulders. "Well, tonight," he said softly, "you've found a friend."

"A *friend*?" For a moment she remained frozen, her eyes on the mirage of the town shimmering across the bay. Then she looked across at him. "It's much, much worse than that. If I'm not careful I could start loving you, Damian."

"That *is* pretty bad," he answered, "because I don't do women."

"That's all right," she answered, "because I don't do love."

They both listened to the lulling waves, the distant disco, the Caribbean night.

"We really did dance together once, long ago, didn't we?" Damian asked dreamily.

"If we haven't already," she replied, "then I promise you someday we will."

EĪGHTEEN DAYS

It's all about power, Maia.

It was Damian's words the night before that drove Maia from her sleepless bed before daylight. Stepping out of a cold shower, she walked out on the beach, scattering water droplets like silvery diamonds on the crystal sand. She found their footprints in the cool gray light, still ringing the beached catamaran. And she stood very still, watching the purple sky explode into rich scarlet clouds that rose like a curtain above the golden dawn.

It didn't matter if everyone on the island told her that Wisdom no longer existed. Maia didn't care if the tourist books had erased the roads, the hills, and any mention of the estate. She didn't care that she'd lost three precious days trying to decide how to proceed.

It was time to act. Time to find and use her own power.

Her face bright with the clean morning sun, Maia made her decision. "I need a car," she mused aloud. "I need a car that will get me over rocks and rivers, if that's the only way to Wisdom. And I've got to find

---

45

a map. Somewhere on this island there's a map that will show me the way. They can lie to me, play games with me, and even try to frighten me off. But nobody is going to stop me from doing what I came here to do. I am going to find my way to Wisdom."

Much later that day, Emily Paulette Johanssen Fairchild—known by everyone on St. Croix as Paulette—stood on the terrazzo terrace of her glass home on Shoys Beach and watched a lone sailboat cut along the molten edge of the twilight horizon. After the frustration of that morning, she'd managed to save the rest of the day by meeting a friend for a Caesar salad luncheon, followed by an afternoon of rambling through the boutiques of Gallows Bay. Afterward she'd done thirty laps in her pool and laid in the late afternoon sun. Now her skin glowed a deep honey against her ash-blond hair, and her blue eyes seemed to leap out in the softening light.

An ice cube whispered its demise as she systematically lifted a rock glass to her lips. The glittering of her pear-shaped diamond and heavy stone earrings could be seen from far away; her body cut a statuesque silhouette against the metal railing. In the background her husband, David Fairchild, sang loudly in the shower, triumphant over having defeated her brother Clay in their umpteenth game of golf.

The livid sun on the western horizon was a perfect backdrop for her anger and frustration at what had happened in Christiansted that morning. Paulette had gone looking for her cousin Severin and found him in the island's dilapidated hospital, a yellow-skinned, bald-headed scarecrow whose bent knees looked like the spine of a tent beneath the sheets. She sat down next to the scratched metal bed and bent forward, squinting carefully for a closer look.

Severin saw the ice-blue eyes before anything else as he emerged from another pleasant conversation with Pete. "So you find me, did you, Cousin?"

"Only after sending David to search every brothel in town. Why the hell didn't you tell someone you were going into the hospital?"

"Everybody know."

"Nobody knew. Not even Mimi."

"Mimi no tell you. But everybody talk. I tell one person and everybody know."

"So which one person did you choose to tell?"

"Tina."

"Tina is no person."

"More woman than you."

"You don't know anything about real women."

"You mean *white* women," he said, managing a dry chortle. "Don't want to know anything about no white girl!"

"There's nothing wrong with finding your own women attractive, Severin."

"Nothing attractive about ball-crushing bitches!"

Paulette leaned back in her chair. "So you're playing rasta with me today?"

"Fuck you."

She crossed a leg, then flicked a baby cockroach from the nightstand. "You should have at least gone up to Miami. This place is a nightmare."

"So what you come for?"

"I came to find out if you're dead or alive."

"Sorry, Cousin. You don't get Wisdom, yet."

"No part of Wisdom comes to us, Severin. We are fully aware of the terms of your father's will—"

"Go home, Paulette," he spat. "If I decide to die, let me die in peace."

"You should let us help you—"

"My pretty little cousin only want to help herself."

"You're disgusting, Severin."

"That's right. And when I die, I leave the house to anybody but you."

A silence held them apart. Paulette's eyes swept the bed, hoping for some idea of the extent of his illness. "When are you going back to Wisdom?" she inquired.

"When my vacation's over."

"I'm only asking in case you need a ride."

"Look out the window," he responded. "See my truck?"

"Will you be well enough to drive?"

"Don't matter. Got plenty friends to see after me."

"Tina and Carlson are not responsible, Severin."

"That's not your business, Cousin."

Exasperated, she stood. "So I'll tell Clay not to come."

"That's right. Tell your shitty brother not to come. And tell the same to your idiot husband."

"David had no intention of coming here. He didn't even want me to come."

"Smart white man."

"Better than a stupid white man who doesn't even know he's white."

"*Home*, Paulette."

She ignored Severin's evil stare as she walked out, undefeated. As she passed the black women in uniform at the nurses' station, she straightened her shoulders to accentuate her great height. The fluorescent lights cast a sheen on her perfect blond hair and honey-alabaster skin as she vised her attention on the head nurse, raising her voice so that everyone in the corridor could hear.

"I'm Severin Johanssen's cousin, Paulette Fairchild. My cousin's room is filthy! You need to get someone in here to spray. And he needs a bath. He actually smells."

The nurse nodded politely. "Mr. Seven refuses anything more than very basic care—"

"His name is Severin Johanssen, not Mr. Seven!"

The nurse paused, her face expressionless. "Excuse me, Mrs. Fairchild, but Seven and I played together when we still wore diapers. My name is Vashti Peterson. My father was the foreman at Wisdom and I grew up there."

Paulette halted. She had a vague memory of the nurse Vashti as a serious child who refused to accompany Severin and her brother Clay into the grape trees growing wild along the beach beneath the house. Hiding just behind a clump of thick twisting trunks, Paulette had heard the foreman's daughter say with dignity, "No playin' dirty, Seven."

"No dirty," he had answered with mocking eyes. "Sweet play, Vee. So very sweet."

Now the nurse continued to speak calmly.

"Mr. Seven is doing well and we are giving him every service he consents to. Thank you for making me aware of your concerns. I'll see what I can do about them."

Now standing on her balcony, the hickory smoke from a neighbor's grill drew Paulette back from her memory of the useless morning. But just as quickly her mind was filled with a sudden, violent longing for the noisy feasts the Johanssen family used to throw on the beach beneath Wisdom during her childhood. She remembered the black man Peterson hollowing a pit in the sand and lighting a bonfire as the children flitted through the grape trees. Late into the night they chased each other through the shadows and up the steep hill to the mill, while their parents sank into a stupor of flamed meat and rum. Sometimes the servants' children were allowed to join them, and Tina appeared from her hiding place, her golden eyes luring the boys into the undergrowth. The nurse Vashti must have been there too, but she kept a careful distance, as if her father's position of respect on the estate automatically destined her for something better.

The shower ceased and David trundled out onto the adjoining balcony, wearing nothing more than a towel about his waist. Paulette eyed the tanned, firm muscles of his chest and shoulders and had a fleeting memory of his undulating hips when she'd discovered him one day on top of one of the black girls, partially hidden by the bushes. She had run all the way back to the great house, her heart thumping and her skin prickling. For months she had savored the memory of his white buttocks grown red in the sunshine and the low satisfied moans that had drawn her to their forbidden pleasure. She had decided then, when she was eleven years old, that one day she would be David Fairchild's wife.

He stretched, throwing his arms out to the evening. "Let's go to Chéz Alexander tonight. I feel like having grilled salmon." Taking the Scotch from her hand, he raised it to his mouth, then winced at the taste. "This isn't Glenlivet!"

"It's Chivas."

"This is the limit, Paulette! I want you to get rid of Rose."

"I will not! Rose's parents worked for my mother and father and I consider her part of our family!"

"She's a servant!"

"You don't understand the ties that bind us on this island, David!"

"Yes, Paulette," he said angrily. "You never let me forget your proud, slaveholding heritage."

"Shut up, goddammit. This has nothing to do with Rose. *I* bought the Scotch! The store didn't have anything else."

As if by magic they heard the servant's voice, calling out to Paulette from the kitchen. Paulette gave a snort of exasperation and went back into the house to deal with whatever was required.

David Fairchild lingered a moment on the terrace, aware that his wife's slow-burning anger had far more to do with Wisdom than with their incompetent maid. Paulette had been terribly preoccupied about Severin's latest illness—and very worried that if she left him in the hands of the blacks who surrounded the estate, he might well end up leaving it all to one of them. David knew that his wife was particularly bothered by the thought of Tina, Severin's lover of more than two decades. Tina was a woman of fierce, violent sensuality whom all the men on the island desired and many had bedded. Yet Severin always took her back, no matter where, and with whom she'd been sleeping. It was Paulette's greatest fear that Tina might one day marry her cousin and become the mistress of Wisdom.

Severin had preferred black women since his childhood, and had only slept with white tourists when his mood—and the rum—was right. Like most of the white men born into the leisure class on the island, he'd learned all about sex with the poor black girls whose parents worked on the estate—David, too, had often indulged in this, the guiltiest of pleasures.

Unlike the other white boys, Severin had not grown beyond this forbidden taste, preferring to eat, drink, and live with the blacks. He'd never played golf, because he liked to spend his days riding practically naked across the barren, sun-bleached hills of his family estate. He'd never learned a profession for he'd given up school the day his older brother died, making him heir to the family fortune. And he'd never married, though plenty of women from the old island families would have been willing to try and civilize him.

No, Severin Johanssen, much to Paulette's endless consternation, was a law unto himself. A man of full, clear, deep lusts. A man who answered to no one. Well, perhaps that would soon change, now that the years of rum and nicotine were finally catching up with him. Rumor had it that he had cancer. That, in fact, he was dying.

A few feet away in their white-tiled bedroom, Paulette kicked her husband's sweaty golf clothes toward a wicker laundry basket and wondered again how she'd managed to marry a man who had none of the qualities she valued. David had never sought her out; he had no particular interest in the Johanssen land holdings. He thought of nothing more than his next momentary pleasure—of the condition of the water-starved golf greens; of the availability of the newest and best set of irons. He didn't even care about the portfolios he supposedly managed at his father's brokerage. Paulette knew that if there were any chance of ever gaining control of Wisdom, she'd have to do it alone.

"Hurry up and dress, David," she called up to him now. "It's getting late."

"Of course," he answered, entering the bedroom. They stared at each other for a long moment, each wondering how they had come to spend their lives with a perfect stranger.

SEVENTEEN DAYS

The ride from the hospital to Wisdom the following morning was slow and silent, but for the roar of the engine and the voices of the people who waved at the truck as they passed on the highway. Severin's glassy eyes took in everything and nothing, and both Tina and her brother Carlson knew him well enough to understand that he was still very sick.

Carlson practically carried Severin from the truck into the house, which Mimi had managed to clean. Someone had called the exterminators and gathered up his torn, stained shirts, replacing the rags with new white clothing. The jalousies were open and a sea breeze freshened even the long hidden corners of the master bedroom. Severin sat weakly on the bed, peering around him as if he had not been born in that very chamber. "It only so clean when Pete die," he whispered, leaning back on the pillows.

"Vashti come by my place after her shift at the hospital," Mimi explained as she fretted about the room with a dust cloth. "She say the doctor keep you until we fix the house up."

Severin smiled vaguely at the thought of the head nurse, who still had the character of the serious little girl who never let the white boys touch her. "She strong, Vashti," he whispered.

Tina observed him, her hands on her soft hips and thighs drawn apart in the attitude of command. She had slept in that room more nights than she could count; she had enjoyed the pleasures of that very bed and had seen the sun rise many times through those windows. Yet never before had it occurred to her that this man might need her to be more than the mistress of his mattress. Never before had she seen him in his fragile, fetal nudity.

"Vashti say you must eat, Mr. Seven," Mimi continued. "No more rum. No more cigarettes. You must eat food if you want to get well."

"Vashti is no doctor," Tina snapped. "She don't know what's best for Seven."

"*Kuté fam-la!*" Mimi insisted. "Listen to the woman! She want him to live, that's all."

Tina sucked her teeth loudly and turned back to her crumpled lover. Her mind raced over the images of thirty years—the boy whose unnamed anger drew her close and bound her forever to his need. The teenager who touched her before all the others, and whose body still fit so perfectly into hers. The man whose face and voice still called to her day and night, and even in her dreams. Looking down at this bald, trembling heap of suffering, she wondered where the Severin who rode bareback across the gutted fields of her life had gone. She was so lost in thought about the Severin of her youth that she failed to hear the grumble of the Jeep as it pulled to a stop at the foot of the drive.

It had taken Maia almost two hours to find her way, despite following the snaggle-edged, yellowing map she'd discovered the day before in a dusty corner of a lonely tourist shop on the very edge of Christiansted. The map dated back to the nineteen-fifties and still showed the estates that had since been sold or broken up for new development. Estate Wisdom was drawn as an immense property encompassing the entire northwestern coast of the island. The road to Wisdom was a thin, wavering line that took weird turns along the coast, like an unraveled thread waiting for the scissors of Fate.

After driving through neighborhoods of neat asphalt roads and landscaped, ranch-style homes, Maia passed the island's handsome university, which was set off from the highway down a long drive framed with swaying palms. She spotted the airport, a sprawling modern shopping center, and a Catholic school with bright yellow classroom buildings.

Then, trusting the directions indicated by the crumbling map, Maia thought that she had entered a time warp. She guided her rented Jeep—the biggest and toughest looking vehicle she could find—north toward Maroon Ridge. The clean brick dwellings of St. Croix's black middle class grew scarce, replaced by tumbling stone structures and wildly thatched hills, each crowned with an abandoned sugar mill. The carefully tended gardens bursting with bougainvillea and hibiscus vanished, replaced with rocky fields of dried grass, deforested during centuries of cane cultivation and bleached to baldness by the equatorial sun.

She mounted a sharply curving rise, feeling the rotted asphalt decay into a dirt road that spat up chunks of gravel as she mounted the hill. At the summit she let the Jeep's engine idle as she stared out at the distant, blue-black sea. Drawing in a deep breath, she pressed down the clutch and forced the engine into gear, determined to find whatever lay ahead.

The wandering dirt road hugged steep cliffs that were marked by neither guardrails nor signposts. Even in the meridian light the road was eerily lonely, with blades of wild grasses throwing whiplike shadows across the ruts. Beneath her the hills dove sharply seaward and the sky grayed under a gathering of heavy rain clouds. Struggling with the madly tilting steering wheel, she found herself imagining the desperation of the "maroons"—the fugitive slaves who'd had no hope of escaping from this remote and hostile place.

Maia drove west, carefully avoiding potholes large enough to swallow up the front of her Jeep. After nearly forty-five minutes she came upon a rusting chain-link fence running down from the road clear to the sea. Behind it were storm-beaten outbuildings that might have once been stables. The charred carcass of a tractor and a number of rusting scythes were scattered among large boulders. Up ahead an unpaved driveway vanished through crumbling stone gates.

She climbed out of the Jeep and stretched her aching back. A mongoose shot out of the trees and across the road, and she sprang back in fear. Turning slowly, she inspected the yawning drive that was overshadowed by gnarled plain trees. The house was invisible, but she caught sight of the tip of a sugar mill standing sentinel on the top of a steep, rocky hill.

Her breath caught in her throat. This must be it. This scene matched her grandfather's description of Wisdom. Throwing the Jeep into gear, she drove into the unmarked drive, barely able to hold back the tears that sprang into her eyes.

White afternoon heat was wrapped around the house. The elderly Mimi swayed back and forth, singing, *"Scalambay, scalambay, scoops scoops, scalambay,"* as she scrubbed the rusty sink. The door to the great room stood open, and she could see Severin's pale legs propped up on the rotting wood of the balcony railing, slightly reddened from the sun. The rest of him lay shaded beneath the thick branches of the great oak tree that had been planted as a sapling when the house was young. Tina sat gloomily beside her, shaking out the loose sleeves of her caftan to cool her bouncing underarms.

The two women had little to say to each other, though they were second cousins. Mimi had worked at Wisdom since her childhood and had always disapproved of Tina's free reign on the estate. There had even been times in the old days—when Tina was sharing Severin's bed—that she had treated the old woman as her own personal servant, ordering her to bring food and drink, or to wash the soiled sheets. Severin had ignored the antipathy between the distant cousins, rising and leaving the room when their anger erupted into shouts. Like most men, he ignored the uncontrolled emotions of his women. He often left the house, wandering out to the horses he'd kept stabled in a barn on the edge of the estate, the sound of their rage fading into the humored wash of the sea. He'd select a horse, strip to his shorts, and ride all afternoon, slowly winding his way past the ruined windmill and deserted beach, returning only at sunset to find the great house still perched on its wooded cliff, silent and empty.

A half hour earlier the women had argued hotly about Severin's unwillingness to eat, and it was the strained silence between them that probably allowed Maia to stand a whole minute in the doorway, waiting silently for someone to sense her presence. When she cleared her throat Mimi looked up nervously, but Tina took her time turning her head, as if nothing and no one justified any intrusion into their virulent hostility.

"Excuse me," Maia said politely. "Is this the Wisdom estate?"

The two women looked at each other, then back at the visitor. Suddenly Tina burst into hard laughter, flinging her head back and letting her raucous voice knock the high ceiling, the scarred furniture, the unpainted walls.

"Here is Wisdom," Mimi said. "No stranger call in here for many years. What you want?"

Maia stood uncertainly in the doorway. "I was hoping to visit the house."

"This no museum. Owner sick."

"I see. Is there someone else I could speak to about—"

"You talk to me," Tina interrupted firmly. She took in the sundress and straw hat, instantly recognizing the Statesider from Brandy's bar. Tina's scowl razed the sun-browned limbs and froze on the sunglasses that hid the woman's eyes. "There's a museum to see back on Centerline Road."

"Could I just have a look around the grounds?"

"This house private. You go now—"

"I just—" Abruptly she stopped talking and both Mimi and Tina turned to find Severin propped up in the doorway.

"What's this?" he wheezed.

Tina grunted. "She think here is for tourists."

He stared at Maia a long moment, then turned away without responding.

"Excuse me—" the stranger insisted, raising her voice as if to leap over the hurdles of Mimi and Tina. "My name is Maia Ransom. I'll only be on St. Croix for a few days and I wanted to have a look at the estate."

The two women stiffened. Severin looked back at the visitor and suddenly he went very still, his body bent strangely in the doorway. Finally he managed to speak. "It's over. Finished. Nothing more here," he murmured as he shuffled back into the shadows.

Tina's eyes still scoured the visitor. "I remember you. I see you at Brandy's."

"The bar down on the dock? Yes, I go there sometimes."

Mimi and Tina slowly exchanged glances. Tina stood up slowly and magnificently, her voice acquiring a Yankee plainness.

"This is no place for visits. Good-bye."

Maia didn't move for an obstinate thirty seconds or so. Finally she hoisted up her woven grass bag and turned on her sandal, briskly descending the curving drive. Tina walked to the door and observed her descent, waiting for the sound of a car engine from below. After a few moments she turned back to Mimi.

"What you think she want?"

"She looking for her family, Tina. She think her people here."

Tina nodded slowly, one thick hand coming up to her hip. "She got no people here," she remarked, more to herself than to her elder cousin. "She got no business at Seven's place."

"Why you worry?" Mimi said. " 'The machete blade leaves no cut in the water.' It don't make no difference if she take a look."

"She got no business at Wisdom," Tina repeated darkly.

Without answering, Mimi picked up another pot, hoisted a deep sigh, and began to rub.

Maia turned her rented Jeep around and drove slowly down the rutted, overgrown drive shaded by its enormous, listing oak trees. When she reached the entrance to the road, which was broken by huge potholes and decaying asphalt, she turned off the engine and slammed her fists against the steering wheel, shouting into the cagelike tree trunks.

"I've traveled too goddamned far—and worked too goddamned hard—to be kicked off this estate five minutes after I found it!" She shot an evil glance over her shoulder. "Can you get that? It wasn't even that shriveled-up white man who chased me away. It was a black woman—and she might even be my goddamned *cousin*!"

Maia climbed out of the Jeep and turned back to the house, squaring her shoulders.

"My people sacrificed their lives here," she said aloud. "And now you want to treat me like I have no right to set foot on this property?"

Steadying herself against her sudden desire to return to the dilapidated heap and tell them all to screw themselves, she stood very straight and still, listening to the wind climbing painfully through the tangled branches. A bird called out overhead, but the only answer was the distant murmur of the sea. Maia breathed in the scent of salty loam and bladed grasses, closing her eyes to the rage she'd felt only seconds before. When her eyes opened she was filled with a new determination, buttressed by the truth that she had yet everything to learn about her ancestral past and absolutely nothing to lose.

Climbing back into the Jeep, she calmly slid the engine into gear and roared away, deciding that nothing and no one would stop her from getting into Wisdom.

"So? What's it like?"

"A mess."

"A mess like Monticello? The White House? *Tara?*"

"God, no." Maia lowered her glass without tasting the unsweetened iced tea, and gazed at Damian's opaque sunglasses. The two were stretched out on towels beside the pool at his Danish employer's estate. The boss was in Europe tending to her other businesses, so Damian looked after the empty Spanish-style mansion, supervising the gardener and housekeeper and walking the three Great Danes. Two swordfish steaks grilled slowly on a hibachi beside the deck.

"It looked pretty typical for the Caribbean," she said thoughtfully, dipping her finger in the heavily chlorinated water. "One floor. A central great room and wings extending out to either side. I guess one part was for servants. The other part was probably for the owners. But I couldn't really tell. I was only there for about five minutes and it was extremely run down."

Damian pulled a cigarette from his slender lips and exhaled a fine ribbon of smoke into the hot evening. "So what else did you see?"

"Well, the property obviously extends down to the water. I could make out some ruins of outer buildings from the road. Probably stables. And there's an abandoned mill up on top of a hill."

"Any ghosts wandering around?"

"Sure. They offered to give me a tour."

He grinned, flicking the ashes into the hedges, and pressed the tip of his beer bottle against his lips. Four other empty bottles stood forlornly near his feet. "Is the owner rich?"

"Probably was. But he's in the poorhouse now. The wood's about to warp off the hinges and nothing's seen a paintbrush in decades. Smelled pretty evil, too."

"He can still afford servants."

"I can't imagine what he pays them."

Damian grunted. "You should be thanking your lucky stars that your ancestors got smart and got off this island. Otherwise you might be one of those women you met in that kitchen."

"God forbid," Maia agreed, staring up into the motionless midday palms. "What really hurts is that it was a black woman who chased me away."

"What do you expect? She figures you're rich—"

"I sure as hell am not!"

"And you're gorgeous!"

"Gorgeous? What planet are you from?"

"Come on, Maia. Spending your life in some ugly nurse's uniform hasn't changed the fact that you happen to be a very beautiful woman."

"Oh, please, Damian! I'm not trying to flirt with that broken-down piece of white man!"

"His girlfriend doesn't know that! As far as she's concerned, you're everything she'll never be. She doesn't want you getting any ideas about her little piece of plantation!"

"I'll only be down here for two more weeks."

"God made the whole world in much less time than that." Damian chuckled, rolled over, and stubbed his cigarette into the ashtray. "Maia, you should see what wandered up last night!"

"Fine?"

"A Guinean gladiator!"

"Oh, please, Damian!"

"No, really. Strong and passionate and unspoiled by white blood."

"You're half white!"

"And *mein Gott*, don't I regret it!" Damian laughed again, looking thoughtfully into the pool water. "You know, I spent the first twenty years of my life trying to forget my German mother. Then she showed up on my twenty-first birthday and invited me to live with her in Europe."

"And?"

"I had to go with her, Maia. I had to find out who she was and why she gave me to those American missionaries. Why she let me grow up in America, where everybody hated me because I wasn't black or white." He sat up and sighed, his face empty. "And you know the only thing I learned from surviving three years in Munich? *Ich habe Deutsche gelernt*: I learned how to speak German."

"Are you sorry you went?"

"If I hadn't gone I would have spent my whole life wondering who she was. Wondering if I belonged in that culture. What part of me really is German." Damian sucked hard on his cigarette. "Maia, I forgave my mother when I saw the life I would have had growing up in Munich. I'm black and I'm gay. I would never have fit in there. It hurt like hell to discover those things. But at least I don't have to spend what's left of my life worrying about it." He reached out and touched her arm. "Now as I see it, you've got to do the same thing. It may not be easy for you, but you've got to find out what part of you belongs here on St. Croix. And what part of you still lives at Wisdom."

The pool water lapped softly, and a red-winged bird landed on the flamboyant tree by the guesthouse. Damian's expression cleared. "Want some ice cream?"

Maia laughed softly. "I've never seen anybody eat like you and stay so thin."

"Thin?" He faked outrage. "I'm a master of illusion, darling. Actually, I'm six-foot-four and weigh two-eighty-five."

"That's all right, baby," Maia laughed. "Some of us prefer an easy fit."

"Easy fit?" He removed his glasses and winked at Maia. "If you only knew . . ."

A few moments later he returned from his guesthouse with two bowls of lime sorbet.

"Why do you hang out with these guys who only want to sneak around in the dark?"

"St. Croix has not yet experienced gay liberation, Maia."

"So does your gladiator have a name?"

"We'll stick with Caesar."

"Caesar?"

"He's got a wife and five kids, baby. He's got to sneak to keep his oldest son from seeing him."

"Damian—"

"I know, I know. But that's just the way things are down here. And in most other places in the world, I'll remind you. In fact," he added quietly, "my black parents told me not to come home after I came out. They could accept the fact that I was the bastard son of an alcoholic German woman and an unknown black serviceman. But they couldn't take it when I told them I'm gay. I don't have any family in the States to return to."

"I'm sorry."

Damian laughed, but kept his gaze fixed on the lapping pool water. "Sometimes I miss New York," he added softly.

"Hey," Maia said brightly, "you're seeing more men than I am."

"But you could have Juan just by whistling."

"True, that," Maia responded in a deft echo of the island dialect.

"So why don't you give him a try? I guarantee you he wouldn't be a bore."

"He'll think he owns me."

"But that would keep all the other bowwows away."

"What if I meet someone I like?"

"Honey, anyone who pleases Maia Ransom will come from a much finer breed."

They laughed lightly, savoring the sharp taste of sorbet mixed with cigarette smoke.

"So," Damian said suddenly, "you think the servants will throw you from the top of the sugar mill for having a closer peek at your great-grandfather's happy hunting grounds?"

"They'll have to catch me, first."

"Then," he laughed to a puff of Marlboro, "they'll put you to sleep with the rest of the Ransoms."

"Well, we're all gonna meet up with our ancestors sooner or later. I might as well go ahead and introduce myself."

FiFteen Days

The next morning Maia, outfitted in a good pair of hiking boots, drove to the edge of the Wisdom estate. She left her rented Jeep in a thick clump of grape trees, and climbed over the fence. Avoiding the rusting farm implements, she began a long secret trek across the wildly over-grown fields. With some difficulty she mounted a dangerously steep slope to the well-preserved stone mill, and sat for a long while on a huge boulder just beneath it, looking out over the sea.

From her perch on the boulder she could see the great house, con-structed graciously on a swelling crest of rock so that the rear windows faced the private beach below. The rusted metal roof was now warped and reddened under the beating sun, and even from a distance Maia saw shoals of tiny lizards scuttling in and out of the cracks. The windows were tall and narrow—French doors, actually, and those that still had glass reflected the lush vibrancy of Caribbean undergrowth.

Maia made her way laboriously down the rocky hill and snaked her way through the dense undergrowth, finally finding her way to the rear of the house. Through the thick bushes she could admire the carefully detailed woodwork, often called "gingerbread," that laced the arched windows and added a gentle Gothic touch to the house. The hand-carved patterns were rotting in the constant salt spray and unrelenting heat, as was the wide wooden terrace that flanked the great room.

She crept right up to the terrace and peered over the stained floor into the open chamber. She could see the edge of a bed. Worm-feasted furniture and shredded draperies haunted the room. Beneath the piercing odor of cleansers she could still smell raw sickness, and when she heard tortured coughing from the stained mattress, she ducked down into the sheltering grape leaves and stole away.

Maia understood that the owner, that peeling, emaciated man, was too ill to really care who walked around his estate. But she also knew that his woman—that bratwurst with yellow eyes—would rip her to tatters if she caught her on the grounds.

Yet she couldn't stop herself from returning, and within two days Maia knew her way around Estate Wisdom with certainty. She was drawn again and again to the abandoned sugar mill—now an echoing stone tower on its lonely cliff above the sea. From the mill she could see ships that were like mosquitoes on the horizon. She could make out the blue echo of St. Thomas, thirty nautical miles away. And best of all, when she sat on the thronelike boulder with the woods rolling out beneath her, she could hear Ransom voices whispering and singing to her in the hot sea breeze.

Late one morning she was cooling off in the shallow waves of the white sand beach, her gaze drawn inexplicably to an old boathouse that seemed abandoned to the grape leaves. Raising her sarong up high around her hips, she had just decided to explore the rotting structure when she heard a rustling voice as distinct as her memory reach out from the bushes. Turning, she stared into the shadowy silhouette of a man crouching in the foliage.

"You here."

"Yes," she answered, rising boldly to her full height.

There was a pause as the broken voice gathered up its strength. "What you want?" The sound was desiccated, agonized.

"I want my people."

Again he waited, as if the waves might write his lines. "Your people not here."

"My people are here." She said it factually.

"Where your people?"

"Beneath every plant, every tree, every flower," she intoned, slowing wading from the sea to stand before him. Water rushed down her legs and she lowered her skirt so that little more than her calves was visible in the crystal water.

Severin grunted. "I been here my life long. Who your people?"

"My great-grandparents left eighty years ago. But their ancestors lived here and worked here since Africa."

"Africa! Oh, please!" He made a rough, hacking sound that she recognized as a laugh. He chortled as if the myth of her kinship to that place was too ridiculous to believe. "Who tell you that? What a tale!"

She stared into the shadows, her features hard and calm. Severin moved forward, his face almost coming into contact with the blazing sunlight. "Listen, girl," he whispered, "you need to forget all that. They make it up. They tell you that because it sound good."

She waded out of the water, approaching him despite her cloying sense of distaste. "What difference is it to you?" She stopped in the wet sand, finally making out the contours of his hollow sockets. A wash of pale hair had begun growing on his scalp and chin.

"This is my place," he said, a note of childishness creeping into his memory of a voice.

"I just want to spend some time here."

"Even if it's a lie?"

"It's my truth," she answered, and to her surprise he laughed again. The sound ended in a weak groan.

"You tough, right?"

"I'm tough, all right."

An exasperated cry startled them both, and Maia watched as the thick, slit-eyed Tina waddled her way down the steep embankment toward them. Severin turned stiffly, then sighed.

"Why you here, Seven? It's too hot! You need to be at rest, now!"

"I want to go swimming, but water already taken," he muttered, slipping back into their dialect.

"You get back to bed, like doctor order!"

Acknowledging her command, he shifted as if seeking the strength to rise. The only sounds were the soft wind in the leaves and the murmur of the sea. Severin winced and grabbed at the swaying trunk of a young palm, trying to hoist himself up to his feet. He staggered and sweat washed down his face. For a moment it seemed he might pass out. Then Tina's voice yanked him up and sent him turning back to the uninvited guest.

"And you, tourist!" she shouted. "I already tell you this place private. You go to museum if you want play visitor!" Tina's voice gained volume as she evaluated the patterned sarong tied over the firm hips. Maia's arms were wrapped across her chest, denying the other woman a view of her bust.

"I'm not going anywhere until your employer asks me to leave," she said clearly and slowly.

"My *what*?" Tina blurted like a blowtorch.

"Your employer," Maia repeated clearly.

"You get off this property before I hurt you!" Tina shouted, clenching her body as if it were a fist.

"I think that he's able to speak for himself," Maia responded, looking toward Severin.

"When he sick I speak for him!" Tina hurled, taking a heavy step forward and sinking into the soft well of sand at the foot of the embankment.

Maia snorted and turned away.

"What you laughing at, you black-ass cunt!" Tina snarled.

"Hey, Tina! Stay cool, baby!" Severin garnered up his strength and found enough voice to keep Tina from leaping toward the American.

"What this bitch think? She no belong here!"

He swayed a bit, but kept his voice light. "She want to find her people—"

"No people here!"

"But she look, and then she see and then she go!"

"Wisdom your place, Seven. She got nobody here."

"Let it be, Tina," he said with a gentle desperation.

Maia watched the strange exchange between this man and his

servant—or lover—or whatever Tina was. She remarked that the white man was able to switch between the local dialect and American English at will—if indeed, he really *was* white. It was damned hard to tell, despite his blanched color. She also noticed that he coddled the woman, speaking to her sensuously, gently, teasingly, as if she were a cocky but beloved pet.

Now he looked back at Maia, still speaking to Tina.

"She don't do no harm, Tina. Forget it. She take a souvenir. A rock or a handful of sand. Then she satisfied."

Tina sucked her teeth loudly, in Caribbean fashion. Severin tried to hold his smile, but the pain he felt suddenly erupted and he staggered forward, sinking onto one knee in the deep sand.

Tina's eyes leaped from the trespasser to her lover and she moved toward him in concern. To her surprise, the other woman came forward, too. Severin lifted his eyes helplessly, but remained in his painful crouch.

"What you doing, Seven? Get up!" Tina cried. She grasped his upper arm and pulled at him. Her efforts were met with a groan. Maia knelt beside Severin, reaching for his wrist with one hand while expertly running her other fingers along the base of his throat and chest.

"Don't touch him, you bitch!"

"You need to get someone to carry him!" Maia responded with unexpected authority.

"What you mean? Don't you—"

"I'm a nurse, and from his pulse, I'd say that he's in trouble. Who's his doctor? We need to get him to a hospital!"

Tina stared at Maia with a hatred that might have frightened the other woman, had not the sound of Severin's labored breathing frightened her more.

"Get someone, fast!" Maia commanded, and despite her rage, Tina waddled toward the hill. She lumbered up the embankment, her stubby feet sinking into the sucking mouths of sand. Almost bent double and dripping with sweat, she paused at the top of the knoll and took a quick look back. In the shallow waves of a sullen sea, Tina's lifelong lover lay immobile in Maia Ransom's powerful arms.

THIRTEEN DAYS

This was so very different from the other times.

Before, she had struggled with the sensation of stealing something. Of deceiving an unknown authority whose power might hurt her in an indescribable way. Of trespassing into a history that excluded her, although she knew it was her own.

But this time she was a part of the caravan that moved toward Wisdom with the purposefulness of manifest destiny. She was supposed to be there. She was a part of this Truth.

They were moving so slowly up the tortured dirt road, her Jeep lurching and staggering behind the ambulance as it scrolled its way between the potholes, that she had time to examine the ragged scrub brush, low-growing thistles, and red-toned rocks that hugged Maroon Ridge. She had time to mark the little inlets of barren land that unfolded as they rounded a curve, and to admire the blue-green sea that gently licked at the pearly shore far below. She had plenty of time to go over the events that would now permit her to enter the house built by her forefathers.

One day earlier she stood with the doctor as he bent over Severin, examining the unhealed wound where the latest biopsy had been performed. He stirred and the doctor reached forward to adjust the bandages so that the raw flesh was covered. A filthy cough erupted from deep inside his lungs, but when he tried to move his arms he discovered that he was tethered to his bed.

"Take it easy, Mr. Johanssen," the doctor advised quietly. Severin's frightened eyes wandered around the room. He grimaced at the sight of the plastic bottles emptying their contents into his body via an elaborate weaving of tubes. His legs were bound tight under the sheets. The doctor's Canadian-trained eyes met his and he made a remark that Severin couldn't fully understand. The American woman—yes, the tourist—was standing beside the bed. Realizing that he was awake, she looked at him and smiled.

Then they went on talking about him as if he weren't there. He thought that he was frowning, but couldn't reach up to his face to find out. After what seemed an eternity the doctor ambled off, leaving him alone with the woman. Weakly he motioned for her to come closer. She leaned forward, automatically reaching for his wrist.

"Why you here?" he rattled after clearing his throat.

She spoke while staring at her watch. "You almost died."

"Why you here?"

"I came here with you."

"Why you here?"

She dropped his hand. "I'm a nurse, Mr. Johanssen."

He felt waters rushing through him at those words, the words that he no longer could ignore, and he tried to move forward, rasping, "What's your name?"

"I already told you. It's Maia. Maia Ransom."

"Oh, no," he groaned.

She stood and smoothed the sheet over his wasted thighs. "Your medication was way off."

"You're a nurse," he whispered belligerently, "not a doctor."

"And you're probably alive because this *nurse* was with you during your attack. You had toxic levels of medication in your blood. Don't you ever eat before taking your pills?"

The door opened and the doctor returned, Severin's chart in his hands. "Mr. Johanssen, you'd better be thanking somebody that Nurse Ransom was nearby when you passed out."

Severin's eyes began to water with contempt.

"I think," the doctor was saying, "that I not only let you go home too soon after your surgery, but I sent you off without the proper follow-up. When you leave tomorrow, you need to have someone with you who knows something about medicine."

Severin turned over several answers as his system was beginning to roar with the lovely liquids that took all his troubles to another universe.

"I've been talking to Nurse Ransom," the doctor continued.

"Talking to her? About *me*?" Severin twisted his head weakly to see Maia, who looked back at him steadily.

"You need a professional at the house, and she's agreed to spend a few days with you at Wisdom until your health improves."

"I don't want *her*!"

"Just a few days, Mr. Johanssen. Or next time you might end up in cold storage with a tag tied to your toe."

Severin stared at Maia through slits of frustrated rage. "Hey," he rattled. When she didn't answer, he choked the syllable out again.

"You will address me by my name," she responded coldly.

"All right, *Nurse* Ransom," he mocked. "How long you stay on the island?"

"That's my concern."

Severin looked back into the doctor's eyes. "You give me the right medicine and I won't need her."

"If you're not careful you won't need anybody."

Warily, Severin met Maia's unwavering gaze. "What's in this for you?" he rasped.

"You already know, Mr. Johanssen," she said in a dry voice. "I get to look for my people."

Thus Maia's position as Severin Johanssen's "home care support" had been arranged in a brief conversation between the Canadian doctor and Vashti Peterson, the dignified head nurse who always seemed to be on duty. Maia had admired the woman's quiet demeanor and intelligent watchfulness. She also appreciated the nurse's willingness to speak to her candidly about her patient.

"The doctor's written prescriptions for several painkillers," she explained as they waited for the orderlies to wheel Severin's gurney to the waiting ambulance. "But I'd keep a close watch on how many tablets he takes."

"He's going to be in a lot of discomfort until those sutures heal."

The nurse placed her hand on Maia's arm. "Just watch him carefully," she said quietly. "As we say in the islands, 'Where the fence is low, the cow will jump.' Keep the medications in your possession. And make sure he doesn't have a bottle of rum hidden somewhere."

Maia looked at her in surprise. Vashti shook her head slowly. "I've known Seven for a long time, Miss Ransom." A brief smile softened her stoic features. "St. Croix is small. We take care of each other, even if it doesn't seem to make much sense."

The attendants arrived with the mummified Severin, who was whining about needing more drugs to survive the trip to Wisdom. The two women exchanged glances as he was loaded into the ambulance.

"Miss Peterson," Maia said as the doors closed on the sound of the sick man's complaints, "Why does everyone refer to Severin as 'Seven'?"

"That's no mystery," Vashti said. "He's the seventh. The last of the Johanssen men."

Finally the ambulance cleared Wisdom's crumbling stone pillars and entered the long, root-entangled drive. Maia angled the Jeep carefully around a wormy mongoose carcass that lay beside the gates. A sudden darkness seemed to fall over the vehicle as she entered the tunnel of interlaced trees, and Maia was actually relieved when they arrived at the base of the overgrown circular drive.

The old woman Mimi emerged from the house. Behind her Maia could make out the silhouette of the cat-eyed woman in the doorway. The driver and ambulance attendant managed to maneuver the gurney up the broken slates while Severin cursed them in a wheedling voice. Maia was just pulling her suitcases from the back of the Jeep when she heard the cry: "*Awa! Sa pa sa!* What does that bitch want?"

She looked up to see Tina waddling down the drive while the old woman hovered in the shadows. Severin broke into a fit of coughing and Maia took several steps toward her patient.

"You better not touch him!" Tina warned, placing herself in front of the gurney.

"I'm here to help."

"*Mwe sav ki-mun u ye!* I know who you are!"

"I'm a nurse and—"

"You get in your car and go."

"Mr. Johanssen is very sick—"

"And *you* going to be sicker!"

"Tina, you must let her come," Mimi interrupted. "The doctor say so."

"What?" Tina wheeled on her cousin, who stammered out a reply.

"Vashti—she come to my house last night. The doctor want the American here one day or two."

"Vashti say that?" Tina repeated in outrage.

"She said one or two days. That's all."

Tina turned her Medusa stare on Maia. "I know why you here. I know what you want. But you will never, ever have Wisdom."

"Seven need her," Mimi insisted softly. "You want him dead?"

At these words the sick man reached forward and grasped weakly at Tina's fingers. "Tina," he rattled. "It's only you. Never nobody but you."

For a long moment, Tina stared intently at her lover. Then she waddled slowly down the drive, coming so close that Maia could see her own reflection in the hate-filled eyes.

"I going now," she announced in a growl of stale beer and tobacco. "But remember: I not going far."

Maia hoisted up her shoulder bags and mounted the steep drive, pausing for a brief moment at the threshold. The ambulance driver and attendant had hurriedly placed Severin on a dilapidated daybed, and now pushed by her as if afraid to remain in the house a moment longer than was absolutely necessary. The reasons for their discomfort were immediately apparent: Wisdom was a nightmare.

"My God," Maia murmured in dismay as she stepped inside. The unpainted walls of the sickroom—she instantly surmised that it had once been the house's great room—were cracked and pocked with wormholes. Faded areas suggested that paintings had once filled the wide, empty spaces, but now the walls were bare. The floor was rotted, the planks twisted up in some places to reveal the foundations of the house below. Wide doors that led out to the rear balcony hung slightly off their rusted hinges, and the wooden jalousies were cracked and broken away from the window frames.

Although the sheets were clean, the mattress on the bed sagged, and the metal headboard bore scars of its own. A low table beside the bed was full of plastic bottles, some full of pills, others practically empty. The other faded pieces of furniture might have been a century old.

There was nothing else in the room except the competing odors of vomit and bleach. Mimi was evidently doing everything in her power to hold the house on its hinges. But it was a losing battle. Maia knew within five seconds that Wisdom, and any evidence of the Ransoms that it might be hiding, were doomed.

She walked slowly toward her patient who, thanks to the large amount of medication he'd begged for during the trip, was fast asleep. She looked down at the emaciated, bald-headed figure and wondered if all families who based their wealth on the exploitation of others eventually came to look like this. "Shit," she whispered softly. "Thank God I don't have any Johanssen blood in my veins."

She turned to find Mimi standing hesitantly in the doorway. Walking forward, Maia held out her hand.

"I'm Maia," she said softly with a glance over her shoulder. "You've taken care of him for a long time, haven't you?"

The old woman ducked her head shyly. "I been here when Seven's grandmother was young. I take care of all the Johanssens."

"Do you live here, now?"

"No. I got my house down in the valley. My grandson bring me up in the morning and pick me up at night."

She followed the old woman along a creaking corridor to a room at the rear. Maia sighed as she stepped into the crumbling chamber. The ancient wallpaper was peeled back to reveal the raw planks of the outer walls, and there were wormholes in the floorboards. A mosquito net was draped over the sawed-off limbs of the former canopy bed and the jalousies on the windows were strung together by threads. Everything smelled of rot.

"I guess this is the guest suite," Maia said lightly.

"Seven don't look after the house since his brother dead," Mimi explained apologetically.

"Well," Maia replied as she spied a gecko slipping through a crack in the wall, "I guess I'll survive for a couple of days."

Mimi pointed to a faded towel on the foot of the bed, then turned to leave.

"Mimi," Maia asked quickly, "is there anybody else around at night?"

The old woman paused, wondering if she should mention the fact that Tina was always somewhere close by, lurking in the shadows. Instead she shook her head.

Maia stood mute, suddenly consumed with a feeling of complete inadequacy in the face of such overwhelming obstacles. Did she really belong in that place? Was there anything she could do for its pathetic resident? Could she really hope to find any trace of her ancestors in the middle of this destitution? Could they possibly have lived like *this*? Perhaps Damian was right: She should be thanking God that her great-grandfather got the hell off the island!

"You must be hungry," Mimi said softly, and Maia looked at her with grateful eyes.

"Yes, I could stand a bite to eat."

"Well, you come on out to the kitchen and we'll see what we got in the larder."

"I'll be right there," Maia answered. When she was alone, she sank slowly down on the bed, tears filling her eyes. There has to be something more, she thought. This can't be all that's left of my people!

A scrambling noise drew her attention to the warped window frame and she looked out, catching a glimpse of the brilliant sea through the thick grape tree leaves. In the distance she could make out the stone tower on its steep hill, still guarding the land of the Johanssens.

"You're out there," she whispered. "You're out there and I'm going to find a way to you. I just don't know how, and I have so very little time."

A single tear broke free from her lashes and she brushed it away, stepping back into her nurse's persona.

TWELVE DAYS

The silver Mercedes wound its way cautiously along the steep, rutted dirt road, tracing a reluctant path up Maroon Ridge toward Wisdom. From the driver's seat, David Fairchild cast occasional glances at Paulette, who was staring at the highway, her head held magnificently erect. Even now, in her mid-forties, Paulette had lost nothing of the regal bearing of the legendary Johanssen women.

It was said that her ancestor Solomon Johanssen had followed a woman named Marie-Paule Emilie St. Severin from her plantation in Martinique all the way to France to ask for her hand in marriage. Solomon Johanssen was rich; far richer than the crumbling French family ensconced in their Revolution-ruined estate outside Paris. In the end it was fortunate that he had caught a glimpse of Marie-Paule in her carriage at the market of Fort-de-France, and obsessively inquired after her identity until he'd finally found her.

Solomon and his bride had settled on his enormous estate on St. Croix, producing two sons, Jakob and Issak. Issak died young, but

Jakob's own son was grandfather to Peter and Severin, Paulette and Clay. After the plane accident that took Peter's life, Severin became the sole heir of the remaining portions of the original estate, the rest having already been divided between the cousins.

And of course Paulette wanted it all for herself, if for no other reason than to keep the likes of Tina out. David knew that Paulette would stop at nothing to get it. She had inherited her ancestor's great sense of obsessive purpose, and believed deeply in the importance of her family name. He found her ambition quite appealing, if a bit absurd, and thus tolerated her endless desire to defeat Severin.

"We're going to have to get a better car if you plan to start doing this more often," he commented as he steered them carefully around a mammoth hole.

"The only car better than this is a Bentley, and you know there's no dealer on the island," she replied dryly.

"I meant that we need a four-wheel drive with a manual transmission—"

"I won't be seen driving one of those ugly bulldozers, David. Anyway, we've made it, so the discussion is moot."

They passed the crumbling gates and emerged from the copse of thatched trees to swish up the circular drive. David climbed from the sedan, his darkly tanned face hidden beneath a pair of heavily tinted glasses. He offered a hand to Paulette, who was still brushing her blond mane as she swung her long legs to the weedy flagstone path. She was immediately aware of an unexpected odor and she stood aloof, her head tilted so that she could better flair the unexpected scent of life from the ruined house. Was it possible that someone was baking bread?

Inside the dingy kitchen Mimi stood by the gas stove, stirring a big pot of something that seemed to be a gently spiced soup. This surprised Paulette, who knew from a lifetime spent with servants that island women cooked everything with their hot peppers and plenty of garlic. Mimi nodded at the Fairchilds, but did not speak. David stood behind his wife, inspecting the place.

"Is Mr. Johanssen here?" Paulette asked.

The old woman nodded again.

"In his room?"

Still stirring the soup, Mimi glanced toward the closed doors as if unsure how to respond. Paulette stepped forward, then hesitated at the thought that Tina might be somewhere nearby.

"Is he alone, Mimi?"

Still stirring, the old woman obstinately refused to answer. Throwing back her heavy mane, Paulette strode across the foyer and flung open the double doors to the great room and found herself face-to-face with a stranger.

"Who are—"

The woman's hands came up in a silencing gesture and Paulette froze, despite her surprise. The woman stepped forward, forcing Paulette to back up toward the kitchen, where David leaned in the doorway.

"I asked who you are—"

The woman, dressed in a simple cotton dress, spoke calmly. "I'm a nurse. I'm here to look after Mr. Johanssen until he has recovered some of his strength."

"Who hired you? Did you fly down from Miami?"

Maia looked patiently into Paulette's face, quickly noting the colorless lashes and brilliant turquoise eyes. There was a long pause.

"No."

The resistance in Maia's even gaze might have silenced a weaker woman, but Paulette held a pedigree from generations of plantation wealth and leisure, and was not likely to be stood down by a working-class woman of color. "I asked you—"

"Are you related to Mr. Johanssen?" The question, quietly stated, nonetheless resonated like a saber thrust.

"What do you mean, asking me—"

"Mr. Johanssen is resting now and needs absolute quiet," was the cool response. Maia closed the doors firmly behind her without dropping her gaze.

In the kitchen, the spoon in the soup pot stopped. David chuckled quietly from his perch in the open doorway, switching legs so that his weight was balanced inside the peeling doorframe. All Maia could make out was the silhouette of a tall man blocking the afternoon sun. Paulette continued to look hard into Maia's face, as if trying to weigh the true extent of her composure. "I'm Severin's cousin, and since he has no other relatives, *I'm* the person who looks after him."

"Well, I am Maia Ransom. Mr. Johanssen's doctor suggested that I stay here for a few days, until he's back on his feet."

The tension vibrated like a high-tension wire as Paulette waited for further explanation. Then, realizing that she might be waiting all afternoon, she lifted her chin and struck her finest pose. "And when will Mr. Johanssen be 'back on his feet'?"

"I'm sorry, but the details of his treatment are confidential. I cannot discuss this any further with you, unless he consents."

Paulette blinked, speechless. Maia lifted her head calmly and stared into her eyes. The silence began to feel like an undetonated explosive.

In the doorway David shifted and sighed. "Come on, Paulette. I need to see a client in Judith's Fancy."

"But David, I have to—"

"If you want to see Mr. Johanssen," Maia said, "I'd recommend that you stop by in the morning. I'm trying to keep him quiet during the hottest part of the afternoon." The air resonated for another beat, then shifted to the grade of a temporary cease-fire. Paulette whirled around angrily and stomped past her husband into the afternoon sun. Mimi began stirring the pot again.

When the Mercedes had cleared the bottom of the drive, Mimi's face melted into a grin. She had never seen anyone back that Paulette bitch down, and would never have dreamed that a *black* woman could do it. Even Tina, who made sparks fly whenever she was in Paulette's presence, had never managed to defeat the last of the Johanssen women.

Mimi was saturated with secret delight. In fact, the only thing that would have delighted her more would have been a similar showdown between the American and Tina—something which, for reasons she didn't fully understand, had not yet occurred.

"Mimi?" Maia's voice brought the old woman back from her reverie. "He's waking up. How's that soup coming? I've got to try and get him to eat."

Through the cracked great-room doors Mimi watched as Maia listened to Severin's heart. The American obviously didn't recognize how important her patient was. Yes, he did look terrible, but cancer did that to people. Still, couldn't she see how grand the house is—well, *was*? Couldn't she tell the importance of the family by the size of the estate? And by the way that everyone responded to the Johanssen name?

The nurse didn't care, of course. Because even if she was a Ransom, she was from America, where everybody was rich. Americans had never seen a house as historic as Wisdom. They couldn't understand what it meant to work for a Johanssen. To have free reign on the estate. To eat from the china purchased by his ancestor Marie-Paule after her long-ago wedding in Paris.

Yes, the nurse said she wasn't exactly a tourist. So why had she come here, anyway? Was she running from something? A man, perhaps? A broken marriage or a desertion by—

Maia again appeared by Mimi's side. She bent down to taste the soup and stood up with a quiet smile. "It's real good, Mimi. Thanks for going so light on the spices. With all the stuff he has to take, his stomach won't be able to handle much."

Mimi beamed up at her, unaccustomed to compliments. *"Vié kanawi ka-è buyô,"* she said in patois. "Old pots make good soup!"

They both heard Severin's voice, still rough despite the extra sleep and decent food he'd been getting since Maia's arrival. Mimi brought the bowl to him and watched as the nurse pushed pillows behind his back, tucking the single sheet over his thin legs.

"I'm not hungry," he muttered. Maia ignored him, taking the bowl and spoon into her hands. She sat beside the bed. "Take this spoon, Mr. Johanssen, or I'll have to feed you."

"I don't want—"

"Eat."

He took the bowl on his lap and looked at her slyly, his face as close to smiling as he'd been capable of for a long time. Then he resolutely put a spoonful of the rich broth into his mouth, and grimaced, pretending to find it vile.

"Don't bother," Maia said. "It's my recipe and I've stayed alive on it for years."

His eyebrows shot up.

"That's right," she continued, taking his medications from her pocket. "Years. Believe it or not, some of us manage to preserve our bodies without pickling them in alcohol."

"What's wrong with rum?"

She looked across the bed. "If you start drinking again, you'll die, Mr. Johanssen."

"Shit, woman!" he rasped. "Can't you stop using my slave name?"

"*Your* slave name?"

"Don't you think the name Johanssen makes me a slave?"

"To what?"

"To my family."

"I don't think that the privileges afforded to you by your family are a form of enslavement."

"You have no idea." Severin's smile faded into a weary bitterness and Maia watched him carefully.

"Eat, Severin." For the first time, her voice was nearly gentle.

He consumed the soup with trembling hands, more to be finished with it than to give sustenance to his wasted flesh. Then he shoved the bowl toward her.

"Good," Maia approved. She sat on a stool beside him, administering his pills with a glass of cool milk, and he dutifully accepted the medication. Then Maia went away and returned with a pan and a cotton cloth. She helped Severin out of his faded T-shirt and washed his face, his neck, his sunken chest.

"You see anything you like?" he asked weakly.

"Oh, yes." Maia averted her eyes as she washed his underarms, stroking slowly. "You're one sexy hunk of a man."

"I used to be," he bragged pitifully.

"I'm sure that's true."

"I have pussy all over the island," he rasped. "Any woman I want—giant or midget, butter-soft or bone-crunchy. I like them mellow yellow, blue-black, and chocolate brown." He paused, then grunted ironically. "Don't want no white pussy. White woman feel like death. Don't know how to fuck."

Maia began humming softly to shut out his monologue. He rolled over, and she began massaging his wasted back as he rambled on.

"White woman always want to be mistress. Need to control everybody. They know black women are more beautiful, so they make black women into slaves. Always try to break black woman's spirit—"

Maia interrupted him. "By the way, a white woman came to visit you earlier."

"Paulette," he said with satisfaction. "You took care of her."

"You were listening?"

He made a small broken sound, then stretched out his arms and took the wooden bedposts in his grip. She stroked harder.

"Paulette is my cousin," he croaked.

Maia pressed into his lower back and he managed to grunt out another statement. "This place—she can't—she's not going to—unless I leave it to her—"

Maia stopped. "What are you trying to tell me?"

"Paulette," he whispered, "is a fucking bitch."

"I don't care," Maia stated dryly.

"You should, you should."

"I have nothing to do with any of that."

"But your people—" he mocked her softly. "Your people are here—"

"Are they?" she asked, a trace of anger entering her words.

"You said they are."

"And you said that was a lie." Maia buried her hands in his bloodless flesh. "You said I have no people." She pulled on his tendons, her hands becoming deep and cruel. He reacted by tensing what was left of his muscles, but he didn't cry out.

"Your people," he gasped.

"What about my *imaginary* people?" She was pressing so hard now that he was nearly voiceless.

"Paulette hates them," he gasped.

"And you don't?"

"You want to find them?"

"I will find them."

"No," he groaned, "you won't."

"Yes, Severin, I will."

"I—can—help—you."

"I don't need your help!"

"Yes—yes—you do!"

"Fuck you."

In the kitchen, Mimi could hear the rocky meanness in the nurse's tone. There was a desperately whimpered answer. Mimi listened hard, but heard nothing. After a while Maia came out of the room with a blank face. Closing the great room door, she entered the kitchen.

"I'm going into Christiansted for a while" were her only words. Then she stood washing her hands in the sink for a long, long time.

The curved lens of Noah Langston's sunglasses magnified the Magic Plum smile of the young woman behind the glass counter. Her name was Miranda and she had come to St. Croix from Bayamon after spending two years in the Bronx. Her ears bore three tiny gold hoops and her deep brown hair was twisted in an elaborate knot and secured with a rhinestone clip that glittered in the store's low lights.

"She will love this cream," Miranda was saying in a voice of pure seduction. "It makes the skin very nice. You see? I use it myself."

He saw. Miranda's face was cast in the deep copper of the black Puerto Ricans', but her eyes were a wicked apple green. She'd shaped her brows into whispers over her fringe of black lashes, and her mouth was a perfect, lush fruit.

"Actually," he began, "I was thinking about buying some perfume." Miranda squealed in delight. "I have exactly what you want, Mr. Langston! Look! We just got it in from Paris! It's Anya's newest creation, 'Myrrh.' " Miranda carefully untied the golden sash of a purple velvet sachet and reached inside to reveal a heavy, pear-shaped flask. Setting it gently on the display case, she lifted off the beveled stopper, stroked it sensuously along the soft skin just beneath her palm and lifted her wrist toward his lips.

Noah inhaled.

"You like it?" she murmured. "I'm sure that it will please you."

"Actually," he answered, "it's got to please my mother."

"I'm sure I could find a way to please you both," she purred. They both looked up as the store manager walked over and reminded

Miranda that there were some new shipments in the warehouse to be unpacked.

When he stepped out into the sun, Noah's heart was exceedingly light. The Miami trip had been fruitful—he had managed to purchase some software to help him catalogue his ongoing property cases—but he was glad to be back.

"Hey Lawyer Man!" someone shouted, and Noah glanced up in time to see a dreadlocked man take a swig of malt liquor and spit it on the sidewalk near his feet. Passing the bottle to his companion, he cocked his head in the defiant hope of a fight.

"You lost your mind, Perry?"

"What? I dirty the lawyer's pretty Bally shoes?"

"You dirty yourself sitting out here like a dog."

"Because I don't have no Armani?"

"Because you don't have no pride," Noah replied, slipping into the island dialect.

"I got to work for white man to have pride?"

"You need to be working for somebody."

"That's right," the man smirked. "You more important than we. You got important case with white judge today. You got to get to your office in white man's court."

"You be glad I there when the cops haul you in for public drunkenness!" Noah snapped in irritation.

"I won't be able to find you when they come for me," the man answered. "When I look for you, all I see is white."

"And when I look at you I see talking pisswater. You trade your manhood for the gutter and dishonor Jah's people with them dreads in your hair."

"What you know about Jah people, Mr. Lawyer Man? You go to white man school and live in big white man house and drive white man car—"

"I free," Noah said softly. "You still in chains, my friend."

"At least we not kneeling between no white man thigh!"

The pair burst into thigh-slapping laughter. *Fuck they!* Noah thought as he turned away, too disgusted to continue the argument. He crossed the waterfront, nodding perfunctorily to Juan and Rico as they sat on the dock, then greeted the boatman who was waiting patiently beside the hotel ferry. The hotel ferry! Suddenly he remembered the woman he'd met in his courtyard the other day. What was her name? *Maia.*

Glancing at his watch, he thought he might give a quick call to the hotel before grabbing a sandwich at Brandy's. After all, he deserved a new amusement. Something to take his mind off his work. And to take his mind off the fact that no matter how much he achieved for his people, some folks were more jealous than thankful for it.

Juan had heard about Maia's move into Wisdom from Tina's younger brother, Carlson, who liked to fish with him on quiet afternoons in Christiansted harbor. Leaning against the dock supports, the two discussed every aspect of island life, from the antics of the elected officials to Severin's latest exploits at Wisdom.

"She come there with the ambulance yesterday, and move right in!" Carlson explained to his disbelieving friend.

"How Seven get her?" Juan screeched, instantly picturing his elusive dance partner in a sensual embrace with the white man Severin. "What she want with him?"

Carlson, short and burly like his sister, shook his head. "Money, man. Seven *rich*! And now he sick! The American bitch not stupid!" Carlson threw a stone into the water and sneered. "Him dying, man. Not much left. She see that. She a nurse. She take him money!"

Juan thought of his afternoon sailing trips with Maia to deserted beaches. He focused on the night they'd danced in the disco. That night, he thought, she was only a thread away from becoming his lover. He *knew* that she wanted him. *That's* what had driven her away that night! She couldn't handle her attraction to a *real* man!

"Bitch. Bitch . . ." Juan chanted quietly. He turned to his fishing partner. "You go out to Wisdom and check on Seven, man. Next thing you know, they standing at the altar!"

Carlson sucked his teeth loudly. "Shit, no—Seven only marry when Tina say so." They both laughed, certain that Tina was still in charge of the estate, but a little seed of doubt sprouted in Carlson's mind. "Mimi no let that happen. Mimi watching while she cook. She know how to keep the house from a stranger."

The two men ruminated on the thought that perhaps the estate would pass into the hands of the American woman—a thought more unbearable than the idea that Tina would not somehow marry Severin and inherit Wisdom. Even more unbearable than the outside chance that Paulette and David Fairchild might someday sleep in the great room.

"Naw, man—it must not happen," Carlson remarked, gently slapping the dock with a measure of rope. Juan grunted in response and broke a stick in his strong brown hands. The two stared out over the horizon, both wondering how this foreign woman could insert herself so neatly into a place that they were barely allowed to enter.

At that moment, Maia came out of the pharmacy and made her way quickly along the narrow stone passage of Christiansted's main street. Dressed in bright yellow, she took deep breaths of the hot salty air, as if savoring the cleanliness of the world outside of Wisdom.

She looked out across the shimmering bay toward the island hotel she'd lived in before moving in with Severin. Then her eyes traveled the length of the port, coming to rest on the vagrant figures of Carlson and Juan. Ignoring the men, she strode through the lobby of the small hotel by the boardwalk and down the narrow passage to Brandy's Bar. Aside from two or three tables of tired, sunburned tourists, the place was empty. Dressed in a low-cut emerald green dress, the barmaid looked up from the counter and smiled. "Well, looks like you really are going to stay!"

"No," Maia answered coolly as she slid onto a stool. "My plane takes off in eleven more days."

"We still haven't managed to make you forget Michigan?" Brandy teased. "Or are you getting homesick?"

"I'm too busy to even think about going home."

"Enjoying the beaches?"

"Actually, I'm working for Severin Johanssen out at Wisdom," Maia replied, looking directly into Brandy's eyes. For a long, awkward moment the barmaid didn't speak and Maia waited with a cool smile. Then Brandy bent busily over the sink and began to jostle a tray of washed glasses.

"How did you find your way to Wisdom?"

"It wasn't easy," Maia answered. "No one seemed to remember how to get there."

"And so?"

"And so I kept looking until I found the right map."

"And Seven gave you a job?" Brandy asked without looking up.

"Something like that," Maia replied. "Still serving passion fruit?"

Brandy reached into her refrigerator and stood, her face expressionless.

"Wisdom is no place for tourists."

"I'm not a tourist. My ancestors lived and died there."

"What difference does that make?"

"I have a right to know what happened to them."

Brandy's eyes darkened and she leaned over the counter toward Maia. "There is something you need to understand, Miss Ransom. Every inch of this island is soaked with the blood of someone's ancestors. Every estate, from Butler's Bay to Grapetree, holds the forgotten stories of thousands of black people. We have no monuments to mark their lives. There are no cemeteries to mark their deaths."

Glancing across at her white customers, Brandy lowered her voice. "Look around you, Maia Ransom! Every one of these buildings was raised by slaves' hands. But you won't find their fingerprints in the mortar. Look at the stone mills up on the hills. Our people carried those stones. Every fence and every field on this island represents our ancestors' labor. But you will never see their sweat or hear their voices."

She stared into Maia's eyes. "Do you really think your ancestors are any different from mine? Or from the rest of us?"

Maia blinked hard and straightened her back. "You may have made your peace with the past, but I haven't."

"How do you know that?" the other woman said softly. "Because we smile when we're serving the tourists you think we like them? Because we don't burn down the hotels you think we enjoy changing the nasty sheets—"

"Excuse me, Miss!" a man's voice rang out. "Can I get another Corona?"

"Coming right up!" Brandy answered brightly, her eyes never

leaving Maia's face. "We don't have the luxury to come here and bang on doors and demand to know the 'truth' about our people! We don't have the money for restaurants and hotels, or to walk away from our employment. We don't have the arrogance to believe that everyone we meet should be ready and willing to help us."

Maia stared at her wordlessly and Brandy lowered her voice to a whisper. "Above all, Miss Ransom, you must understand that the white people you are challenging for the truth about your family are the same white people who hire us, pay our rent, and feed our children. We don't necessarily like them, or want to protect them, but until things change we have to look out for ourselves. After all—" Brandy paused. "We will live and die on this island. Your plane takes off in eleven more days."

Maia closed her eyes as the green dress swept past. She heard the barmaid speaking pleasantly to the Americans about rum punch, coral reefs, and scuba equipment. The sound of their banter almost drowned out Severin's mocking words: *"your people where are your people are here are here are here—"*

A sudden loneliness erupted from the bottom of her heart. She stared blindly beyond the cheerful patio umbrellas and felt her soul being drawn from her body by the endless expanse of Caribbean blue. In the grayest winters of Michigan and the longest days of rain, Maia had never known anything like the abandonment she was feeling. Clasping her trembling hands together, she tried to focus on a distant sail that separated the water from the cobalt horizon. But it was useless. There, in the exquisite warmth of the sun and the sea, she suddenly knew how alone she was. Her mother was dead. Her father was a being without a future or a past. She had no children and no lover. She was dying. And she belonged to no one.

Maia pulled her gaze away from the sea and lifted her eyes to the mirror behind the counter. A woman stared back with hollow eyes. Her russet skin bore the hues of an unknown ancestry. Her features recalled the stark geometries of Europe and rolling fullness of Africa, but she had no idea when the cultures had mated. She had no memories beyond the empty rhythms of routine days, for her life had never been punctuated by the mark of a real love. There were no fading photos of Ransom kindred who shared her lips and nose; no bedtime stories of precocious cousins and irritable aunts. She had no past, either mythic or real, except the past she sought in the rotting walls of Wisdom.

Staring into the mirror, Maia finally grasped with her mind what her heart already understood. When her father's last memory faded, his mind emptied by his illness, the *Ransom family would die*. This was her one and only chance to learn the truth about the Ransom past. And it was her only hope to give meaning to the future!

The green dress returned, and Maia focused on Brandy's smooth arms as she began making a pitcher of rum punch for a group of men who had just ended their shift at the oil refinery.

"Brandy," she began in a halting voice. The barmaid grunted, but went on with her work.

"Brandy," she repeated, "I'm sorry."

Something in her voice caused the barmaid to look up and their eyes locked. For a long whispery moment they drank in each other's gaze, and when Brandy blinked, something had changed.

"What you sorry for?" she asked gruffly.

"Everything," Maia stammered. "My assumptions. My arrogance. My bad attitude."

Brandy sucked her teeth musically. "That place where you're living would give a rock a bad attitude. And," she added, "Seven is no easy man." Reaching across the counter, she grasped Maia's arm. "My mother cut cane on the Wisdom estate. I knew Seven when he still had his milk teeth." Brandy sighed. "They were wild, the Johanssen boys. They ran free all over the island. Their father spent his days drinking in Christiansted, and their mother did what she could when she could find them.

"Severin's older brother Peter was handsome and good in school, and he got all the attention. He was engaged to a girl from another old Danish family when his plane went into the water. He had gone to St. Thomas to take care of some business because their father was drunk, and his mother never forgave the old man for Peter's death. It wasn't long before they both drank themselves into the grave."

Brandy shrugged. "Severin wasn't a bad boy, but he got lost in all that tragedy. So he refused to grow up, I guess. But a child's mind in a man's body can be a dangerous thing, you know. Many of us care about Seven, but none of us can make him do what's right."

"Not even Tina?" Maia asked.

"Tina is like a sister to me," Brandy explained. "Our mothers came to St. Croix together from St. Lucia. But she was always different from the rest of us. I remember when a young white woman came down from Texas to teach at the school. Tina thought the boys were paying more attention to the white woman, so she hit her with a stick and broke her nose."

The barmaid chuckled wryly at the shocked expression on Maia's face. "You should stay out of Tina's way. She don't play when it comes to Seven."

Brandy walked past her with the pitcher of punch and Maia sat alone, staring into her passion fruit. Suddenly she sensed someone standing behind her and caught the reflection of a familiar face.

"I've found you, Maia!"

Wheeling around, she looked up into Noah Langston's winning smile. Before she could answer he shook his head. "I just called your hotel and they said you'd gone. Don't tell me you've found your way to someone else's rooms!"

"Actually I'm working. Something came up and I moved out of the hotel."

"So where are you staying, now?"

"Out at the Johanssen estate."

"The Johanssen—you mean, Wisdom?" For the flicker of an instant he paused. "How'd you manage that?"

"Good or bad luck, depending on how you look at it."

"I'd like to hear about both."

"Does your dinner offer still stand?"

"What about tonight? I can pick you up at seven."

She glanced at her watch. "Let's make it eight. I'll meet you in your courtyard." She slid off the stool but he put his hand on her arm.

"Don't leave so soon! I'm not due in court for an hour."

"I really should get back to Mr. Johanssen."

"*Mister* Johanssen?"

Ignoring the open disdain in his voice, she answered, "I'm a nurse and Severin is in my care."

"I see," he sighed. "I'd heard that hard living finally got tired of old Seven. Well, Maia, I'd say you've got your work cut out for you. He's always intended to go down like a flare." Noah emitted a short, hard snort, as if enjoying the news of Severin's infirmity.

He called out to her as she walked away. "Just in case you start feeling guilty about going out this evening, just remember: If Seven's survived this long, one night without you won't kill him."

Paulette Johanssen Fairchild rolled her eyes in exasperation. David, having recognized a group of his golfing cohorts getting noisily drunk at the bar, had hardly spent a moment at their table that evening. So she sat alone, her shoulders thrown back in her sleeveless linen dress, her head lifted to reveal her fine collarbones and sharp, Scandinavian profile.

The restaurant she'd chosen for their evening meal, the Marienbad, was built precariously on the crest of a volcanic cliff, its open terrace peering down over piled condominiums built to the specifications of the golf-and-tennis rich, each apartment equipped with its own private pool. The restaurant itself was an enclosed garden. Lazy evening breezes swirled the fronds of palm trees standing in wooden boxes along the slate floor, and a jazz pianist who played only Sinatra and Bennett lounged a few melodies out from the bar.

Murmuring guests sampled the island's fresh dolphin steaks, sizzled on a charcoal grill and laced with a fine lemon sauce. Imported French wines were impeccably matched to each dish on the dinner menu, and salads were prepared tableside, to the specifications of the diners.

Paulette picked at a bowl of cool melon, papaya, and pineapple slices while waiting for their grilled fish to arrive. She peered through the twilight, noting which of her friends had put on a pound or two during the exceptionally hot summer, when those who didn't have a pool tended to fall behind on their exercise. Bonny McKinnon was there with her second husband, a retired dentist from Massachusetts who'd come down as a tourist to celebrate his divorce and never got away. Betsy Collington was at the other end of the terrace, deeply engaged in conversation with two of her bridge partners and their golf-bronzed husbands. Marietta Van Arnheim, who had made a fortune handling the real-estate transactions of the island's elite, chatted easily with David's college roommate, Harold Morton. And one of the Darian daughters, a successful photographer, was tête-à-tête with a very prestigious looking Statesider.

Paulette sighed. Her sense of irritation could only have been calmed by something so grand as the unexpected appearance of a film star or vacationing politician, but the restaurant offered nothing so excitable that night. At the bar she could see David leering at the syrup-colored, big-breasted, blond waitress. And most of the other couples on the terrace were transplanted from the States and had only a parochial interest in land ownership on the island. Certainly they did not share her interest in maintaining the purity of her ancestral home.

Her gaze was arrested by a subtle movement, a kind of flowing gesture followed by a fine silk fabric. From behind a deep red bougainvillea she could see the elegantly cut, Stateside design of the sleeve. Her mind raced—*lovely dress*—unusual for one of the island blacks. She squinted, forgetting for a moment her silent promise never to subject her skin to unnecessary wrinkling—and realized with a start that she knew this woman. My god—isn't it that bitch who had been standing guard over what was left of Severin out at Wisdom? And where had she found a black man with enough cash to bring her up to the Marienbad?

Curiosity drove Paulette to her feet and, ignoring the casual glances of the other diners, she made her way slowly across the open terrace, stopping at other tables, greeting her friends, keeping her eyes fixed on that silken sleeve.

"So you're getting along out there at Wisdom?"

The man's rich voice carried lazily on the evening breeze. Paulette cocked her head as she kissed one of her bridge partners on the cheek, desperate to hear the murmured reply. The man laughed and he leaned forward, his face coming into view. Of course. It had to be. Noah Langston.

"Sev's keeping you busy, then?"

Again the reply slipped away, and Paulette's rage inflated like a balloon. How dare that woman discuss the Johanssen family with strangers? She was a mere employee, hired to empty Severin's bedpan and change his dirty linen. And how in the hell did she meet up with the one black man on the entire island who thought himself important enough to frequent the Marienbad, the most private enclave of St. Croix's wealthy and powerful whites?

How, in fact, could she have found her way to Noah Langston?

A few tables removed from Paulette's stare, Noah let his deep laugh roll forward while he too, watched his guest. He'd been shocked by the animal beauty of the woman in the sheer flowing dress that grazed her ankles when she emerged from the stone passage to meet him in the courtyard earlier that evening. She was, in fact, a study in elegance. She'd moved toward him slowly and gracefully, and he found it hard—even though she was nearly a stranger—not to slip his arms around her waist and pull her close.

As he bent forward to give her a welcoming kiss, he caught the scent of her body oil and glimpsed the pearl-sized, burnished gold cowrie shells she wore as earrings. Her dancing eyes seemed to enjoy his appreciation and she offered him a full, open smile. For a few moments, he hadn't known what to say. All right: He had already made note of Maia's powerful, full thighs—every island man's delight—but tonight he was captivated by her thick lashes and soft short hair and the sight of an ankle bracelet beaten out of a gold so fine that it was barely a whisper against the sun-browned skin. Such ornamentation was forbidden among the women of his class on the island—and yet Maia seemed to wear the gold filigree like a declaration of love.

So rather than taking her to a popular bodega frequented by the blacks of Fredriksted, he chose to drive her to the East End, the white folks' territory—both to watch the way she reacted to the ostentatious display of indifferent, unapologetic wealth, and to have her entirely to himself.

"So after law school," he was explaining to her, "I took a good look at race relations in the States and made the decision to come back home. I knew I'd have a bigger impact here on my own territory, so I opened my practice, then began consulting for the government. Of course, my mother now fully expects me to run for governor."

"And?"

"Perhaps I will. When I've found someone suitable to be Mrs. Governor."

"Interviewing candidates?" she asked, her brown gaze wrapped in a secret smile that he read as languidly sensuous. A more religious man would have sensed the smile's sadness, but Noah had long ago surrendered his faith to ambition.

"So why'd you become a nurse?"

"I'm attracted to the smell of blood."

"Dangerous attraction."

"Well, there's good blood and bad blood. It just takes wisdom to know the difference."

"And that difference is?"

"That very small distance between death and life." Her eyes nagged the darkening horizon. "The important thing is not to be afraid."

"Something tells me that you're not afraid of anything."

"I've got my fears," she responded lightly, "but I respect them rather than run from them."

Noah observed his dinner guest carefully. On the way to the restaurant, he'd tried to get her to open up about Severin Johanssen. Island gossip supposed that he was quite near death. But Maia had been strangely evasive about her patient. Now, intrigued by her cool, even mysterious responses to his questions, he decided to try once again.

"I think," he said slowly, "it must be tough for you out at Wisdom."

"I've been a nurse for a long time."

"But Seven isn't an easy patient."

"His housekeeper's there to help during the day, and he sleeps most of the night."

Noah waited for her to continue but she stopped speaking. "You know, Sev and I go way back," he said, hoping to elicit a more detailed response from Maia. "In fact, we went all the way through school together."

"I'm starting to see that everybody on St. Croix knows everything about each other," she answered smoothly. "In fact—" Her eyes roamed from his face to his shoulders, then lingered on the space just below his waist. "—I'm sure there are plenty of women around here who could tell me everything I want to know about you, Mr. Langston."

Noah was momentarily disarmed. Not by her words. Nor by the granite in her voice. Not even by the sudden midnight in her expression. What took his breath away was her lethal combination of strength, beauty, and intelligence.

So despite his years of courtroom success, and despite a childhood of careful training at the blue-blood prep school and the Ivy League colleges and the countless cases he'd presented with intelligence and grace, Noah Anthony Langston *Esquire*, began to chatter.

"Have you been out to the beach at Cane Bay? It's wonderful for snorkeling. And you really need to visit the national monument at Point Udall—"

The evening breeze teasing at her flowered sleeves, Maia listened to Noah's banter. Slowly she placed the leaves of an artichoke between her lips. She admired his perfect skin and decisive eyes as she drew the flesh of each leaf against her white teeth. Then her gaze explored his soft black brows and neatly trimmed mustache, the fluted nostrils and firm jaw. She savored the sharp taste of the oil and vinegar while imagining the sweet soft pressure of his full lips. She glanced at his strong ringless hands, clasped lightly on the table. She imagined him, tall and sleek, on a midnight beach. Flooded with desire, she reached for the next prickly leaf.

Maia wondered why the lawyer was so interested in her patient, although after a lifetime on an island still owned primarily by whites, Noah's obvious disgust with Severin Johanssen's dissipated lifestyle made sense. Yet there was something cloying in the lawyer's questions. Something irregular. Almost indecent.

But, Maia thought, she had no real reason to protect this man who lived in a state of virtual abandon, on property that was turning to dust around him. Severin had lived in his filth for so long that even his skin had taken on that grayness of unwashed people. His teeth were rotting; his hair was patched with blond and white and greasy gray. His eyes were trapped in a squint and his hands would probably always shake, even if he did stop drinking.

So why did she feel such a grudging, almost *unhealthy* desire to protect him? Why did she give Severin so much more than the simple professional care that he was paying for? Why feed him the same quality food that she ate? Why massage his sweating, wasted muscles? Why even exchange words with a man who chose to live like a dog? *I don't even* like *his nasty ass!* Maia thought, her face closing in disgust.

She had agreed to work for him for one reason only: To gain access to the estate. To explore the rolling hills and broken buildings. To touch the trees and swim in its waters. And to remember the song sung by the distant woman whose presence Maia sensed whenever she sat on the enormous boulder by the ruined sugar mill.

Noah watched the moodplays on Maia's subtle face, wishing that he could step away from the table and watch the other guests as they watched him watching Maia, who was quickly becoming the most fascinating quest ever laid before any hero.

Suddenly Noah caught the glint of Paulette's glowing hair as she swept toward them, and instinctively he placed his soles flat on the flagstones beneath the table. He knew Paulette Johanssen Fairchild—knew her mind and her manner. He sensed that her appearance at his table, on just the evening when he was dining with the nurse from Wisdom, was no coincidence. He saw her crablike approach, obvious and oblique. So he reminded himself to stay loose. Reaching out, he gently grasped Maia's left hand, as if to steady her against the inevitable impact of whatever drama Severin's cousin intended to stage.

Then she was standing beside them.

"Good evening," came the low voice of unconcealed annoyance. The glacial greeting drew little more than a single raised eyebrow from Maia.

"Good evening, Paulette," Noah chanted, an island tone drifting instantly into the words.

"I just came over to say hello." She spoke without looking at Noah.

She was staring at Maia. "And I certainly do want to greet my cousin's *nurse*," she added, the final word little more than spit on concrete. "He must be doing much better, since you've strayed so far from his bedside tonight."

Maia cocked her head even as Noah's grip tightened on her fingers. "I thought I'd made it clear to you that I don't discuss my patients' condition," she replied, her eyes so calm that he heard the breeze in her lashes.

"I didn't ask about his condition—"

"Then you have less than nothing to say to me," Maia concluded.

Noah struggled not to react, although his soul roared at the enraged defeat in Paulette's eyes. He saw her quick appraisal of what was to be gained or lost in challenging Maia in full view of her moneyed peers. He knew that she had already exposed herself badly by coming to the table of the only blacks dining at the exclusive Marienbad. She certainly couldn't afford a public shouting match with an unpredictable black Statesider!

Paulette threw back her blond hair even as Maia yawned. An extravagant yawn. A deliberate, rude, unimpressed yawn.

Paulette didn't speak. Noah would remember for many years the manner in which this member of the island royalty pulled together her skinned-up dignity, already deciding that it was victory enough that she was white, stunningly handsome, and unquestionably rich. She smiled darkly, theatrically, and spun away.

"What was *that*?" he asked Maia softly.

"Laying a siege."

"Private war?"

"Meaningless skirmish."

"You're the general?"

"I'm more of a hostage," Maia said, closing the subject with an irritated sigh. The lawyer appraised her once again.

"I've never met a tourist who fit in so fast on our island," he said in ironic admiration.

"It must be my Ransom blood," she shrugged with a smile.

Something in his face changed. *"Ransom?"* he whispered, shifting in his chair. "Are you a Ransom?"

"In the flesh." She replied ironically, then paused, watching as he tried to hide his surprise. "Now," she said, again raising a curious eyebrow at his intense expression, "suppose you tell me the truth, and nothing but the truth, about what my name means."

Noah moved a little bit closer to the lovely woman whose quiet strength now seemed like a buoy in the sea of his future. He raised his hand, signaling the waiter to return with the menus. He would need to spend a bit more money this evening. That is, if he was going to find out what he needed to know.

eLEVEN DAYS

Severin raised his head from his soaking pillow and watched Maia as she patiently washed his chest clean of sweat. A storm had blown in at dawn and the late morning was a dripping sponge. Rain pounded the rusting steel roof, yet he could still hear Mimi and Tina's sharp voices in the kitchen.

"You should be glad Seven feeling better," Mimi was saying. "The nurse save his life."

"The nurse will soon be leaving," Tina answered, loudly enough to be standing just outside Severin's door. "Even if she thinking about staying."

Severin chuckled. Emerging from his illness had provided him with new and unexpected knowledge. He had discovered just that morning that Maia really did have a face. For the past two days he had looked at various parts of her body: Her nose as she leaned over him. Her ass as she walked away. Her fingers as she handed him his medication. And her mouth as she bullied him into eating yet another bowl of her famous soup. He was shocked when, for some reason, her features arranged themselves into a pleasingly discernible unit.

Maia had a luminescent beauty, although Tina had been far more beautiful before alcohol destroyed her fierce, feline visage. Yet—at least under the influence of the codeine—the American held her own against his lifelong lover.

Maia wrung out her cloth and, ignoring Tina, began working on his arms. She then dressed him and walked him like a sagging scarecrow to a chair near the decaying window, and seated him carefully. The rain had momentarily abated and he listened as she hummed, stripping the tattered sheets and sweeping out the room. Mimi came in and, smiling at Maia, helped her to beat at the pillows, remove his soiled clothing, and replace the pitchers with fresh water.

"*Mwê ka-alé.* I going home, now," the old woman announced as she left with his dirty linen.

"Let's see: *Mèsi*—that's thank you—and *boswè*—good evening," she answered in her tentative patois.

Mimi laughed delightedly as she walked away.

Maia turned to look at him. "Severin? You okay?"

He lifted his head from the rotting window frame. She wore an expression of such honest concern that he found himself again fascinated. "Yes, Nurse," he managed in a nearly normal voice. "I'm doing better than I should be." A week without cigarettes had even given his throat a chance to heal.

"You mean, better than you deserve."

He could have laughed, but he still resented the idea that she should make the jokes. It was, after all, his estate, his illness, his island. His house. His world. When the hell did she get so damned cocky? He raised his head: "Some rum will take care of it."

Maia shot him a sideways glance, a mixture of humor and irritation, then turned away, as a sudden, unexpected trembling forced her to lean against the bedframe. She took a deep, slow breath, and then another, feeling a cool sweat break beneath her shirt.

"I want more pain medication," he announced in a whining voice.

To his surprise, the patience she usually showed to his childish moods vanished. Her body tensed as she returned to stand over him.

"You need to get off this stuff," she said coldly. "Either try to get healthy or don't be surprised if you end up back in the hospital. Next time I'm not doing anything to revive you when you start jerking around on the floor."

He stared at her, wondering where the daggers had come from. "Yes, ma'am," he retorted impotently. She twisted the top off a plastic bottle and poured a single tablet into his palm.

"That's all you're giving me?"

"That's all you need."

"How do you know?"

Something crossed her face. "You make me tired, Severin." She dropped the plastic bottle into her pocket. Outside, fat drops of rain again began to splash against the balcony, the sound a soft pattering on the metal roof overhead. The kitchen door slammed as Mimi and Tina departed with awkward steps through the gathering storm. Maia walked to the bedstand to pour him a glass of milk.

"You came in late last night," Severin rasped, watching for her reaction. "Found a boyfriend?"

She ignored him, beginning to sing quietly.

"You planning to stay on my island, then?" he persisted, eyes intent. "You won't be happy with no Crucian man!" he declared as the rain grew steadily louder. "You too skinny. We like woman with big tits and ass!"

She raised her voice, singing louder against the timpani of rain.

"Besides, we don't like women with bad attitude."

She broke off suddenly and looked out at the indescribably green branches braced against the weeping blue-black sky. "You know, I had a boss once who said that I'm too hard to be a nurse and too soft to be a doctor."

"I don't see no softness."

"There isn't much left, I guess." For the first time, a note of vulnerability entered her words, and they both looked surprised. "You think St. Croix is so tough?" She shook her head. "I grew up in tough. Went to school when all the boys were getting strung out on drugs and all the girls were getting knocked up by those boys. In a place where most of my classmates ended up in jail, in mental wards, or dead." Her voice went reedy as she glanced at the balcony. "I've worked around sick people for fifteen years. Believe it or not, I've seen more sun here in one day than I saw in my entire life."

"The sun don't shine in America?"

"Not when you're trapped in that darkness."

"No husband?"

"No." She laughed suddenly. "Not that I didn't try. Almost got married in college. Then I caught him in the sack with my roommate. Got engaged to a minister. But he wanted me to bake chicken all day and go to church every night. So then I tried a schoolteacher who, as it turned out, preferred very little girls. And finally I got so desperate that I hooked up with a high school boyfriend. Musician. But he just liked the idea of screwing me until he found a better prospect."

Severin whistled and shook his head. "See, down here it's much easier. You love the one you with and if you feel the spirit, you might get married after the baby comes."

"I don't believe that," Maia retorted. "There must be twenty churches between this place and downtown Christiansted. Don't tell me they don't keep people in line."

"No, the church is for *after* the baby arrives. First the baptism, then the wedding. Or maybe the funeral if the man don't marry the woman and her father own a gun."

She shook her head, and Severin grunted. "I been lucky, I guess. So far the bullets missed me."

The pounding rain increased as she gazed down toward the windswept beach. "I'm not like you, Severin. I still see some dignity in being alive."

He followed her gaze. "Everybody I ever loved is long gone, except maybe for Tina. Why should I make a big deal out of my life?"

"I can't speak for you," she answered, "but I'm looking for one minute of peace, Severin. One moment of understanding. Of connecting to something bigger than I am before I die."

He gazed jealously at the whole, strong body standing beside him. "And what have you discovered, Nurse?"

"That if this is all that's left of the Ransoms, then I'm already long gone."

He laughed hoarsely, the rain almost drowning out his answer. "I like you, Nurse. I like you because you're lost, like me."

"No, Severin. I know exactly why I'm here. You can barely remember what you did one hour ago."

"But I don't care," he answered. "The day you're really free is the day you die," he declared as he turned to face angry, gray sea.

He heard her walk away. For a moment he sat in the stifling heat, listening to the rain. Then something in her words—*one moment of connecting to something before I die*—began to cloy in his gut, leaving him strangely curious. He listened to the silence outside of his chamber, at the other end of the house. Like a child suddenly realizing that its mother had a life beyond the limits of its vision, he began to wonder exactly what Maia did when outside of his presence. Moving carefully, he hoisted himself up and followed her. There was no movement in the kitchen, so he shuffled weakly toward the rooms he'd lived in as a child.

Mimi had given the nurse the largest of the old bedrooms. The corner chamber had windows on two sides, allowing the slight breeze to lighten the load of mosquitoes, geckos, and the giant cockroaches that the Crucians affectionately described as "Mahogany Birds."

The room was also special in that the walls still bore faded traces of the delicate lacy wallpaper imported decades ago from Martinique when it served as the bridal chamber of Marie-Paule Emilie St. Severin, Solomon Johanssen's French bride. The bed Maia slept in, an immense cathedral of dark cherry, had once sported a curtained canopy draped in fabric that matched the paper. But the canopy was long gone, hacked off by one of the Johanssen men after Marie-Paule's death. The cavernous wardrobe, pushed into the corner behind the door, was the last piece of the room's original furnishings.

Bracing himself weakly against the wall, Severin crouched outside the door. He heard her moving about; he heard paper tearing and plastic bottles snapping open. She muttered something, then sat heavily on her bed. Moving stealthily, he instinctively reverted to his childhood game of spying. Then he realized that with the wind blowing in from the southwest, she would never hear him over the rippling rush of grape leaves outside her window.

Severin peered around the cracked doorway and made out Maia's long legs as she sat on the edge of her bed. There was a calm, almost eerie silence in her virtual stillness. He looked into her face and found her eyes cast down. He stirred and she glanced up.

"Get out, Severin!" she hissed in a low whisper. "Give me some privacy."

"What you doing?"

"Leave me alone!" she spat at him.

Confused, he stared at her blankly. "What's wrong with you?"

She pushed her palm across her face, trying to dry her eyes.

"Why you look like that?" he insisted. "Why you sitting here?"

She paused, then surrendered. "Because I'm sick, Severin. I'm sick, just like you, and I don't know what to do about it."

"What you mean, you sick?"

The look in her eyes was enough.

"No way—I don't believe that."

"Neither do I," she murmured. "Neither do I."

"Then, that's why you came here? To this place? To my home?"

"*Our* home, Severin. I keep telling you that my great-great-grandfather—"

"Sick from what?"

She hesitated, exasperated. "A growth in my ovaries. It's big and getting bigger."

"How do you know?"

"I'm a nurse."

"Talk to another doctor."

"There aren't any more doctors."

"Surgery."

"Pointless."

"They saved *me*!"

"A miracle," she said acidly.

"You're just giving in?" His voice went dry with disbelief.

"Why do you think I'm here, Severin? Why do you think I put up with your self-pitying bullshit? Why I'm sleeping in this, this—" she looked as if she wanted to spit "—this filthy ruin—"

"You here because you want my land."

"No! I'm here because I want my *people*! Don't you understand? I won't die without knowing, or at least without trying to know as much as I can about the Ransoms!"

Severin's eyes narrowed. "So you don't want to claim Wisdom for yourself?"

"*Claim* Wisdom?" Maia almost shouted. "Claim this rundown wreck? Even if I did want to claim this mess, I'd be ashamed to do it. You're living in some kind of booze-induced fantasy. You're living in filth." She indicated a crack in the wood beneath her windowsill that was wide enough for them both to see the leaves of a bay rum bush outside the house.

"The house needs work, but—"

"The house is the least of it. Your land is useless. The stables are empty. The wells are dry. This could be such a beautiful place, even for you."

"So you *are* interested—"

"Listen, you asshole! My family lived and died on those hills outside. They washed their clothes on those beaches. They ate the fruit from those trees. They might even have served your lazy white ancestors in these very rooms. Of course I'm fucking interested! But I'm sick, Severin. Soon there may not be a Maia for you to worry about."

She stood up wearily. "Don't waste your energy on whether or not I'll try to stake some claim on this shanty. I don't even respect this place enough to die in it."

He squeezed his eyes shut as she pushed past him and moved noisily down the hall. The front door slammed and the house shook, a fine powder of dust shimmering down from the rafters. He listened for Mimi, but there was nothing. He listened for Tina, then Peter, then his mother and father. And never moving, he stared out into the past through the split wall boards into the brilliant emerald, turquoise, and ivory that lay just beneath the splintering vestiges of his heritage.

David Fairchild had co-captained the basketball team with Noah Langston during their sophmore year at Rosemeade Academy. Noah remembered well the mediocre talent of the white boys, who played in the desperate hope of being a bit more like the Americans they saw on

TV. He also remembered the flitting hungry eyes and waist-length braids of young Paulette Johanssen. Severin was but a smear on the canvas of those years, though his brother Peter, the one who died just before his wedding, stood out as an Olympic-caliber swimmer and president of his class. None of them had acknowledged Noah's existence, though being the sole black at the island's most private and exclusive prep school made him hard to miss. The students, for the most part, simply ignored him, going on with the ritual mating games that inevitably led to the matches decided years earlier by their wealthy parents.

The four years at Rosemeade Academy had been difficult. Not because of the rigorous courses in math and literature, but because of the different world Noah came from. He easily succeeded in mimicking the white kids' speech. He was an honor student and chaired the debate team. He was occasionally invited into the glass homes built along the golf courses and allowed to swim in the private, terraced pools. But he was clearly an outsider. And he had never gone near the white girls. Most of them, even those who had nearly become his friends during those four years, barely spoke to him now.

All right—that was partially his fault. After all, he had broken all the rules.

Noah Langston had graduated *summa cum laude* from Rosemeade—still the only black ever to do so. He'd then made island history by taking a B.A. and a *juris doctor* from two Ivy League colleges and choosing to return to the island, rather than succumbing to the temptations of a New York law firm and the Manhattan sweet life. He'd represented many black islanders in land-possession suits against the white landowners—his former classmates—ensuring that he was hated among the local white gentry. Noah had also made sure that his mother had come to possess a good portion of the land surrounding Fredriksted, the island's second city.

And now it didn't much matter whether the whites spoke to him or not. It didn't matter if they approved. In Noah Langston's mind, his people had built that island and it was their right to own it. His father had brought him up this way, and he believed very deeply that his father was still watching over everything he did, even now. Yes, Noah would dedicate his life to displacing his former classmates. And God willing, he was going to see that Maia Ransom—and yes, of course he knew the meaning of her name—got her due, too.

So the morning after their fateful dinner at the Marienbad, he went to work on it. Closeting himself in the dank, airless tunnels beneath the government's seafront fortress, Noah couldn't hear the storm raging outside as he patiently dug through the island's rotting archives. A morning's labor of peeling apart the delicate leaves of birth and death records, census forms and tax forms recording the sale of human beings and their offspring, yielded him much more than he expected.

The Ransoms were, as a matter of fact, the stuff of truth and folklore. First of all, there were Ransoms all over the island. Their name was taken from the ship that brought the original group from Africa. They'd been purchased in Christiansted from an English dealer, and their story was recorded precisely because the eldest member claimed to be a healer. And healers, on an island plagued by drought, insect infestations, and outbreaks of fever, were always deemed useful. Indeed, the overseers bid boisterously all afternoon for the group, thinking that introducing even one of the Ransom clan into their plantation society would somehow enhearten the rest. At least, that's what the local broadsides had written about the auction almost two centuries earlier.

And so they were splintered out across the island's numerous estates, and their children and children's children populated the island, the name surviving because their masters had felt a certain, inexplicable pride in owning a Ransom. By the end of the first morning's research, Noah Langston was sure he could prove that there was Ransom blood in all the principal estates on the island. And most certainly within Wisdom.

With his lawyerly mind, Noah knew that Severin had recognized the Ransom name, too. As did Paulette. And every other indigenous white islander who took a good look at Maia. He knew the power of the name. The sense of uncertainty it provoked in the whites. He only wondered how much Maia knew about her own family. And her own right to sleep in the owner's suite of the great house where she, like her ancestors, was now but a servant.

He emerged from the government archives and squinted blindly at the fierce noontime sun that was scattering the remnants of the mid-night storm. The humid streets of busy Christansted were criss-crossed with lumbering tourists, their totebags clutched nervously over bal-looning bellies. A handful of rastas crouched inside the town's band-shell, their dreads swinging to the artificial reggae pumped from a boombox. Noah bought two crab samosas from a street vendor and approached a windy bench near the pier.

"Hey, Lawyer Man!"

He saw Juan's silhouette, darkened against the noontime sheet of blue-green sea. The sailor pulled the tarps off of his boat, and threw a sinewy leg up on the edge of the pier while he tied the lines around the iron stays.

"So who you robbing blind today, Lawyer Man?"

"Show me what white man need it most."

"I reckon all them white folks could share some of they wealth," Juan answered, rubbing his chin speculatively.

"How's business?" Noah nodded toward the small vessel, aware that Juan hadn't managed to entice any of the tourists to let him sail them out to nearby Buck Island.

"Not bad," Juan said. "Have a new girlfriend from Stateside. Every day out to Buck Island. She like me so much, she ask me to marry her and go live with her in New York. When I tell her I can't give up my boat, she decide to take a job and stay."

"Yeah?" Noah laughed, shaking his head at Juan's tall tales of conquest.

"For true. She out at Wisdom. Nursing Seven while he sick."

The lawyer froze, the samosa halfway to his mouth. "Seven?"

"Yeah. She fine. *Muy, muy bonita,*" Juan added, making curving gestures with his hands.

"And she wants to marry you?"

"Excellent taste, eh?" Juan said with a wink. He went on bragging, describing Maia's body, the delight of beholding her in a swimsuit, the joy of holding her in his arms. He spun tales of passionate couplings in the grape leaves along the pristine, deserted beaches of nearby Buck Island. "I give it to her real good," he declared, his voice growing louder as Carlson and Rico joined them. His talk got even raunchier.

Noah rose and shook the crumbs off his pants. They barely noticed as he walked away, face closed in disgust.

"That man is worse than the roaches on Avenue C!"

Maia laughed softly at her companion and he rolled his eyes. "It's not so bad," she said. "Severin really demands a lot of attention, but I leave whenever I've had enough. Whenever," she lowered her eyes, "it gets too heavy."

Damian rolled over on his inflatable pool mattress and breathed out a stream of cigarette smoke. Coughing harshly, he leaned up on one elbow and ignored the water that came pouring onto the raft. The late afternoon sun was back, more relentless than it had been before the sky was conquered by the morning storm.

"Why are you working for such a wretched piece of shit?"

"It gets me into the house."

"I think he fascinates you."

Maia paused. "I've never met anyone like him."

"He's bad for you. Do you hear me? Bad. Bad. Bad bad bad bad."

"I didn't say I was attracted to him—"

"But he's attracted to you."

"Oh, come on, Damian."

"You just don't understand, do you? You are beautiful, Maia. You don't even know how beautiful you are, sister!"

She laughed and shook her head.

"Quit that stupid shit and come stay here with me," Damian insisted. "My boss won't be back for another six weeks and the guesthouse is way too big for me alone."

"Six weeks? I only have ten more days. And besides: How alone are you?" Maia asked from her lawn chair, perched close to the side of the pool.

"I'm pretty alone. Except for sometimes, when Caesar turns up."

"You can't find anybody who doesn't have to sneak around?"

"That's the way things are done here in the Caribbean paradise."

"I don't need to be here when the party starts."

"We wouldn't keep you up."

"My dorm days ended a long time ago, Damian." She reached down and brought up a handful of water to pour over her face. "And besides, I like spending time out at Wisdom."

"Feeling those ancestral vibes?"

"I don't know. There's something special about the beach and that mill."

"So the place really is haunted? That's deep, sister."

"I didn't say it's haunted. It's just that on the entire estate, I feel most comfortable in the water and up by that tower."

He grunted ironically. "I still think you'd be better off here, with me."

"I'd be bored here with you."

"Bad, Maia. Repeat after me: This man is bad for me."

Maia smiled down at Damian. "Sometimes I think you're the only really sane person I've met since I got here."

"Well, I'll tell you one thing," he replied. "I'm the only person you can trust."

"That may be true."

Damian rolled over and placed his hands behind his head.

"Why'd you become a nurse?"

"Don't know. Family tradition, I guess. Everybody always worked in hospitals."

Damian pursed his lips as if he wanted a better explanation.

"Okay, okay." She sighed. "I went to nursing school because it's what everybody expected me to do. The thing is—" she shrugged "—I'm really good at it. I'm not afraid of illness and I get along well with patients."

"But?" Damian prodded, sensing an unspoken reluctance in her answer.

"I really wanted to do something more. I always dreamed of getting out of Michigan and seeing the world."

"Why didn't you leave?"

For the first time she seemed unsure how to respond. "I don't know, Damian. I always got involved with the wrong men. Then my mother was sick for a long, long time. After that, my father went downhill fast. I guess I never had the chance to get away."

He nodded and reached for his Marlboros. "Well, I was doing fine until I decided to come out. I was in my junior year in college when word got back to my family that I was living with a guy. My parents threw me out and I had to go to work. I took a job at the first restaurant I could find, and I've been in food services ever since."

"What were you studying?"

"Accounting," he said with a laugh. "Can't you just see me with an office, a blue suit, and a secretary?"

Maia looked carefully at the stick figure whose cigarettes were barely thicker than his fingers. When his hair was wet she could see the flesh of his skull, browned from long afternoons in the pool, and his pelvis formed fossil ridges beneath the loose spandex.

"Damian, are you seeing anybody?" she asked gently.

"I told you—just the long-after-midnight crew."

"No—I meant a doctor."

He grew still with the quiet of someone who wanted to hide the truth more from himself than from others. "Do I look worse than when we met?" he asked in a whisper.

Maia sat up on the lounge chair and let her head sink between her shoulders. "You look like somebody who's planning to ignore it for as long as he can."

"I'm broke. Insurance-free. Family-less. Lover-without." He tried to smile.

"Your employer should insure you, Damian."

"Pointless. Everyone who works for her is seasonal. When the tourists vanish, so must I."

"To go where?"

"Does it matter? And what about you? You're playing house with that white buddy of yours."

Maia laughed despite herself. "The difference between you and me is that with the proper medication you can stay alive for years. I've only got months. And my quality of life won't deteriorate until the very end. If you take good care of yourself, you can lead a nearly normal existence."

"Maia," he said. "Look around you. I'm living in a guesthouse, swimming in my private pool. I play all day, work evenings, and make enough money for Marlboros and beer. I have sex a-plenty and at this very moment I'm soaking in the Caribbean sun. Jesus, child! Why would I want a *normal* existence?"

"I guess you only want normal if normal's been good to you."

"Right. And normal for me has never been pretty," he agreed.

They were both quiet for a few moments. Damian slid his feet into the water and kicked himself toward the side of the pool. He took a deep swill from a tankard of iced cranberry juice and lit up another cigarette.

"I let a lawyer take me out last night," Maia said suddenly. "My mother would have been pleased."

"Just like a Statesider. Always coming down to the islands to steal away the few good men these poor girls have to vie for."

"There's something to it," she concurred. "He spent a wallet-full to show me how the white folks live. And when the evening ended, he didn't try very hard to get something back for it."

"What's his name? Maybe he's been here after hours."

"Noah Langston. Has an office in Christiansted."

"No. Not one of mine. That doesn't mean he's not married or seeing fifteen other island beauties, of course."

"Of course," Maia agreed and they both laughed. "But I'm really not sure what the evening was about."

"You like him?"

"I do. Although its pointless, really—"

"Oh, *please.* You can't have a bit of sport while waiting for the Reaper? Child, take a hint from me: Since nothing bad can happen to you now, you might as well have some fun!"

"But it wouldn't be much fun if I started to care—"

"If he's a typical male he won't let that happen."

"It's hard enough to keep my shields up when I'm with Severin."

"You can let them down with me," Damian said softly. "But if you've found a guy who has some looks, class, and money, then you'd better count your blessings!"

"He is somewhat bountiful to behold." Maia chuckled.

"Tall, dark, and handsome?"

"And no knucklehead, either."

"Lordy—send him to me if it don't work out!"

Their laughter exploded and threatened to go on for so long that Maia had to dive underwater to calm her throbbing heart. When she surfaced beside Damian's raft neither could tell if her face was wet with tears.

Tina managed to hoist most of her hips onto the padded barstool at Brandy's. The poolside bar was busier than usual, and her friend had scarcely spoken to her the entire evening. Some of the guests were tourists who required Stateside service—that is, they expected the barmaid to trot back and forth between their tables and her counter while serving as an informal travel agent and unofficial island hostess.

Tina kept her face coldly impassive as one of the men in a polo shirt and seersucker trousers smiled at her and let one of his eyes flicker in a wink that might have been excused as anything else. She knew that they could not fathom the idea that a black woman sitting at the bar could be anything other than a prostitute. She knew that the hotel management often suggested to male guests that the hotel could see to "all of their needs." She knew that if Seven died, she might indeed find herself smiling back at these breakfast-cereal imitations of men.

If Seven died. If he died. No, Seven couldn't die. The seventh Johanssen? The one who cared least about the legacy and yet always seemed to survive it? Her first real lover. The only person she had ever come even close to loving. The father of the three babies she'd gotten rid of. The man-child she'd worshipped and desired from the time her older sister pointed him out to her as he rode a pony through the workers' shanties with his brother, Peter. No, Seven wouldn't dare die and leave her!

"*Wavét!* If the tips weren't so good, I'd tell them all to—" Brandy's whisper was interrupted by a tourist calling her from the other end of the patio. She waved pleasantly and balanced a tray full of iced rum punches on her shoulder. Tina watched her childhood friend move gracefully through the tables as the white men surveyed her hips.

A handful of workers from Antigua came in and sucked their teeth at the sight of so many Statesiders. They wanted to watch the cricket game on Brandy's bar TV, but she had the set tuned to CNN.

"Hey, Tina," one of them greeted her. "Where Carlson at?"

"He and Juan up to something. I no see him for two, three days."

"You staying out at Wisdom?" asked another.

"Wisdom my home," she responded firmly. "Seven fine now."

The men let out a collective laugh. "Nothing kill the bastard!" someone remarked. Tina shifted uncomfortably and caught her own reflection in the mirror. She had been adrift since the American woman moved in, displacing her to a primitive boathouse at one end of Wisdom's beach. Now Tina had nothing to do but eat the fried fare at roadside stands and drink beer, and her skin was acquiring the dimpled pallor of boiled chicken.

"Ooooh! Look at what show up here!" Brandy crooned at her island clients. "Where your wife, Thomas? You, Pedro!" she teased, accepting a kiss and hug from every man in turn. "I know, I know! Barbados against St. Lucia!"

She glanced ruefully at the tourists, knowing that even if they tipped better than the islanders, she could not survive without the patronage of the local customers. Without another word she flicked the remote control to the cricket game. The men let out a hardy cheer and at once gathered on the barstools, ordering rum and Cokes. Silenced by the loss of the television link to their safe, CNN lives—and the sight of so many boisterous blacks—the tourists became eerily quiet.

Brandy served the men and finally moved to the end of the counter to speak to her friend.

"She still out there, Tina?"

"She come, she go. Seven looking better."

"So the nurse finish soon."

"Maybe. But Seven talk only about his nurse. Nurse this, nurse that, always the nurse!"

"She go, soon, Tina. Don't vex yourself!"

Tina lifted her glass and caught the eye of one of the island men in the mirror above the bar. "No," she whispered into her rum punch. "It don't make sense to get vexed."

Brandy let out a sharp breath. "Seven never want nobody but you," she said in patois. "Even when he was with me, he was thinking about you."

"How you know that?" Tina asked automatically. The man in the mirror jerked his head gently toward the hotel rooms.

"*Mwe kònèt*. I know it," Brandy answered, her ironic tone lost beneath the excited roar as St. Lucia scored. Tina slid from the stool and smoothed her skirt as the man laid five dollars on the counter and exited in the direction of the front desk. Tina's gaze crossed Brandy's and the barmaid instantly understood. Turning back toward the television, Brandy picked up the tip and placed it silently into the cash register.

TEN DAYS

"I want to see if you're really a Crucian," Noah murmured to Maia as they stood at the end of the long pier in Fredriksted. During the winter months cruise ships docked there, spilling thousands of sweating tourists into the small town, but that evening the tiny seafront bustled with the sounds of laughing black voices, strains of lively music, and the occasional roar of a car engine. Before them the bloodred sea lolled gently against a deep purple sky. A scant wisp of shredded clouds lounged lazily at the world's end.

"So this is some kind of test?" Maia asked, reluctantly turning her gaze from Noah to the enraged ball plunging into the horizon.

"It's more of an initiation," he responded, slipping an arm casually around her waist.

There was a long silence, for both of them were slightly abashed at how confused they became when their bodies were so close. Maia breathed in Noah's bay-rum scent and savored the whisper of his silk sleeve against her bare skin. She counted the strokes of his fingers as he drew his palm along the swelling rise of her hip. He cleared his throat softly and she stole a glance at his face.

It had never occurred to Maia that a man's lips, nose, and eyes could tell her so much—not only about his moods and desires, but about the character of the people whose blood he bore. In the hot red light of the Crucian sunset, Maia was startled to find herself looking into a face as ancient as those images found on African masks. Graceful and fine-boned, with swiftly arching brows, Maia recognized the strong gaze of a hunter, whose every perception was honed to razor sharpness. She saw the proud lift of his nostrils and the firmness of his lips, and understood his pride in that which was black. His pride in that which emanated from his ancestral homeland. That which had remained pure and undiluted in his blood.

He glanced down at her and she turned her eyes away, certain that he would see the wonder in her gaze. Thoughts churning, she looked back toward the water at the instant the burning ball dissolved into the water.

"What the hell was that? There was a kind of—of a reflection or something!"

Noah chuckled and cheered her softly. "Well, well, well. You've passed, Miss Ransom! You've seen the green flash."

"Oh, right! This phenomenon is only visible to native Crucians and their descendants?"

"Something like that," he chuckled. Reaching up, he placed his hands on her shoulders and turned her to face him. "The legend says that if your heart was sealed away from us, you'd never have been able to see it."

"So." She steadied herself to look into his eyes. "My heart's open to you?"

"Wide," he answered. With that word, Noah pressed his lips gently against her temple and pulled her close. Breathing in the clean scent of her hair, his nose brushed her earlobe and launched tiny needles on a race along her spine. Maia held her body tight, slightly resisting the sweetness of his touch.

"Is this a normal part of your practice, Attorney Langston?"

"I try to render only the best service," he murmured, bringing his lips to hers.

The horizon had already gone purple and deep stars were striding into the sky as Noah and Maia retraced their steps along the pier toward the town. "Tonight I want to show you *our* end of the island," he said. "I want you to see the place where I grew up."

A group of ebony and bronze fishermen, seated on plastic drums in their tank shirts and shorts, grinned and raised their beers at the couple. Addressing each one by name, Noah moved slowly and deliberately so that they could admire Maia's beauty.

"What would you like to eat? Ribs or seafood? Indian, Chinese, Puerto Rican, or home-cooked Crucian?"

Maia glanced up at her escort. "Surprise me."

They dined in a small courtyard where a steel-drum player spun out the most delicate music imaginable. There was no light save the softly swaying patterns thrown from paper lanterns strung across the tables, and the savory smoke from an open grill chased the mosquitoes away. Although the restaurant was full, the voices from the tables were joyfully melodic—a sharp contrast to the restrained conversation of the Marienbad.

"You passed Test One with flying colors," Noah quipped after the waitress left their table. "Are you ready for Test Two?"

"I'll give it my best shot."

"What do you think of the town where I was born?"

Maia's answer surprised them both. "I think the blood flows deeper on this end of the island."

He laughed, genuinely curious. "What do you mean by that?"

"I mean—" She paused, glancing around her. "I read in a book that the revolt that ended slavery on St. Croix began here, in Fredriksted in 1848. And I think that the children of those slaves hung onto that and fought to keep this town, even when the Statesiders moved into the other end of the island."

Noah laughed appreciatively. "There's something to that, Maia. The truth is that Fredriksted is the most fertile end of the island. The rain forest is here. And it's much more hilly."

"So it was always more useful to farmers—"

"And to the maroons—the fugitive slaves. Many of our people have taken refuge in these hills when necessary." Leaning toward her, he lowered his voice. "We've had more to struggle against than slavery, you know. Life was hard after abolition. St. Croix didn't even become American until 1917. Some of the old people on the island still speak Danish."

Maia nodded. "Mimi, the housekeeper at Wisdom, learned Danish in her childhood."

"Yes. And my interest is in keeping as much of our island as possible in the hands of the people who really deserve it." Noah glanced around them. "I don't want my children to wake up one day and discover that every inch of their home is owned by outsiders."

"That makes sense," Maia responded.

Noah sat back in his chair and contemplated her. "Is it just intuition that tells you so much about us? You already know more about this island than many Statesiders who've lived here for years."

She shrugged. "Part of me is Crucian, Noah."

"You don't have to remind me," he responded softly. He took a sip of his drink, his gaze wandering slowly over her face and hair. Their eyes met, and for one intense moment the world swirled around them in a rush of smoky sound and dancing shadow. They both looked quickly away, deeply moved and inexplicably shy.

"I'm—I'm sorry to stare," he said. "I just don't think I've ever met anyone quite like you."

"Come on," Maia laughingly protested, but he held up his hands.

"I know the world you come from, Maia. I know that you're surrounded with blond skeletons, and told from the moment you're born that you have to admire them. But this is another place, and we don't see things in quite the same way."

"All right," she said. "How do you Crucians see things, Attorney Langston?"

"First of all, I'll enter into evidence that island men like some flesh on their ladies."

Maia felt herself flush, but she laughed anyway. "And what do the Crucian ladies like on their men?"

"Manhood," he answered simply. "Our women expect men to take care of them, protect them, and provide for them."

"And what do they have to give up for all that?"

"Their loneliness," he replied. She rolled her eyes and he cocked his head. "Don't you believe me, Miss Ransom?"

"Let's just say that you have yet to provide probable cause."

"Actually, I think it's more like a hung jury."

Now they laughed together. "You're very smooth, Noah Langston."

"And you, Maia Ransom, are beautiful."

Maia's breath caught in her throat as she thought of Damian's words: *You don't even see how beautiful you are, sister. . . .*

He paused, looking steadily into her face. "Maia, I've been doing some research on your family."

"My family?"

"Well, I used the island's archives to try and locate some of your relatives."

"Why? You didn't have to—"

"Let me explain—" At that moment the waitress intervened, placing a heaping platter of fragrant samosas on the table. She looked boldly at Maia, then shifted her glance to Noah. Finally turning on one heel, she went away. Noah cleared his throat.

"Columbus first visited our island in 1493. It was settled by the English, French, and even the Knights of Malta before Denmark took over in 1733. Denmark occupied St. Croix until the island was sold to the United States in 1917."

"All right," Maia responded.

"Well, the Danish kept meticulous records of everything—births and deaths, deeds to property, sugar harvests, and so forth. When you mentioned your interest in finding out about your heritage I thought I could help. So I had a look in the island's archives.

"You know," Noah continued, "Ransom is not an unusual name on St. Croix. In fact, the records suggest that there was a whole contingent of Ransoms here at one point. Quite possibly they came from the same region in Africa. Perhaps even the same village."

"But they weren't called Ransom in Africa."

"No. The group was bought from an English slave ship. The *Ransom*. Hence the name."

"You found a record that shows my family's arrival?" she asked in wonder.

"I even found a document detailing the sale of the group to various estates across the island." He sipped his rum, watching her closely over the rim of the glass.

"And did you find out anything about Wisdom?"

"Yes, Maia. I did."

For a moment she sat in utter stillness, one hand tightly encircling her glass, the other gripping the edge of the table. He could see her chest rising and falling, her eyes lowered, lips pressed together. "Hey— are you all right?"

When she looked up tears beaded her cheeks. "Who were they?" she whispered.

Caught up by her emotion, he reached silently into his wallet and removed a sheet of paper. Holding it high so that he could read it by the lantern light, Noah began to recite. "Eighteen hundred and three: Oba of the *Ransom* ship, some eighteen years of age, sold to Solomon Johanssen. Eighteen hundred fourteen, a woman named Dembe was given to Oba Ransom in marriage—"

"The Johanssens recognized their marriage?"

"Evidently."

"But if they were slaves, why didn't they bear their masters' names?"

"Well, it appears that there was something special about this group. Something to do with African religion. The Ransoms were shaman. Healers. The whites seemed to think they should be singled out from the other slaves on the island. There were several stories about strange illnesses and even stranger cures worked by the oldest members of the Ransom clan."

"You're kidding, right?"

Noah smiled. "I forgot for a moment that you're a nurse, Maia!" He put his hand over hers. "I don't mean to frighten you. This isn't a story of zombies or possession or anything supernatural. It just seems that this group stood out, so the masters let them keep the Ransom name. But that's not all I discovered."

He was again interrupted by the waitress, who set their drinks down and then lingered by the table, openly examining Maia.

"Everything is fine, Inez," Noah announced patiently as the waitress turned her appraising gaze on him.

"You go for tourist, now?" she asked, smiling darkly.

"Don't worry," he answered, moving instantly into Crucian, "I no marry no woman but you, sweetheart."

Momentarily appeased, she strolled away and Noah turned back to Maia.

"There's no mention of a Ransom at Wisdom in any records for some years after the marriage. Then, in the eighteen-fifties there are three males—Adam, Jeremiah, and Mattias—each with the Ransom surname. They weren't slaves any longer, so they're listed in turn as foremen at the estate. It appears that they might have been the grandchildren of Oba and Dembe."

"Three brothers listed as foremen? Did they take turns or something?"

"No. I think—" The restaurant grew noisier, and Noah began speaking very slowly, enunciating every word. "I think that they managed different parts of the estate. One might have been in charge of the cane crop. Another of the stables. The third, the mill. There was a fourth child too. A daughter called Zara. It seems that she actually ran the great house. You see, Wisdom once had a great many servants and workers. It was one of the premier properties on the island."

"It still is, according to Severin."

"Today it's hard to imagine how beautiful it was, even in my childhood," Noah remarked.

"So you think that the Ransoms once played an important role at Wisdom?"

"Actually, I do." He paused. "There was one other record. The birth of a son to Zara Ransom. The child's name was Abraham—" He stopped as Maia clutched at his arm. Her face had tightened and her eyes were once again filled with tears.

"Abraham was the name of my great-grandfather!"

"I think I've found his birth certificate," Noah announced.

"My God, Noah. Thank you so much! I don't even know what—" The words stumbled and she covered her face with trembling fingers. Surprised, Noah reached over to stroke her shoulder and saw that her lips were wet with her tears. For a moment he watched in wonder as this woman who controlled her reactions so carefully broke down like a child. Fighting the urge to press his mouth against hers and kiss away her tears, he simply chanted, "It's all right, Maia. It's okay, love. Please, please don't be sad. . . ."

Most of the restaurant had been inspecting them with openly amused eyes, even before Maia's sudden distress. Now Inez again appeared at the table, this time with a box of tissues. She boldly leaned down, placing her face near Maia's.

"Don't let him tell you nothing," she crooned. "He a lawyer. Same thing as liar! I can't stand to see this man break another sister heart!"

Maia's hand came away from her face and she stared up at the waitress in confusion. Then her gaze went to Noah, who was almost glaring at the islander.

"Thank you," Maia said to the waitress. "I promise to kick him under the table every time he says he loves me!"

The waitress sauntered away and a titter went up from the nearest tables.

"Maia, I didn't mean to upset you," he apologized.

"Upset me? God, no! You've just given me my family!"

"I'd like to give you something more, if you'd let me."

"More?"

Noah Langston straightened his back and reached for both of Maia's hands. He began speaking in the voice he used only for very private consultations with very special clients.

"I'd like to give you Wisdom," he said.

"What do you mean?"

He could see that he'd already told her enough for one evening. Part of his training as a lawyer was to know when—and how—to inform clients about important details. He knew that the rest of his research could wait—that he should give her time to work through everything he'd already told her. Time to become curious about what else he knew.

Time to come to rely on him for the truth. Perhaps even time to whet the desire for something more than a professional relationship.

But when he looked at the unexpected, deeply profound gratitude written on her face, he forgot about her full brown breasts and muscular thighs. He stopped thinking about the taste of her tongue and began to wonder whether he could make her happy—*truly* happy—in a way she'd never felt before.

"It has to do with Abraham," he heard himself saying. "How much do you know about his life?"

"I know that he left St. Croix with his wife and eventually came to the States," Maia said. "They settled in Florida with their son. Their son, my grandfather, came to Detroit to work in the car factories. That's where both my father and I were born."

Noah cocked his head slightly. "Did you ever hear why your great-grandfather left St. Croix?"

"No. I always assumed that after the United States bought the Virgin Islands, lots of people came north to find jobs."

"Then you never knew anything about his heritage?"

"We all assumed that everything about our family was lost."

"Maia, it's possible that although Abraham was called Ransom, he should have been named Johanssen."

"I don't understand," she said, confused.

"Maia, I believe that your great-great-grandfather might have been Jakob Johanssen, the owner of Wisdom."

"Abraham's father was white?"

"Yes. Abraham was Jakob's first-born son."

Her brows came together and she turned her head slightly, as if trying to be sure she understood. "But he was illegitimate."

"I'm not so sure about that. Something happened at the estate between the Johanssens and the Ransoms. I found an article in a broadside published during the period suggesting that there may have actually been some sort of legal bond between Jakob and Zara before he married Isabella Haagenssen, the daughter of another wealthy Danish planter."

"But what about my great-grandfather?"

"It appears that some whites in the community—not to mention Solomon Johanssen, the family patriarch—turned against his black grandson. The boy, Abraham, was driven out. I think he had a claim on the estate, so the landowners offered him a choice: Emigrate or die. So he left."

"That's crazy! If my great-grandfather were a Johanssen, that would mean that Severin and I are cousins."

"That's not all," Noah concluded, opening his palms slowly. "It would mean, dear Maia, that ownership of the estate should have been passed on to Abraham, his first-born son, and not Jakob's son by his white wife. In other words, Wisdom belongs to you. Severin Johanssen is sleeping in your house."

These words were met with silence. Noah watched curiously as a number of emotions flooded her face: outrage, frustration, and fatigue.

"What happens now?" she asked quietly.

"Give me a few more days. I need to find some kind of document that legally establishes the relationship between Zara and Jakob."

"A few more days," she echoed softly. She looked up, her voice troubled. "Noah, I want to go now."

"Of course." He signaled to Inez, who was observing them carefully from the kitchen.

Together they made their way slowly toward the pier, stopping beside Maia's Jeep. Noah's shining BMW sedan was parked a few cars away.

"I'll lead you out to Wisdom."

"You don't have to do that."

"It's too late and too far for you to go out there alone. And especially in that—" he eyed her rented car "—that contraption. Besides," he added softly, "it's the perfect night for a drive along the coast. Full moon, low tides, and no storms on the horizon."

"Even in separate cars?"

"Just say the word, Miss Ransom, and nothing will ever separate us."

She smiled despite the tears that were trapped in her lashes. "You're too charming, Attorney Langston," she began, but her words ended with the look in his eyes. Suddenly she was in his arms. He had meant to kiss her, but he found himself holding her in an instinctively protective embrace, as if the things he'd told her were serious enough to cause her bodily harm. Her head lay pressed against his heart and he lowered his face to her sweet, smoky hair, drowning in the desire he'd felt for her since he first found her in his courtyard.

And yet he couldn't treat her like other women, turning this hug into a series of caresses that would eventually land her in his bed. He wanted to touch her—he wanted to peel away her resistance in the same way a lover undresses his partner, gently pulling her dress away from her shoulders and opening her bra to free her own desire. He wanted to explore the parts of her that were cool and distant, as well as the sensual immediacy of her intelligence, her curiosity, her lack of fear. The sadness he sometimes read in her eyes moved him, too, and he truly believed that in telling her about her family, he had removed every obstacle that lay between them.

She stirred, gently running her hands along his full upper arms, then over his shoulders to pull him close. She leaned up to kiss him, opening her lips so that the tips of their tongues met very gently. Instantly their mouths opened, their bodies flooded with a deep and urgent desire.

"Noah," she whispered as she pulled back, shaking her head. "Noah—this is too much for me. It's too fast."

He closed his eyes. "There's nothing wrong with us being together."

"I have to go back to Wisdom," she murmured, struggling against the pleasure of his touch.

"Later—"

"No. No. I can't give—" She broke away from him and went straight to the little Jeep. Her mind was roaring with thoughts of his hands, hips, and powerful flesh. Her fingers were shaking as she gripped the steering wheel. Barely able to stop herself from climbing down from the vehicle and running straight into his arms, she looked neither left nor right. She slammed the stick into gear and leaned on the accelerator, steering herself back to the highway.

"This is the right thing to do," she said aloud over the engine's roar. "I can't get involved with anybody. I have to deal with Severin. I have to deal with my health. The last thing I need to do is—" She took a deep, deep breath. "Is to fall in love."

She wasn't sure if Noah was following her until she turned off the highway and began the treacherous ascent to the deserted hills so far from the rest of the island. Looking into the rearview mirror she saw the arcs of his headlights making their way calmly, protectively, and even lovingly, behind her.

Her steps were halting in the midnight dark, and she stumbled over a curb that jutted out from the slave-cobbled street. The heavy locked grills on the windows of jewelry stores and tourist shops met her groping fingers as she felt her way blindly toward the town square. She stepped on something thick and soft and cried out in fear, then began jogging lightly despite the pitch blackness.

There was no sound behind her. Had he given up so easily? Something told her he would leap out from behind an arch, pull her into an alley or doorway, and she cursed herself at the thought that she could survive in a world that spat her out so long ago!

Dripping with sweat and almost panting in terror, she finally emerged in the town square. Faint street lamps in antique sockets glowed from the old stone fortress near the bloodred auction block. She could see the hurricane lamp hanging by the ferry landing and she thought she could make out the figure of the ferryman, sitting in his little booth by the black, lapping water.

It seemed an eternity before she stepped into the tiny skiff, and she reached down to steady herself as the boatman threw the engine into throttle. She looked back to thank him and at that moment the figure rose up from beneath her, and she felt his hands grasping her arms and her throat, groping at her breasts and sliding downward toward her thighs. Crying out in terror, she used all the force in her body to jerk herself from his clutches and felt the floor of the boat ride out from under her. She was falling, falling, falling with a slow and steady grace into the colorless warmth of the oil-black water, as black as the sky and as black as her mind as her breath vanished and sound ended and the blackness of his eyes became the last sensation she could—

"Nurse! Come here, Nurse!"

Maia ripped herself up from the damp, twisted sheets and fumbled for her watch, thrown on the floor beside the bed. It was late—late in the night, but still too early for the sun to bring hope back into the sky. She could hear the shrill soprano of mosquitoes on the net near her head, and the low warble of a hidden bird outside the rotting walls. Severin was turning restlessly in his bed at the end of the hall and she concentrated hard, hoping he'd be lulled back to sleep by the insistent promise of the sea.

She lay back, ignoring the sweaty pool of mattress and threw her arm over her greasy forehead. Eyes trained on the ceiling, her thoughts bounded back to the sudden, deep desire mixed with a wrenching wave of despair she'd known when Noah kissed her deep and hard as they stood beside his car.

For a moment Maia wasn't sure how she'd gotten home. Then she remembered that he'd followed her rented Jeep in his own car all the way to the estate, leaving her at the base of the circular walkway before the great house, after asking repeatedly if she wanted him to see her inside. No, she hadn't wanted that. She didn't want Noah to see the manner in which she was living—or worse—the manner in which she was dying. She didn't want Noah to know about any of that. For now, she wanted him to be a man, and she simply wanted to be a woman. If anything could ever be that simple.

"Nurse! You hear me calling you?"

Dutifully Maia pushed back the net and made her way through the darkness into the great room to check Severin's pressure and his temperature, and administer his medication. Eyes closed, Severin was nonetheless wide awake. And he was evil.

"You smell like Saturday night without the sex, Nurse."

"Since it's well after midnight, I must smell like a clean Sunday morning."

Severin emitted a dirty chuckle. "My whole life smelled like Saturday night, so it don't make a damn bit of difference to me what fucking day it is. But I know you got a man, Nurse."

"Christ—everything in this place needs scouring. Starting with your mouth," she muttered.

"He not man enough for you," Severin said sharply. "You need to go out and find somebody to give it to you good, woman. You so tense all the time."

He rolled over, ignoring her as she crossed the room to turn out the light. Closing the jalousies that led out to his crumbling balcony, she took a good look at her patient in the lamplight. His flesh had thickened. His skin was beginning to look vaguely human again. And his bald pate was shadowed with a soft yellow down, like a schoolboy's September hair. Despite the steely odor of medication that poured from his sweat, Severin almost smelled like a man again. And his eyes could focus—watchful, amused, thoughtful, even cruel, when he looked into her face.

Maia knew that she had saved him. And that meant that she should leave. Catch the plane that would take her back to her other life, her real life, in nine days. Take the things she had learned about her family and make a lovely scrapbook to admire on cold Michigan evenings. Put this crumbling house and its disgusting owner behind her and concentrate on somehow healing herself.

But standing in the center of what was once the grand drawing room of the estate's great house, she felt a sudden, crippling need to stay. She needed time to learn every inch of Wisdom. She wanted to lay her footprints on the sands of the beach. Touch the mossy bricks of the ruined mill. Breathe in the air of the old stables. Explore the cracks and crevasses of the pockmarked, wooden boathouse.

She wanted the chance to finish her war with Severin and make her peace with the Ransoms.

From somewhere deep in the traces of her memory she heard her father's voice:

"My granddaddy, he said he loved the grape trees with their big fan leaves hanging down over the water. He loved the way the sands curved along the water's edge like somebody took a paintbrush and

closed their eyes and made a curving line, separating the white and the blue. . . ."

Maia stood looking down at Severin as the medication took effect and he drifted off into a muttering sleep. "All right, Pete," he whispered. "I'll get rid of it now. . . ." The light threw a yellowing shadow on his parched face against the peeling wall. Moths bounced angrily against the shade, momentarily forgetting the dangers of the beckoning light.

"He said it was the finest on the entire island. The most elegant great house you ever saw. A big drive in a circle going right up to the door. And a veranda around the entire rear with a view of the sea. A great room with a spinet and Delft china come all the way from Holland. Even a chandelier. He said the leaves on the trees by the mill sang songs with the waves at night, and you could hear the horses calling up at dawn from the stables. . . ."

She wandered slowly down the hall, away from the light, and into her own dank chamber. Climbing under the net and onto her narrow bed, she wondered if Abraham had ever slept in that room. Her thoughts traveled along the sill to the empty shelves built into a wooden cabinet near the door. Perhaps Zara, Abraham's mother, had once cleaned this very chamber. Perhaps she had sewn here, or ironed here, or even made love with Jakob Johanssen—the great-great-grandfather she shared with Severin—here, within these walls.

"They had hand-laced curtains from Brussels, and sheets purchased in Martinique. The mistress kept fresh flowers in the rooms every day. The house was always cool because the breezes swept up from the sea, and they never had to worry, because even the worst storms couldn't bring down the walls of Wisdom. . . ."

Maia lay in the vibrant stillness. She didn't care anymore about Tina. She didn't care about Severin's illness or that bitch Paulette. She didn't care about any of the other whites who had trampled on her people for so long. And she didn't even care about the death that was swelling inside her with each passing day. She only knew that the Ransom spirit had brought her to Wisdom to know, and she'd have to know, fully and completely, before it was over.

NINE DAYS

Rose carried the crystal platter of crisp romaine lettuce to the terrace and set it beside the home-baked rosemary bread. Mr. and Mrs. Fairchild and their guests were still drying themselves off on the pool patio below, but the maid knew that everything had to be ready the moment they came up the steps.

A pitcher of iced tea with peppermint leaves sweated beside the white wine set to chill in an Italian ceramic pot. Rose had placed the basalmic vinegar and Greek olive oil in the shade of a deck umbrella, near a bowl of frozen blueberries. She'd bring out the platter of grilled steaks when the guests were comfortably seated. Until then, she could slip back into the kitchen and enjoy a surreptitious bowl of lime sherbet, followed by a forbidden cigarette.

Something was amiss in the Fairchild house. It had begun with Seven Johanssen's most recent illness, which was the talk of the entire island. Rumor had it that he was getting better (as Vashti reported after Severin's last checkup with the Canadian doctor). And it was said that a private nurse from Stateside—whose last name just happened to be *Ransom*!—had been hired to look after him at home (Mimi repeated all the details on her own front porch every evening). There was even talk that Tina had taken a lover. Brandy said he was a technician who'd come up from the oil refinery in St. Lucia.

Everyone knew that if Severin died without an heir, Paulette would inherit Wisdom. The land was priceless: Several of the island's real-estate developers (all white men from the States) had hounded Severin for years to sell it. One developer had even submitted plans to the government for an exclusive hotel complex with the Wisdom great house serving as the casino.

At one point the local historical society had approached Seven about turning the estate into a nature preserve and museum, but he had all but chased them off his property. He also refused access to an animal rights organization that wanted to turn the old stable into a large animal hospital.

Everyone knew that Seven was living in alcohol-induced poverty with the last dollars of his inheritance. The white families were aghast at the thought that one of the most successful slave-holding dynasties should fall into ruin at the hands of its own son. But for the blacks, Rose included, the wreck of the Johanssens was divine retribution for the suffering his ancestors had caused so many blameless people for so many decades.

Rose's reverie was broken by the sound of the luncheon party mounting the garden steps. Mrs. Fairchild led the way in an emerald sarong that matched her Miami-purchased maillot. Her brother Clay followed with his date, a graduate student from Toronto who'd soon be returning to Canada. Bringing up the rear was Mr. Fairchild, who had already made himself a gin and tonic at the poolside liquor cabinet below.

The maid was startled into action by Paulette's irritated voice. She stepped out onto the terrace to find her employer glowering from her seat at the head of the glass table.

"Rose! You were supposed to have everything ready! Where's the butter?"

"Sorry, Mrs. Fairchild! It is still in the refrigerator—"

She ducked into the kitchen and rummaged in the enormous, over-loaded double fridge while the guests continued a heated conversation begun at the pool below.

"So you're trying to tell me that Severin knows what she's up to?" It was Mrs. Fairchild, of course.

"Sev's not quite as stupid as he pretends," her brother answered.

"But he's very ill," she insisted.

"He's been partying pretty hard for years."

"This is different, Clay. You have no idea because you didn't go to see him."

"He doesn't want to see me, Paulette. And besides, I know I can count on you to stick your face in it and report back to me."

"*Someone* should care what happens to the family legacy," she declared loudly.

"What are you two arguing about?" David Fairchild said equitably. "Nobody can do anything about Wisdom until Sev's gone."

"Paulette is scared that our cousin Severin will leave the family estate to his girlfriend," Clay explained to the silent young woman at his side. "That thought has plagued her since we were kids."

"That's because he's run after those women since we were kids!"

"Those women," Clay said to his date, "are black. And that drives my sister even crazier."

"I don't care what you did when we were young," Paulette said with a cool glance across the table that also swept up her husband. "What matters is what you do now that we're adults."

"If Severin wanted Tina to have Wisdom he'd have married her long ago," David Fairchild said patiently. "I think this whole conversation is nonsense."

"But you can't pretend you didn't see his so-called nurse with Noah Langston," Paulette hurled at her husband. "And you know damned well what that means!"

"Calm down, honey. Just because that woman from the States was having dinner with Noah doesn't mean that they're planning some secret—"

"Noah's built his reputation—and paid for that BMW—on cases just like this. He's hoping to do to us exactly what he did to the Desmonds and the Sutherlands."

"Noah can't do anything to us," Clay said irritably. "We're not even in line to inherit Wisdom."

"If Severin dies without an heir then the estate comes to me," Paulette almost shouted. "He's been letting it fall apart for the last twenty-five years. I'll be damned if he gives it away to one of those parasites who take advantage of him."

"Nobody could exploit Severin if he wasn't drunk all the time," David argued quietly.

"I can't stop him from drinking," Paulette replied, "but I intend to stop him from handing our family's land to those people who pretend to be the descendants of our slaves."

The young woman from Canada spoke up. "I've never heard of any land restitutions being made on the basis of slavery."

"Me, either," Clay said.

"And what difference does it make?" David asked diplomatically. "I wouldn't want to take on the rebuilding of that house. The whole place is a wreck."

"It's not *your* house!" Paulette shouted. "Your family did not live and die there!"

"My family has been here for a half century," David said meekly.

"Your parents came here for their honeymoon on your father's G.I. bill and never left!"

"I'm sorry," David responded icily, "that you married a commoner, darling."

Quietly Rose stepped out to the terrace. She put the butter in the center of the table, trying hard not to be visible. To her relief the conversation continued.

"All right. So you think that Noah is going to help this nurse exploit Severin in some manner?" Clay asked patiently.

"I'm sure of it," Paulette snapped.

"And Noah's reward will be?"

"I don't know. Maybe he's working for one of the developers."

"That doesn't sound like Noah," David put it. "He'd never help any whites get a piece of the island. No—if he's involved with this, it's only for himself."

"But how would he stand to profit from helping that nurse get control of Wisdom?" Clay inquired.

"Maybe," the Canadian woman inserted, "he plans to marry her or something." She froze at the surprise on their faces.

"Noah Langston's still single?" Clay asked with his brows raised. "Christ! I haven't seen him in years."

"That's because you're too busy drowning your last brain cells in that beer you're drinking," his sister snapped. The Canadian woman flushed in embarrassment and lowered her eyes, but Clay merely stretched his arms out wide.

"Staying drunk between golf games is the greatest benefit of being the proud descendent of very successful slave holders," he quipped, hoping that someone would laugh.

"I'd love to see your family's estate," the young woman said quietly. "I've never known anyone who actually owned a plantation."

The entire table looked at her as if seeing her for the first time. Paulette took note of the young woman's remarkable hickory skin and light brown hair drying in the afternoon sun to an almost unnatural gold. Her eyes were green and her full lips opened to strong white teeth. Paulette saw her husband's eyes as they roamed appreciatively along the woman's long arms, folded to partially obscure her lean, full-bosomed form. She had swum slow, patient laps while the others drank cocktails on the deck, and in the heat of the conversation no one had paid her much attention. Now it was evident why Clay had brought her into their circle. She was beautiful. Unusually beautiful for a Statesider. Almost, in fact, as beautiful as Paulette.

"Where in Canada do you come from?" Paulette now inquired.

"Toronto. But my father's Brazilian," she said in answer to the unasked question.

"Bianca spent part of her childhood in Rio," Clay explained.

"And I'm still not used to snow," she joked. The others chuckled politely.

"Where are you living?" Paulette asked.

"My roommate from college is doing research in marine biology. I came over to spend the summer with her."

"So you're enjoying your stay on St. Croix?" David asked in his most gracious voice.

"I love the beaches. I just got my scuba certification."

"We'll have to take you for a dive at Buck Island," David said. "The reefs are almost indescribable. And the water is amazingly clear. You even see the occasional dolphins—"

"Christ, David!" Paulette interrupted. "You sound like a hard-up travel agent. I'm sure that Clay is quite competent to show the sights to Bianca."

Paulette watched her husband watching the lovely Bianca as she ate her lunch. Clay was watching his brother-in-law too. He didn't know Bianca well enough to be certain that she didn't prefer middle-aged, graciously graying men who stayed in excellent shape by engaging in a variety of sports and fastidiously avoiding any kind of stress. Once or twice Paulette and Clay's eyes met and the brother and sister looked quickly away, embarrassed by the transparence of their shared insecurities.

The meal done, the party moved casually into the pastel living room. Rose appeared, now wheeling in a bamboo cart with lime sherbet in bowls shaped like open blossoms. Of course, David went straight for the bottle of vermouth and Clay asked Rose to bring him another beer. Bianca sat down on the edge of the white leather sofa and followed the conversation with her smoky green eyes.

"Well, I don't suppose anyone has any ideas about Wisdom," Paulette declared from her pose near the sliding door.

"Not I," David responded.

"Nor I," Clay chimed in. The two men laughed in unison.

"All right," Paulette said in irritation. "But don't be surprised when property that's been in our family for generations is suddenly beyond our reach."

"Don't worry, big sister. Wisdom's not going anywhere anytime soon. And knowing old Severin, nothing's going to change with him, either."

"Let's face it," David added. "If Severin dies, the house is yours, anyway. And as long as he's alive, he has to pay the taxes and keep the roof on. I think we should just calm down and give it some time."

Paulette saw that her husband and brother were already thinking about the golf game they'd arranged later with some friends. Bianca saw it too. She asked Paulette whether she might take a shower, and was shown to the guest suite in the rear.

When Paulette returned she walked straight to her brother. "You've made a lovely friend. Why don't you take her out to see Wisdom?"

"I don't know. I can give Mimi a call tonight and see how Severin's feeling."

"Why don't you just surprise them?"

"It wouldn't be right, Paulette. You yourself said he's very sick."

"What you mean is that your golf game is more important than our family." She shrugged. "I'll take Bianca on a little tour this afternoon. I want to look in on Severin, anyway."

Clay knew that his sister really wanted an excuse to get into the great house and analyze the Statesider nurse's influence over their cousin. He sighed, then decided that if Paulette wanted to waste her time, he certainly wasn't going to get in the way. After all, he'd watched Paulette struggle against the inevitable their whole lives. And if Bianca was under Paulette's supervision, it was very unlikely that David would manage to have a go at her. If there was one house that his sister could control, it was her own.

In the corridor Rose waited for the party to break up. She still had a load of laundry to wash, and Mrs. Fairchild would be furious if the living room wasn't restored to its spotless state before dinner. She wished that there were some way to warn Mimi and Tina about Paulette's plans to visit Wisdom. But there was no phone at the decaying estate. And anyway, Mimi would be all right, no matter what. She had worked for the Johanssens—and survived their madness—for a long, long time.

"Piss on you! I been swimming every morning for the last thirty years," Severin declared to Maia from the edge of his bed, "and even the day you showed up on my beach. It's probably your fault that I damn near died!"

"You're doing much better, Severin. It won't be long before you can get back to working on your tan."

He watched her as she straightened up his bed table, organizing his medication bottles with a nurse's intrinsic neatness. "Hey, Nurse," he said, "make me a deal: If I can walk down from the house to the beach, you'll go swimming with me."

"I'm not getting anywhere near the water, but I'll watch you have a heart attack and drown," she said pleasantly and he grinned slyly.

"I can't believe you're going to let the cell doors swing open for a little while!"

"You need some sun, Severin. I've truly never seen a man as white as you."

"I'm doing my best to get over it!" He chuckled, his voice still raw from the years of cigarettes and alcohol. But he hoisted himself up and immediately shuffled toward the door.

"Whoa—where you headed?"

"Guess," he said without looking back.

"Oh, shit," Maia muttered. Then she turned to the kitchen. "Mimi—could you get these sheets changed while Severin's up for a while?"

She held his arm as he half-walked, half-skied through the thicket of grape trees and thorny scarlet bougainvillea down to the alabaster beach.

"Jesus! What'd they do to me at that claptrap hospital?" he gasped as they reached the bottom, his heart nearly leaping out of his porcelain chest.

"They kept your scrawny ass alive till I could take over," she answered.

At last they were standing on the velvety sand, the warm turquoise waves caressing their feet. Severin's eagerness to enter the water was moving, but Maia still cried out when he stripped himself naked, hurling his tattered underwear toward her.

"Put your shorts back on, you idiot!"

"Born this way—die this way—*swim* this way!"

He splashed into a froth of white and vanished beneath a wave. For a moment she saw nothing from her place on the shore, but then Severin's white buttocks appeared, followed by his blond frill of hair, and finally, his rotating twiglike arms.

"Disgusting!" she muttered, shaking her head. Moving back into the shade, she sank into the sand and rested her chin on her knees. Although she couldn't do much to save Severin if he swam too deep or got caught in a strong current, she felt it was her duty to supervise. She could see parts of his body rising and falling in the pearly surf. He was rolling from his belly to his back like a chicken on a rotisserie, eagerly offering up his blanched flesh to the salt and the sun. Every few seconds she heard him cry out in rough ecstasy, the water holding him like a cruel, adoring lover.

Maia let her gaze wander, pressing her toes deep into the sand and clutching at handfuls of powdery crystals. She breathed in the sweet jasmine while watching the great circles of grape leaves twitter like green wind chimes. Two fat pelicans blew lazily out toward the reefs, looking for fish. In the distance a sail cut a restless triangle on the tide.

The Ransoms were buried there. In that red earth, and beneath that silken sand, and even in the roots of the trees and flowering bushes. Her blood watered every fertile stalk and fragrant bough. This was her land. Her home. Her sea. Her endless blue sky. *This* was the world that Abraham Ransom had wanted for his descendants—

"Maia!" Severin's rough voice was carried with the waves toward the shore. She looked up and saw his thin arm waving frantically. "Come help me, Maia! I'm too tired! Can't make it back!"

It seemed that he was balancing on a shoal, some hundred feet out. He was visible from the waist up, and his shoulders were already red from the unaccustomed exposure to the hot sun.

Slowly she stood and shook off the sand. She was wearing a cotton dress styled like a long polo shirt. She hadn't had time to change into her swimsuit—and Severin knew it. So he'd posed her a choice: Come into the water fully clothed or undress on the beach and swim in her underwear. Clearly she couldn't take the risk of leaving her sick patient alone in the water while she returned to the house for a swimsuit.

"Maia," he cried hoarsely, "I don't feel too good!" he shouted. It seemed the water had grown deeper around him—as if the undertow was moving out quickly.

"Just swim back, Severin!" she shouted in exasperation.

"I can't make it."

"Lie on your back and float!"

"Come help me, Nurse!"

"You don't need my help!"

"I'm sick, Nurse! Sick!" The water was suddenly up to his neck, and without another thought Maia pulled her dress up over her head and ran into the water in her panties and bra. She began to swim against the surf, wrestling with the fresh morning waves while trying to keep Severin in her sight. The ground disappeared beneath her and she was in deep water. She swam onward, making steady headway through the rough foaming current toward his flailing figure.

Suddenly she found sand beneath her feet, and she realized that by stretching out her legs she could walk through the water toward her patient. She was only waist deep, but he seemed to be in much deeper. She pushed herself forward, feeling the hungry sea bed snatch and hold her toes. As she came close Severin reached for her, his face grim, and she held her arms out to grasp him before he got into worse trouble.

And then she felt him pull her firmly toward his body and place her easily over his bent knees. She saw that he was sitting calmly on a shallow bank of sand where the water was less than knee deep. Swiftly he managed to get his arms around her waist and bring his face close to hers.

"Thank you, Nurse," he whispered in mock relief. "I was fearing I might drown!"

"You bastard!" she shouted. "Now you're about to get strangled!"

"You wouldn't kill your helpless patient!"

"I might send him back to intensive care—"

"Come on, Nurse Ransom—" He playfully splashed water down her exposed back. "You're supposed to be healing me!"

Irritated beyond words, Maia struggled to release herself from his embrace. Severin, however, pushed her off his knees so that she went backward into the surf. Instantly he was on top of her, pressing her into the thick sand while the warm waves poured over both their bodies.

"Severin—get off of me!" She choked and sputtered as she took a mouthful of salty spray.

He laughed and put his arms around her, rolling her deftly so that suddenly she was on top of his body with his thighs wrapped over her hips. She could feel the thickness of his penis pressed against her.

"You like it better this way?" he murmured, running his lips along her neck as another wave poured over their shoulders and faces.

Maia was amazed at his unexpected strength, matched only by the boldness of his embrace. She pushed her elbows into the sand and tried to lift herself away from him, but the force of the water knocked her off balance and after a brief struggle she found herself once again lying beneath him. He vised her thighs open with his knees, still laughing.

"Severin," she said, fighting to remain calm despite her rage, "I want you to let me up now."

"Why, Nurse?" he answered, his voice distinctly deeper and more masculine than she'd ever heard it.

"Because I don't want you." She managed to steady herself against the next insistent wave.

"You'll like me," he promised with a softness that blended gently with the hiss of the retreating sea. He pressed harder against her. "It's real good like this. . . ."

"Severin," she called through the tickling foam, "get off of me!"

"They wanted it like this. The Ransom women. And *she* liked it, right here, just like this. With *him*. Let yourself go, Nurse," he urged, running his hands the length of her back to pull her hips forward. "Oh, my lord, woman—it's been too long—"

"Let me go, Severin," she cried, knowing there was no one to hear.

He pushed up against her, simultaneously pulling her body closer, and kissed her again, his tongue finding her lips even though she tried to twist away. Maia screamed into his mouth and pushed so hard that he fell backward into the surf. Severin lay beside her in the warm water, panting and laughing. Another wave crashed over them both.

"Listen, you fucking asshole," Maia ordered, wiping her mouth and spitting into the water, "don't you ever put your hands on me again. Do you understand?"

"You're so beautiful I can't make any promises," he said, splashing the water joyfully over his face and running his hands down his thin chest. "And besides," he added, "the tomb's a pretty nice place, but nobody gets some in that space!" He laughed even harder, sending the water flying off his forehead. "My English teacher taught me that poem in school. I think it's perfect for you and me!"

Maia pulled herself up and began wading to the shore, unsure whether or not her soaking underwear was completely transparent.

When she was again on land she turned back to her patient. "Please drown, you dickhead!"

She had only gone a few steps up the steep slope when she felt a presence in the bushes. Tina stepped out from behind a wall of grape trees, her despising yellow eyes slitted against the noonday light. "You playing a hard game, Nurse."

Maia glanced down, knowing that no matter what she said, nothing would dispel the notion that she was nearly naked on purpose. She was holding her dress away from her dripping body, and sand crystals coated her panties and thin bra. Tina's flesh, sausaged into the sleeveless dress she was wearing, was an effigy of fatty foods and alcohol.

"It's you he really wants," Maia said clearly, but Tina reached swiftly forward and gripped her arm.

"He don't give a shit about me no more."

"Don't worry," Maia barked. "I'm gone!"

Tina's eyes widened slightly, then narrowed. "You leaving Wisdom?"

"Hell, yes!"

"You leaving St. Croix?"

Maia hesitated and Tina looked back out toward the water. "As long as you on the island, Seven will still be sick for you." She hawked and spat into the sand at Maia's feet. "Get out and don't come back. I'm warning you: *Piti hash ka-bat gwo bwa*—little axes can cut down big trees!"

"Fuck *both* of you!" Maia shouted, continuing her climb up the steep, sandy slope. At the top she looked down to see Severin floating on his back, rocking peacefully in the surf. She could also see the other woman crouching in the grape trees, staring toward the sea, hidden from view in the bushes below.

By the time she reached the top of the hill, Maia's anger had coa-
lesced into action. She would change clothes, pack her things, get into
her Jeep and find another place to stay until her plane took off. All she
had to do was leave!

The house was staggering in the unwavering noon heat and Severin's room was patch-worked by the broken slats of the shutters drawn
close against the meridian sun. Still throwing off droplets of water as
she walked into the kitchen, Maia avoided Mimi's surprised stare by
wiping her face with the only thing she could find—a faded dish towel.
"Mimi—" she began, then stopped, silenced by frustration.

She went into the moldy bath and began washing herself. "I have
to go," she muttered. "It's time. Time to get out. Severin will never let
me get any closer. He'll never let me find out the truth."

She had almost finished when she noticed it—a faint vein of fresh
blood, tie-dying her panties in a nagging statement. Maia pressed her
forehead against the mirror, calculating and recalculating the days and
knowing very well that this blood was nothing so healthy as her period.
Knowing that this blood was a flag. A silent warning. Undeniable evidence that her time was running out. Her body would soon refuse to
play the game of denial.

She returned to her bedroom and dressed. Severin entered the
house with Tina; he spoke to her in muted tones. Then the front door
closed and the world seemed to hush. Maia took a deep breath. She
closed her suitcases, then made her way to the great room.

Severin was sitting on the edge of his bed. He was wet and salty and
his eyes were evil. "What's on your face, Nurse?"

"My face?"

"Don' bullshit me!" he growled so forcefully that his hot breath
reached her across the room. "I been all the way, you know. I stared at
it. Smelled it. Even tasted it. So I know its shadow. Dark paint. Like
somebody put a black net over your eyes—"

"What the hell are you talking about?"

"The Fear." He stood up and moved toward her slowly. "How did it
catch up with you? Some sneaking ugly memory? Or—" He paused.
"Or is that thing in you getting bigger?"

He had fallen back into Crucian dialect, and the gently rounded words captured her attention just long enough to delay her rage. Their eyes locked and he reached up, touching her forearm. She started, pulling away.

"I'm leaving, Severin."

"Stay, Maia," he said as if baiting a trap. "I can take care of you."

"Take care of me?"

"You can't go. You can't leave this island. You can't leave this house. And Maia," he throttled, "you can't leave *me*—"

"I have to go," she replied, expecting him to argue, but instead he continued to speak quietly, his gaze sweeping the dank, cluttered room.

"You're safe, here, Maia Ransom. Whatever happens out there don't matter. Your people won't let nothing bad happen to you at Wisdom."

Maia's eyes snapped at the bold absurdity of the statement, yet she realized that Severin was voicing one of her deepest, most secret thoughts—so secret, in fact, that she'd practically hidden it from herself.

"There, there," he said with a low chuckle, his voice emptied of its mocking slang. "I understand what you feeling. I understand because I have to stay at Wisdom, too. You think I would still be alive anywhere else? It's this place that keeps me breathing. Look at me—more rotten than these rotten walls, this rotten roof, that rotten mattress. Wisdom is what keeps me alive."

She looked away, her eyes leaping involuntarily to the balcony and the hilltop sugar mill silhouetted by the blazing sun. "I wish it were true," she whispered.

Suddenly outraged, he spat toward the balcony. "Don't you see, Nurse? You were meant to come here. You're *supposed* to be with me—"

"No. It's Tina who wants to be with you, Severin."

"Tina," he chuckled, lowering his voice. "She my love. My first love and my last love. But Tina love rum and meat and party, too. Tina love my truck and Tina love that when she with me, she don't need no island man. She spend her life looking up at Wisdom from those huts down below and wanting to be inside. And when she sleep here, she become the mistress like all the white women she hate." He paused, his eyes moving out to the boughs fixed in the heat beyond the balcony. "She never know me for the man inside."

"You're always too drunk to show her that man."

"For true," he agreed. "And I took Tina into the bushes before she had a chance to know a man any other way. But I didn't know a woman any other way. I was like my father, my brother, like all the Johanssen men."

"And still trying to be the master," Maia mocked.

"This is not America," he answered. "A woman wants a man to be a man in this world."

"No woman wants a man who can't tell the difference between making love and rape—"

"Then let me show you how a Johanssen makes love." She felt his rough hands reach forward and find her waist. He looked into her eyes, almost begging for something that neither one of them could give. "Maia," he whispered. "Maia Ransom."

"Let me go, Severin—you know I can't do this."

"Why not?" his voice flattened out, his words clear and urgent and strong. "You're not married. You're not my sister. And I'm a man, Maia. Even if you've seen me dying, half-dead. Even if you've wiped my ass and held me while I puked, I am still a *man*—"

His flesh was close in the hot room and she was smothering in the scent of his fierce desire. Her eyes closed and she heard him panting as he pushed her back against a massive oak commode. Half-lifting her, he found the strength to bend his body between her thighs and brace her back against the wall, the seams on his shorts chafing the soft inner skin where her skirt had ridden up high.

For a strange instant Maia removed herself from their sweating bodies and looked down from a safe, distant corner at his urgent attempt to couple with her. She saw herself protesting—but not loudly enough to bring Mimi out of the kitchen. She saw herself pushing back at Severin, urgently repeating his name, but she couldn't tell whether she was feeling a forbidden pleasure or a joyful outrage.

"Don't be afraid, Maia. I would never hurt you," he promised in a low rustle, one hand reaching behind her to bring her hips closer, the other fumbling with his pants. "I would never hurt—"

Her hands moved to his shoulders, and she felt something of the wasted strength that must have once guided horses through the rugged foliage; the power that had pulled his body through the rough waves off Wisdom's beaches. Her head fell back and he kissed her, taking her words into his mouth as her resistance reluctantly gave way.

"I need you, Maia Ransom. I need you—"

And then she saw herself in another time, her hair bound in a white cloth and her linen dress pushed high above her thighs. There, in that room, with the raging sea roaring beneath them, she knew the bitter pleasure of Jakob Johanssen's touch, and he called her name—*Zara!*—as he pressed her damp body hard against the wall and forced himself inside her like a piston—

No, she thought, fighting the mounting sensation of pleasure that seemed to come not from Severin's yellowed flesh, but from the pulsing grip of a tall, full-bodied man whose hands were rough from the reins, whose flowing wheat-toned hair was streaked from years in the fields beside the Ransoms—

"I love you, Zara,"—his voice a leaf stirring on the breeze.

No, she whispered. She felt his lust wrench at her, like a listing buoy in a sea of words and emotions far too great for her to control. He was stroking her, kneading her, telling her that he loved her. He loved her, and he would take her and make her his own. Spinning into a vortex of helplessness, Maia searched frantically for the only thought strong enough to grasp and hang on to. "No," she panted. "No, no—*Noah!*" The name exploded frantically, desperately: *"Noah! Please Noah, please!"*

Maia's senses suddenly ruptured into machete focus and she found herself drowning in Severin's hair and hands and insistent, promising hips.

"Oh, my god, no," she said softly, reaching up to hold his face. "Stop, Severin. Please. Please, Severin. This isn't right. You're too close, Severin. You've got to stop—"

It was the register of deep trouble beneath the words, and not the force of her command, that halted him. He, too, looked down at her and realized in a mixture of shock and pleasure that his manhood had returned—*that she had given him this strength*—and that he was using it as a weapon against her.

He wavered, awash in a newly discovered emotion: shame. Stumbling back, his eyes came to rest on the raw skin of her inner thighs. She looked up slowly, tears in her eyes, and he threw back his head and barked out his best imitation of laugher.

"That's right!" he said roughly. "You think my Johanssen ancestor had to force himself on your Ransom ancestress!" He stared at her, his sunburned chest still rising and falling. "It wasn't always like that, Nurse. It wasn't always that way."

"What do you mean?" she asked, jerking her dress down over her legs.

"It wasn't rape, Maia." He stared into her face. "I know that he loved her."

"What do you know about them?" she cried. "What do you know about my family?"

For a long, ragged moment neither of them spoke. Severin's face was like the door of a safe, its knowledge sealed away. "I know someone needs to make a woman out of you."

She slipped down from the commode and walked painfully toward the front door.

Instantly his voice grew softly pleading. "Don't go, Nurse. There has to be more between us. There has to be."

"You think so?" she murmured, her chest rising and falling.

"It don't matter what I think," he answered. "It only matter what Wisdom want."

Maia stumbled past the kitchen and out into the blinding noon light. Running to the bottom of the drive, she braced the butt of her palm against the Jeep to steady herself. At that moment her thoughts were spinning too fast to care whether Severin was right or wrong.

Once again she entered Noah's quiet courtyard in the center of downtown Christiansted. She stopped to stare at its gently swaying palm trees and scarlet bougainvillea, her mind racing at the thought that these thick walls, now painted a bright cheerful yellow, might have watched the wealthy Danish landowner Solomon Johanssen purchase Oba, newly arrived from Equatorial Guinea on the sailing vessel *Ransom*. She stood for a moment, awash in the strange destiny that brought Oba's blood into league with his master's. The destiny that created her forefather sent him into exile, only to guide her unerringly back to the very same courtyard where it all began.

NOAH LANGSTON ESQ., ATTORNEY AT LAW leaped out from a burnished plaque beside an immense, iron-ribbed wooden door. Surprised by its weight, she managed to creak it open enough to slip into a dank foyer and grope her way up a worn marble staircase to the second floor.

There was no secretary in the airless, cluttered anteroom. A desk, barely visible beneath a number of leather-bound books, was pushed against one wall. Several overloaded file cabinets stood rusting beside it. There was one small barred window in the tiny chamber. Maia had to lean over a dusty, overstuffed chair to look out. The sea formed a firm turquoise ribbon beyond the neighboring rooftops and Club Pan stood just across the arcade. She could hear the voices of children rising above the roar of a garbage truck below, but the building itself was deathly quiet.

"Maia! What are you doing here?"

She started up to find Noah, almost unrecognizable in a somber suit and dark tie, and practically hidden from view behind an armload of yellowing papers. "I'm sorry to show up like this," she said. "There's no phone at Wisdom."

"I was in court this morning," he answered, "but I'm coming up from the archives just now. Let me put these documents away and I'll be right with you."

Maia followed the lawyer through the doorway to his private office and stopped in surprise at the threshold. "Oh, Noah!"

"Do you like it?" He chuckled. "It was once used as a jail."

The expansive walls of the vast, low-ceilinged chamber were alive with vibrant, joyous paintings of Haitian market scenes by a number of different artists.

"They're originals," he said, following her gaze with evident pride.

"I did some consulting in Haiti several years ago when the Americans were helping restore the democratically elected government."

A giant speckled croton in a fired ceramic pot brought a burst of color to a wall stacked with leather-bound books. Two tennis racquets waited in a corner beside a butler's table bearing a bottle of Cruzian Rum. Noah had just set down the stack of papers when Maia caught sight of the softly dancing rainbows thrown from a row of cut crystal prisms hung above the window.

"They're beautiful, Noah."

"They're a bit of Crucian history," he explained, his eyes gently washed with reflections of violet and gold. "They were taken from the chandelier of the old governor's residence when the house was destroyed by a hurricane some years ago."

She moved to the window, touching the tips of the prisms with a tentative finger. Slipping off his suit jacket, he put it over his chair and walked over to join her. "Is everything all right?"

Severin's voice whispered in her head. *It wasn't rape. I know that he loved her.*

Maia's eyes flickered. "To tell you the truth, nothing's all right."

He reached for her but she stepped back, slipping out of his grasp. *There has to be more between us. There has to be.* She crossed the office to peer at a framed black-and-white photograph near the door. Noah slowly followed, coming to a stop just behind her.

He quickly appraised her appearance. The shirtdress she was wearing was smudged around the hips and thighs. She was disheveled, her hair looking as if she had driven very fast on that very dangerous road from Wisdom. She had on no earrings and no other jewelry. Even the lovely ankle bracelet was missing.

Even more unusual was her sudden—and obvious—distaste of his touch. He could feel her reluctance to stand so close to him, even at that very moment. Was this the same woman who seemed to struggle with her desire to make love with him only the night before?

"That's my father's family," he explained, showing her an old photograph on his desk. His voice betrayed nothing of his burgeoning concern. "My father's people originally came from Antigua. We've been on St. Croix for three generations."

"Do you think," she began quietly, "that they ever wanted to leave?"

Nurse. You must not leave the island.

"No," Noah said simply. "Life was better for them here."

"Do you miss him?"

"My father? No. I guess it sounds crazy, but—" He paused, realizing he had never spoken these feelings aloud, before. "But I really believe he's here. Watching over me. All the time."

She didn't answer, but her gaze remained fixed on the photograph. While she stared—longingly?—into the assembly of smiling people he took note of her hunched shoulders and the lengthening silence. She had wrapped her arms protectively over her breasts and her eyes were somber.

Slowly she turned around to face him, her gaze coming to rest on his crisp white shirt. She looked up, her eyes meeting his.

Nurse. You must not leave the island.

"I have a feeling that you want to take my deposition, Attorney Langston."

"That thought is crossing my mind."

Nurse. You cannot die yet.

"First, could I make a statement off the record?"

"Naturally."

It don't matter what I think. It only matter what Wisdom want.

"I was hoping that you might be able to show me those rooms your mother rents out."

"Not a chance," he responded, his eyes never leaving her face. "There's only one place on this island for you, Miss Ransom. And that's with me."

It happened so swiftly that Noah wasn't sure it was real. One moment they were standing in his office, as awkward as strangers. The next moment they were walking toward the parking lot, moving purposefully through the crowded afternoon.

Of course, every woman he'd ever dated on St. Croix was standing in front of a building, or next to a car, or coming out of a store, or waiting to cross the street. Everyone on St. Croix was staring straight into his BMW as he pulled the sedan out into traffic. "Shit!" he murmured. By evening the entire island would know that he'd helped the Statesider Ransom into his car in the middle of the day. He glanced neither left nor right, unable to meet anyone's eyes, as if the nature of his mission were somehow shameful. And although he realized that he'd spent the last few days wanting her more than he had wanted any woman for a long time, he hated the whole world knowing it almost before he'd admitted it to himself.

"You're pretty quiet," he remarked as they moved in fits and starts up the congested, potholed street. Tourists milled around the open arcades, wandering in and out of stores with duty-free perfume and jewelry store shopping bags. Maia stared straight ahead, her thoughts hidden away. He moved his right hand across the car, wanting to touch her in some way, but then held back, fearing that he might break the fragile bond her words had woven.

But suddenly she seemed to come alive, waving enthusiastically at a stick figure emerging with a nervous gait from Chéz Alexander.

"Hey, you foxy rascal!" she called, tugging at her window. The fragile man, his sun-browned skin wrapped so tight over his bones that it was nearly transparent, whipped around as if prepared to fight. But recognizing Maia, he scuttled across the street, bringing a pickup truck loaded with bricks to a screeching halt as he stuck his head into the car and kissed her warmly.

"Noah, this is Damian—a good friend."

Damian stuck out his hand and looked hard at the lawyer. "*Scheiss!* So you're Noah," he said with a sly grin. "*Everything* I've heard about you is true!"

"We're checking out real estate," Maia announced.

"For rent or for sale?"

"You know I'm in no position to buy."

"I hear you, sister," he said with a sigh. "Well," he added, glancing appreciatively at her escort, "enjoy yourself, Maia. All right?" He was out of the car, swinging his narrow hips back into the crowd so quickly that he almost seemed an apparition.

"Somebody you knew at home?" Noah asked coolly.

"Someone I've known forever," she answered.

He shot her a glance. "Living on the island can make things seem much simpler than they really are."

She laughed ironically. "Things have never seemed more complicated to me."

They passed the dock where Juan and Carlson were sitting on inverted plastic buckets. Noah glanced at them and was relieved when they didn't recognize his passenger.

"Maia," he asked, trying to keep his voice casual, "how did you fill up your days before you started working at Wisdom?"

"Before Wisdom?" She shrugged, her gaze wandering toward a milling crowd of cruise-shippers. "I was just a tourist. I went out to Buck Island a couple of times with Juan—you know, the guy who rents out his boat for the afternoon. I snorkeled and laid around in the sun."

"Was he good company?"

"Excellent. He left me alone and gave me lots of time to think."

"That must have been pretty difficult for him. I've known Juan for a long time and let me tell you—he has a hard time leaving any woman alone."

"Then it must have been torture for him." She met Noah's eyes and looked away in distaste. Relieved, the lawyer exhaled silently.

Soon they were driving past the old hospital in La Grande Princess. Rows of neatly painted townhouses swept down to the beach, where a desalination plant purified the seawater for drinking. Noah soon turned north, heading toward Kirkegaard Hill, the highest point on the island. The BMW roared up a steep, winding drive that was largely overgrown with blooming flamboyants and wild tongues of aloe.

Noah's house had been constructed only a few years earlier, after the last major hurricane had nearly decimated the island. Using insurance money gleaned from several ruined rental properties located too close to the water, Noah bought land that was tucked deep against a sheltering face of rock at the height of the sharp incline.

"There's a reason why I'm hidden away up here," he explained as they cautiously wound their way up a twisting, narrow road and entered the single-laned street leading to his home. "Winds can't reach it, floods can't submerge it, and thieves give up before they find it."

The property was less lush than the land at the foot of the mountain, nearer the rain forest. But the plateau offered a stunning view of the sea from every direction. A kind of wild, flowering scrub grew between iron-red stones that were scattered across the earth by some deity's hand. Bougainvillea bushes sponged the hill with smears of deep purple.

"What do you think?" he asked, almost before the house was in view. Maia gasped at the sight of the palatial two-floored structure with vaulted arches across its face. The drive formed a perfect semicircle up to the double-doored entry. Hibiscus bushes lined the asphalt from the street to the property, culminating in two potted rose trees on either side of the entry. The windows on the lower level were open and Maia fancied that she could hear traces of cheerfully syncopated music wafting from inside.

"Very, very impressive, Noah."

"It's my design. I thought about architecture as an alternative to law, but believe it or not, I couldn't manage all those physics courses."

Maia understood his comment to be self-aggrandizing, but she also clearly comprehended the reasons for his pride. There were very few such houses on the island, and even fewer owned by blacks. The house was elegantly conceived, solidly built—and incomparably superior to Wisdom.

He pulled his car up in front of his castle and they climbed out. The music was louder now and they mounted the steps. He opened the doors and followed her inside. Maia found herself in a fern-filled atrium, a stone staircase rising gracefully at the entrance and disappearing into a light-filled upper hall. Beneath the atrium was a spacious great room filled with delicate glass animals, illuminated by windows looking out over the hill toward the sea. The white-tiled floors reflected the endless blue of the sky and distant water, and all the furnishings were bleached wicker and glass.

"Ma, I'm home!" Noah yelled like a teenager.

The music stopped abruptly and was replaced with quietly padding feet. A tall, lean woman appeared from a side chamber, wrapped in a turquoise batik kimono. Gray braids formed a thick crown around her head. Her face was a coppery mirror of her son's. She grinned at the couple, hands on her hips.

"You bring home a friend and don't call?"

"No time, Mother," he said in his Statesider voice. Quickly he introduced the two women, noting with satisfaction that Maia had no trouble looking directly into his mother's eyes.

"You call me Pearl, not Mrs. Langston, sweetheart. When I was teaching, everybody had to use the titles. But now I'm retired and I want the world to know that I've earned the right to be *nobody*!" The woman winked and began guiding her guest toward the screened porch. "First, you need something cool to drink—"

"Not yet, mother. I want to show Maia the apartment."

"The apartment?" His mother turned to look at him for a moment. Then her smile deepened. "Be careful, Maia. My son will lock you up in there," she warned. "I want you to come on back down and spend some time with me."

The upstairs studio apartment, a small kitchen flanked by a spacious living room and bath, looked out over the rear of the house. Although sparsely furnished, everything was clean and new. The kitchen fully equipped and the view over palm-spiked hills to the sea was extraordinary.

Noah walked back and forth, opening the jalousies. "My mother furnished this for my sister, who decided to pursue her studies in St. Thomas."

"I see."

"Now I use it for off-island clients. You can stay here as long as you'd like," Noah said, leaning against the doorframe.

"The rent?"

"Free."

"Why?"

"Because you're a Ransom," he said, then quickly added, "and because you're Maia." Reaching over, he pulled her firmly into his arms and pressed his lips softly against the corner of her mouth.

"Would your mother approve of this?" she asked, gently pulling herself free of his scent of bay rum and stirring desire.

"There are times when it's appropriate to be a son," he answered. "Then there are times when I need to be a man."

Maia lowered her eyes, hesitating before speaking. "Noah, there's something you've got to understand. If I move into this flat, I'll pay for it. And—" She spoke slowly and clearly. "You'll respect the meaning of closed doors."

"That's fine," he purred, running his hands gently down her shoulders. "But only if you'll promise to stay for a long time."

"Noah, I'm serious."

"And so am I." He wavered a moment. "I don't bring every woman I meet to my house. Or to my mother."

Maia smiled wryly. "Well, you haven't given her much of a chance to get a look at me, have you?"

"Once Pearl Langston gets her hands on you, I'll never get a word in edgewise." He gave a mock sigh. "Let's go get your things from Wisdom. Then we'll stop by my office and pick up your Jeep. After that I'll surrender you to Pearl."

"Do we have an understanding?" she repeated calmly.

He took a step back, pretending to return to his lawyer's persona. "All right, Ms. Ransom. Since you insist, one hundred dollars a week. Agreed?"

She nodded slowly. "That's perfect. As long as the doors have locks."

"I'll respect your space," he said, hardly able to contain his pleasure. "As long as you'll keep it close to mine."

To Maia's surprise, the front door of Wisdom was hanging open and Mimi was not in the kitchen. She could smell frying meat and hear the sound of voices, so she stepped slowly into the dank foyer. She felt a presence beside her and looked around to see Noah standing behind her in the doorway.

"Just came in to help you carry your things," he said, aware that he had not been asked into the house.

"My room's at the end of the hall," Maia explained softly, "but first, let me check on Severin."

"I thought you quit this morning."

"Noah, I'm always a nurse, whether I'm getting paid or not."

She stepped into the great room, following the sound of the voices.

The double doors to the balcony were thrown open and a trace of laughter swept in on the breeze. At that moment Mimi came in from outdoors, a tray in her hands.

"*Bodieu!* You startle me! Seven say you gone!"

"I'm here for my things, Mimi. Is he all right?"

Mimi hesitated before answering, her aged face flooding with discontent. "I do what I can," she said softly, "but it's no use. We have a saying: *Bô tsè kwab bay kwab mal do:* crab's good heart give crab a bad back. He don't want to be better, Nurse. You must move on before he causes you harm."

Another laughing breeze caused both women to look toward the open doors. Mimi sucked her teeth hard.

"Who's out there?" Maia asked.

"Go see for yourself," she answered, walking on toward the kitchen.

Maia took in a deep breath and crossed the great room. At the balcony doors she stopped. Severin, still dressed in his shorts and naked above the waist, sat propped up in his favorite chair, his feet balanced on the rotting rails. A familiar figure in white stood beside him, facing the sea. A third person, honey-skinned with extraordinary waves of sun-streaked hair, was perched on the edge of the porch, exclaiming her delight at the sight of the hill tumbling steeply toward the water.

Sensing a new presence, Paulette turned around to face Maia.

"Severin said that you'd finally realized your uselessness," she snapped as if dismissing a servant.

Maia's eye traveled across the scene, noting that all three of them were holding sweating bottles of beer. Severin blinked when their eyes met. He lowered his bottle to the floor with a child's shamed discomfort. "You not gone, Nurse Ransom?" he asked quietly.

"I'm gone," Maia said simply, turning on her heel.

"That's right," Paulette said loudly to her back. "Severin's in the hands of his family now."

Heart slamming against her chest, Maia found Noah at the kitchen door speaking in low tones with Mimi. She led him back to her chamber. His eyes ricocheted around the broken furniture, peeling walls, slanting window shades, shattered panes. He saw her suitcases, already packed. He noticed that she paused, breathing heavily as she looked around the room one last time.

"What is it?"

"It's hard to explain."

"Tell me, Maia."

"Abraham Ransom might have been conceived here," she began very softly. "His life might have begun on this bed. Some part of me belongs here, Noah. And it's hard for me to leave."

Her voice broke and he stepped forward, placing his arms around her waist. He drew her close, marveling at the volatile mix of strength and sensitivity in this woman. She leaned against him, a sob breaking free from deep, deep inside.

"You'll be back, Maia. I promise you. I won't let you lose Wisdom."

She pulled in her breath and wiped her eyes quickly. "Let's go," she said.

"So you've actually discovered one of them?"

Glancing at her son, Pearl Langston nodded her head toward Maia. "You know, if it's true, then she's probably the last pure Ransom."

"*Pure?* Really, Mama!" Noah said with a smile as he brought a pitcher of iced tea to the table. "You're talking as if the Ransoms were a rare breed of animal!"

The trio was seated at a white wicker table on the screened-in porch at the rear of the Langston house. Only a few minutes before, they had enjoyed a quiet meal to the lulling sonatas of evening birds and insistent insects. The evening air was rolling up dense and humid from the coast below, and Maia thought she could taste a tang of the sea in the breeze. Now she settled back to take in the easy banter between the mother and son, rather amused that they were so much alike.

"Well, you know what I mean!" Pearl looked appraisingly at her guest. "All the others married into other clans years and years ago. Today its virtually impossible to find a real—"

"You see where I got my interest in Crucian genealogy," Noah interrupted. "My mother is a regular griot."

Pearl laughed. "That's true. My late husband's family came here three generations ago. But my name, De Windt, goes back to the time when this island belonged to the Knights of Malta."

"The Knights of Malta?" Maia raised her brows and again Noah spoke up.

"I'm the son of a long, long line of Crucians."

"And now," his mother added proudly, "he's making sure that our island is given back to the people whose blood was shed here. I suppose that Noah's told you all about his work—"

"No, I haven't had the chance to explain everything to Maia," Noah said quickly. He glanced anxiously at his mother, who was too busy praising her son to notice.

"Noah has won five lawsuits against whites who tried to keep land that had been legally deeded to former slaves. He's an excellent attorney and a local hero," Pearl stated. "He's successfully blocked several attempts by outsiders to develop our natural resources into tourist attractions."

"That's very impressive."

"And he's become quite a landlord, too." She leaned toward Maia and lowered her voice. "We possess quite a bit of the land that the whites abandoned after the last hurricane. Noah has decided to let it remain vacant for the time being. We're certain that the value will only increase with time."

"So he could have been an accountant, too?"

"Noah could be anything he chooses," his mother said, twisting in her chair to address her son. "I think he could build a very strong political career on the work he's doing."

"You must be very proud," Maia said evenly.

"I don't know where he got his skills," Pearl concluded with false modesty. "He's always been able to outthink everyone else. Even when he was a child. And you should have seen him when he went to school with those white children. I didn't want him out there all alone. But his father said, 'Let the boy go, Pearl. He'll learn the way they think. He'll learn how to beat them at their own game.' I guess his father was right."

"Hang on, Mama. You mustn't exaggerate."

"And I'm sure he was excited to meet a *real* Ransom," Pearl continued. She took a sip of her tea, grimaced, and began pouring sugar into the glass. "You know, there's a long-standing story that the whites drove the last of the Ransoms off the island after some dispute over an estate. It seems that one of the Ransom women had given birth to a son who should have been the heir. Of course, the other whites wouldn't stand for that. Which estate was it?" She turned to her son, whose face had gone ashen in the fading light. "Don't you remember that story, Noah?"

"Perhaps it was Wisdom," Maia suggested without a trace of irony. "I've heard that story, too. But I didn't realize that it was so well known. I thought, in fact, that Noah had just discovered it in the island's secret archives."

"Oh, for heaven's sake!" Pearl cried, her laughter ringing through the house. "The story of the banished Ransom son is an island favorite. The problem was that none of those Ransom kinfolk here on the island could ever prove they were the direct descendants of the one who got sent away. And without proof, there's been no way to sue the Johanssens for the property."

"So everybody's been waiting for the right Ransom to reappear?" Maia said with a darkening glance at Noah.

"Well, of course!" Pearl laughed. "It would be the most interesting land-restitution case our island has ever seen."

"Imagine that," Maia murmured. "The Johanssens must be very afraid that somewhere in the world, a 'pure' Ransom might just be getting ready to take an innocent vacation in St. Croix, only to stumble on that lost inheritance."

"I'm sure the Johanssens know the story better than anybody," Pearl said in a low, gossipy voice. "In fact, there was always talk about that last son—the one you knew in school, Noah—and his preference for colored women. Seems he inherited that from his ancestor, who was said to have left the estate to his own black son."

Maia stared open-mouthed at Noah, her anger now hard to disguise. "This is also a part of the well-known story?"

"Some of the blacks who worked on the estate claimed to be

descendants of the Ransoms," Pearl continued, oblivious to Maia's growing anger. "And that last Johanssen son has been fooling around with one of those black women since he was a boy—it's been the talk of the island for years—but even she couldn't get the family lines straight. So it's been of no use to her to claim to be a distant Ransom relation."

The only sound was a warbling bird on a branch nearby. Maia clasped her trembling hands together to still them, then addressed Noah in a carefully controlled monotone.

"Am I understanding this correctly? The story of my family is common knowledge here in St. Croix? So every time I've introduced myself—everybody from the hotel desk clerk to the pharmacist—has known who I am, where I came from, and who my ancestors are?"

Noah cleared his throat. His mother cocked her head, surprised at the anger and distress in the young woman's voice.

"Do you mean to tell me," Maia continued, "that Severin knew all along that what I told him was true? That my people *did* live and die on that estate? And that half the people I've met in St. Croix are probably distant cousins of mine?"

"Well," Noah said cautiously, "it would partially explain the hostility you've felt from Paulette."

"Well, naturally!" Maia nearly exploded. "It would explain why Tina immediately hated me. Why Paulette is waging an undeclared war against me. Why that idiot Juan thought it was so important to be with me—the potential 'heiress' of Estate Wisdom. And why even the doctor at the hospital was so supportive of the idea that I move out there with Severin. Christ! This whole island has been manipulating me without my even knowing it!"

"What are you talking about?" Pearl asked, eyebrows raised.

"Noah had me thinking that the story of my ancestors was some long-hidden secret. He pretended that he went into the island's archives and found out the truth for me."

"Don't get angry, Maia," Noah began. Pearl looked with bewilderment from her guest to her son.

"Angry? I just want to know why you went to so much trouble to concoct that complicated tale about discovering my heritage. You should have told me from the start that my family story is common knowledge here in St. Croix."

"The story of the Ransoms is a popular folktale," he confessed. "But until you arrived I never took it seriously. That's why I went into the archives. I wanted to know the truth. And now we have the records to prove it."

"But why? So that you can sue the Johanssens and get control of that land, too?"

"So that I can give it back to you."

"Back to *me*?" She stared at him a moment, then began laughing as all the stones fell into place. "You want to give *me* a chance to take control of Wisdom? Why don't you tell the truth, Attorney Langston? You want to take the estate away from the Johanssens. You want to punish that lazy, useless Severin. You want to crush Paulette and her wealthy friends. But most of all," she said, shaking her head in disgust, "you want the chance to bolster your reputation by winning the ultimate lawsuit against the whites. You want to return the most valuable piece of real estate on St. Croix to the blacks!"

"Hold on, Maia—"

"Of course, you might also want to buy the land for yourself, or simply come into possession of it by making love to the woman who would inherit it—"

"Miss Ransom—" Pearl began, but Maia was too angry now to curb her words.

"So that's why I'm here, right? You've wined and dined me, found a clean bed for me, and even researched my family for me, just so that you could get a crack at Wisdom?"

"If I've done these things, it was only for you, Maia."

"Not to get a whole lot richer? Or maybe, to help you in your run for governor?"

Noah glanced involuntarily at his mother. Pearl remained silent, looking at their guest.

"Maia," he said, "let me explain."

"I'll hear nothing but the truth, right?"

"The truth is that I met you, became interested in you, and then I—" He paused, suddenly encumbered by Pearl's presence.

The silence was as heavy as the eye of a hurricane. Maia stared across at him and he waited, his breath trapped in his lungs. Finally she stood. "Is that your very best defense, Attorney Langston? Am I supposed to find you innocent on the grounds that you can't lie fast enough?"

She was standing at her open suitcase, staring through the fog of her rage at her few belongings when the gentle tapping on her door perfectly matched the pounding of her heart. She thought of ignoring the sound, of testing whether or not, in fact, Noah was capable of respecting her need for privacy. But it was Pearl's voice that called out to her gently.

Maia stepped aside self-consciously as the tall woman swept quietly into the room and seated herself on the wicker armchair beside the small kitchen table. She crossed her long legs at the ankle and leaned slightly forward in a calm, thoughtful pose. When she began speaking, Maia heard the teacher addressing a deeply troubled pupil.

"Noah explained to me that you didn't know anything about your people until very recently," she said evenly. "Please forgive me for being so insensitive. I had no idea that the Ransom story would be so important to you."

Maia observed Pearl's open face warily before responding. "I'm sorry, too. I shouldn't have been so rude. But everything is so deceptive here. On the surface it seems so easy, so beautiful, so restful. Yet there's so many secrets, so many hidden things."

Pearl sighed. "It's because the best parts of this island remain in the hands of a very few people. It's been that way for hundreds of years. So people have had to play very complicated games to survive."

"Then why go along with it? Why don't the blacks just elect people into the government who'll support changes—"

"Not even all the blacks on this island agree about what should be done," Pearl explained calmly. "Some come from other islands and have no stake on this land. Others come from poor families and feel a certain jealousy toward the wealthier blacks. We are a people of many different cultures and histories, Miss Ransom. We are still living in the mind-set that we learned over hundreds of years in slavery. That's one reason why Noah's work is so unique. He's determined to uncover the lost heritage of this island. He's giving all black people, rich or poor, a chance to recover what's rightfully theirs."

Maia turned her head, holding back a wall of sudden tears, and Pearl rose and walked toward her. She felt the older woman put her arm around her shoulders. They were practically the same height, and when Pearl spoke her soft words seemed to bloom inside Maia's frustration.

"Listen, Miss Ransom: My son came home a few days ago and told me he'd met a Statesider Ransom. He said you spent the evening together and that you were smart and strong and—" She laughed softly. "He even said that you're very brave."

Pearl paused, choosing her words carefully. "He was worried about you living out at Wisdom with Seven. You see, that boy has quite a reputation for misbehaving in just about every way. Noah said that he was going to try and prove that your family was the lost Ransom family. I think he planned to tell you everything when he was really sure he could prove it—and not before."

Slowly Maia raised her hands to her temples and sighed. "It doesn't matter. I don't care what he discovers. I don't want any part of the estate. I don't want to sue anyone for the ownership of Wisdom."

"Noah wouldn't suggest a lawsuit unless he was certain he could win."

"No. You don't understand," Maia insisted. "I won't be here long enough for a lawsuit."

"You wouldn't have to be here," Pearl said. "Most of the work is in finding the right documents, anyway."

"That's not what I'm saying." Maia faced Pearl squarely and placed her hands on the woman's forearm. "When I leave, I won't be coming back to St. Croix."

"The trial only takes an afternoon, then the judge renders judgment some weeks later, after studying—"

"No! That's not what I'm saying," Maia cried, her voice rising sharply. "Please listen to me!"

Pearl frowned. "All right. Go ahead."

Maia exhaled sharply. "I've never had any interest in possessing the estate. The house is in ruins and the land would serve me no purpose."

"Not now, perhaps. But what about the future? If you should ever think of having any children—"

"There won't be any children."

"Oh, many of us feel that way when we're young."

"I'll never know what it feels like to be old," Maia said, finding the confession strange even as it escaped her lips.

"What?" Pearl furrowed her brow; her sharp eyes foraging for the source of her guest's growing distress.

"I'm sick." Maia's voice had become hoarse and low. "I'm sick and I can't stay on this island. I can't live at Wisdom. I can't fall in love with anyone. I can't even dream of having children. The only thing I can hope for is a few more months of pain-free living."

Pearl's head was moving from side to side. "What are you telling me, child?"

"I'm telling you that I'm dying."

Pearl's eyes pierced the strong young woman with a look of disbelief. "You must be mistaken!" she whispered. "You're the picture of health—"

Steeling herself, Maia turned abruptly away and fixed a hard stare at the scene through the window. "That's the thing about ovarian cancer: I can't see it. Can't feel it. But it's there, working it's magic in the deepest part of my body—"

"You haven't given up?" the older woman murmured.

"No. No, I haven't. But every day that I'm here is a day without treatment. You see, if I stay on St. Croix to fight for Wisdom, I may already be surrendering my life."

There was a long, appraising silence. Then she felt Pearl's hands take her shoulders from behind.

"Where's your mama?"

"It already killed her."

"Your father?"

Maia shook her head silently.

"Have you told Noah?"

"No. I don't want his pity."

"Then you're living with this all by yourself?" Pearl asked with the softness of love.

Maia tried to hold back her breath, but it exploded in a sob. The older woman turned her gently and took her into her arms. "Not anymore," she said once, then twice. Then, as Maia began weeping in earnest, she repeated the words again and again.

EIGHT DAYS

"I tell you, Mimi say she gone," Carlson announced.

"No," Juan replied, "it's not so easy."

"She gone. Mimi say she take everything and don't even fight when Paulette show up."

"I still don't believe it."

The two men sat at the counter of Brandy's Bar, drinking beer while the waitress served a group of overweight white shoes straight off a cruise liner docked in Fredriksted. Vaguely hoping that some of the tourists might want to take a boat trip, Juan ignored Tina as she stared disconsolately into a glass of orange juice spiked with rum, her "morning tea."

"We came here for our honeymoon many years ago," a tourist announced in a nasal whine. "We just *had* to come back for our fortieth anniversary. But everything looks so different!"

The tourist's eyes rested on the black men, whose shredded shorts revealed much of their heavily corded upper thighs. Their stained T-shirts were bleached to transparency, and when they raised their bottles their upper arms bulged like insolent melons.

"The hurricanes are our architects and decorators," Brandy pleasantly explained, her struggle for patience carefully hidden beneath her mask of hospitality.

The tourist went on talking, ignoring her. "There were no cars, no parking lots, no telephone poles back then. Everything was so *natural*. . . ."

"Why don't you take a boat trip around the island?" Brandy suggested brightly. "That gentleman sitting at the counter can show you St. Croix's beautiful coral reefs."

Carlson turned to his sister. "Tina, you said Seven still looking for her."

"I know Seven wondering where she gone," Tina answered, a half-chewed plastic mermaid between her teeth.

"Maybe she found somebody richer," Juan put in. "She used me. She'll use somebody else."

Tina sucked her teeth and rolled her eyes. "What she want with you? All you got is a rowboat and a sunburn. Anyway, Paulette bring some other bitch out yesterday. Mimi say she from Canada. But she look like Guyana or Venezuela to me."

"Paulette want Seven thinking about something new," Carlson asserted with a grunt.

"So what you gonna do?" Juan asked, his attention drawn away as Brandy returned to the counter.

"Don't need to do nothing," Tina said angrily. *"Zâdoli sav ki pyé-bwa i ka-moté."*

"What?" Juan asked.

"The lizard know what tree to climb," Tina said. "Seven will come back to me. No white woman satisfy him."

Carlson looked at his sister, noting that the loss of her lover had stretched ten more pounds on her polyester-clad hips and thighs. His gaze crossed Juan's and the two men shared a sour thought.

"What are you all scheming up?" Brandy asked as she dug in her refrigerator.

The three went silent. Brandy stood up and looked into Tina's eyes. "You don't cause no trouble, Tina."

The woman sucked her teeth in response. Brandy loaded her tray with more beer and bustled back to the tourists.

"So what about the nurse?" Carlson asked his sister.

"We got to find out where she staying," Tina responded with irritation. "I know she not finished with Wisdom."

"Then what you want to do?"

"Convince her to leave the island," Tina said with finality.

A shrill laugh brought their attention to a reed-thin figure that appeared at the end of the deck. The man was wearing sandals and his T-shirt and jeans were ironed to crispness. He hugged Brandy and the two began talking with great animation.

"Look at that aunty-man!" Juan growled in a low voice. "What Brandy want with that?"

"Oh, she just talking nonsense," Carlson responded without interest.

"But that the aunty-man who go with the nurse," Juan said, his voice still flat with his humiliation from the night at Club Pan two weeks before.

Now the other two took a long look at Damian. He was speaking delightedly with Brandy about Chéz Alexander, the restaurant he managed—a restaurant that none of the three had ever entered. The two chatted briefly about the difficulty of getting food delivered from the States before it spoiled. Then they made a few remarks about how good business had been for the last few days. And then Juan heard the word they all wanted to hear.

"Maia's staying with her lawyer friend," Damian told Brandy. "She called me last night."

"Really?" Brandy said, guiding Damian a few more steps away from the counter and lowering her voice.

The two went on talking, with Brandy taking one casual look over her shoulder at Juan, Carlson, and Tina. Damian glanced over at the counter and seemed to instantly understand the reasons for Brandy's wariness. He lowered his voice, kissed her cheek, and he went on his way. Brandy returned to the counter.

"Before you even ask," she said calmly, "I can only tell you that the nurse is finished with Wisdom. She will not come back. She plans to leave for the States in a few days."

"Then why she with Noah?" Juan asked, realizing that the lawyer had certainly discussed with Maia the boatman's lies about their relationship.

"Hotel full," Brandy said with a shrug. "Noah has rooms."

They all remained silent, each knowing that there was some truth even in these lies. Tina looked across the counter at her lifelong friend and wondered why she would try to protect the Statesider. Juan wondered how Brandy had become friends with that queer, Damian. And even Carlson, who had left school in the fifth grade and never put any stock in the need to reason, asked himself whether they should trust Brandy's claim that the American Ransom was finished with Wisdom. After all, she was now in the hands of that lawyer who took away white people's land. And he was determined that one day, sooner or later, his sister Tina was going to be the mistress of Wisdom.

Noah had known Pearl to be stubborn. He had, in fact, grown up the son of one of the most shrewd, powerful, passionate, and obstinate women in all of St. Croix (the islanders often described Pearl Langston as downright *vexin'*). Yet never had he seen her more moved by, more protective of, and more allied with another woman. She had spent the better part of the night upstairs in the little studio apartment.

Still, early that morning, as Pearl prepared her cup of Earl Grey, he made a brave attempt to beseige the fortress.

"What happened last night, Mama?"

"That's private business, son."

"Well, when's she coming down?"

"Whenever she's ready."

"But—"

"Understand this, Noah: That young lady upstairs is a guest in our home. Not your pet. And certainly not your toy!"

It was as if that evening had forged an unbreakable bond between them. As if the two were blood. As if, well, as if Maia was drawn to the house not by his desire, but by his mother's will.

And the silence his mother was carrying was almost more disturbing than the bond itself. Late in the night Pearl had walked out of the room she'd prepared for her foolhardy daughter (everyone in St. Croix knew she had followed a married man to St. Thomas and was only pretending to study at the university there!). Behind Pearl stood an invisible wall, a kind of force-field keeping him away from Maia. Each time he tried to get closer to the stairs, the phone rang or his mother's dog started chewing on the wicker or she needed him to open a jar or kill a centipede, and he was drawn away.

Something was going on. Like a sorceress, Maia had walked into his courtyard ten days before, handed him the most important case of his career, and come to live in his house. No, she had done even more. She had yawned in the face of Crucian royalty and embraced her own black past with a passion he'd never seen before. She had kissed him until his heart was slamming, then leaped into her Jeep and driven away. Without even looking back!

Maia's physical closeness made it so hard! He'd spent the night lying awake in his room, ruminating on her features. Her short hair. Her deep eyes. Her full body. He wanted to hear her voice and the laugh that he was starting to treasure. He wanted to touch her. To drive the entire length of the island to the nude beach behind the bluffs of Grapetree and swim with her, naked and free. He wanted to make love with her, very slowly, in the heat of the day and the long dark night. He wanted to build a future—

A *future*?

For a moment he considered whether it was really possible to spend his life with one woman. It wasn't his fault, after all, if St. Croix was a male paradise. Women of every age, size, color, heritage roamed the island. Women who spoke Spanish, French, Creole, English. Even Dutch and Portuguese. Women who were smart, but not unnecessarily intelligent. Women who knew how to wear clothes. And how to wear no clothes. Women who enjoyed eating, and knew when to stop drinking. Who knew how to dance late into the night. Women who loved making love as much as men.

And what about making love?

Sunlight. Moonlight. Sandy beaches and shady groves. Cool terraces and poolside patios. Sex with and without clothes. Sex with or without rum. And the occasional puff of ganja.

Never, in Noah Anthony Langston's thirty-seven years on Earth, had he seriously entertained the idea of marriage. Dating? Yes. Living with a woman? Perhaps. But the permanence of marriage? Forty years of nagging? Decades of sex with a single partner? Respecting curfews and sharing his bank accounts and letting a woman drive his BMW? Never.

Well, maybe. For Maia Ransom, maybe.

"Why your face dragging in the dirt?" his mother asked as she joined him at the wicker table.

"What you mean?" he answered, pretending ignorance.

"She sending you over!" his mother laughed.

"I don't have time for games," he said gruffly, but Pearl set down her teacup and shook her head.

"Thirty-seven you and still want your mama to make your toast! I shouldn't be in this house, Noah. You should be here with a wife!"

"I don't have time for serious romancing," he argued, trying to keep the conversation amusing, but she sucked her teeth like the Crucians on the street.

"Meson," she said quietly, "you're just too selfish to share any of your bounty with a woman."

"Come on, Mama. I see lots of women!"

"That's not sharing," Pearl said crisply.

"You've never thought any woman was good enough for your son."

"You've always been afraid to find one who was," she countered, looking him squarely in the eyes.

"So something is different with Maia?" he asked.

His mother stared at him. "This woman will never bend down to serve you, Noah. She will make you stand taller to reach her height," she said softly.

Noah felt the insistent pull of his mother's words as he finally mounted the stairs, his mother watching calmly from below. His knock pulled Maia out of a deep sleep; the deepest and safest sleep she had known in many months. She opened her eyes and glanced around, momentarily surprised that she wasn't at Wisdom. But then she remembered.

She slipped into a dress and ran her fingers through her short hair, then opened the door to Noah's curiosity.

"Sorry to wake you," he began, then stopped at the sight of her swollen face. She'd obviously been crying a good deal, and his heart wrenched at the thought that his words had caused her such pain.

"I—I didn't realize—" he began, but she motioned him to sit down at the table. She went to the sink and began running the cold water.

"I'll be all right," she said in a ragged voice.

Noah made himself look away from her brown legs as she washed her face and drank a glass of water. Finally she regarded him with a heavy sigh.

"I owe you an apology," she said. "I was very tired last evening and I lost it."

"I should have told you everything. I hope I didn't hurt you."

"I'll survive," she said flatly. Then she laughed. "Your mother beat up on me pretty badly for giving up so easily."

"She did?"

"I have a feeling," Maia added, "that it's hard to let Pearl De Windt Langston down."

"I might have felt that way once or twice," he agreed.

"Well," she said with a resigned smile, "is there anything else about the Ransoms that I should know?"

"Do you remember those papers I had in my arms when you came to my office yesterday? Well, those are all documents from Wisdom. I had intended to go through them today."

"Mind if I come with you?"

"I was hoping you would," he answered. "With you by my side I have a feeling we'll find exactly what we need." He stood up. "I'll be waiting downstairs."

Maia reached out and touched his arm as he moved toward the door. "Thank you, Noah."

They drove to Christiansted and climbed the stairs to his office. He emptied his desk and pulled a chair up beside it. Then he set the stack of papers on the floor.

"There's no correct way to do this," he explained to Maia. "We'll just look at each document and see what we discover."

Five hours later they were exhausted. The floor was littered with tattered and crumbling sheets, some of them water damaged, others worm-eaten. Frustrated, Noah had walked to the window of his office and was now staring out across the street at Club Pan. Maia was breathing slowly, evenly, as if calming a deep sense of inner discord.

"It's here," Noah said quietly. "I know it's here."

"We don't even know what we're looking for."

"We're looking for the one document, the one paper that proves Jakob Johanssen's recognition of Abraham Ransom as his son."

"If there had been such a document they would have destroyed it."

"They didn't destroy anything else. Look at all this, Maia! Receipts for sales of livestock and wine and fabric imported from Belgium—"

"And slaves," she said, reaching toward a paper witnessing the 1835 purchase of "Ana," a ten-year-old girl from Cuba, by Solomon Johanssen. Maia touched the wax seal on the bill of sale—an image of a sugar mill on a steep hill—and wondered what had become of the child who had been bought to labor at Wisdom.

Noah stared at his dusty hands. "They were fucking vermin, weren't they?"

Maia heard the angry despair in his voice. Working beside him throughout the long afternoon had shown her how much he hated his dependence on the good record-keeping skills of the slave masters. It was a sad irony that without their bills, receipts, and deeds, he was practically powerless in his quest to return the land to the descendents of the slaves. Maia also understood how the long, lonely days spent poring over such detailed evidence had led him to the point of obsession.

"I'll help you get these back to the archives," she said quietly.

Together they carried the papers down the stairs and out into the bright sunlight. Maia followed Noah across the courtyard and into the tall building that faced the harbor. Noah nodded at the security guard, and the two descended a dank, steep corridor into a low chamber that was lined with wooden cases, pitch-sealed barrels and staggering bookshelves. Maia watched him thread his way carefully into a darkened corner of the catacomb, where he placed his load alongside more stacks of discolored cardboard folders.

"I'm going to do my best to see that all these papers are properly preserved," he said, his voice swallowed up by the closed space. "I've already introduced a motion to the government to build some protective cases down here."

"Why doesn't St. Croix move them out of this cellar?"

"Because of the hurricanes," he answered. "Even if they're damp, those heavy stone walls have kept these things safe for centuries."

Maia stood very still, drowning in the untold human stories that were lost in the rotting pages that surrounded her.

"Have a look over here," he said, and Maia joined him in the dark recesses of the chamber.

"All of these documents come from Wisdom," he said with a sweep of his arm. "Can you imagine? It's going to take weeks to get through everything."

"Listen," she said gently. "We'll do our best. I know you have other cases. I know you can't drop everything else just to help me."

"Oh, Maia," he began, his voice catching at the sight of her eyes. "There's nothing and no one else as important as—"

"What's that?" she interrupted. She was looking over his shoulder at a thick brown object emerging from a pile of papers stacked crookedly against the cold stones. Noah steadied the crumbling mountain with the length of his arms and she gently extracted a palm-sized object without the other documents falling.

"Check this out," she whispered. "I think it's a book."

Blowing the dust and dirt off its surface, Noah held it carefully up to the faint light. Enclosed in rough leather, the covers were held together by a tightly knotted blue ribbon that had decayed to a frayed spider's web.

"This doesn't look like an official record."

"Does it have a name on it?"

He paused. "There are some marks on the leather, but it's too dark in here. Come on—let's take it outside."

They walked to the doorway, where Noah stopped. "Maia," he said, "I want you to slip this under your dress and carry it out that way."

"Why?"

"I have to sign an affidavit for everything I remove from this room, and I don't want them to know we have this."

"Won't the guard search me?"

"He'll certainly look at you," Noah answered with a smile. "But he's not allowed to touch. And anyway," he added, "it's me they feel they need to keep an eye on."

"We're breaking rules, Attorney Langston," she said as she pushed the book into her underwear.

"And in the very nicest way," he answered.

•

Bianca Vasconcellos took a deep breath before mounting the circular walkway to the great house of Wisdom. Although she had been preparing herself for hours, it still took some real psyching up to do it. Especially alone.

Even in the broad daylight the place looked hexed. It hadn't been painted in years, and the decaying wood revealed peeling generations of eggshell and periwinkle and even a creamy yellow hue that must have made the house delightfully welcoming in decades gone by. Now the slats of the blinds were broken and the windows were missing panes, and even the drive was cracked and root-veined. The house might have been deserted.

But she had promised Paulette she'd visit. And she wanted to, really. Not only to see how things were going, now that the infamous nurse had finally taken off. But to see how things might go, now that Severin was well enough to communicate with the outside world.

Bianca found it strange that he chose to live in the house alone. It couldn't have been a lack of money that was making him choose poverty—the land alone was worth millions. And surely it wasn't because no woman wanted to be mistress of the estate. Hell, Paulette had been pretty forthcoming in her description of Severin's countless lovers.

So what was wrong with the guy?

Bianca saw his eyes on her first visit. She figured out pretty fast that

Severin liked to see a lot of leg and a lot of breast. At least, that's where his eyes spent most of their time. This was an improvement over Paulette's brother, Clay, who worried more about his golf game than about sex. Even though he, too, was a very eligible bachelor, Bianca saw pretty quickly that dating him was likely to go nowhere.

So after visiting Wisdom with Paulette, Bianca thought she might be ready to strike out on her own.

The door to the house was propped open when she approached the top of the circular drive. From inside she caught traces of contented singing, and for a moment she thought that the American nurse was back. Then she realized that it was only the servant, Mimi, straightening up Severin's room. Bianca stepped boldly into the chamber.

The old woman looked up. She was making the bed. Her eyes caught the mane of coppery-golden hair and the short skirt split nearly to the hip. Without missing a note she continued her song, turning her back on the visitor.

Ignoring Mimi, Bianca made her way to the balcony. Severin was there, his legs raised to the cracking rails, a flyswatter on his lap. His head had fallen back, his mouth slightly open, but he stirred from his sleep at the sound of her steps. He looked up, his guardedly hopeful eyes narrowing into an expression of contempt.

"Oh, so the little cub is here without the big lioness!" he remarked, wiping his growing hair away from a bristling face and grinning as if deeply amused.

"You invited me to stop by," Bianca said coyly, crossing the terrace to press her lips against his stubbled cheek. A hint of gardenia swirled from her hair and the sick man pulled himself up on the chair and slowly inspected her.

"Paulette choose that outfit?" He reached out lazily and grabbed her thigh.

"Of course not!" she said as she took a quick step back.

Severin snorted. "But she sent you over here."

"She has nothing whatsoever to do with my visit."

"Bullshit. I know my cousin. And I think she has plans for you and me, little vixen."

"I don't have the slightest idea what you're talking about."

Severin's head went slowly to the side. "You said you a college student?"

"I'll be starting my graduate work next fall."

He laughed again and stretched out his arms. "Well, even if you got seven or eight degrees I guess it would be hard for you to understand this jigsaw place. And my cunning cousin."

Bianca stood pressed against the rotting railing as if trying to make herself appear smaller. Severin watched her, his eyes opaque. "What do you want, girl?" he suddenly spat, his voice rude and low.

"Would it—would it be all right if I sat with you for a few minutes?"

Severin smiled at the tremble in her voice. "Sit with me? Hell, you can move in if you want to. There's a free room in the back. Or you can sleep in my bed. I'm sure I'd like that."

The woman flushed but remained silent. Severin's attention moved to the scene beyond the balcony, watching a figure move through the grape leaves below.

"Thinking about going swimming?" she asked, following his gaze.

"No."

"I just thought—"

"What did you just think?"

"Well, I thought you were looking at the water."

"That's what you thought?"

"Your beach is just so beautiful."

He didn't answer. His gaze was fixed on Tina's silhouette.

"I've got my bathing suit in the car," Bianca said hopefully. "Want me to help you down the hill?"

"You might not want to do that," Severin answered without turning his head.

"Why not?"

"Because then I might help myself to you."

"Pardon me?"

"Please let me help myself to you," he repeated.

"You mean—"

"I mean I'd really like to fuck you," he said, fixing her with his unsmiling eyes. "So if you continue to sit so close to me, little leopard, you can expect something hard and fast."

"Is that some kind of threat?"

"You're on my property, right next to my bedroom, and a few inches from my bed. Although," he added, "I don't need a bed for what I want to do to you."

"You have no right to talk to me this way—"

"I don't remember asking you to come here this afternoon. I know I didn't call you, because I don't have a phone. I don't even remember that you knocked. So if you come here, you take what I have to offer."

"I didn't come here to be raped."

Severin burst into a cruel laugh. "You didn't come here to be raped! Well, beauty, what are you here for? To keep an eye on things for my bitch cousin? Or to make her faggot brother jealous? Or maybe just to see what might be here for *you*?" Reaching forward, he grasped a handful of her wild, sunlit curls. "This is dangerous, you know. Didn't Paulette tell you that I only get it up for black women? That I got those nasty, secret genes from our nasty, black-loving forefathers?" He threw his head back, chortling out a raucous laugh. "I guess she didn't say too much about that. After all, her husband suffers from that little tendency, too."

Bianca stood up quickly. "I don't know what kind of medication you're on, but you sound like you're—"

"Oh, please don't be offended," he said through a sardonic squint. "I know that you sophisticated university women aren't used to such rough and tasteless discussion."

He thought for a moment that he detected a glint of tears in her eyes, so he delivered the crowning blow. "I can tell by the way you *move* that you don't know a goddamn thing about fucking."

She quickly drew in her breath and he rolled his eyes, realizing at that instant that she was much more his cousin's tool than her spy.

"Oh, shit! Why can't I control my dirty mouth?" He softened his tone, smiling up at her. "Bianca, sweetheart. There's some beer in the fridge. Go and get yourself one. Get one for me too. But promise not to tell the bitch goddess about it, all right? My cousin would savor the thought that I might once again be on the verge of drinking myself to death. If you promise to be very nice, I'll sit with you and behave myself—at least, until all my beer is gone, all right?"

Obediently Bianca walked back through the now silent house. As she passed the hallway leading down to the bedrooms something stirred in her pulse, but she ignored the strange sensation, instead moving just a bit faster. When she returned to the terrace Severin had fallen asleep again, his hand loose around an empty medicine bottle. Bianca took a seat beside him, wondering whether or not to risk waking him up.

Instead of returning to the office, Noah led Maia to his car and drove them out of Christiansted. To her surprise he passed the highway that led to his house, instead taking the East End Road several miles in the opposite direction. Noah drove with an intensely focused silence until they came to a clearing in the thick blooming foliage. He opened Maia's car door and took her hand, leading her wordlessly along a narrow earthen path that climbed over a short, steep rise to a tiny peninsula reaching out into the water, below. The rocky beach was surrounded by a grove of wild bougainvillea. The only sounds were the calm lapping of the water and the breeze in the flowering trees.

They sat together on a flat stone near the water. "This place is called Buddhoe's Cove," he explained. "I know it's crazy, but I've come here since I was a kid. This is one of the only places on the island where I can be sure that no one will see or hear what I'm doing." Their eyes met and he glanced away shyly.

"Well," Maia said, "let's see what we've got." She pulled out the little book and together they stared at the leather cover. "What's that?"

The leather cover of the book bore the image of a sailing ship, its center mast rising high from the deck to form the sign of a cross. Noah examined it for a moment, his brows drawn together. "It's a seal of some kind, but I don't recognize it. It's definitely not the Johanssens'." He placed the book in her hands. "You found it, Maia. You should be the one to open it."

With trembling fingers she tugged at the rotting blue ribbon. It came away easily from the leather cover and the book exhaled an odor of damp paper and India ink. The pages had the thick, uneven texture of homemade paper, and were bound to the cover with a thin strip of waxed leather that had gone brittle with time. Maia took a deep breath and looked inside.

The letters *Z. R.* were written in thick black ink with an uncertain hand. The date "1853" was scrawled below.

"*Z. R.,*" she whispered. "*Zara Ransom*? This is incredible." She turned the crackling page and gently lifted the book to the light. Slowly and quietly she began to decipher the words written with unsteady fingers.

15. march

i hav this book to practice rit. master solomon say that jakob and issak must lern english. when they finish i lern to. he want me to work away from wisdom. but i do not want to go from heer. my brothers is heer. jakob is heer. mistress marie is heer. wisdom is my hom.

Maia's eyes clouded with tears, but she didn't expect to see the tears she found when she looked into Noah's face. They stared at each other wordlessly. Then he reached for her, pulling her so close that the book pressed into their breasts. "I knew it," he whispered. "I knew that we'd find something if you were with me. Go on, Maia."

20 jun

master solomon say i must marree camby rasmussen from estate wite lady in fredriksted. at my age i must be wif and have babys. my brothers also want camby for me. but mistress marie is sik and jakob say i must stay at wisdom to care for her. he say i am a ransom and i can mak her well. master solomon see how i love jakob and how jakob love me. i fear master will send me away.

Maia looked up thoughtfully. "So Solomon knew that Jakob and Zara were in love. He tried to marry her off to someone in Fredriksted."

"And Jakob kept her there by claiming she was needed to care for Marie-Paule. They believed she possessed the Ransom power to heal."

10 dec

Adam bring Camby to me at night. I am sleeping in the boat house with Ana and they come in. Adam says we make wedding now and Master Soloman is happy. I say we are no longer slaves. I am free and I will marry the man I love. Adam go away and come back with Jeremiah and Mattias. They hit me four or fiv times. Jeremiah want to cut my face so Jakob will not want me after. Ana run to Wisdom and Jakob come.

Now I sleep in graat house, Jakob says. He must protect me from my brothers. And we must take care because of Master Solomon. Mistress Marie want to help us, but she is very sik. I am trying with all I know to make her well. Jakob say we must be strong, but I am afrad.

"Jesus," Maia whispered. "Her brothers actually tried to marry her to somebody by force."

"Under orders from Solomon, of course."

"But why would they do that? They were freed five years earlier, in 1848. Solomon wasn't their master anymore."

"No, but Wisdom was their home. The only home they'd ever known. And if the records are right, Zara's brothers had positions of responsibility on the estate."

"So," Maia said, "they didn't want their baby sister messing things up."

"They had nowhere else to go. Slavery was just ending on the other islands. The United States wouldn't liberate its slaves for another ten years. They had everything to lose by leaving Wisdom, and everything to gain by keeping Solomon Johanssen happy."

Carefully turning the brittle page, Maia continued reading.

15 may 1854

My english is so much better, now. The wif of the Anglican priest still come every fortnight and stay two days to teach us. I learn with her in the evening when my work is done. Her name is Jane and she is sad to be so far from her people. Jane say I wood make a good teacher. I can teach black children when I reed and rit very good. Jakob think it good for me to live in town. If I am away from Wisdom he can come to me. My brothers then can not stop us. They can not make me marree a man I do not love.

I must work very hard at wisdom now. I see that food and wash are don. I make certain the house is clean. I tell other servants what to do.

I go to the mill when my brothers are away and sit on my rock. I can see Saint Tomas on cleer days. I dream of a ship taking me and Jakob away. To a place where no one know us. Where we are truly free.

I take good care of Mistress Marie. She is happy to see how much Jakob loves me, but she can not change the heart of Master Solomon. She say she will find a way to give us a future.

Maia looked up at Noah. "So Jakob Johanssen really did love Zara Ransom. And everyone was against them except for Marie-Paule."

"But I don't understand why Solomon was so concerned about Jakob and Zara's relationship. Sex between white men and black women was the open secret of that society—"

"But that's just it." Maia looked past Noah to the darkening water. "This was something more. Look—"

September 26

Master Solomon says he will send Jakob to Denmark if he does not agree to marry Isabella Haagensen.

It is so hard. When I work in the house he comes to me. He finds me on the beech. He follows me into the fields. He always wants to be near me. To be sure I am safe.

But the mill is the only place Jakob and I can be truly alone. We go there very late, when the others are sleeping. We lie together. We talk about the future. When we are ther I am not afraid. He still wants me to go to the town, but I can not leave. I can not live without Jakob.

"That explains it," Noah said softly. "Solomon wanted Jakob to marry an heiress from one of the other estates. The Haagensens were the second or third most powerful family in the Virgin Islands. One of their sons had served as governor and the others were very successful merchants." He exhaled quickly. "That's why the Johanssens were learning English. Solomon was preparing his sons to join the upper class of landowning society. He'd already chosen a white bride for Jakob and he had no intention of letting a black woman get in the way."

They both bent over the little book.

25 December, 1854

Father Edward married us today in the Anglican church in Christiansted. Jane was my witness. Jakob said we must go against everyone's wishes because of the child. He said that he will not allow his baby to be born a bastard.

I will stay with Jane and Edward until after the baby is born. Then I will teach at the mission school. I will have my own small house near the school, and the baby will stay with a nurse during the day.

I am very happy, but I do not know what will happen when Solomon learns of our wedding. I am not afraid for myself, but I wonder what will become of our child. Jakob says that his mother will do what she can to help us protect the baby, and to see that he inherits the estate. But I do not care about Wisdom. I do not want the house. I do not want the land. I want to be with the man I love. And I

"It ends there," Maia whispered, her voice full of tears.

"No," Noah whispered, taking her into his arms and rocking her gently. "That's where it begins."

SEVEN DAYS

On the terrace of Chéz Alexander, a retired investment broker slipped his platinum card back into a sealskin billfold and placed it in the inner pocket of his linen jacket.

"Pretty good grilled swordfish, Damian. Be sure to send my compliments to Caesar."

"Thank you, Mr. Rasmussen. I certainly hope we'll see you again soon!"

Maia leaned against the polished bricks along the side of the terrace, pressing a cool bottle of juice against her flushed cheeks and waiting for Damian to notice her. She watched, slightly amused, as he complimented a pair of deeply tanned, tennis-playing housewives who had come in for chef's salads and the restaurant's famous frozen rum-and-fruit-juice cocktails. Handing their order to a white-shirted waiter, he turned back to the cash register and caught sight of his friend.

"Well, I thought you'd gone missing, Maia! I got so worried about you that I started to send the FBI out to Attorney Langston's magic kingdom!"

She kissed Damian on the cheek and felt illuminated by his hug and radiant smile. "I'm fine! Can we have a dip in your pool this afternoon?"

"Where's your boyfriend?"

"In court."

"Then come back at two, all right? All of the leisurely rich will be back on the tennis courts and golf greens by then."

Maia exited the restaurant and crossed the town square. She didn't notice the two men and snarl-eyed woman sitting in sweltering proximity on the front seat of a truck she should have recognized.

Later Maia lounged on the blue-tiled deck beside the pool, feeling the late-afternoon sun search out every pore of her body. Damian was sprawled across a mammoth orange towel, pouring a thick scented oil over his spidery legs. Maia watched him thoughtfully, wishing that she could tell him about the little book and its contents. But Noah had warned her to share their discovery with no one. He hadn't even told his mother.

"Okay, mysterious lady. Tell the truth. You came, saw, and conquered that gorgeous man *and* his estate!"

"Oh, please, Damian!"

"Don't try to tell me you're not hidden away up in his secret love-nest!"

"No way!" Maia laughed. "There's a mother in the house. And she's tougher than I am, believe it or not."

Damian looked across at her, surprised. "The man in the BMW lives at home with Mommy?"

"I think it's rather the opposite. But believe me, the house is big enough for both of them."

"And there's no wife and kiddies?"

"Not yet. Although I suspect he has used my little apartment to house various female candidates for the job. At least, his mother didn't seem to resist my arrival too much."

"So is she friend or foe?"

Maia paused, putting on her dark glasses. "Pearl Langston is one of the most amazing women I've ever known."

"Okay. What exactly does that mean?"

A pair of bright birds burst from behind the low-roofed glass house and soared over the pool. Damian raised one leg and propped it up on his folded knee. They both listened to the pool water lapping gently in rhythm to the hot blowing wind.

"I think," Maia said in a low voice, "that if I was meant to come to St. Croix, then it might have been because of this woman."

"Not because of the infamous Estate Wisdom?" Damian asked.

"No. Yes. Well—" Maia paused, searching for the right words. "I believe that I found out about Wisdom because of Pearl's obsession with bringing truth to this island."

"So is this supernatural stuff?" Damian sneered. "I mean, does she have some kind of mystical purpose endowed upon her from our ancestors in Africa?"

Maia again paused, both mildly irritated and amused by Damian's teasing. "Believe it or not, there are one or two people in the world who really and truly do have some deep and lasting principles—"

"And Pearl and her handsome son are among them!"

"No. Pearl is one of that group. Her son is just trying very hard to qualify."

"Hence, the lack of sexual relations between the two of you?"

"This isn't just about sex, Damian."

"Meaning?"

"Meaning that although he's made some pretty convincing overtures toward the sheets—and I'll admit that I've been more than tempted—what he really wants is Wisdom."

"He thinks he'll get hold of it through you?"

"Let's just say that he wants to take it away from Severin, and if I can help him with that, he's ready."

"Oh my God!" Damian exclaimed. "What a boring man!"

"Maybe what I need right now is a chance to figure out my heritage and my health, without the added concern of my heart."

"So," Damian said, mimicking a fortune-teller, "you are in risk of losing your heart to this tall, dark, and handsome stranger?"

In answer, Maia rolled over and sat up slowly. Her glasses came away from her face and Damian looked up, surprised by what he saw in her eyes. "What's up, baby?" he asked, thinking that she might be about to cry.

"Nothing makes sense anymore."

"Are you talking about Noah?"

"I'm talking about me. I mean, there's this part of me that thinks about Noah all the time. I mean, when he's not around I can't get his face or his voice out of my mind. And when I'm with him, I'm almost scared to look in his eyes. I'm ashamed of letting him see how much I want him."

"So?"

"So please explain that other part of me that can't seem to get free of Wisdom. I mean, it's as if another woman was living inside of me, making me worry about Severin despite the fact that he's such a disgusting piece of—"

"No, Maia. No. No, no, no. No! You're not thinking about that filthy rat? You're not going to sit here and tell me that you're feeling something for the great-great-grandson of the man who raped your great-great-grandmother!"

"I didn't say I'm in love with Severin," she began defensively. "I said that I'm confused about what I feel."

"I'd say schizophrenic is a better adjective," Damian replied. "In fact, I'd add a dash of psychosis and a pinch of masochism to that little brew."

"He knows something," Maia stated, ignoring Damian's criticism. "Severin knows something about me—about my family—that he hasn't told me."

"Of course! Why should he tell *you* anything? He knows you might try to take his little island paradise away from him. He has absolutely nowhere else to go with his lazy, drunken ass! And quite frankly, Maia, he knows that he'd be breaking with a tried and true tradition of white power if he, even for a moment, treated you with the kind of dignity and respect that you deserve!"

"He was completely under my control when I lived there," Maia began defensively.

"Are you crazy? You were his *employee*, Maia. All the masters lived in constant danger of being massacred by their slaves. But they still managed to keep themselves in positions of power—the same way Severin worked his peculiar magic on you!"

"He didn't do a damn thing to me—"

"Oh, he didn't? Then what made you leave Wisdom so suddenly?"

Maia went silent, but the truth was all too clear in her eyes. Damian leaned close, taking her arms in his hands. "What could you possibly see in that sad excuse for a human being, Maia?"

For a long, long while neither of them spoke. Maia's eyes remained downcast as she wrestled with an answer that would be both complete and true. Damian waited, struggling with his emotions as if Maia were, in fact, his beloved sister.

"He's dying," she finally answered. "He's dying and I'm dying too. And he's alone. He hurts and he's struggling to ignore it. And whether I like it or not, I do share some of his blood."

She looked up into Damian's eyes and cleared her throat. Out came a rough, thick sound. "Damian," she said, "in some ways, he's just like me."

"That doesn't mean he's good for you."

"No. But he said it himself when I left. There's still something more between Severin and me. And it doesn't matter what anyone thinks about it. The only thing that matters is what Wisdom wants."

Noah closed his briefcase and started to the door. Something made him turn back and gaze for a moment at his office, blooming in rainbow fractals from the gently swaying row of prisms. And suddenly, as if a window blew open to reveal a long-hidden corridor to his soul, he knew that the greatest beauty was found not in perfection, but in sometimes dangerously damaged, seemingly broken things.

Things such as Maia.

He locked the door to his office and slowly descended the stairs. The late afternoon courtyard was bathed in shadows. He'd done well in court that day, arguing in favor of a displaced tenant who'd lost everything in a fire. But the whole day his thoughts had really been on Maia.

Not because he was consciously aware that the needle had slipped out of the groove and was sliding noiselessly across the black vinyl. Not because he was aware that he was falling in love with a woman who had decided not to give anyone the chance to love her. He was so steeped in his thoughts about her that he almost missed her rented Jeep as it shot across the town square at an erratically high speed. He looked up as she turned up King's Cross Street and headed west. West toward Wisdom. Without missing a beat he jogged toward his parked sedan, threw his briefcase into the rear seat, and took off behind her.

Noah didn't know Wisdom. He had grown up on the southern coast of the island, in a neat estate of brick homes owned by the new black middle class of teachers and government officials. The children played together in well-tended yards with overflowing gardens, and rode the small school bus to a private Catholic school with plaid uniforms.

It was clearly unacceptable for the children of Noah's bourgeois world to mingle with kids still living on edges of the estates where their ancestors had been enslaved. It was also unthinkable that Noah or his sisters should take jobs in white homes, or consider employment in the service sector, for they were intended from birth to become college-educated professionals.

And it was this ironic fact that made him the ideal candidate to integrate the island's most exclusive prep school. Ironic because it made him, simultaneously, a complete outcast from the world of his white peers. For even if he could hold his own in those competitive academic classes, he was still barred from entering even the most liberal and welcoming whites' homes by his parents' deep stubbornness and pride.

Despite studying with Paulette, Peter, and Severin Johanssen, Noah had only twice before set foot on Estate Wisdom. And both of those times he was with Maia.

So Noah watched with dismay as Maia's little steel Jeep careened along the rutted back roads of the island's north coast toward a destination that he knew all too well—yet not at all.

Up ahead, Maia pulled off the road before reaching the entrance to the estate. Seeing the swirl of braking dust, Noah did the same, guiding his sedan behind an ancient stone wall, where it could not be seen from the road. He listened as her steel door slammed, then slipped from behind the steering wheel of his car and stripped off his suit jacket and tie.

Walking slowly, he caught glimpses of Maia's white dress as she pushed her way through a tangle of hedges and grape trees where the rusted chain-link fence began at the edge of the property. It was obvious that she knew where she was going—that she'd taken this route before. Noah was impressed by this act of surreptitious boldness.

He bent low, pushing thorny bushes carefully away from his eyes, and saw that she was walking with deliberation toward a stony hill. The wind was blowing in from the north, whipping the leaves into a mad dance against the shore. Maia's sandals sent scurrying pebbles down the ridge and into the tufts of dried grass below.

She vanished into an abandoned mill that stood at the crest of the hill. Noah paused halfway up the slope and rolled up his sleeves. His fine-grained shoes were dusty and his pants were unbearably heavy in the sweltering heat, but he couldn't stand the thought of leaving her alone there, in the unmarked cemetery of her bloodline. Moving slowly and carefully he mounted the steep incline, stubbing his toes painfully on loose rocks and trying to remain hidden from view on the open, exposed ridge.

As he neared the top he heard singing. The sound was strangely ethereal in the insistent winds, and he moved noiselessly closer, like a sailor drawn to the sirens' song. Through the empty frame of a window in the ruined mill he could see her, knees drawn up and circled by her arms, sitting on a large boulder facing the sea. She had opened the buttons on the front of her dress. She was facing the water, rocking gently, slowly, in rhythm to the white waves crashing against the rocks far below.

Noah could make out neither the words nor the melody, but lilting echoes of her voice pierced the winds like the haunting voice of another woman from long ago. He was struck by her great stillness, as if she had become a part of the rock that bore her. Or as if she had been conceived and born there, on that stone. Or, perhaps, as if she had come there, to that strange navel at the top of Wisdom's world, to die.

Suddenly she shivered, her whole body trembling as if shoving off a mantle of cold. She stretched forward from the waist, throwing out her arms. Then slowly she rose to her full height, breathing deep and long. Noah watched her drinking in the air of Wisdom, as if it were the sustenance of her life.

She leaped off the rock and began a wild plunge downward, her arms flung open, her face turned upward toward the sun. Noah had to move quickly to catch a glimpse of the flaming white dress as Maia sprinted down the steep hill toward the water, the only sound the small rocks that were loosened by her step to bounce joyfully and fitfully ahead of her.

It took Noah some time to negotiate the pathless canyon that dropped sharply toward the sea. He knew enough about the island to be aware that scorpions were likely to be living beneath some of the larger stones, and that vicious fat centipedes were certain to be found around the scrubby grass that clung to the sides of that hill. He wondered that Maia roamed around this wild place without injury. He, himself, would take no chances.

But when he finally made his way down to the brace of grape trees that grew in thick abandon beside the exquisite pearly beach, he was unprepared for what he saw.

The white dress was strewn on a rock, and Maia's sandals had been picked up by the waves and were already floating gently in the shallow surf. Noah looked desperately out to sea, suddenly terrified that she might simply have decided to walk into the water. He cupped his hands over his eyes and prepared himself to run out into the waves to pull her to safety, if necessary. But then he heard voices.

He knew the man's voice at once. For even if it had been years since they were in school together, the alcohol and nicotine and decades of neglect had not altered it so much. What he didn't expect was the strength and timber of the voice that answered.

"So, Nurse Ransom, you're back."

There was a long pause. Noah climbed carefully through the thatch of grape trees and nestled himself behind the fanlike leaves, where he could see much of what was unrolling on the edge of the surf.

"And you, Severin, are still alive."

"Can't die till you give me permission."

Severin was standing unsteadily on the edge of the beach, as if he had just emerged from the bushes beneath the house. Noah strained to see Maia and at last caught a glimpse of her as she stood, calf-deep, in the waves.

"Can't give you permission to die till you tell me about Jakob and Zara, Severin."

Noah heard the man give a low, throaty laugh. He shifted his weight in the sand, and Noah did the same in his hiding place.

"Nurse, you're trespassing."

"Severin, I'm still searching. I'm a lot closer, but I'm not there, yet."

"I told you—"

"Lies," she interrupted, raising her voice for the first time. "You told me a pack of bullshit because you wanted to be sure I'd come back."

There was a long moment of windswept silence. Then Severin spoke. "And here you are."

Maia stepped forward, coming into full view and Noah's breath caught in his throat. She was wearing nothing but her panties. Her long arms were wrapped around her breasts, but her browned legs and full belly were exposed.

"You can tell me, now, Severin."

"Why should I?" He cleared his throat at the end of the question.

"So that we can move on to something else. Something better."

"You think there can be something better between us?" He grunted. "You come here and show yourself to me after you pushed me away? To pretend I can have you after you fought me like a dog?"

"I didn't come here for you. I came here because she called me."

"I know," Severin said in a voice that was filled with an unmistakable sadness. "I knew she would."

The two stared at each other for a long time, the woman still standing in the waves, and the man still motionless on the beach. Noah watched, his heart leaping at the look he recognized in the man's eyes. "Nurse Ransom," Severin murmured, "how can I go swimming on my beach if you're standing like a ghost in my water?"

"You can have your beach and your water, Severin," she replied, "if you give me Jakob and Zara."

"I don't have them."

"I believe," she insisted, "that you do. And I swear to you that I'll find them before—" Her voice broke strangely, and now the look between the two of them changed.

"You know," Severin said in a voice so low that Noah could barely hear him, "that without you I really might die?"

"Only if you choose to," she answered, swaying a bit in the water.

"Paulette wants Wisdom pretty damn bad. Found a woman to bring round here. Found me some temptation." He laughed his rusty laugh. "Pretty thing. Nice to look at. Nice to touch. What you think, Nurse?"

"If you won't give me my people, why give your life to her?"

"Oh, it don't make much difference," Severin said. "Better to die with a good piece of pussy and a bottle of rum. What do I get if I help you? No pussy and no rum, either!"

Noah let out his breath at these words, but Maia took a step toward the shore, simultaneously dropping her arms. She waded out of the water, a full-breasted, brown Venus emerging from the waves. Severin straightened painfully, unable to take his eyes off her.

"Maybe," Maia said to the withered man, "all of this is bigger than you or me. Maybe it doesn't matter if we live or die."

"Or if we make love," Severin said in a pathetic voice. To Noah's wonder, Severin raised his arms and Maia came into his embrace, almost holding him up as she put her arms around him.

"Severin," she said, her flesh pressed against his thin body. "We are blood. We are *blood*. Blood cannot mix with blood. Blood cannot love blood."

"But I love you," he said in answer. "I knew it when you first came into Brandy's that day. Knew it when you found your way to my kitchen door. I knew you'd be back. I even knew you'd be here. It's just a matter of time before you come to stay."

"I cannot make love with you," she murmured. "I can't."

Her words were mysterious, but even stranger was the fact that she had drawn the sick man close and was holding him gently. Almost . . . lovingly.

And then it happened. Tina waddled out from the trees and moved forward with intense speed, despite her size. She was cursing loudly, her voice rough with rage as she leaped toward Maia. Severin saw his lover coming and tried to shove Maia behind him, but they were standing in deep sand and they staggered sideways to retain their balance. Tina grasped Maia by one shoulder and struck her in the face with a rock, knocking her to her knees. Severin grabbed Tina's arms and pulled her away from Maia. "You bitch! Why you do this shit?"

"Fuck you and your whore!" The squat woman hurled, straining to kick Maia's fallen figure.

Noah threw himself through the grape trees and lurched toward the struggling pair. Tina whipped around in surprise and Severin turned toward him.

"What do you think you're doing?" Noah shouted.

"I'm all right," Maia said in a dazed voice. Tina stepped back, her furious gaze following her victim as Noah helped her to her feet.

Severin's eyes narrowed. "What you doing on my property?"

Noah ignored Severin, instead guiding Maia to the edge of the water. Carefully he wet her forehead, noting with relief that her gaze cleared and she looked full into his face. Tina sucked her teeth loudly and shouted: "*Mwe kay-tsé*! Next time I kill you. You hear? Keep you ass away from Wisdom!"

Severin turned on Tina. "Shut up, you damned bitch. Shut up! You nearly kill this woman! Go away, Tina! I don't want to see you! Never!"

Chest heaving, Tina retreated several steps. Severin now looked hard at Noah and nodded. "I know you," he said softly. "Rosemeade. And now you the big lawyer. I know why you here."

"No, Severin, you don't." Noah had placed his hands beneath Maia's shoulders and pulled her easily toward him. Severin watched, his desire for Maia changing to rage as the full significance of Noah's presence took hold.

"So. You sent her here?" Severin asked. "Sent her to find out what you need to take this land from me?"

"Where's the nearest phone, Severin?"

"No phone at Wisdom. No television. No radio, either. I don't need nothing like that here at Wisdom!"

"Fuck you, Severin," Noah said very quietly. "Fuck you and everything you stand for." He took a careful look around and picking up Maia's dress, slipped it carefully over her naked shoulders.

"You gonna pay for this, Nurse!" Severin called out. "You betraying your people with the lawyer man."

Still dazed, Maia seemed to ignore his comment. She let Noah lead her toward the grape trees, looking back only once at Severin.

Severin let out a barking laugh and dropped onto the sand, as if so much excitement had left him exhausted. "She don't belong to you, lawyer!" he shouted. "She belong to Wisdom!"

Noah slowly guided Maia up the steep hill. He led her to the large boulder beneath the sugar mill, and checking quickly for centipedes and scorpions, helped her sit down. "Are you all right?"

"No," she said honestly. "My head hurts like hell." Gingerly she pressed her fingers along her jaw, visibly relieved when her hand came away without blood. Then she silently buttoned her dress, glancing around her with a sigh. "I guess my people were watching."

"*I* was watching," he replied with irritation. "Why the hell did you come here?"

"You know why: You told me it's mine." She lowered her head to her hands, and once again he was afraid.

"Can you walk, Maia?"

She nodded, standing up slowly.

Together they made the long trajectory across the estate, this time taking a thin, secret path that Maia had used during the days she'd spent roaming in the beginning. When they arrived at the cars, she climbed into the front seat of the Jeep and rested her head on the steering wheel.

"Are you going to be all right?"

Again she nodded. "I just need to rest, Noah."

"I'll drive right behind you," he said.

Noah's mother called Vashti Peterson, who came out to the house and went upstairs to examine Maia. Pearl approached her son, who stood rigid and drawn in the atrium, looking anxiously up the stairs.

"What happened, son?"

"She fell," he lied, unable to meet his mother's eyes.

"She fell on purpose?"

"No, Mother. It was an accident," he said, ashamed to admit that he hadn't been able to keep Maia away from Wisdom.

"Where did it happen?"

"Christiansted. A cracked sidewalk near the courthouse."

"She fell on her face in the broad daylight in downtown Christiansted?" Pearl repeated ironically. "Well, she's lucky you just happened to be there."

Vashti came out of the studio and descended the stairs. "She's fine," she said to the mother and son. "But I think that she should get some rest this evening."

Noah quickly mounted the stairs and paused at the door before knocking. Inside the studio the curtains were drawn, and he could barely make out her reclining figure in the falling night.

"Sit down, Noah."

He pulled a wicker chair up to the bed and leaned forward, his hands clasped between his knees. "How're you doing, lady?" he said in a low, light voice.

"I'm dying."

He laughed gently and reached out reassuringly. "I know you may feel that way, but I promise I won't let that happen."

She didn't respond. The silence in the room grew ponderous and he pulled his hand back slowly. "Listen," he said. "If you feel that bad I've got a friend who practices on St. Thomas. I'll fly you over there if its necessary."

Her eyes were closed, so for a moment he thought she might have fallen asleep. He stirred, preparing to rise when she repeated, "Noah, I'm dying."

"What?"

"I'm dying."

There was no mistaking the honesty in her voice. So this time, he listened.

"I've got a tumor," she explained, the words disintegrating with sadness. "It's been there awhile. For a long time it didn't get bigger and they told me to wait. So I waited. Then, just before I came here, they said that it was growing. Eventually it's going to expand out, everywhere, all over my body—"

"Why didn't you do something?" he asked, shocked.

"I did do something," she whispered. "I got on a plane."

"You're sick and you decided to go on vacation?"

"Better than lying in a hospital bed—"

"How can you say that? How can you throw your life away?"

"I'm not throwing it away," she murmured in a barely audible voice. "I'm trying to find it."

"Oh, Maia," he said, holding back his confused anger and despair by rising and moving blindly toward the closed shades. He stopped at the windowsill and pressed his forehead against the sharp aluminum slats, breathing in their warmth as they marked his flesh.

"You can't let yourself die," he whispered. "Isn't your life worth anything?" he asked without turning.

"It wasn't, then."

"And now?"

She was silent and he felt his breath quicken. "Maia, you've come here and found out that you have a past. You have land. You have friends. You have—you have someone who—" He faltered and looked over his shoulder at the crumpled figure. "Doesn't it matter that my mother cares about you? Or that I care about you?"

She jerked slightly, the bed registering the movement in the rustling of the sheets. He walked back to her, peering down through his wordless despair and realized that she was weeping soundlessly.

Dropping down beside her, he placed an awkward arm over her shoulders and tried to rub her back. She had pushed her hand against her mouth and tears were pouring from her eyes. He felt a wave of guilt with the understanding that this was the cause of all the silence he had felt in her from the first time they'd met. His mind reeled with the kaleidoscope of their encounters: Her wordless wonder as the sun set over the western horizon at Fredriksted; her quiet amusement after defeating Paulette at the hilltop restaurant; her profound delight at the row of simple prisms hung in his office.

He also understood how she had chosen to live at Wisdom, and why it was so painful for her to leave. He understood, in his heart if not with his mind, why she felt called back to the place. And why she climbed to the top of the hill and placed herself on the boulder in front of the ruin to stare out at the boundless sea.

Yes, the hills, the house, the very air of Wisdom was all she had to cling to when every other promise of life was gone. It was the sense of ancestral memory—of Jakob and Zara creating Abraham, perhaps in the very bed on which she had slept. Or sitting on the stone where Zara might have enjoyed looking out over the sea. It was bathing on that pristine beach. Washing away the years and years of wandering pain. Coming home because her people called her back. Back to the core of something lost, something yet to be found.

And then he understood that she did not need to own Wisdom. *She needed Wisdom to own her!*

Noah didn't know exactly when he climbed into the bed beside her. He took her into his arms, feeling his heart rise and tip over and break.

"I love you, woman," he whispered. And he kissed her forehead, as a father might kiss his child. He kissed her and held her and tried to find a way to turn Wisdom into a place of survival for her. Rather than a promise of surrender.

SIX DAYS

It was strange: Maia thought that when he took her it would be painful—an act of lust and rage on her unwilling flesh. But now, as Severin enfolded her in arms grown strong with her gentle care, his body seemed to fit perfectly into and around her own. His face was near, his lashes brushing her forehead as he pressed his chin carefully into the hollow of her cheek. She felt his hands pulling her near, then exploring the caverns of her back, the ridges of her hips, the deep valleys of her thighs.

And she didn't resist. Not because she wanted him. But because this unwilling surrender seemed as inevitable as the sunset. She felt him draw closer, and still closer, while knowing him only on the exterior of her body, as if the melting inner chamber were numb to his probing embrace.

He called out to her, the name as unfamiliar as his touch. And she answered, because answering was what she must do. He pressed ever deeper, as if he had no other choice, and she bore the invasion in the same way that she bore the heat and the darkness and the stinging of the gleeful mosquitoes in the night.

"Zara," he called her. Then "Ransom" escaped his swollen lips. "Zara," he muttered again and again and she answered, drawn so close beneath and around and near him that his name was only a memory.

"Jakob," she whispered.

Immediately the name became an agony and the walls seemed to buckle and kneel toward her, as if they were made of canvas. The touch that caressed only seconds before now began to tear away at her flesh, as if every pore on her body were scourged by the jagged knot of a high-flung whip. She began to writhe beneath the pain, to jerk and to twist herself away from the weight that impaled her, and tearing her mouth free, she screamed.

And screamed.

"I'm not the type who wants a man to come and rescue me."

"Of course not."

"And I'm not going to stay here and take advantage of your hospitality."

"I wouldn't let you do that."

"I will pay for my room, just as I arranged with Noah."

"Naturally."

"And I'll be leaving in a few days, anyway—"

Pearl rolled her eyes as she moved briskly around the studio, opening the windows and arranging the shades so that the hot hibiscus-laden breeze perfumed the room. She pretended to ignore her guest, whose bad mood was caused more by her sense of imposing on her hosts than by the memories of her dream-haunted sleep.

"They come often?" Pearl asked lightly as she ran a cotton cloth along the dustless windowsill.

"What?" Maia asked. She was sitting at the table, a cooling cup of tea before her.

"Those nightmares."

"I don't have night—" Maia choked back the lie when she saw

Pearl's hand freeze in midair. There was a long pause. The two women waited to see what that hand would do, and at last Maia caved in.

"Once in a while."

"What is a while?"

"I don't know."

The hand found Pearl's hip. "You *do* know, young lady."

"All right." Maia lowered her head. It hurt to think of the dreams. And it hurt even more to try and count them. To come up with some accurate sense of their frequency and intensity. To try to view them through a clinician's eyes.

"I'm waiting," Pearl the Schoolteacher prompted, and Maia shrugged.

"Once a week."

"You're fibbing. You haven't slept peacefully since you've been in this house," Pearl said calmly. "Those dreams are your safety valve. Without them I don't know where all those poison thoughts might end up. It's Noah's fault, putting all that nonsense about Wisdom into your head."

Maia was awash in shame, for she knew that she sometimes cried out in her sleep. And she remembered the dreams with absolute clarity. But now Pearl changed the subject, her voice remaining as cool and nonjudgmental as that of a sage.

"You know, you're lucky Noah was with you when you fell yesterday," she remarked casually, removing from her voice all disbelief of the strange story her son had told her. She knew that something had happened involving that damned Wisdom, and she understood that Noah was protecting Maia's pride by creating an absurd, almost slapstick explanation of her "accident." Slipping on some wet stones and cracking her chin on the uneven pavement! *Jah!* Even eighty-year-old women didn't split their skulls on the cobblestones! What Pearl didn't understand was exactly when her son had moved from desiring this woman to actually caring for her.

"You've both been so good to me," Maia said, her eyes lowered. "I don't know how I'll ever thank you." Her hands, clasped around the teacup, were trembling slightly.

"You thank me when you're sure you're not leaving us," Pearl said, keeping it light and chatty. Her remark, however, was met with another heavy silence. She turned to face the young woman. "Why aren't you getting treatment?"

Maia shifted and looked away evasively. "When the doctors told me one to two years, I just decided to spend the rest of my life living. Not dying."

Pearl moved restlessly from the window. "You just quit your job and left everything behind?"

"I had money from my parents' insurance. I put together all my unused vacation time from work and decided to give myself three weeks of freedom."

The older woman stood patiently, waiting for a fuller explanation. Maia's voice hardened. "You know, I spent years looking for someone to share my life with. Finally I understood that the only person who was responsible for my life was me. So here I am."

"Then why give up?" Pearl repeated obstinately.

"For years I've watched people dying. And I don't want to go that way. Strapped to a bed. Weeping relations. Doped out of my mind. Looking like a skeleton. Besides, no one's waiting for me to get better."

"No one?" Pearl echoed skeptically. "You're smart, you're pretty, and you're strong. So why—"

"I just haven't met the right man."

"What's wrong with my son?" Pearl asked, only half teasing.

"Noah? Nothing at all!" Maia said in embarrassed haste.

Her hostess laughed. "I know he can get obsessed with his practice. But that's because he's spent his life trying to please me. He's a good son and a fine man. Look, Maia—" Pearl pointed to the open window. "I have my own house over in Fredriksted. It's nice. New. Not as big as this monster. My nephew's living in it right now. I decided to stay up here until Noah finds somebody better than me to live with."

"But that can't be me!" Maia cried, panic leaping into her voice. "The doctors said—"

"I'm no physician. But it seems to me that the first step to getting better is deciding that you want to." Pearl walked over to the table and sat down. She looked into Maia's eyes. "I don't exactly have to beg women to go out with my son. But I've seen something change in him since he met you." She paused. "I was starting to be afraid that Noah had sacrificed his heart to his success. But now, I see that he's finding his heart again. And that's because of you."

Maia began to stammer out an answer when Pearl again raised her teacher's hand for silence. She got it.

"I don't care about your money, Maia Ransom. I don't care why you left your home. Or why no one in the States is looking out for you. But I do care about seeing a beautiful young woman like you giving up without trying. Especially when my son cares so much about her. I won't just sit back and watch."

She moved closer, placing her hand on Maia's arm. "I've been making some calls. You're going to see someone I know. A specialist from England."

"England? Noah mentioned someone in St. Thomas—"

"No. Catherine is my friend's daughter. Grew up over on Virgin Gorda and practices in London. She's at home visiting her mother and I've invited them both to fly over."

"She won't be able to say much without some tests—"

"Don't worry about that. Vashti will arrange for the hospital staff to do whatever Catherine requires."

Maia closed her eyes, trying to block out the kinds of examinations that lay ahead. She felt Pearl's hand stroking her cheek gently and she forced a smile. "You really don't have to do this, you know."

"Yes I do," Pearl replied. "You need a doctor. And Catherine is an excellent doctor. The hospital has agreed to let you come in on Monday."

Maia sighed. "I guess I should be thanking you."

"Well, if everything goes right, I'll be thanking you. This girl has been in love with Noah for years and if I'm not careful I might end up with her dragging my son off to England."

Maia's eyes widened and Pearl burst into a laugh that quickly subsided. "You may be ill, sweetheart," she said gently. "You may soon be facing our Maker. But I won't agree to let you go on that journey until you've completed the tasks set before you on Earth. And I believe there's something you have to do, Maia. I saw it in you the moment you crossed that threshold. I see it in you, now. I won't let you walk away until you've tried to complete it."

Pearl rose and sighed. "You need to get some rest. So today you're going to stay right here with me. I'm going to make you some good Crucian food. And I'm going to turn up my music real loud, so you can listen to some of our healthy island rhythms. I want you to let go of that evil house and that crazy man who lives there. Do you understand?"

Maia nodded like a child.

Pearl laughed. "And most of all, when he gets home from court tonight, I want you to take a good, long look at my handsome, sexy, intelligent son."

Long after the filly was gone, Severin woke up to find the beer bottles hot and stale beside his chair. Dusk was falling and he brushed away the impatient bloodsuckers, watching the way the grape leaves bowed against the breeze. Would it rain? The hurricane season brought blankets of falling rain, and then the insects would vanish to nourish their nests in the sudden wells of water sprung up in ditches and fields. Even before the torrential rains there were days of gray that turned the flower-heavy island into a dull, dirty place. And once the storms came trundling in from their secret haven across the water, all conversation ceased as the steel roofs thundered under the punishing assaults. Sandy land sprang into surreal green and the air became matte with the weight of its moisture.

The stormy season! Severin could hardly believe that he had lived through another summer. There had to be a reason for it. There had to be.

Why had Maia appeared at Brandy's that fateful summer evening? Why did she come up to the bar at the moment he had reconciled himself to dying? What was she doing on his beach the day he really *did* try to pass over? And how did she convince that damned doctor to let her move out to this place?

Severin's thoughts sharpened as he caught a trace of Bianca on his stained T-shirt. What was he doing with this mindless, meaningless leech, when the woman he really needed was slipping away? How could he let Paulette lead him into something that made him want to puke?

The thought of Paulette ended up in a wad of spit on the railing. He wrapped his wan arms over his chest and squinted into the new night, remembering Maia's tearful eyes and sweet-sweet warmth and deep lulling voice when he was so close—*You have to stop . . . You're too close, Severin. . . .*

"Oh, Maia," he muttered. "Maia Ransom."

He had been there, on the very cusp of possessing her, taking her, ending their search by drowning it in the deluge of their shame. For what else could come of such a coupling? A forced, furtive thrusting in the dark corners of Wisdom? Flesh meeting flesh in the rotting room of their tortured, dying souls? A fully realized dance of sex and death? He grunted, wondering what it would feel like to crush her beneath him, feeling her muscles strain in impassioned outrage. His breath quickened and he smashed an insistent mosquito, leaving a bloody smear across the mottled flesh of his thigh.

The night rolled in over the twilight and he detected a woman's mass in the shadows, standing on the steep slope to the side of the balcony. She was simply standing there, waiting, as she had waited when still a child. Many years before she had waited, while the Johanssen family gathered in the great room, lit by a hurricane lamp, after their meal. Every night she waited until a young and hungry Severin stepped out on the balcony and glanced into the darkness. And when his eyes found her shadow, often darker in the encroaching leaves than the darkness of night itself, he would go back inside and announce to his parents that he was going out. Out into the night. Out into the grape leaves. As his brother and father and grandfather and great-grandfather had done when they recognized their own hunger in the shadows of Wisdom.

And the women of the house—his mother and aunt and even his grandmother, when she was still living, pretended not to know that they were going to those girls who waited by the edge of the balcony, anxious to give their bodies, and even their lives, to the Johanssens.

Tina's beauty was legendary, even then. Her golden eyes glowed against her rich brown skin, and her frame seemed ridiculously frail for the full breasts and high, round rear. Severin's brother Peter wanted her, and David too. Clay tried, but was too effete to snare this wild, slit-eyed girl. The other boys had tried to pull her into the bushes and force themselves upon her (she always laughed afterward, saying none of them could please her). But it was Severin she came for, golden eyes shining in the darkness, the first time, then time and time again.

When he led her into the bushes she came willingly, the first time clumsy and fumbling. Later she returned, teaching him the things the other boys were showing her. But teaching him to do those things the right way, the way that women like them. And he had complied.

"Tina?" he called softly to the womanly figure, gone squat and lumbering with the passing years.

"You don't want me no more, Seven," she whispered in a voice that tore softly at the night.

"Don't want you coming here to vex me," he answered, leaning painfully toward the railing. "Don't want you to kill the nurse."

"What about that toy you have here today?" she asked from the darkness.

An image of Bianca Vasconcellos pranced through his mind. "She truly is a toy." He laughed roughly. "But she break too easy. I don't want no woman like that."

"You play mean game with me?"

"She play game with me," he answered.

"And the nurse?"

"Where she sleep is none of my concern."

"And where I sleep is none of your concern?" she asked, sadness wafting out beneath her anger.

"I know you never far away."

"Even now?"

"You know where the door is," he said softly.

She stood stock-still and he waited at the railing, his profile etched against the night by a dim light in the kitchen. Where Mimi had certainly left another bowl of soup made from Maia's recipe.

"You know where the door is, Tina," he repeated in a hoarse whisper.

"It's open?" she asked, holding back the trembling.

"Never closed," he said.

FIVE DAYS

"How about a glass of Chardonnay to complement our garlic-grilled scallops?"

Noah looked up from his plate and started at the sight of Damian, dressed in a white silk button-down and leaning provocatively over the table. He instantly placed the man as the strange scarecrow who bounded out to the car to greet Maia that afternoon several days before, but he hadn't realized that he was somehow associated with Chéz Alexander, the best restaurant in Christiansted.

"Remember me?" the man said softly, his voice caressing the words. "I'm Damian, Maia's soul brother. I haven't heard from my sister for three whole days and I'm getting ready to call in the marines."

"Maia's fine," Noah replied, trying to sound reassuring as he hastily wiped his mouth with his linen napkin. "She had a small accident a few days ago, but now she's resting quietly."

"A slight *what*?" Damian's response betrayed his distrust of the story, and he squinted, lowering his voice still further. "I hope this has nothing to do with Wisdom."

"You'd better talk with her about that," Noah replied politely.

"Talk with her? I can't even *find* her!" Damian's words were just a tad too loud, and several curious customers glanced in their direction.

"She's out at my place," Noah said quietly. "And I'm sure she'd be delighted to see you."

"Well, where is your place?"

"It's—well, it's up in the hills above mid-island," Noah said evasively.

"Give me directions."

"Most people have a terrible time finding it."

"So how do I get there?" The waiter's question rang with impatience.

Noah paused. Even though he personally had nothing against men like Damian, he wasn't sure that he wanted the entire island witnessing him driving the man around in his car. He looked up, their eyes meeting, and Damian laughed.

"I can afford a taxi, you know. I just want to see her."

Noah was swept with a wave of embarrassment. He wondered how small and prejudiced he seemed to this New Yorker. *And Damian was Maia's friend.* "When do you finish your shift? I'll be leaving my office at about four o'clock today."

"I don't work shifts. I'm the manager," Damian said calmly. "I can meet you any time."

Noah looked at his watch. It was already too late. A pair of secretaries from the court were finishing lunch at the next table, and from the look in their eyes, it would take only minutes for the entire island to be yapping about Noah Langston's chat with the aunty-man with the rings through his eyebrows. He sighed. "Meet me by the fortress at four."

Noah introduced Damian to his mother when they arrived, and he saw Pearl's face tighten into a mask of unusual restraint. Her expression changed, however, when Maia threw her arms around Damian in delight. Pearl then looked at her son, raising her brows, and returned in uncharacteristic silence to the screened-in porch and her book.

Maia was looking better than Damian had ever seen her. Or at least, that's what he thought when she appeared at the top of the steps. She seemed happier, and her eyes were less hollow than when she was staying in the haunted house with Severin. She had even begun twisting the locks of her hair into baby dreads.

Damian trilled like a bird at the view from Maia's little studio, declaring earnestly that if he could, he'd never leave such a place. Maia turned toward him with a deep, throaty laugh, and gracefully crossed the room with a pitcher of iced tea.

"So you found my secret hideout?" she asked as the three sat down at the wicker table.

"I just cast myself away with the handsome prince," Damian replied, cutting his eyes toward Noah.

"Are you sure he's not an evil giant?"

"Fee, fi, fo, fum! I smell the blood of a *fine* Crucian!" Damian chanted, and the two of them again burst into peals of laughter. Noah looked nonplussed and took a great gulp of his drink.

Damian shook his head reprovingly. "Noah said you had a little accident out at the Fun House."

"I'm just glad he was there looking out for me," she answered, reaching out to touch the lawyer's hand.

"I'll bet he's pretty good at looking after other things, too."

"And I think he's looking pretty good himself!"

"Except for that stiff blue suit!"

"It's what's under the suit that counts—" She grinned.

"I'd say he's got that going on—"

"I happen to be sitting here, right beside you!" Noah interrupted, caught in a self-conscious space between embarrassment and pride.

"Don't mind us," Damian answered. "It's a sister thing."

"Be sweet, Damian," Maia chided. "Noah really is the dedicated, serious type."

"Oh, God!"

Maia giggled and brought her head close to Damian's. "All we need to do," she announced in a stage whisper, "is get him into Club Pan!"

"That's true. The Club will fix him—"

"Club Pan?" Noah interrupted. "What in the world were you two doing there?"

"When in Rome, party like the Romans," came the New Yorker's reply.

"Besides," Maia teased, "you can meet some of the island's finest people there."

"It's where you go to meet handsome devils like me," Damian chimed in.

"Or lost souls," Maia laughed, "like me."

"It's the best dance hall this side of Puerto Rico," Damian threw in.

"Puerto Rico?" Noah repeated incredulously.

"All right," Maia conceded. "Let's just say that it's the best dance hall in Christiansted."

"Fredriksted is my home," Noah said haughtily. "I don't waste my time in Christiansted after dark."

"Oh, no! A West End snob!" Damian cried, rolling his eyes.

"It's not snobbery," Noah replied. "It's simply the truth."

"Don't try to pretend there's a big difference between Christiansted and Fredriksted!"

"Everything about us is different!" Noah insisted.

"Come on, friend. St. Croix is only thirty miles from end to end!"

"Still," Noah explained, his voice deeply serious, "many black Crucians spend their entire lives in Fredriksted. Many don't have cars. Most work and go to church within walking distance of home. When I was a child there weren't even any buses. The East End of the island was like another world."

"I'll admit that lots of rich whites are holed up in Christiansted," Damian agreed, bouncing his toe against the wicker to some private rhythm. "I'm sure it almost kills some of them to get off the tennis courts."

"Why should they? They own the best property, control all the businesses, and have an underpaid work force to take care of their every need."

"But not for too much longer." Damian lowered his head and batted his lashes audaciously at Noah. "I'm sure you're hot on their trails, Attorney Langston."

"Someone has to be."

"Well, let me know before you close my restaurant down. I need my job."

"Needing a job is no reason to support those parasites."

"But I really do enjoy living in the guesthouse of the parasite who employs me. And Maia rather likes my parasite's swimming pool," Damian replied.

"What I like," Maia interrupted, "is being with *you*, Little D. Although right now I think you're working our host a bit too hard."

"Chastise the New Yorker in me," Damian replied. "I get rusty if I don't sharpen my wit on someone every few hours."

"I think there are better targets for your practice," she replied, rising and walking to the window.

"All right," Damian said. "Case closed. Or even better—guilty as charged." He looked coolly and critically around the room while Noah stared at him with polite distaste.

"Just imagine being a slave," Maia said, ignoring the men as she stared at the falling twilight. "Even if you followed the North Star, there was nowhere to go."

"Not necessarily," Noah said. "Some slaves escaped into hills like this and lived their lives without capture."

"But even from these hills they could see the water down below, in every direction, holding them here forever," she replied.

Damian pretended to pout. "Are you feeling like one of those slaves?"

Maia grunted softly. "For the first time in as long as I can remember I almost feel safe."

"Safe?" Damian muttered. "What the hell is that?"

Maia shrugged. The trio was quiet for a moment, then Damian followed her to the window and placed his arm gently over her shoulder. "All things considered," he whispered, "it sounds like you're doing okay, sister."

"Better than okay."

"Mr. Langston is treating you right?"

"Mr. Langston is a true gentleman."

"And he doesn't bore you too much?"

"He hasn't managed to, yet."

"And you're staying away from . . . ?"

"Haven't been there for a day or two," she murmured, avoiding his gaze.

Damian looked over his shoulder at the lawyer. "Keep your search-light on her, my friend. This woman believes she has a mystical con-nection to Estate Zombie."

Noah inhaled deeply and stood up. "Excuse me. I'd like to get into some comfortable clothes."

"Wait—let's all go out this evening," Maia suggested.

"I've got to return to Chéz Alexander and be my parasite's proxy," the New Yorker said, winking at her. "But I suspect that Attorney Langston might be willing to spend a couple of hours alone with you."

They both looked at the lawyer, who smiled coolly. "I think I can handle that. As long as I only have to keep up with one of you at a time."

Noah had said Fredriksted, so Fredriksted it was. But it was a different Fredriksted from the town Maia had seen before. And clearly she was with another Noah.

The open-air Bailey's Place was reached by walking up a narrow, darkened passage that led to a large, tiled courtyard. A loosely swaying roof of woven vines formed a green quilt over thick bamboo pillars, and the round tables of warm cherry wood were lit by flaming torches.

The enclosed square was vibrantly alive. Friends and neighbors moved easily between tables, carrying beers and bottles of rum that were passed from hand to hand to explosions of laughter. Babies squalled from quieter corners and two or three dogs sat patiently at their owners' feet. The musicians on the raised podium were tuning up gui-tars against an electric piano, and a glistening, shirtless man had just carried in a pair of steel drums.

Maia was in a black halter dress that flowed out short and loose. No jewelry. Simple sandals adorning her long brown legs.

And Noah was home-style. A simple black T-shirt and a pair of loose-fitting jeans. He was moving differently, too, with a sleekness that smoothed the sharp edges of the attorney into the low, sweet resonance of something peppered and set on the grill.

Following Pearl's orders, Maia was taking a good, long look. This was not Attorney Noah Langston, Esquire. This was somebody else— a man with cool, sensuous grace. The man beneath the facade. Wow! Maia thought with a start: This is what Noah *really* looks like!

He had done something to make the taut skin beneath that shirt glisten, and her gaze was drawn repeatedly to the relief of his nipples through the fabric. Maia was strangely moved by her realization that this was what men felt when gazing at the outlines of a woman's breasts. And his thighs in those pants! Exhaling slowly, she had to struggle to keep her eyes above his waist.

"You okay, Maia?" he whispered as they reached the courtyard's entrance, his hand light on her bare back. She gazed across the crowded space and his fingertips smoothed out to a warm palm. She tried to concentrate on choosing a table as that palm skittered lightly along her shoulder blades, the strokes going wider and wider until he had explored the entire continent of her back.

Slowly crossing the open arena, they pushed coolly through the wave of rollicking voices and critical gazes. They sat as far as possible from the little raised podium where the band was preparing to play. And as far as possible from the packed tables. Away from the eyes. In the velvety black. Under the rustling leaves and peeking stars.

There were no menus. There was no bar. The full-hipped waitresses sauntered back and forth from a leaning straw hut where a man with hams for arms flipped chunks of meat on a sizzling grate.

"You should try the roti," Noah said, "but be prepared: The spices can warm things up."

"Crucians need spices for that?"

"Sometimes our guests do."

Maia laughed. "That doesn't say much for the Crucians."

"It says even less for the guests."

Someone at a nearby table began singing.

"Maia," he said suddenly, "you have beautiful eyes."

"That's because they like what they're seeing."

"And your extraordinary mouth?"

"The better to enjoy those spices."

"And your wonderful skin?"

"Crucian-grown, my friend."

A steel drum tittered and Noah leaned close, brushing his soft lips against hers. "You," he said softly, "could incite me to break the law."

"That's all right," she answered, looking straight into his eyes, "as long as it feels good."

The second steel drum began a laughing conversation with the first, and someone hit a few chords on an electric keyboard. Noah reached for Maia's shoulders and they kissed. And kissed some more.

Maia had forgotten what it was like. Desire. Not that faded copy that she felt when watching TV or movie men, or fantasizing about neighbors or colleagues or long-lost childhood sweethearts.

The fresh, sweet, heart-speeding moment when all of her senses blinked into life. Pulse quickening as her speech thickened. A cool wetness tracing the fine whispers of hair at the edge of her scalp. Nipples tingling. And that great lonely fruit roaring back into pulsing existence.

He moved closer to her and their legs came together, his hard muscles taut against the elastic press of her thighs. The straw she was grasping between her fingers seemed to knot itself as he brought the length of his arm against her naked flesh, the hairs on her arm tickling so that she trembled.

"Maia?" His voice caressed her, and she lowered her gaze, sure that he would hear desire in her swollen answer. "Maia Ransom," he repeated very slowly, holding the consonants against his tongue as if they were thick and sticky and full-fleshed. Consonants like mangos.

"Yes," she rasped, the words looming up against her emotions like metal hurdles. They stared at each other. Noah cleared his throat.

"Can I get you some juice?" He paused, his own voice cracking gently. "Soursop? Guava? Or perhaps you'd like a taste of something *else*?" He laughed a low, sweet sound and swung his head away from her to look across the courtyard.

Maia felt the cool earth through the soles of her shoes. The smooth wooden table clutched gently at her elbows while the ripe scent of the ocean slipped under the urgent sizzle of grilling meat. What would it be like to lie tangled in the surf with Noah, as she had with Severin? What would it feel like to have him lift her to his waiting and eager hips? What would his voice sound like when he was so close, so close that . . .

Unconsciously, her senses gathered up these impressions and laid them beside Noah. The haze that had hung over her life since the date of her diagnosis began drifting away, like morning fog. And the phases of her illness: First, the incompetence of those surly, underpaid lab technicians; second, the lonely screaming into a January ice storm from the railings of a freeway overpass; third, the no hunger no thirst no lust no no no hope that nailed her to her bitter mattress for weeks; and finally the steely *fuck you this is my death and I'm in charge here*— All of that hopeless and bottomless shit suddenly belonged to another woman. Another life.

Because here, everything was different. Here she had come to know scarlet bougainvillea and guava ice cream and the dance of sand crabs on night beaches. Here she had touched the womblike walls of her ancestry. And here, so unexpectedly, was the incarnation of something she had given up on so many years before. Here, sitting so close that his bay-scented pulse sent her earrings stirring, was a chance for—

"Nurse Ransom."

The voice snatched up her breath and crushed it. Tensing, she pulled her lips away from Noah's, her gaze shooting out into the darkness. Noah turned, too, and together they could only just make out Severin's face—little more than a silhouette etched by the torchlight against the night.

"So you still making our little paradise your home?"

He was standing at an odd angle, the hand clenching a cigarette held stiffly to his side. Behind him Maia could make out the wild mane of golden curls and the curve of a breast in something elastic and white. Even in the dim light, Severin's escort sucked all the noise from the other tables.

"And you're back on the streets," Maia responded below the steel drums.

"Got a bodyguard," Severin said as he jerked his head toward the woman.

"Well, I guess my soup paid off."

"You know how much I liked it," Severin chuckled roughly. "You did real good, Nurse. Especially late at night and down in the water."

Noah stiffened and Maia could feel the swell of the black man's ancient rage.

"You don't speak to her in that manner," Noah said clearly.

Severin's eyes slid from her face to Noah's. "Oh, it's Noah the Lionhearted?"

"It might be Severin the Dead," Noah replied swiftly. He started to rise, but Maia caught his arm.

Severin began to chortle a dark, insinuating laugh, but the sound twisted into a wretched choking that pressed him forward at the waist. Maia stirred, her nursing instincts nearly sending her out of her seat, but Severin's amazon leaned forward to pat his back.

Half smothered by the darkness, there was little more to see than the rough cascading hair and abundant breasts, shaking nicely as Bianca hit at him. Severin straightened up slowly and staggered back a step, and the woman grasped his waist. Carefully he righted himself, exhaling a rancid breath of tobacco and rum. Placing an arm around his Rapunzel, he addressed Maia quietly.

"I do miss you out at Wisdom. For a while I was wondering if you got over your last visit."

Noah grunted, turning his head away, but Maia sat transfixed by the strange pair.

"You've found your angel," she said clearly, "and I've found mine."

Severin slid both his arms around the young woman's hips and nodded knowingly at Maia.

"You right, Nurse Ransom. I got my sexual healing now." The woman remained impassive as he ran his gnarled fingers along her firm thighs. "I have to admit she feel much better than you."

The band leaped into a calypso and Seven pushed his companion away, toward the center of the courtyard, though he could barely walk. The flickering torchlights sent writhing images of her body as she worked her way into a dance, with Severin teetering like a mocking scarecrow beside her. Four or five other couples joined them, the women deliberately ignoring Bianca while the men hungrily stared.

Maia felt Noah's hand brace her arm and to her surprise he pulled her up and walked her past the dancers and out into the alley. "Hey— what are you doing?"

"I have no intention of spending my evening watching that dog."

"But I'm not ready to leave," she began, but the face he turned on her was enraged.

"So that's how you operate," he spat, ignoring two or three couples that squeezed past them in the narrow passage. "You came crawling to me because he was finished with you—"

"*Finished* with me? What do you *think* you mean by that?"

Noah blazed down at her. "What was going on between you and Seven?"

"My stethoscope."

"Were you nursing him in his bed?" Noah asked, his eyes like splintered glass.

"Am I nursing you in yours?"

"Tell me the truth!"

"I'm nobody's trash," she cried as her own anger erupted.

"But you wanted him, didn't you, Maia?" Noah's voice reached down beneath the music, growing dark and dirty. "He was all over you, wasn't he?"

"He tried. But I wouldn't have him."

"He was out of control?"

"I controlled Severin—"

"But you couldn't control yourself?"

Maia stared at her companion. A group of women, awash in duty-free fragrance and batik-print dresses pushed by. One woman looked up at Noah and sneered.

"No," Maia said slowly, a great fatigue taking the place of her rage. "It wasn't about Severin. It was my illness that I couldn't control. And my need to know the truth about Wisdom. And my desire to understand my feelings about something I'd never known before." Maia lowered her head and practically whispered the final words. "I needed to figure out how I feel about *you.*"

He stood above her, staring down angrily into her face, and then the word came home. *You.*

His breath caught in his throat. Then pulling her toward him, he pressed her hard and silently against his body. He felt a subtle stirring of resistance in her shoulders and back, but it vanished when he buried his face in her sprouting dreadlocks.

Behind them Severin careened drunkenly across the courtyard and fell onto a stool. His mannequin immediately followed, settling herself on his lap and bursting into loose, inebriated laughter. Severin took a handful of Bianca's hair and pulled her face back. She laughed again before meeting his tattered lips.

In the narrow passage Noah called Maia, bringing his mouth to her brows, her chin, her lips. Maia's arms came up and around Noah's shoulders as her lips opened to his probing tongue. Pulling back gently, she stared into his dark eyes. "Come on," she said.

In the courtyard Bianca's hands grasped her beer bottle more tightly, and raising it high, she baptized them both with a stream of the frothing liquid. He chortled, lapping the yellow liquid off her face and arms.

A sea of eyes watched Severin demean beauty. But can true beauty be so easily destroyed? Everyone knew that if that woman cared for herself, she would never have come close enough to be touched by the last of the Johanssen sons. She would never offer herself, like the meanest slave, to the abuse of the master. Everyone believed that there were few men lower than Severin. For there had been seven sons and all but the seventh were gone. And everyone knows, of course, that the number stops at seven for a reason.

The car was halfway up the hill to his circular drive when he heard her words licking at his ear. "Baby, I want to go to the beach."

They were so close to the comforts of his good bed, warm shower, and fully stocked kitchen that he instantly refused. "It's late now, Maia. The beaches won't be safe."

Her insistent hand came to a stop on his thigh. "Buddhoe's Cove is safe."

"Maia," he pleaded as they reached the house. "Let's just go inside."

She didn't respond. Noah coasted into the drive and turned off the engine. A heavy silence filled the car and he looked at the woman beside him. For a moment he wavered, calculating what he would win or lose by refusing to give into her whim. Then he turned on the motor and opened all their windows so that the sweet midnight air could fill the cabin. It would only take them a few moments to get there. And those minutes wouldn't be lost, he realized as her fingers found his zipper.

Maia cascaded from the car, tearing off her sandals and dress and panties as she bounded toward the beach and the pitch-black sea. Noah left his shirt and shoes and locked the vehicle, following her over the little ridge and down to the water. A trembling white lace of water tickled its way up to the sandy slope, and when he came over the crest of the hill he found Maia already thigh deep in the surf. He heard her laughter above the soft crescendo of the mirroring waves, and saw her silhouette prancing in the sharp moon shadows.

She came up like a dolphin and returned to the waves, sliding effortlessly between the gentle swells. He wondered that she wasn't afraid of biting schools of fish, or flesh stabbing sea anemones, or even the Frisbee-sized sand crabs who appeared on the beaches after dark.

He watched the water stirring: first a hip, then a thigh. Then her whole head emerged from the black liquid, her face raised high toward the midnight sun. She rolled over and her nipples grazed the surface of the water followed by the elusive glimpse of the little frill beneath her sloping, full belly.

And suddenly his breath caught in his throat and he was submerged in the realization that he didn't want to have her. He didn't want to pull her out of the water and onto a cool white dune and press her down beneath him and take her. He didn't want to roll her up on top and suck her breasts while she rode him. He didn't want to take away that great, burgeoning anticipation that made his eyes hurt and palms wet when he gazed out at her joy-drenched figure.

Because he knew that at least for these few moments, she felt truly free. And he deeply regretted his aching need to bind her once again to the needs of the flesh.

He didn't want to merely love her. He also wanted to be loved by her. And this feeling was as new and terrifying as anything he'd ever faced. Perhaps, he thought as she vanished into the silvery water, love was the ultimate courtroom. The only true plaintiff. And the most severe jury.

Noah sank down on the sand dune and rested his chin on his hands. Maia swam in circles, dipping beneath the surface just long enough for the air bubbles to halt their fizzing and the waves to be restored to their rhythm. Then she'd burst out, shattering the oily gleaming surface, and send droplets flying up to the cool wet sand.

And then suddenly she was racing up the beach, leaping toward him and landing warm and electric in his arms. They fell back, her legs pinning him beneath her, and she kissed him until he forgot everything. Even his own name.

Four days

The sun was hard white and high overhead when Noah pulled the sheets away from his sweet exhaustion. The room was bathed in blinding light and he grunted as tears filled his eyes. The first thing he recognized was a brown body he'd seen only once in daylight—then submerged to the thigh in the waters beneath Wisdom—and he reached forward curiously, as if he had not caressed every inch of that flesh the night before.

She was, he discovered, like a refracted image. Throwing off sparks of light in every direction, she shifted in the darkness like the light-splintering prisms in his office. There were even times when her face seemed to ripple and flow into that of another woman as she gazed solemnly at him in the moonlight.

He had called her name, calling to her again and again, as if conjuring someone from within the woman who held on to him with a ferocious tenderness. He wondered, at some momentary intersections, whether he was hurting her when her eyes wandered off into an impenetrable distance and her voice deepened in response to his touch. But she moved with him, against and around him as if her heart were aligned with the trembling pleasures of their limbs, and he gave himself to her with an abandon that he would never have risked in the light of day.

It was strange to be with a woman who wanted nothing from him. Who had no dream of marriage. No desire to be the mistress of his manor. Who didn't hope to become pregnant. Who hadn't asked for his love.

And liberated from all the plots and devices that usually formed the invisible and unspoken foundations for sex, he had discovered a new kind of union, based solely on the fascination of desire. It was truly different to touch a woman who had come to terms with the possibility that she might never be touched again. Every moment was a gift, every sensation a new discovery.

She was full-bodied, her hips and thighs welcoming to his weight. Her breasts seemed lush and ripe to his fingers and tongue. And in the dark of the night, her skin seemed to flow like liquid honey against his own damp flesh. Submerged in her, driving deep into her overwhelming heat, his thoughts vanished into a dizzying sense of completion. For the first time, after countless lovers and many years of lovemaking, he truly understood the indescribable beauty of a becoming one with a woman. And he faced the loneliness that all people seek to deny through love-less acts of mating.

This woman, Noah thought as he looked at her in the morning sun, had already changed his life. Her willingness to trust—to give herself completely to him—was anything but a burden. It was a gift, and he would do whatever it took to repay it.

Maia stirred sleepily, as if she could hear his thoughts. "You're gonna be late, Noah."

He reached down and placed his hand on her hip. "Not today, baby."

"Don't want to interfere with your work," she murmured.

"You can't," he agreed, kissing her forehead.

"Then it's okay if you have to go—"

"I don't have to go, Maia. It's Sunday."

"My God," she laughed, smiling as she slowly stretched her arms above her head. Noah watched the tips of her nipples harden and his own body responded in turn. She was looking at him through swollen, gently amused eyes. "You've made me forget everything, Noah. Even the day of the week."

"At least you remember my name," he said, leaning forward to kiss her forehead.

"Come to think of it, I remember a couple of other things about you," she teased. Noah pushed out a short breath and looked away from her quickly.

Maia began stroking his chest. "You'd better behave, or I'll be expecting more nights like that."

He laughed lightly, caught somewhere between shyness and pride.

"Oh, look at you! I swear you'd be blushing if you weren't so manly."

"That's your fault," he answered awkwardly, unaccustomed to his own discomfort.

"Well, you can blame me as much as you want," she whispered in a hoarse voice. "As long as you blame me real good. . . ."

And he did. Some time later, Noah fell back and sighed.

"What's your mother going to say about this?" Maia asked sleepily.

"I suspect," he replied slowly, "she'll want to know whether she should open up her box."

"Her box?"

"She has a secret box hidden somewhere in the house where she keeps her valuables," he explained. "And deep inside that box is a ring her great-grandfather gave her great-grandmother when they were freed. I was raised with the understanding that it has to be passed on to the next generation of Langstons."

"Meaning?"

"Meaning that I'm to put it on the finger of the woman who'll become my wife."

Maia struggled to sit up, suddenly wide awake, her face darkening. "And what do you plan to say to her?"

"I'll tell her the truth," he answered. "I've found that woman. But I don't know if she's found me."

There was a long silence, broken by the strident call of a bird on the terrace. Maia looked away, sudden tears in her eyes. "Don't ask for more than I can give, Noah."

"Please," he said gently. "Please."

The pleading in his voice pulled her head around and she finally met his eyes. "Aren't you forgetting some things about me?"

"I feel them more deeply than anything I've ever felt in my life," he answered. "But nothing changes the fact that I've found you, Maia."

She slid off of the bed, stood up and slowly turned to face him. "Look at me, Noah. Look carefully at my body."

Silently he regarded her, trying to still the quickening he felt at the sight of the rich valleys and plains.

"I thought I knew this skin, these arms, these thighs," she began. "I thought I knew what it meant when I got a stomachache or a sore throat. That every twenty-four days, like clockwork, I'd bleed. That I could cure my colds by eating garlic and drinking hot mint tea. I could eat right and go to the gym and everything would be all right.

"And then there was this trace of blood." She paused. "Wrong time. Wrong color. Wrong everything. And I went straight to my doctor because I knew it was nothing. How could it be anything? I'd never been sick. Never been depressed, or on medication, or addicted to anything or—" Her voice broke but she raised her hand to stop him from moving toward her.

"And then my body became a stranger," she murmured as her arms opened out wide, her nudity cloaked in sadness. "All the things I've wanted—a husband, a family, a chance to be loved—they all just evaporated with that one word: *cancer*. Because Noah, I can't tell you what it was like to nurse my mother through the chemo and radiation. What it was like to watch her starving to death right in front of my eyes. And then to see what passed over the doctors' faces when they asked me if there's a history of cancer in my family."

She inhaled very slowly. "When you talk about me knowing you, or about my knowing myself—well, Noah, the only thing I know is that right now I'm a pilgrim in one of the world's most lonely and pathetic lands. My own dying flesh."

"Oh, Maia," he whispered.

"Everyone tells me to fight. Everyone says that I'm wrong for giving in. But nobody understands that I haven't given in. I just don't know how to begin."

Noah pulled the sheet away and got to his feet. Holding out his hands, he drew her close to his own warm skin. She was shivering despite the heat of the sun, and he pressed her head against his shoulder, rocking her gently.

Something inside him tightened unbearably as he felt her tears and heard the choking sob. He held her closer, and she began to weep. He pressed his face gently against her forehead and rocked her from side to side. And as he stood with her in the morning light, he felt her surrender to the pain, the fear, the hopelessness that had held her enslaved for many lonely months.

Suddenly Noah Langston understood that loving him only brought into focus the grains of sand tumbling through the hourglass of Maia's life. How could he know such pleasure in touching her, when their union only heightened her awareness of her looming death? Making love was meant to create life, yet for Maia, their night of loving was just a marker on her journey toward death.

Feeling tears rise to his own eyes, Noah held her tighter.

He couldn't let this happen! How could he make her choose life? How could he make her desire that ring, hidden away in the secret vault of his own family's history and heritage?

She pulled away from him, wiping her eyes with a courageous, obstinate fist.

"I don't know how to handle what you make me feel," she said with heartbreaking honesty. "Before last night I thought I could keep some kind of balance, some kind of peace with the inevitable. But you—and your mother—are making it so much harder."

"I'm so sorry," he answered, knowing that words alone would never describe the feeling of frustrated helplessness that he, too, was feeling.

Some time later Maia stepped from the shower and pressed her face against the bathroom mirror. Purple shadows formed deep wells beneath her eyes and she noted that her lips were swollen—whether or not from Noah's insistent kisses, she couldn't say. Her hair sent cooling droplets rolling down her shoulder blades to her thighs and she sighed at the memory of Noah's mouth tracing wandering highways on those fertile landscapes. The awakening brought about by his touch had been almost unbearable—as if she were virginal once again, filled with the awful hunger to know the greatest of all mysteries: the sharing of her flesh with another.

He was extraordinarily gentle with her, sometimes flinching as if he were himself wounded by the fierce tenderness of their lovemaking. And yet he never spoke, never shattered the perfect harmony of the sensations they shared. It had been so easy, the way they moved together, the tips of their fingers first drawing the heat away, then sending it crashing back to the pulsing center of their union. He bent to kiss her even when he might have moved away to jealously harbor the intensity of his own pleasure. He brought her with him slowly, carefully, judging by the trembling of her lashes and the music of her breathing, until they came swelling upward and outward, the joy so powerful it bordered on pain.

Maia stared sightlessly into the mirror, still sensing his hips braced between her thighs, still tasting his cool mouth and drenched in the lingering lilt of bay rum. Who was this man who had found her, guided her, taken her away from her drifting? Who had come so close—too close—to the terrified woman who hid herself away behind a wall of strength? Maia felt his growing understanding of her immense loneliness, and the sense that they were One, although fleeting and elusive, once again brought tears to her eyes.

Now she wandered out into her room, glancing only once toward the mattress stripped bare. She bent to gather up the salty sheets and then heard Noah's voice, raised in anger in the hallway below.

"You shouldn't have done that without speaking to me," he was saying as Maia cracked the door softly.

"This has nothing to do with you," Pearl countered, her voice loud, but unflinchingly self-assured.

"She'll only get in the way!"

"That's exactly what I'm counting on!"

"I'm not talking about Maia's illness," Noah asserted in a low, gruff voice. "I'm talking about our relationship."

228 • Heather Neff

"I know exactly what you're talking about," Pearl answered, sliding into angry Crucian dialect. "You plan to keep Catherine in the dark, just in case you want to fly over for a sweet visit!"

"Catherine knows I see other women!"

"She been waiting on you for years!"

"I never gave Cat a reason to wait!"

"Then it won't be hard for you to come clean with her!"

"What's that suppose to mean?"

"Now that you're *finally* in love, you can liberate Catherine to find a future!" Pearl declared triumphantly.

"What I say to Cat is my decision, Mama."

"She not coming here for you, Son. It's Maia who needs her."

"I already called Felix Robertson in St. Thomas."

"Maia will never agree to go there!"

"But Cat can't practice here in St. Croix."

"I'm on the board at the hospital. I've already talked to Vashti Peterson. They will not refuse me."

"All right," he conceded. "But you still should have spoken with me."

"Listen to me," Pearl said in a low voice. "I know how much you've started to care for that girl upstairs. So we're going to get the best for her, and the best is Catherine. I don't care how it makes you feel. You are not important right now."

"How do you know she'll agree to help?"

"She'll do it for you, Noah."

"You expect her to ignore the fact that Maia and I are—"

"I expect you to make it clear to Catherine that you are no longer in love with her."

"And she's supposed to stay and treat her rival?"

"She's a surgeon. You will ask her to practice her profession."

"And if she decides to catch the next plane?"

"Then you'll use the same skills of persuasion on her that you use in the courtroom. After all," Pearl added, "you've convinced quite a few other women do to exactly what you want!"

"So when is she arriving?" he asked after a pause.

"Seven o'clock. You go pick her up. You talk to her. You ask her to help."

"Mama—"

"What's wrong with you?" Pearl shouted, walking back into her kitchen. "You're a lawyer, Noah! You scared to ask a doctor to do her job?"

Defeated, he grunted and Maia heard the front door of the house open and close. Her heart banging in her chest, she met the tears that had already poured into her mouth, down along her chin, and onto her breasts with a sad, lonely moan.

"What in the hell is this?"

Paulette stood in the doorway to the great room, her eyes taking in the scene with icy disbelief. Behind her Mimi shook her head and turned away, throwing a towel resolutely over her shoulder as she vanished into the kitchen.

From within the darkened room came a slow stirring followed by a deep, bitter groan.

"Holy fuck," Severin rasped, pushing his wasted chest up between his chicken elbows. "If it isn't Queen Bitch."

From beneath and behind him the bronze curls trembled and a long leg emerged from a tangle of grayed sheets. Severin glanced over in surprise, and chuckled ironically as his memory of the woman crystalized.

"Well," he finally said. "Here we are."

"Are you both out of your minds?" Paulette nearly shouted. "It's two in the afternoon and this place smells like a pigsty!"

"Oh, forgive us," Severin retorted. "We forget we have an audience with royalty today."

"Bianca! What do you think you're doing?" Paulette's eyes narrowed at the sight of the young woman vainly trying to cover her naked rear with her Godiva hair.

"You send her to me. You find her with me," Severin replied.

"This is disgusting!" Paulette continued, ignoring him.

230 • Heather Neff

"Don' talk like that to my little sweetheart," Severin sneered. "You'll hurt her feelings."

Paulette took a step into the room, closing the door firmly on Mimi's listening ears.

"Even if you enjoy living like this, you should keep your filthy hands where you know they belong!"

He burst into raucous laughter. "Mimi! Mimi! Can you hear what she say, *meson*? She thinks my hands only good enough for the likes of Tina and *you*!"

Something clattered loudly in the kitchen and Paulette took two more steps forward to speak in a harsh whisper.

"Don't try to twist what I'm saying, Severin! This woman is no slut for you to use and throw away. She's a guest on our island and you should show her some respect!"

He laughed again. "I don't hear nothing from this side of the bed," he added, reaching behind him to grasp and shake Bianca's thigh. "I think she likes it with me."

There was a long silence as they waited for some response. Finally Bianca swallowed hard and peered up through her curls at Paulette.

"Sorry I missed our lunch date," she said with a touch of sarcasm.

Paulette squinted to assess the young woman's subtly stubborn tone. Quickly she noted that Bianca had not reacted to Severin's rudeness. In fact, she hardly seemed moved by the fact that she'd been discovered wallowing in his filthy, reeking bed.

"You both make me sick," Paulette said haughtily, and turned abruptly on her heel. Severin laughed out loud, but Bianca took the bait, calling out for the older woman to wait.

Soon a half-dressed figure staggered out to the winding drive. Paulette was leaning on the Mercedes, her cigarette ashed to her knuckles. Dark mirror lenses hid her raging eyes, and she looked the younger woman over with measured restraint.

"I don't care if you're sleeping with Severin," Paulette announced before Bianca could speak. "But don't expect me to lie to my brother about it."

"Clay doesn't give a shit about me," Bianca answered, using her palm to shield her aching eyes from the meridian sun.

"Neither does Severin," Paulette replied plainly.

"Well, at least Severin knows I'm alive."

"All he knows is what you've got beneath your underwear," Paulette snapped. "And he's been with enough women to be an expert on that."

"I'll take my chances."

"What chances?"

"I have nothing to lose with Severin."

"No, Bianca. You have nothing to gain with him." Paulette tossed her cigarette butt into the grape leaves and folded her arms across her chest. "What exactly do you want? Severin's certainly no Prince Charming. Although you may be on some kind of Beauty-and-the-Beast trip—"

"I'm not in love with him!" Bianca said acidly.

"And he doesn't have any money, which should be fairly obvious."

"I'm no whore."

"That remains a matter of conjecture," Paulette responded dryly. "There's only one thing you could be aiming for: Wisdom."

Bianca tried to throw back her head defiantly but Paulette snorted and focused her blazing gaze on the younger woman. "Let me tell you something, little girl. I grew up on this island. I know every inch of this property. Every plank on that house. Every tree, bush, and rock. And I know Severin."

She stared at Bianca without blinking. "Wisdom was never intended to be his," she explained. "It was all meant for Peter, his older brother. Peter knew what it meant to be a Johanssen. He understood the responsibilities of carrying on our lineage."

"Severin's not too old to have children—" Bianca began, but Paulette continued to speak over her.

"Severin is going to let all of this crumble into dust for reasons that you can't understand."

Bianca shook her head slowly. "I don't know what you're talking about."

"It's because of our past. Because of things that happened before we were even born—"

"Are you trying to say that you're cursed or something?"

"I'm trying to tell you that you will never be able to change the man that Severin has become. The best thing that could happen would be to let the estate pass into Clay's hands—or mine—so that we could oversee it properly."

"And you're afraid that if he gets interested in me you might never get control of it?"

Paulette removed her glasses slowly and looked down at Bianca.

"Right now, Severin is only interested in screwing you. Chances are that soon he won't even be interested in that. And at the rate he's drinking, he won't live long enough to marry you or anyone else."

Bianca glanced quickly up toward the house, catching her lower lip between her teeth. Paulette laughed for the first time. "I understand. You're just trying to get the timing right. Let's see: How much alcohol would it take to get him to marry you before he dies? Making big plans, aren't you?"

"Isn't that why you brought me here?"

"I brought you here because you asked to see the house. And once I realized that his so-called nurse had taken off, I thought I should check up on him more often."

"Well, maybe I'm doing the same."

Paulette steeled herself and once again covered her eyes. When she spoke, her voice had fallen an octave. "I don't care how often you visit him, or how much you drink with him, or how easy you make it for him to screw you. You may be planning to get rich by marrying Severin and selling Wisdom to developers. But Wisdom will never, ever be yours."

When the car door slammed, Mimi moved back from the rotting jalousies where Bianca's fractured image jigsawed its way back toward the house. The young woman passed the kitchen without looking inside, unconcerned by the black housekeeper's presence.

In the great room Severin had once again drifted off to sleep, his ravaged body ghostly in the sweltering shadows. Bianca stood above him for a long appraising moment, then gently shook him awake and offered him a tumbler of rum from a half-emptied bottle.

* * *

Pearl watched both Noah and Maia leave the house within minutes of each other, and her heart fluttered at the thought that each of them drove away with a private bitterness, though no words had been spoken between them.

Perhaps Maia's hurt bloomed in the fact that Noah hadn't climbed the stairs to see her after the argument with his mother, despite what they'd shared the night before. Or perhaps it was because Maia herself needed to take her freedom, rather than waiting like a princess in a tower for her prince to return. In any case, Maia had certainly seen her lover climb into his car, seating himself carefully to avoid soiling his fine attire. She had certainly realized that he was doing everything in his power not to glance up at her window overhead. And Pearl was not naive enough to think that their guest hadn't heard at least part of their shouting match over Catherine. Although angry and disappointed by her son's behavior, she was more immediately concerned with how Maia might respond.

Pearl tried to understand exactly what Maia would be feeling about it all. Because after all, she had come to St. Croix prepared to accept death as an imminent reality to be met with quiet dignity. She had never asked for medical help or emotional support. She had borne her illness with great courage and self-respect. It was the Langston mother and son who had exhorted her to struggle against it. And now Maia knew that Noah still had feelings for the doctor Pearl had summoned to help her.

So when she left the house that evening, dressed in dark clothes and moving with steely determination, Pearl prayed that her desperate attempt to change destiny had not already been in vain. What could she do? She needed to protect Maia—and Noah, for that matter—from any harm that might befall them. Determined to find some way to help, she moved into her cool, glass drawing room and picked up the phone directory.

"Vashti?"

"Miss Pearl?" The head nurse's voice rose in surprise at the unexpected call. "Is Miss Ransom all right?"

"Yes, thank you. But I thought I'd better confirm that she'll be

234 • Heather Neff

coming in for a complete physical, tomorrow. Doctor Catherine Cole-man will be arriving from Virgin Gorda to take charge of the examina-tions."

"Ah," Vashti said softly. "I remember meeting Dr. Coleman when she toured the hospital with you just after the hurricane."

"Yes," Pearl said. "She was instrumental in getting us those portable X-ray machines, if you remember."

"Yes I do. As a matter of fact," Vashti said, "I'm glad you called. You're not the only person who's concerned about her well-being, you know."

Pearl shifted the phone to her other ear and sat down on her wicker love seat. "Really, Vashti? Have other people been asking for her?"

"Mimi—well, she takes care of Seven Johanssen out at Wisdom—came by my house yesterday to ask after Miss Ransom. Mimi was afraid that she had been done serious harm when Tina attacked her."

Pearl's heart sped up, but she managed to hide her surprise. "Was it Tina, then?" she asked, her mind flicking quickly through the catalog of children she'd taught during her many years in Crucian classrooms. Yes—she found the file and pulled out the image of the yellow-eyed girl distinguished by her almost predatory cruelty. Pearl recalled the teen fighting with other girls over so little as a lost plastic comb. It came as no surprise that she might attack Maia, now. And especially if it came to Wisdom. Why hadn't Noah told her the truth?

"Where is Tina, Vashti?"

"She left the house when Miss Ransom came to care for Seven. She's off and on at the estate, now. But Brandy—you remember her? She runs the bar down on the waterfront in Christiansted—tells me Tina's been staying with a 'new friend' from time to time."

Pearl understood Vashti's euphenism to mean that like any dis-placed house pet, Tina was sleeping wherever she could.

"Miss Pearl," Vashti went on, "I hope that Miss Ransom realizes how serious Tina and her brother are about Seven and Wisdom," she said quietly. "Brandy hears them talking about her with that fisherman Juan every day. Brandy has known Tina since they were girls, and if Brandy is worried, there is good reason to be afraid."

"Well," Pearl said with an anxious look at the wall clock, "I'll certainly let Miss Ransom know that she should be on her guard for Tina and her friends. If all goes well, we'll see you early tomorrow morning."

The phone in its cradle, Pearl stood up restlessly and wondered how long it would take Noah to return. And how they would manage to find Maia.

The palms were casting violet shadows in the quickly fading light when Noah slid his sedan into a slot on the outer edge of the airport parking lot. The plane had just arrived and he'd seen the attendants wheeling the portable staircase out to the machine as he approached the hangar. He had to jog the distance from his car to the airport entrance, cursing silently at the thought that he'd look like a sweat-stained building contractor when Catherine cleared Customs.

Catherine Coleman. Cat. It had been two, almost three years. And then some. Because the last time they'd parted he'd made some promises he simply hadn't been able—or maybe *willing*—to keep. Like coming over to visit her in England. Or thinking about opening an office on Virgin Gorda. Or scouting out the possibility for her to set up her own practice on St. Croix.

Travelers were already emerging from the open terminal when he pushed past the line of waiting taxi drivers, and he had to peer through a thick group of seersucker Americans before spotting the figure leaning casually against a pillar, reading a magazine.

She turned when he called out to her, glancing over from beneath a wide-brimmed straw hat and tortoiseshell sunglasses. He saw that she was wearing a loose dress of rust-toned linen; that she was sporting a single leather suitcase; and that she was poised and calm and as breathtakingly fine as ever.

When he bent to kiss her, his lips were met with her full copper mouth, and she threw her arms around him with warmth.

"Well, Noah," she remarked with her lovely British accent, "at least you haven't forgotten how to do that."

"Some things just come naturally," he answered, hoisting up her bag.

"I guess the Crucian girls do keep you in practice." She laughed and took his arm. "I'm glad to see you, you monster. I shouldn't be speaking to you at all. And here I am, leaving London just when the director of the local hospital was on his knees and about to propose. Just so I could come here and listen to some more of your empty promises!"

They paused at the entrance to the terminal and Catherine scanned the parking lot. "Let's see: It will be the biggest and the shiniest. And it will be parked the farthest away from the local wrecks. Ahh—" her dark eyes alighted on the BMW. "Since there's no Jag present, I guess that other rolling bank account must be yours!"

She held on to him tightly as they crossed the wide expanse of concrete. A furious airplane lifted heavily off the runway behind the terminal, drowning out all other sound for a few moments. Noah had forgotten how easily Catherine fit into this world, and how it always felt as if she'd never left when she returned, no matter how long it had been.

In the car she swept off her hat to reveal her hair tucked into a loose knot at the nape of her neck. She began to chat about the long flight from England, and how glad she'd been to return to her mother's house on Virgin Gorda. She inquired after Pearl, his most recent court cases, the reconstruction of the island since the last hurricane. And then, without a moment's hesitation, she looked him straight in the face and took a big bite.

"So whose heart are you breaking at the moment?"

Noah cleared his throat and kept his eyes on the road. "It's been rather quiet, really," he began, but Catherine burst into laughter.

"Is that why your mother called so suddenly? Did she think it might be the proper time to try and convince her errant son to settle down?"

Noah shot her an uneasy glance and found her looking at him curiously. "Your silence is starting to worry me," she said, her British accent elongating the words.

"There's nothing to worry about," Noah said smoothly. "And my mother will never stop matchmaking me. But—" He paused, choosing his words carefully. "I think there's another reason why she wanted you to come over right now."

"She's not ill, is she?" Catherine reached over and touched his arm in concern.

"No, no of course not. Pearl DeWindt Langston survived eighteen hurricanes, thirty years of teaching Crucian urchins, and nearly forty years of marriage to my father. Now that she's finally a happily retired widow, the last thing she'll ever do is let herself get sick!"

They both laughed. "Actually," he said in a light voice, "my mother wanted you to take a look at someone else," he said.

Catherine's eyebrows shot up. "Don't tell me that after all these years of trying to make me give up my practice and accept the quiet life of a solicitor's wife, she suddenly wants me to prove I really did finish medical school!"

Noah ignored her sarcasm. "Mama worked every day of her marriage, and would never expect you to give up your profession, Cat."

"But everyone knows that teaching is the most *noble* profession. Especially for mothers." She snorted coolly. "But doctoring: Now, there's an element of the grotesque. So much blood, and gore, and so many unclothed bodies. And for a woman to actually become a surgeon—well, I'd say that's nothing short of *hubris*!"

"My mother has always had great respect for your gifts. That's why," he added quietly, "she asked you to come over right now."

Catherine sighed. "So this is work, not play. All right: Who is it?"

"A tenant of ours. A woman who's living in Precious's rooms at the house."

"Have you taken her to hospital?"

"Not yet. There's no one on the staff who can treat her."

"You know I've taken the oath and all, but this is my holiday, Noah."

"It would mean a lot if you'd examine her. She's very important—" he cleared his throat "—to a lawsuit I'm about to file. The biggest case I've taken on yet. I really need her to be involved in this."

Catherine glanced at the sea, just a blue stripe laid flat on the top of the sand dunes. "So this is about a lawsuit?" she asked, her voice level.

"Yes," Noah answered.

"A lawsuit that will make you even richer and more desirable?"

"Certainly," he answered, keeping his eyes on the highway.

"Then of course I'll do it," she said. "But only for your mother, Noah."

They drove a while in silence, with Catherine pushing loose hairs out of her eyes. She seemed genuinely happy to be back on St. Croix as she looked for familiar landmarks along the way.

"You know, you haven't asked me the first question about London!" she said suddenly.

"Sorry. I was thinking about the case."

"Oh, my. It must really be important if you can't make small talk with the woman you've been stringing along for years!" she laughed, but he knew that she was serious.

"I'm glad to see you, Cat," he said, his words sounding more formal than he intended. "And you look more beautiful than ever."

"Remind me never to ask for a letter of recommendation from you," she replied. "That was positively the least complimentary compliment I've ever had!"

"Do you need yet another compliment? You already know that you're brilliant, beautiful, and amazingly accomplished."

She laughed. "I'm also not quite kinky enough to grab Noah Langston's attention and keep it, though I've been trying for years."

"Maybe I'm just not worth it," he said.

"I suppose that could be the case," she said. "But I suspect that I've just never gotten my timing right. I mean, you were just over your Ethiopian friend when we met, right? And then there was that young lady from—"

"That was a long while ago, Cat."

"I know, baby. But that's really been the long and short of it. I fell in love with you the first time I laid eyes on you, and you fall in love with me each time we meet. The only problem is that I go on loving you, and you forget me as soon as my plane is out of sight."

Noah was very relieved when they reached the top of the hill and mounted the drive to the house. He noticed that the Jeep wasn't there, but momentarily arrested by his mother's figure at the open door, he didn't have time to think about where Maia might have gone.

* * *

She had sworn she wouldn't do it, and during the daytime her promise had currency. Now that night was falling, however, she could no longer fight the other woman who still seemed to be waiting in the shadows of her daylight self.

Maia began to vanish in the growing dusk, and that hidden woman struggled to take her place. Gripping the scalloped wheel of the rusty rented Jeep, Maia strained to hear the sea above the roar of the engine, and she wished that she had wrapped a cloth around her hair to keep the road dust at bay. A head wrap would have been ideal. A head wrap like the one her great-great-grandmother Zara Ransom wore when she appeared to Maia in her dreams.

The potholed asphalt threw her back and forth as she fought to stay on the road, twisting and turning her way along the darkening cliffs, toward the hills of Wisdom.

She left the Jeep on the side of the road and climbed to the edge of the property, only to find a silvery new barbed-wire fence segmenting Wisdom from the rest of the world. She ran her fingers along the sharp teeth, testing and weighing them, then scaled the low brick wall and stepped carefully over the wire. She knew that even if getting in was easy, exiting the estate would be another story, for the wall was much steeper on the other side, and there were no large rocks to use as stairs. She also knew that Tina roamed the estate at night, waiting and hoping for some sign from Severin. Back when she was taking care of her patient, Maia had often seen the woman moving restlessly in the shadows beyond the balcony.

And yet something in the air told her that Tina wouldn't be there. Or, at least, that she wasn't there. Yet.

Why am I doing this? Maia thought as she took a cautious step forward, finding the landscape much rougher and more dangerous in the twilight. She also found that the air was much sweeter, as if saturated by the quaint perfume of white roses. But there were no roses near the great house—no one had tended the gardens there for decades—and she hadn't noticed any during her other forbidden peregrinations across the estate.

Why did I come tonight? As always, her path led her up the steep incline to the ruined mill and the rocky cliff that overlooked the sea. The stone silo stood dark and forbidding in the quickly falling night, as if standing guard over her hidden past. Breathing heavily, she crested the cliffs and reached the boulder where she often sat to sing. She gazed out at the endless indigo that decorated the newly starred horizon. Lifting her arms to let the evening breeze cool her wet flesh, she realized only then that the air was hushed and heavy and absolutely still. Even the crickets had halted their reedy song.

It was the hush that made her listen so intently to the tumbling night. A night so heavy that even the sea held back, its waves breaking soundlessly on the rocks below. Maia sensed it again—white roses—and she stepped behind her singing stone, where she was invisible from the mill above. Then, within seconds, she learned why she had been called back to Wisdom, and why she'd been summoned with the falling night.

Severin's drunken steps were strangely assured in the darkness, as if he'd traced that path a thousand times before. He was muttering, speaking to another person who wasn't there. Maia could clearly make out the words in the tense darkness, and she poised herself even more carefully to better understand what he was saying.

"Of course the little golden mare, yes," he laughed as he moved toward the stone silo. "Pretends she likes the steed! Well, it's foals she wants; foals to fill the corrals and stables."

He paused, hardly able to draw breath after the steep climb from the beach below.

"Yes, brother. She want Wisdom for herself. Want to be mistress of the manor!" He gave a low, dirty laugh. "But you know, being greedy chokes the puppy! I make her pay for it, Peter. Make her pay the price for taking the place of the Ransom."

Maia froze. Severin stumbled and paused to find his balance, still mumbling. "The little blonde mare don't like it up here, Pete. Won't come for an evening walk with me, her beloved. Say it's haunted. She scared of ghosts, Pete. Can you imagine that?"

Another chuckle escaped his lips, and he cursed softly. "Don't none of them love Wisdom, really. None of them but her. The nurse. And she scared because it take her too close. Moth in a flame. Coming closer and closer and then pulling away."

He shuffled forward again, and Maia peered around the boulder in time to see him enter the mill's dark silo.

"Peter!" he suddenly yelled, his voice echoing weirdly in the enclosed space. "Pete! Why you want to go away and leave me with this? Don't you know I can't be like you, brother?"

He broke into roaring laughter that quickly disintegrated into a series of choking sounds that Maia recognized as despairing sobs. "I'm not strong, Peter! It's too much for me. I hurt, Peter. I don't want to be alive no more!"

Maia listened to the man's tortured tears, wrenched from deep within his failing body and flung outward to a silent, blackening night. The moon had risen and a white light was turning the world into a photo-negative reality—all color bleached away, and all form visible only by the shadows imprinted on the darkness.

Severin seemed to have climbed to his feet, for now he grunted heavily and moved around inside the mill.

"I know what to do," he grunted to himself. "End it all, right now. Be finished with the bullshit secrets. The fucking lies. Make sure nobody gets it. Not that pussy Bianca. Not that bitch Paulette. Not her pansy brother and not her asshole husband. None of them. Not even the Ransom. Nobody—" he began mumbling inarticulately.

She heard things shifting—rocks being pushed with desperate exertion—and once he cried out as if he had injured himself. At last she heard a rustling, the sound of very old papers being carefully unfolded, followed by his irritated muttering.

"I burn it all, Pete. I burn it and no one ever know. You say destroy it twenty years ago, but Severin too drunk to listen. Nobody know a goddamn thing, eh, Pete?"

His voice had gained a mocking anger and he was neither laughing nor crying. She heard another sound, like the fevered flicking of a cigarette lighter. "Burn it and be finish. Burn it, like you say back then, Pete. I listen to you now!"

Maia heard the tip of the lighter snap and snap. She sensed

Severin's silent concentration. She felt the hot wind pick up, scratching the dried scrub against the rocks. The scent of roses grew so intense that for a moment she felt dizzy. Severin was muttering and the lighter was snapping and the wind keened low in the shimmering grape leaves.

She suddenly knew that he had it. The paper they were looking for. The document that would prove, once and for all, that Abraham Ransom was the legal heir to Wisdom. It was there, in the mill. It was inches from the cigarette lighter in Severin's shaking hands.

Fear exploded in Maia's chest and she felt herself stumble forward, her eyes groping for a path through the scattered rocks to the yawning entrance of the darkened mill. She saw an angry spark in the blackness of the tower and Severin cursed, furiously ruffling the papers. Maia scrambled up the steep incline, smashing her fingers on falling stone and scraping her knees against a gnarled tree stump. She was only a few feet away when her ankle twisted beneath her and she cried out, her voice soaked up weirdly by the wind.

Severin shouted something unintelligible. She heard the lighter clatter to the rocks, exit the mill, and bounce end to tip down the steep incline toward the cliff below. Then there was nothing. Severin's silence at the mouth of the silo above was well-deep and complete as he listened, uncertain if what he'd heard was real.

"You there, Tina?" He tried the night softly. "Tina, don't play, now."

Maia lay unmoving, hidden by the night, her breath a tightrope against the muscles of her heart.

Severin jerked forward, his sickly white silhouette emerging in the silo's opening. "Eh, Tina? Come on, *meson*. Tell me it's you."

These words were followed by a long, uncertain pause. Abruptly he turned, again launching himself into the darkness of the mill. Maia heard furtive scraping and a firm grunt as he moved the stones inside, and she crept sideways until she was hidden in a thick patch of grape leaves. When he again appeared in the opening she could see that he was dripping in sweat, his face blackened with dirt and his hair stiff and greasy.

Now silent, he wavered a bit, unsteady on his feet. There was fear in his face and an emptiness in his being that she had once mistaken for his illness. Now she knew, as he stumbled forward, working his way like a spider toward the house, that Severin was a man of calculated destructiveness and deliberately inflicted cruelty.

Carefully she crawled to the top of the hill, reaching the mouth of the mill in seconds. Ignoring the dust, dirt, and total darkness, she stepped inside and dropped to her hands and knees, hoping against all hope that he had forgotten to hide even a shred of what he had come to destroy.

Her knees banged against rocks and her hands were scraped bloody as she frantically grabbed at the cold, rough walls. She pulled at stones, hoping to dislodge some secret hiding place. Her nails broke and the skin of her knuckles tore in the darkness. Blinded, desperate, despairing more with each passing moment, she dug and pressed and pulled at the stones until she could have screamed her frustration into the blackness.

But there was nothing.

And she was helpless, digging for something she had never seen in a place that was lonely and dangerous, even in the daylight.

Daylight.

Maia knew she'd have to come back in the daylight. When she'd have a fighting chance to discover what secrets the mill would offer. No matter what the danger.

Brandy saw the danger.

When the seventh beer bottle rolled off the table and crashed on the deck, her last group of Statesiders had risen from their table and moved away, shaking their heads in disgust. In return, Juan had held up an unsteady middle finger, muttering something in Spanish. Carlson only laughed. And Tina, her head buried in her arms, was already too far gone to care.

"Listen!" Brandy began in a hard whisper, "You all need to—"

She was surprised at the insult hurled back at her by Juan, whose face was clutched up in a kind of rage that bordered on hatred. Using her most calming voice, she walked toward the table. "It's time to go home now."

"Suck my dick, you filthy white man's bitch!" Juan growled as he rose to his feet to face her.

She took a step backward, retreating slowly behind her counter and preparing herself for the first time in her twelve years of running the bar to use the gun hidden in the rear of a cabinet.

"Ah, chill out, Juan," Carlson said to his friend, reaching across the table to shake his arm. "Let's just go. Come on, *vamanos*!"

Juan peeled his eyes from Brandy's tense figure, glared at Carlson for a beat, then looked slowly and deliberately toward Tina.

"What you gonna do with this tub of lard, man? She weigh two hundred pound. I not going to carry her."

Carlson shrugged at his snoring sister's doughnut shoulders and flicked his cigarette out into the night. "Leave her. Brandy wake her up when she close. Or maybe," he sneered, "some white gentleman offer her his room for tonight."

"You cannot leave Tina here like that!" Brandy cried. "You got to get her home, Carlson."

"You shut up, Brandy! We got things to do," Juan replied. "When we finish, then we come back for Tina."

Brandy watched in dismay as the two rose unsteadily and slouched across the deck. They had consumed eighteen bottles of beer between them, paid nothing, and driven her other guests away. And they had left a pathetic human souvenir behind.

Brandy crossed the deck and began shaking Tina's shoulders. The woman stirred, reaching out blindly and nearly knocking another empty bottle to the floor. Brandy grabbed at her, pulling her upright.

"Tina! You got to wake up!"

Tina's swollen lids slid open and her golden eyes, bathed in scarlet, sought Brandy's.

"You here, sister. You here," she muttered, her head rolling forward.

"Try to get up. I go get you a room," Brandy said. "You chase all my guests away."

Tina laughed. "Got a cigarette, Brandy?"

"Get up, Tina. Try to walk, *meson*. You need to lay down."

"Why I walk if I need lay down?" Tina laughed again.

"What wrong with Juan and Carlson? Why they leave you here like that?" Brandy asked in exasperation, not expecting a reply.

"I in de way," Tina muttered through thickened lips. "They don't want me there when it happen. But I tell them I want to see. I have a right to see."

"See what?"

"See them get that bitch," Tina murmured, her eyes narrowing despite her semi-blackout.

"Who you talking about?"

"That yellow-hair bitch Seven play with. That bitch Seven sleep with." Tina's features crumbled and she let out a sob. "Seven don't love me, Brandy. Seven don't want me no more!"

Brandy stood up straight, making sense of what Tina was saying. The men were on their way to Wisdom. They were going after that young woman from Canada—the one Paulette brought to Seven after Maia abruptly went away!

Brandy knew this meant trouble, because there was no one out at Wisdom after Mimi closed up her kitchen for the night. No one, that is, except the weakened, ailing man, and the young woman herself. And Brandy knew that whether Severin actually cared for the young woman or not, he would never permit Juan and Carlson to come onto his estate and take anything from him. Least of all a woman.

Brandy thought fast, her mind reeling with the various possible outcomes.

Both men were drunk. But Juan was drunk and enraged. And she had seen Juan like this in the past, when his anger touched the hot fuse of his inebriation. When he was capable of anything.

Carlson was likely to carry out Juan's orders without question.

And Severin? By now he was probably drunk, as well. And he was in no condition to fight with either of the men—and certainly not with *both* of them—over that woman.

And what about that woman?

Brandy had seen her, as had most of the island, flitting her way through both the highs and the lows of island society. The Crucians were used to women like that: Women who came over from the States craving the travel poster promises of unlimited sun and sea, and the television fantasies of romance with rich white men and beautiful black men, under the Caribbean sun. Most of them stayed the winter, and vanished with the next season's tide.

Many handsome women had shared the beds of Severin, Juan, and even Carlson. Many met their island lovers in Brandy's Bar. Some of the luckier ones had managed to find their way into the island's money-eyed elite—like this young woman, who'd been Clay Johanssen's escort for a time.

But her move to become the Mistress of Wisdom had been a miscalculation that only an outsider could make. For everyone knew that Seven's bed was only for short adventures—not for women who planned to come and stay. The moment she declared herself a candidate for a permanent position she had gained more enemies than she could have imagined. From her evening porch Mimi had vividly described the young woman's drunken nudity, adding that Tina often watched from her station in the bushes.

So who would protect her, now, from the likes of Carlson and Juan? Brandy didn't much care what they did to her. Brandy's only fear was what they might do to Seven in the process. For even if Seven had truly abandoned Tina for this Canadian whore, Brandy still could not forget the nights they had spent together, when he touched her with a gentleness that almost let her forget how alone she was.

There was no phone at Wisdom. No way to warn him of the men's cruel mission. And she had no car. She couldn't abandon her bar, anyway, even if those fools had driven all her customers away. And there sat Tina, barely holding her head up, a stupid grin on her face.

Brandy looked around frantically, trying to think of a way to put things right before they could go too terribly wrong. And then someone walked around the corner and asked with a sigh, "Am I too late for one of your rum punch specials tonight, fine lady?"

THREE DAYS

The phone rang just as Cat emerged from her room, feeling much refreshed after a cold, cold shower. She was starting to think she should get right back on the plane. After all, it was clear that even if they needed her, nobody really wanted her to be there.

Noah's mother had hugged her hard, almost knocking her straw hat from her head, then pushed her away with the comment: "You still haven't found anybody to cook for you in all of London, Catherine? You're way too bony, sweetheart!"

"No time to eat, I guess. My work keeps me—"

"From meeting the right man!" Pearl threw a menacing look toward her son, who cleared his throat theatrically and swept out of the foyer, Catherine's leather bag on his shoulder. Cat noted his anxious glance toward the upstairs apartment, and understood his desire to remove himself from his mother's range of fire.

"Momma was really sorry she couldn't come with me, Aunt Pearl," she said pleasantly. "She's in charge of a huge wedding next week and nothing has arrived yet from London. She told me to tell you that she'll be over as soon as she can get here."

The two women walked into the spacious living room, practically overflowing with delicate blown-glass birds and framed photographs of the Langston kin.

"You've done a lot with this room since my last visit," Catherine said by way of compliment.

"All these things are old!" Pearl declared. "You just don't remember them, dear!"

"But the house is really lovely," Catherine insisted, and Pearl put her arm around the younger woman.

"Your own mother came over to help with the curtains, Catherine. She stayed an entire week and we made them together, like in our school days. Gave us lots of time to talk about our busy, successful children!"

"I don't believe that. All Momma wants me to do is come home and get married."

"All we want is for both of you to find the right person," Pearl said. "We understand how vexing that can be."

There was general laughter, but Cat could feel the tension like lead wind chimes in the air. She sensed Noah standing behind them, but when she glanced around he turned away, moving toward the stairs.

"Don't bother," his mother called out. "She left an hour ago. I don't know to where. And I don't think that things were right."

"I think I know where she went," he said darkly, but his mother shook her head.

"Maybe she needs some time to think, that's all."

"But if she went to Wisdom?"

Pearl's face tightened, then she shook her head. "Lord, I hope she's not so crazy."

Cat looked from mother to son, growing more annoyed with each exchange. Finally she turned and walked out to the screened porch, leaving Pearl and Noah alone. When Pearl joined her a few moments later, the two women stood silently, side by side.

"Noah said your guest is instrumental in a very important lawsuit," Catherine remarked to the falling night.

"Yes," Pearl affirmed quietly.

"And she has something the local doctors can't treat."

"Yes," Pearl repeated.

"And I suppose you're keeping her here because she's in some kind of danger?"

"Yes," Pearl said, her answer both simple and evasive.

"Do you want to tell me anything else?"

"Yes," Pearl replied, "but I think I'll wait until you meet her."

They waited. No one admitted that they were waiting, but throughout their late supper and into the real blackness of the night the trio found it impossible to relax. Noah asked her dutifully about her friends and Pearl asked her about her work, and they all shared stories about life on the island, but both of the Langstons were listening for something—the sound of a car, or the phone, or a step, or the doorbell. Finally Catherine began listening, too, although she didn't really know why.

Then, as the hands on the clock approached midnight, she excused herself and went to her shower, stripping off her clothes and bathing cold to clear her thoughts. And to put some clarity on her emotions.

Noah had aged in the two years since she'd seen him. But the aging had done some serious good. He had ripened, matured, mellowed in indescribable ways. He seemed to have learned the value of silence—of listening rather than working so damned hard to hear the sound of his own voice. And he was dressing so differently! Gone were those absurd button-downs that he had worn after his return from New England, even when at home in the evening. And he had let his hair grow in a bit, softening the stark African structure of his handsome face.

But the greatest change was in his eyes. Eyes that had lied with practiced dexterity, making and breaking promises in a single, sensuous blink. Even their expression had deepened, growing unusually pensive and—dare she imagine? Almost caring.

Eyes that— *So who the hell was this mysterious guest?*

Noah had left his meal untouched, and Pearl hadn't even scolded him about it. When the first tape finished on the stereo, no one changed it. The ice melted in the iced tea. The rice grew rubbery and the steaks blackened on the grill. After the stories they told to fill up the silence left by the empty place at the table, they couldn't think of anything else to say.

So after getting her fill of their oppressing awkwardness, Cat took it to the cold water of her shower.

And then, she heard the phone. She stepped to the threshold of her room, still rubbing her hair with a hand towel, and looked upon a kind of chaos.

Noah was slapping at his pants pockets, frantically searching for his keys. His feet were thrust into his sandals, but the straps were still undone. The silk shirt he was wearing was stained black with a substance that might have been coffee. And he was so preoccupied with his missing keys that when their eyes met he practically jumped in surprise.

"Good God, Cat! I almost forgot you're here! There's been some kind of accident—or attack—I don't know which. I just got a call—"

She lowered her arm, remaining steady. "Do you want me to come?"

"Yes, please. I don't know how bad she—it—is. Could you come right away? I'll pull the car to the front."

Catherine returned to her room and pulled a small first-aid kit from her leather bag. As silly as it seemed, she had grown up in the Caribbean and she knew that things such as sterile bandages were never easily found when you needed them fast. So she packed her little kit, like a dutiful girl ranger, whenever she traveled.

By the time she arrived at the front door Noah was already waiting. Pearl was standing outside, her hands clenched together. Cat climbed into the car and looked back at the older woman's face and saw tears. This houseguest, whoever she was, really had to be something to make the likes of Pearl Langston weep.

Noah said nothing as they wove their way through the jetty blackness of the night. And Catherine could see nothing of the neighbors' houses, for they too were tucked far back up into the thickly screened hills. The pockmarked asphalt dipped and twisted, and if Noah had not known the way so well, Cat would have been afraid.

When they reached the bottom of the hill he turned to the northwest—the opposite direction from the hospital.

"I thought we were headed to town," she said.

"I wish we were," was his cryptic reply.

Although Cat had visited St. Croix many times, there were areas of the island that she had never seen. The road Noah selected followed a tortuous path toward the barren stretch of coastline known as Maroon Ridge. They could hear the surf, slow and sullen in the darkness.

"Who lives out here?" Cat asked, more to gauge the extent of his tension than to get an answer.

"The man we're planning to sue," he answered, never taking his eyes from the road.

"Then why would your guest come to this place?"

Noah's jaw tightened. "Because," he mumbled, "I let her down."

It seemed like a long time before they came around a final bend in the twisting, broken road. What they discovered was a scene from a horror film: a car pulled askew and open-trunked, its emergency lights blinking wildly. Two figures kneeling beside a third that was stretched out on the road and covered with a soiled, bloody cloth. Catherine was certain she was looking at a hit-and-run mortality.

Noah cursed and pulled his own car up beside them. He hit the instrument panels and leaped out, running into the hot white arcs of his headlights. Cat followed him, already assessing the situation.

"What the fuck happened?" Noah shouted as he bent down beside the figure. "Did that goddamned asshole do this?"

"What fucking difference does it make?" a skeletal figure barked back. The third person, a woman in some kind of lacy costume, glanced up while shaking her head.

"We find her like this. They already gone."

"Who, they?" Noah yelled.

"The men who done this." She said the words with the certainty of actual knowledge, and as Cat pressed close, the other woman stood slowly and moved away.

Carefully Catherine touched the shoulder of the fallen figure. The body was pulled up into a fetal position, the clothes ripped and stained, the face already blackening from a beating. Shards of glass were stuck in her cheeks and lips, and the hand she was lying on was probably broken. Catherine's fingers moved skillfully to the base of the throat, the neck, then the spine, feeling, judging, evaluating.

"Is she all right?" the skeleton asked, his voice wavering under his show of strength.

"Let me have a little more space," Catherine said softly, and she reached down to cradle the blood-smeared face.

Noah looked up. "Why are you here?" he almost screamed at Damian.

"Me? Why is *Maia* here?" Damian screamed back, his face twisted in rage. "You were supposed to be taking care of her!"

"My home is not a prison and Maia's no one's slave!" Noah answered stupidly, but Damian hardly gave him time to finish.

"I knew you were trouble as soon as I saw you! I knew exactly what you wanted from her! Maia only came here to find her home—she never wanted to get involved in any stupid fucking lawsuit—"

"Be quiet, both of you!" Cat ordered. The victim was beginning to stir.

Carefully, the doctor assisted the injured woman to turn over. Maia let out a deep groan, her head rolling in the dirt, and when her arms fell back from her body they could see the cuts on her breasts and thighs in the naked glare of the headlights.

"Jesus Christ," Damian muttered. "Jesus Christ. Those sick motherfuckers raped her!"

Brandy took a step closer, looking over the shoulders of the two men and the doctor. She turned away immediately, then moved into the roadside bushes. A moment later they heard the sound of vomiting.

Cat again took Maia's pulse, then looked up at Noah. "Can you call an ambulance from your car?"

He moved away instantly, leaving her alone with Damian. "Was anybody here when you found her?" she asked as she opened her portable first-aid kit.

"No," he said, "but I think they had just driven away. She couldn't have been here long. I'm sure of that."

The ambulance arrived in due time and Catherine oversaw the attendants as they carefully loaded the fallen woman into the truck. Two policemen came as well, and after greeting everyone with great familiarity, invited Damian and Brandy to accompany them to the station.

"I'll be there after I take my friend home," Brandy promised, pointing toward the borrowed car. One policeman walked over and looked into the rear window at Tina and smiled wryly in recognition.

"You come straight after," he said to Brandy.

"I'll drive *him*," Noah said with such force that the policeman shrugged and climbed back into his vehicle.

Without a word Catherine boarded the ambulance, never looking into Noah's face.

"All right: Tell me," the lawyer said to Damian as soon as they were alone in the sedan.

Ignoring his tone of command, Damian lit a cigarette and opened the car window.

"Put that shit out!" Noah barked.

"I don't care if this cigarette makes you puke," Damian replied clearly, "because you make me puke. I thought you were going to watch over her, and now you come with this shit about your house is no prison and you're not her master! What the hell *are* you good for, other than a very narrowly defined kind of fucking?"

Noah gripped the wheel so tightly that his knuckles began to sweat. His right foot longed to press the pedal to the floor of the car and send this stuck-up aunty-man flying over the cliff to the sharp rocks below. The road was barely visible in the moonless night, and he knew that if he unleashed his anger they might both truly die.

Pulling together the shreds of his self-control from some deep inner well, Noah managed to speak in an almost normal voice.

"I fucked up, all right? You don't know how much I already regret it. But now I need to know what you saw, Damian. I need to know it so I can go after the motherfuckers who did this."

Damian whistled sarcastically. "What are we about to see? A shoot-out at the Crucian corral? High Noon in Christiansted? Gunsmoke under the Caribbean sun?"

"Damian, are you going to help me?"

"What? Are you going after them with another one of your highly effective legal strategies?"

"Cut the crap!" Noah screamed. "Tell me what happened!"

Damian threw the cigarette out and closed his window, trapping his hands between his quaking knees.

"All right, Attorney Langston." He paused, organizing his own self-control carefully. "I happened to stop by Brandy's after closing. Brandy was there alone. Well, except for Severin's former girlfriend, who was drunk to her eyebrows. Brandy seemed to think that Juan and the ex-girlfriend's brother had cooked up a scheme to get rid of Severin's new girlfriend. So she wanted to go out to Wisdom and stop them."

"But what does Maia have to do with any of that?"

"Nothing. Maia wasn't even a part of the equation. Brandy borrowed her boss's car and asked me to drive with her because she couldn't handle her beer-saturated buddy alone."

"Then how did Maia end up—"

"*You* should be able to answer that!"

"Do you think they followed her out there?" Noah shouted.

"No!" Damian shouted back. "They were after some other woman! They thought Maia was living with you. So it seems to me that she must have been in the wrong fucking place at the wrong fucking time."

The two men were silent for the rest of the drive. When they pulled up in front of the police station Damian sighed. "I'm not going to be able to tell them very much. All I did was ride in the car with Brandy. I didn't see the men. Didn't actually hear their plans. And neither one of us witnessed what happened."

He slammed the car door and turned back to Noah. "I hope that doctor you found will help her more than you have."

The attending physician, a Puerto Rican who had played an occasional game of tennis with Noah, now brushed by him with a face of steel and vanished into the surgery. Directed by the nurses into the hospital's small intensive care station, Noah found Cat standing in the darkened room amid blinking monitors, staring thoughtfully at the mummified figure on the bed. When he approached she looked over at him, unsmiling, then glanced back at Maia.

"She'll live. She's been badly beaten. They didn't manage to break anything, but her left hand is badly sprained. And I'm afraid she'll carry some of those scars to her grave."

Noah forced himself to look at the bandaged face and felt tears start in his eyes. "Did—did they—"

Cat nodded. "They didn't intend for her to survive, Noah. Whoever did this wanted her dead with a vengeance."

He looked away, overcome. Cat touched his arm. "This is the woman who's staying out at your place, right?"

He nodded, unable to speak.

"Well, I had the surgeon take a few tests. We'll send the labs over to Puerto Rico. I should get the results tomorrow. Why didn't you tell me that you have an MRI here now?"

He knew she was deliberately ignoring his tears, and he saw that she already understood that his grief was driven by more than any stupid lawsuit.

"What exactly happened to her?" he rasped. Catherine turned away, adjusting several knobs on a bedside monitor. "I think they hit her with something hard. Got her down and beat and raped her. I don't know how many—"

"Two," he choked. "Two men."

"Well, she clearly put up a good fight. Most of her cuts came from glass and rocks on the roadside. Except for the marks on her face. The cuts look deliberate to me."

Noah heard a muffled sob and turned to see Pearl standing in the doorway. She came slowly toward them and looked up at Cat, her eyes registering her horror.

"She's heavily sedated," the doctor explained. "She'll sleep through the night but I think she'll be able to talk to you both by noon, tomorrow."

Pearl looked at Noah. "That Johanssen man did this?"

"No, Mama. It was someone else."

"Someone else," she echoed softly. Moving away, she pulled a chair to the bed and took Maia's uninjured hand. "Why?"

Because all of us want her, Noah thought. Severin, Juan, and even Carlson. All of us have looked at her and longed for her. He glanced at his mother.

"I think," he said in a low voice, "that it was a very tragic coincidence."

Pearl began to weep as Cat motioned for Noah to follow her into the corridor. When they were outside she looked into his eyes. "Maybe the police should take a trip out to the property where this happened to see if the owner was aware of anything."

"He was probably dead drunk," Noah said, looking back through the windows at the figure of his mother leaning silently over Maia.

Cat watched for a moment, then spoke up. "Noah, she had some injuries that seem to have occurred earlier in the evening. Some cuts on her hands and legs that might have been made by metal. Barbed wire, perhaps."

Noah exhaled slowly. "Maia doesn't always listen to reason. She's been going out there alone and . . ." He searched for words. "That's one reason why we were glad she came to stay with us. We were trying to protect her. And Mama—well, you know, after Precious left—"

"It's clear that your mother has really taken to her," Catherine agreed quickly. "And I hope that the hospital will be able to release her in a few days. There's only one thing—" Cat lowered her eyes. "I'm not sure she should stay in St. Croix."

"I'll take care of the men who did this."

"That's not what I mean." Cat sighed, then gave him her most professional face. "You wanted me to examine her because of her tumor, right? Well, I took a look at the CAT scans and MRI and unless those labs prove me wrong, she needs to get into treatment as soon as possible."

"Immediately?"

"If she wants to survive any length of time. What troubles me is that she's a nurse. She must be aware of her condition. And what she needs to do about it."

"I can't make her do anything," Noah conceded helplessly.

"You mean, even the influence of Pearl and Noah Langston haven't convinced this woman to choose life?"

Noah looked wordlessly at Catherine and she smiled. "This Maia Ransom must truly be a woman of strength. I'll see what I can do, Noah. Although," she added in a low voice, "it won't be easy."

"What?"

"Convincing her to hang around long enough to take you away from me."

"Cat, I—" For one awkward moment he looked into Cat's eyes and saw how much she truly loved him.

"I think I'll check on Maia," she said softly, turning away.

Ten hours passed before the injured woman spoke. Catherine was adjusting the flow of medication into an IV when the fractured voice escaped the bandages. The surgeon hurried around the bed and leaned down over the figure, her head close enough to feel Maia's warm breath.

"Severin," she whispered, "don't do it."

"Severin's not here, Miss Ransom. You're in hospital. You're safe."

"Hospital?" The word had the exhausted acceptance of someone on the way to the guillotine.

"Do you remember how you got here?"

Maia shook her head, her eyes frantically searching the ceiling. Cat leaned closer.

"I'm Noah's friend, Catherine. I'm a surgeon. I came in from the B.V.I. yesterday. I'll be taking care of you."

"Noah?" The voice was weak, but then found its focus. "Pearl? Where's Pearl?"

Catherine went to the door of the intensive care unit and saw Noah and his mother both sleeping upright on the steel waiting room chairs. She had barely walked two steps when their eyes sprung open. Noah leaped up, knocking over a tray of Styrofoam coffee cups and half-eaten doughnuts.

"Is she awake?"

Cat placed a professional hand on his arm and looked at Pearl. "I want to talk to Noah for a moment," she said calmly. "Would you go in to her, Pearl?"

This was the first time that Catherine had ever addressed Noah's mother by her first name, but no one noticed. Pearl moved quickly around the couple and went into the aqua darkness of the intensive care unit, the door swishing closed behind her. Cat motioned for Noah to sit down, but he ignored her, his eyes trained on the ICU entrance.

"What did she say, Cat?"

"Nothing. Nothing at all."

"Then why—"

"Because I think she needs a woman. A mother," the surgeon explained quietly. "Does she have any family here?"

"No family anywhere," Noah responded, his shoulders falling. Cat looked up at him, recognizing a nurturing instinct that was as new as his apparent love for the woman. All the years she'd known him; all the nights she'd slept with him; all the time they'd spent talking about a shared future had never put this look in his eyes.

"So you're in love with her?" She posed the question directly, the way a physician questions a patient about the onset of a medical condition.

His eyes found hers and he seemed to remember that she was more than just a doctor. More than just a friend.

"I don't know what to say—" His lawyer's composure failed him. "I never intended for anything serious to happen between us. She came here from the States to find out about her family. I wanted to help her. Then she had no place to go and ended up living out at the house."

Catherine knew that the Langstons owned property all over the island. "Well, whether she gets better or not, I don't suppose I can change the inevitable," she replied quietly.

"Inevitable?"

She laughed lightly. "I can't have it all, can I? I've got a splendid career in a city I love. I've got a large flat, a host of friends, and all the social and cultural events that London can offer. Why in the world would I expect to snare a handsome, intelligent black man, too? A man with a career of his own? A man whose destiny is clearly linked to a little island where London is no more important than a fur-hatted man on the label of a gin bottle?"

The door behind them swung open and they both turned to see Pearl gesturing. In the room Maia was groaning softly. Catherine leaned over the instrument panel beside the bed and began to adjust the flow of medication into the IV unit. Noah sat on the edge of the mattress, gently clasping her uninjured hand.

Maia spoke to him through swollen lips. "Thank you." The words were a dry mumble.

"It was Damian and Brandy who saved you."

"Please believe me, Noah," she rasped, a tear escaping and running along her face to the gauze that lined her jaw. "I didn't go to him. I didn't go to Severin!"

"You don't have to tell me now," Noah began, but she made a low noise, her hand squeezing his more tightly.

"It's there, in the mill," she whispered. "There. Hidden in the bricks."

"What are you talking about?"

"He was going to burn it, but I stopped him."

"You mean, Severin? He's hiding something up there in the mill?"

"Zara left it there," Maia insisted, her rough voice trembling. "Left it there for me . . ."

Her words softened to a blur as the tranquilizers hit her system. He hovered close, his face inches away. When he finally looked up, he was surprised to find two women staring at him, both recognizing at the same moment that they had to lose their son and lover in order to gain a man.

He stirred and slowly stood. "Will she be all right?"

"I'll stay with her," Catherine responded.

"Momma, did she tell you anything?"

"She kept repeating that she was sorry," Pearl said sadly.

"When the police come—that is, if they even bother, don't send them out to Wisdom."

"What do you mean, son?"

"Just let them think that this was an unfortunate incident. That Maia got lost up there on the highway and met up with a couple of drunks."

"But you know damned well who did this," Catherine protested.

"Of course we do," he answered. "But one of them is the police chief's nephew. And if they're looking for a scapegoat, the blame is likely to fall on—"

"Seven," his mother said shrewdly. "It would make sense, of course. She used to live there. And Tina put it out all over the island that Severin was obsessed with her."

"Severin even spoke to Maia when we were out for dinner the other night," Noah added. "Half of Fredriksted saw it."

"You think the police might arrest him?" Catherine interrupted. "Even knowing he's innocent?"

"They'd love to get Seven for something," Noah said. "And it would be a convenient way of taking those two bastards off the hook."

"But if Brandy and that American fellow already talked with the police, then there's no point in our keeping silent," Catherine said.

"Brandy won't implicate Carlson and Juan," Noah argued. "They grew up together and—" He snorted. "She'd never get another Crucian customer in her bar."

"And the American?"

"Damian?" Noah snorted again. "This isn't London, Cat. No self-respecting Caribbean police officer is going to listen to a man who looks like *that*. And besides: Damian admitted that he didn't see anything. He can't identify Maia's attackers."

"So we're supposed to help them get away with this?" Catherine blurted out.

"No. We're going to buy ourselves a little time," Noah stated.

Pearl looked at him. "Maia doesn't have much, son."

"I know that. But what's keeping her alive, right this moment, is her belief that she's somehow connected to that place. I need to go out there and find out what Severin knows about the Ransoms. And I don't need the police barging in and trying to arrest him in the middle of it." Noah looked back toward the sleeping figure. "If Severin gets scared enough," he said as a dark afterthought, "he may even try to destroy whatever he's got hidden in that mill."

An hour later Noah pulled the BMW into the weedy drive and parked it carefully beneath a copse of overgrown grape trees. The stones that once lined the gracious entry to Wisdom were shattered to rubble, and he cursed as he twisted his ankle climbing out of the car.

The sun was blazing through a thick afternoon haze, and an ominous herd of black clouds braced the western horizon. It was viciously hot and humid, and Noah was aware that on a normal Monday he would be in the air-conditioned peace of his office. In fact, this was the first time in many months that he wouldn't spend the afternoon at his desk.

Yet he didn't give a shit. This was no simple lawsuit about titles and contracts. This wasn't merely about white people ripping off the sons and daughters of their slaves. This was quite literally about life and death.

He wondered if Mimi had already arrived. Wondered what she had heard about the assault. About who had done it. Surely the black half of the island already knew. Twelve hours had passed since Maia had arrived at the hospital. And everyone from the ambulance attendants, to the nurses on duty, to the doctors themselves, would be captivated by the intriguing tale of the Statesider Ransom, who was once Severin's nurse out at Wisdom. Who was now a resident at Noah's mansion. Treated in the hospital by a London-trained surgeon. Kept under vigil by Pearl DeWindt Langston!

If Mimi knew, she would not be helpful to Noah. For on the island blood ran thicker than anyone's notion of wrong and right. It was only the family, after all, that one could count on in good times and bad. After hurricanes. Theft. Unplanned babies. Joblessness. Homelessness. Death.

Tina and Carlson were Mimi's family. They were distant cousins, of course, but they were still family. Mimi wouldn't do anything to bring trouble to Carlson. And no matter who Severin was sleeping with at the moment, island wisdom still believed that Tina might some day marry him and become the mistress of Wisdom.

Slowly he mounted the drive, listening intently for any sign of life. There was nothing. Nothing from the kitchen, whose broken jalousies were partially open. Nothing from the main entrance, which was dark and dusty in the white morning light. Where in the world was Mimi?

Gently he pulled at the cracked slats of the front door. A hot gust of wind pushed the door forward, and he was met with the bitter perfume of bleach and vomit. He paused an instant, his instincts revolting against entering this version of hell. Then his logic guided him forward, and he walked quietly toward the great room.

How did Maia stand this place? How did she bear seeing the Ransom land reduced to this open latrine? How could she have laid down and closed her eyes with that filthy dog just down the hall?

The house creaked as another fist of wind shoved its way down the corridor and out the door behind him. He took shallow breaths, avoiding the scents of death and addiction and mundane despair that filled Severin's life. Placing his hand on the knobs, he pushed open the double doors and peered into the shadows.

Severin's spidery limbs formed a rickety pile on the dirty mattress. Beneath him a fleece of thick golden curls cascaded downward. The two were so silent that Noah drew in his breath, horrified by the sudden thought that perhaps Juan and Carlson had made it all the way to Wisdom after all.

His heart nearly leaping out of his chest, he stepped forward slowly and peered into the mass of flesh and hair.

No blood. No blood. No blood.

The lovers were snoring very softly, the image of inebriated tranquility. Noah took a deep breath and leaned over the couple. "Severin, wake up."

"No, Pete!" the man cried out, jerking in fear as he heard his name.

"Wake up, Severin!" Noah repeated more loudly.

Bianca groaned and shook her hair, pushing Severin to the side as she tried to free her legs and arms of his weight. This, in turn, seemed to liberate her lover from the depths of his nightmare and he stirred, groaning deeply.

Both were suddenly aware of the stranger's presence, and in a moment the three were staring at one another with the clarity of fear.

"Goddamn," Severin snarled. "What the fuck you doing here, lawyer?"

Noah responded with the calmest authority possible. "I need to know the truth, Seven."

Oblivious to his nudity, Severin belched and looked around him while Bianca turned on her side so that only the curves of her hips and shoulders were visible in the semidarkness.

"Seven. I want you to tell me what you've got hidden in this place," Noah repeated.

"I no tell you nothing," Severin responded hoarsely as he leaned over to pick up a broken cigarette from the floor.

"If you don't tell me now," Noah said very softly, "she might die. And neither one of us wants that."

Severin squinted up, trying to see Noah's face in the shadows. "Hey, *meson*," he responded in his half-voice, "we both know you lawyers make careers on lies."

"Listen to me, man!" Noah reached forward and shoved him back against Bianca. "They tried to kill her last night. They beat her and raped her and left her out there in the road behind your place—"

"Who did that? What you mean, beat and rape?" Severin's expression changed as the thoughts crystallized through the fog of his hangover. He shook his head, trying to rise from the soiled mattress, but then sank back down, unable to negotiate his own weight. "Where is she?" he asked.

"She's hooked to a machine with tubes all over her body," Noah answered. "She's half-dead and the doctors don't think that she has the will to make it—"

"What I have to do with that?" he whined. "You come here and tell me I'm to blame?"

"No, Severin. The men who did this didn't even intend to hurt Maia. They had no idea she was here. They were on their way to get *her*." Noah nodded toward Bianca, who was staring sullenly out from behind Severin's back.

"Why that?" Severin asked stupidly.

"Because all of you are worse than animals," Noah answered. "You live in filth and you fight over your women and your run-down hovels and you do nothing but shit all over yourselves—"

His voice broke and he wavered on his feet, overcome by frustrated rage and exhaustion. "Tell me what's here," he whispered, looking down at Severin's withered face. "She's dying and she can't possibly do anything to hurt you!"

Severin shook his head as if nothing the lawyer said could pierce the darkness. "I don't tell you nothing," he croaked in a whisper. "I born a Johanssen and I die a Johanssen."

"Then go ahead and fucking die!" Noah screamed. "You don't have to kill her, too!"

"Yes, I do," Severin stated simply. "You see, Lawyer Man, she's more than my nurse. She's my *blood*!"

"What the fuck are you talking about?"

"When I die, she die. She's part of me."

"You're insane!"

"I am the seventh. You hear my name? The seventh. And I will be the last one, because it must be so." Severin began his raw, growling laughter, and his laughter widened out to a sound that sent the gulls shrieking away from the balcony. The cracked croaking blew with the hot wind through the tattered curtains and down the lonely halls to reverberate against the Frenchwoman's bed and through the double windows to the mill standing sentinel over the Johanssen past.

Noah drew in his breath, his chest rising and falling. He saw the woman lean very gently forward and press her lips against Severin's wasted shoulder. And he understood that the master never frees himself from slavery because without slavery, the master ceases to exist.

Turning on his heel, he burst out of the house. Mimi was walking slowly up the drive, her tattered cleaning bag balanced on her hip. She looked up in wonder as Noah came crashing toward her.

"Where would he hide it?" Noah asked her, his voice high with frustration. "He's got something here, Mimi. Something that could make everything right."

The old woman moved her head in shallow nods, squinting up toward the house. "Don't know, Mr. Langston," she said softly.

Noah followed her gaze to the open door. "Mimi, he can't hear us. He's still lying in bed with his—his woman. Please tell me if you have any idea—"

She paused, her face closed.

"Mimi," he whispered. "What they did to Maia was wrong. You know that, don't you?"

The old woman's gaze dropped and she lowered her head as if ashamed.

"Please," Noah begged. "Please help me."

After a long moment Mimi looked up. Seeing the desperate fury in his eyes, she clutched his sleeve in her gnarled fingers and pulled him close. He lowered his head to her lips.

"I clean house for fifty years, Mr. Langston. I know every plank of wood. Every corner. Every cupboard." She spoke very slowly and very clearly. "What he got to hide—he don't keep it in the house."

Noah's breathing slowed. He looked down into the old woman's eyes and found himself staring into a continent of selflessness and unexpected strength. Her eyes were not, in fact, unlike his mother's. Momentarily steadied by her powerful gaze, he stood up straight.

"Where would he keep it?"

Her grip tightened on his sleeve. She turned her head, and he followed her gaze. His eyes were drawn upward through the trees by some invisible hand to the tower of the mill, barely visible through the darkening jungle of trees.

"What happened?"

Maia's voice was clearer than Cat would have expected, and she was drawn to the bed to look down at the bandaged face. "You were attacked last night, Miss Ransom, on Maroon Ridge."

Maia's eyes registered an amazing clarity, considering the trauma her body had undergone and the medications that were coursing through her system. Cat leaned a bit closer and lowered her voice to a professional hum.

"Do you remember anything?"

"No," Maia said a bit too quickly, and her eyes flickered up to the doctor. "You're Noah's friend, aren't you?"

"Yes. I spoke with you for a few moments earlier today."

Maia's gaze turned inward and she seemed to be reassembling her memories. Her expression showed no confusion or uncertainty. In fact, she seemed oblivious to the seriousness of her condition.

"You've got a concussion, a number of lacerations, and a badly sprained left hand."

"Wonderful."

"And you know that you were raped. We've begun you on a course of very aggressive antibiotics in case—"

"I was exposed to HIV," Maia said dully.

"Naturally, if you can identify your attackers to the police we can have them tested for infectious diseases."

Maia went silent, but she squeezed her eyes shut as if to hold back tears.

266 • Heather Neff

"I take it you're not in any pain," Catherine said in a gentler voice, glancing at the bedside monitor.

"It hurts like fucking hell," Maia responded weakly. "But I'm used to it. I've been living with pain for quite a while."

Cat walked around the bed, keeping her eyes fixed on the patient.

"Have you been getting any treatment for your condition?" she asked quietly.

"I'm a nurse," Maia whispered. "I know there's no point."

"With the proper intervention you might beat this, Miss Ransom."

"The proper intervention is almost always worse than the disease."

"That's really not true," Cat said. "My clinic in London has had tremendous success using alternative methods to treat conditions far worse than yours."

"Worse than mine?" Maia squinted up at her. "What do you know about my—"

"We did a CT and MRI when you came in. We had to check for internal injuries. Miss Ransom, I've treated several women with tumors that were both larger and located in more sensitive regions of the ovaries."

Maia exhaled slowly. "I've watched people die for many years, Doctor. No one seems to understand that I'm leaving my life the way I want to."

"What about the people who care about you?"

"Nobody cares."

"Pearl cares. And so does—" She stumbled over the words. "So does Noah."

Maia grunted. "I overheard them talking. Noah's in love with—"

"You." Catherine said in a strong, clear voice. "You may not believe him when he says it, but you can believe me. Because trust me, Miss Ransom, it's not at all easy for me to give Noah Langston away."

"Then don't," Maia snapped. "Just stick around. You can comfort him at my funeral."

"Do I detect a little bit of attitude?" Cat laughed. "Could it be that there really are some things worth living for?"

Maia went silent and turned her head away. Cat took her pulse, then wiped her face with a warm cloth. "Noah says that you came here on a quest. And it seems to me that you haven't fulfilled it, yet."

Maia remained silent.

"All of us want to help you," Catherine continued, her voice cool. "But you'll have to help us, too—"

"I don't need your pep talk," Maia murmured. "I know what I have to do."

"There's nothing wrong with accepting help. You'll be up in a day or two," the doctor continued. "We'll get these stitches out, and then I'll have to get to work on that other thing as soon as possible."

"To prove to Noah how noble you are?"

"Actually," Cat replied wryly, "I was rather hoping to get my name in the medical books." She looked into Maia's eyes and the two women regarded one another. A tear finally escaped from the wounded woman's lashes and rolled over her cheek to the white pillow.

"I don't know if I can stand it," she whispered.

"The pain?" Catherine leaned close, her voice gentle.

"Letting myself fall in love with him, and then having to die."

"Then don't die," the doctor replied. "I think we can help with the latter part of your problem. But I suspect it's already much too late to do anything about those first symptoms."

TWO DAYS

Noah's shirt was sweat-dampened and his trousers were damp with mold when he climbed out of the cellar beneath the courthouse late that afternoon. Head spinning with hunger and lack of sleep, he sat heavily on the bench in the quiet courtyard and buried his face in his hands.

He had spent much of the night at the hospital, rising before dawn to again make the treacherous drive up Maroon Ridge to Wisdom. Scaling the barbed-wire fence, he'd spent the morning on his knees inside the sugar mill, digging in the dirt floor and chipping at the stones until his hands were blistered raw. Then he had searched the grounds outside of the mill, his grimy clothes clinging to his body in the unforgiving sun. He pulled away the shrubbery that grew near the tower and crawled through the grape leaves, desperate for some evidence of a recent disturbance— footprints or scratchings or any sign of a new excavation.

But there was nothing.

Frustrated beyond all measure, he returned to the archives in Christiansted and waded down into the stacks of documents from Wisdom, hoping against all hope that whatever was hidden on the estate might have a duplicate in the crumbling government records.

But that effort, too, was in vain. Yes, he'd found more receipts for the purchase of animals and laborers. More orders for supplies. More inventories of furniture and equipment. He'd found a packet of school records recording the mediocre achievements of generations of Johanssen children. Even several photograph albums dating back to the First World War. But there was nothing about Abraham, Jakob, or Zara.

Unused to failure, Noah felt himself wracked with an indescribable sense of powerlessness. He knew he should go back to the hospital, but he couldn't bear to see Maia without being able to tell her something—anything—about the document hidden at Wisdom. He knew he should speak to Catherine, but he wasn't ready to listen to her mocking comments about his feelings for Maia. And above all, he couldn't face the recrimination in his mother's eyes, for he knew that his childish behavior about Cat's arrival had sent Maia out alone into the night.

For one of the rare times in his adult life, Noah Langston was at a complete loss about how to proceed. Everything he was used to counting on, including his uncanny ability to figure out the riddles of heritage, ownership, and race, had failed him. His treasure trove of ancient documents had yielded him nothing. He'd failed as a lawyer, lover, and son, while Severin Johanssen had absolutely lived up to his reputation as a useless piece of sh—

"Hello, Noah."

Looking up, Noah was surprised to see John Kimball, the vicar of the Anglican church standing beside him. They had gone to Rosemeade Academy together many years before, but unlike the other wealthy children of the island, John had returned from the States with a degree in theology and had welcomed the life of a humble clergyman.

Now John sat down beside him, an expression of concern in his eyes. "Looks like you've had a tough day. Anything I can do?"

Noah's first instinct was to say something rude to the priest, but instead he exhaled slowly and tried to find the words to explain. "I've been down in the dungeon all afternoon and I just can't find what I'm looking for."

"The dungeon?"

"That's the name I use for the government archives," Noah said, struggling to keep his voice friendly.

"I see. Deep into another one of your famous lawsuits, I presume?"

Noah hesitated, unsure whether he should speak frankly to the priest, who had been raised, after all, among the people whom he now sought to displace. "Actually, I'm looking for something for a visitor on St. Croix. It appears that her family once lived here and I'm trying to track down any proof of it."

"Do you know which estate they lived on?" the priest asked.

"Wisdom. Her great-great-grandfather was born there."

The priest paused, pursing his lips. "You know, it's strange that you should say that," he remarked, glancing thoughtfully into a patch of scarlet bougainvillea. "Just last week I was going through the church records and I found a satchel of documents dating back over a century. Some of them were unmailed letters from the vicar's wife to her family in England. It appears that she spent quite a bit of time out at the Johanssen estate."

Noah stared at the priest, his mouth gone dry. "What was the vicar's name?"

"Let me see. It was Colin Longworth. And his wife was called Jane."

"Do you think," Noah asked over the pounding of his heart, "that I might have a look at those letters?"

"Of course. Come along with me. I was on my way to the church just now."

Soon Noah was seated at the desk in the priest's study, his hands clasped before him in a pose of remarkable self-control. John's figure was a silhouette in the falling darkness as he opened cabinets, looking for the satchel that he'd put away somewhere for "safe keeping."

"After the last hurricane it occurred to me that these things need to be stored somewhere safer," the priest remarked as he glanced beneath a stack of bulging manilla files. "Lost the roof off the sanctuary during

Hugo, you know. We were lucky that the rectory sustained so little wind damage."

Noah grunted in polite agreement.

"Perhaps," the priest continued, "I'll have the church documents boxed and sent down to the archives—"

"No!" Noah said so sharply that the priest looked over his shoulder. "It's already dangerously overfilled," the lawyer added wearily.

"Anyone looking at you right now wouldn't have any trouble believing that," John laughed. "Oh, there—I've found it!"

He carefully lifted a thick leather packet from a drawer beneath the window. "It's also rather moldy, I'm afraid. But it's survived quite a long time, so we can ignore the nasty smell, can't we?"

He set it down on the top of the desk and turned on a lamp. Noah stared at the rough surface of the leather with its tarnished bronze clasp. Then he reached out and ran his fingers over it, closing his eyes as if in prayer.

The priest watched, then leaned forward. "Is everything all right?"

Noah looked up at him with exhausted eyes. "Not quite yet, John."

Opening the clasp, he reached carefully into the satchel and brought out a handful of brittle, neatly folded papers. Some were closed with wax bearing the seal of the diocese; others were tied with blue ribbons.

Blue ribbons.

Zara's little book had been tied with blue ribbon. Zara's little book had been made of brown leather. Zara's book was marked with a seal, too. His breaths coming faster, Noah picked up the first of the letters and held it up to the light. The sealing wax bore the mark of a sailing ship, its central mast crossed by another beam to form the shape of a cross.

Barely able to breathe, he took a silver letter opener from the priest's hand and slid it gently beneath the seal. The paper rustled in protest, then crackled open. Noah's forehead had gone shiny and his fingers had begun to shake so much that he had to put the letter down on the desk. Suddenly he heard Maia's broken voice—*Please believe me, Noah . . . I didn't go to Severin*—and he knew why he had laid in the dirt, ripping his hands raw at that hillside monument to slavery.

Why he had wept when he could find no answer in that paper tomb beneath the court. Why he was here, now, when every cell in his body begged him for food and rest.

Maia loves me, he thought. She loves *me*! He plunged into the thought and felt it wash over him in a wave of hope and steadying strength, and he was swept up in a flush of joy unlike anything he had ever known. There could be more to life than the legal cases, cars, and houses, and the consuming need to avenge his people's suffering on the island whites. He could use his talents to create the kind of community that his woman and children could live in. Out of the past's misery and pain they would find a way to build a world based on love. Love!

Once again he lifted the letter to the light. He opened it slowly. A spidery hand scrolled out a name and address in an elegant script. *Jane Stevens Longworth,* it read. *Christiansted, St. Croix.* And the date was written beneath: *December 25, 1854.*

An hour later Noah was on Northside Road, racing through the darkness back to the hospital. He had washed himself off in the priest's bathroom and changed into a clean T-shirt he found in the trunk of his car. He had purchased a box of Swiss chocolates from a duty-free shop along the way. The satchel of letters rested on the seat beside him. Silently he repeated one of his father's favorite proverbs over and over again: *"The words of God roasted meat for me to eat . . ."*

Soon he was jogging briskly down the hospital corridor, nodding with wordless elation at the bemused patients and staff. He arrived at the door of the ICU just as Vashti Peterson came out.

"Evening, Vashti. How's everything?"

"All right, Noah, considering the excitement."

"Excitement?"

"The police coming in here and showing no respect at all. They act like the other patients are invisible—"

"They came this morning?"

"This afternoon."

"They were talking to Miss Ransom?"

"They tried. But she couldn't remember anything about the attack. She told them someone hit her from behind. So they finally left her alone."

"Was Dr. Coleman with her?" he asked, hoping that the all-too-honest Cat had missed the officers' visit.

"No, Noah. She'd just left for lunch." Smiling with complicity, the nurse added, "I believe she was with your mother."

Noah grinned a bit sheepishly, realizing that the hospital would be awash with speculation over whether both Catherine and Maia were his lovers.

"Thanks," he said, adding quickly, "Is Miss Ransom awake? I just wanted to talk with her for a few moments."

The nurse looked surprised. "Miss Ransom? She's not here. The assistant said that she dressed herself and left about an hour ago."

"Did Dr. Coleman sign her out?" Noah asked.

"No. She signed herself out."

"She wasn't well enough to leave!"

"She said she could handle things."

"She couldn't walk!"

"The orderly pushed her in a wheelchair."

"She didn't even have any clothes!"

"She borrowed a uniform from one of the technicians."

"You don't let patients leave at night!"

"She insisted, Noah."

"Who took her home?"

"Actually—" Vashti paused. "She said you were coming to pick her up."

Noah's jaw clenched tight. "But Vashti—"

"We couldn't keep her, Noah. She was perfectly aware of the risks. She's a nurse, after all."

"How did she leave? There was no one here to drive her."

The nurse hesitated. "Well, if she isn't with you, then there are only two possibilities. Either she took a taxi or—" Vashti took a deep breath "—or she left with Seven Johanssen."

"Seven?"

"He came in after Miss Pearl and Dr. Coleman left."

"But Maia was in intensive care!" Noah shouted. "How did he get in to see her?"

"He told the nurse on duty that he and Miss Ransom are family."

* * *

"What they do to you, Nurse?" His face loomed out of focus just above the white wall of her bandages.

"What didn't they do?" she murmured, certain that she was addressing an apparition.

"It was a mistake, you know," he said apologetically, bringing his swollen face even closer.

"You're fucking right," she replied as she tried to shut her eyes against the bloated vision.

"No, Nurse," he explained. "Juan and Carlson did not want you. They wanted the little golden pony. They wanted to punish her for trying to take Wisdom."

The golden pony? In her morphine-induced haze Maia slowly realized that the face wavering above her bed was a living person. Her stomach reacted before her mind caught up and a terrified wave of bile vaulted upward into her throat, literally lifting her halfway into a sitting position. Severin leaned forward quickly and steadied her as she choked on the rancid wash of painkillers spewing through her lips. From somewhere he brought a towel to her mouth, and he wiped the bitter syrup away as she spat out the rest into a metal dish.

Maia fell back and he vanished into the blinking haze of the darkened intensive care station. Then just as she again reconciled herself to the certainty that she was hallucinating, he returned. He lifted a plastic bottle of ice water to her face and cooing gently, guided the straw carefully between her torn lips. "Easy. Easy," he whispered, helping her lie back on the pillow. Then he dragged a chair across the room and lowered himself beside the bed, his sour odor of unwashed flesh and alcohol bringing her close to vomiting again.

"That lawyer came out to the house," Severin whispered, his lips close to her ear. "He wants me to give him my family. But you already know that I will never give my family to anyone but you, Maia. And you know why, don't you?"

Maia managed to raise her uninjured hand. Her fingers wavered weakly before Severin's face and he reached out and grasped her palm.

"You know why," he repeated, the words a statement rather than a question.

She shook her head imperceptibly and he came so close that she could see the hairs sprouting beneath his nostrils and the broken veins near his cruelly lonely eyes.

"I love you, Nurse," he rasped. "I loved you from the first time you looked into my face at Brandy's Bar. I loved you when you came to my kitchen, and when you asked to speak to Tina's *employer*." He chortled quietly at the memory. "And when you were crawling around beneath my window. You thought I didn't know, Maia. But I felt you—I felt how close you were, even then! And I loved you so much I nearly died when I finally found you on my beach."

He made a sound deep in his throat. "I love you, Maia. And you love me. You weren't thinking about the lawyer when you held me in your arms, Maia. You held me tight on the beach and wouldn't let me die."

"Severin," she murmured, "you don't understand."

"Yes, I do. You love me because it's in your blood."

"No, Severin—"

"You love me just like Zara Ransom loved Jakob Johanssen."

Maia's whole body jolted in response to his words. "Severin," she said through the reeling thickness of the pain medication, "how do you know she loved him?"

"She came to him at Wisdom. They were together every night. She loved him and wanted to be with him. And Jakob loved her, too."

"Then you know about Abraham—"

"I only know they were in love," he insisted obstinately.

"Help me, Severin. Please help me find my people."

"I'll help you," he answered. "I'll give you the house, if you want. You can have the land and the beach. You can have all of Wisdom. But you have to stay with me."

"Stay with you?"

"I don't want the pretty little filly. Paulette brought her to make me forget you. But every time I look at her I think only about you. Every time I touch her I remember what it felt like to touch you. And the longer I'm with her, the more I need you there with me."

"I can't be with you, Severin. And you know why."

"I'll pay for your doctors. I'll rebuild the house. I'll give you—" He leaned forward, bringing his lips to her forehead. "I'll give you a child. Like Jakob and Zara."

Maia felt her body float strangely out of its battered flesh and she looked down on the scene, much as she had done that day in Severin's bedroom. He was staring into her eyes and gently caressing her face.

"I'm—I'm too sick for a baby," she whispered.

"You'll get better. I'll stop with the rum and cigarettes. We'll make the house beautiful again. Just the way it was when I was a boy."

He had begun to plead with her, his eyes softening and his voice becoming clear and low. Maia stared at him and saw the man he might have been—or might have become—if destiny had not stranded him in the mausoleum of the Johanssens.

"What about Tina?" she whispered.

"She only wants the house. Tina don't want a future."

A future? Straining against the painkillers, Maia's answer crawled from her lips.

"I can't live with you."

"You marry me, Maia Ransom."

"You know I can't."

"I know you can."

"We're blood, Severin."

"It was a century ago."

She closed her eyes. "Zara wouldn't have wanted this."

"Yes," Severin said with certainty, "she would have. And so would Jakob. Don't you see, Maia? Their blood brought you back to Wisdom."

He stood slowly and pressed his lips against Maia's mouth. She was surrounded by his hard odor and deep, deep desire. Wisdom leaped up before her eyes, with its crumbling drive, its rotting beams. And its tower, staring down from the crowning hill.

"Will you come to me," he whispered, "like Zara came to Jakob?"

Maia stared into his face, unable to speak. He brought his lips to her forehead once more. "You have to come, Maia Ransom. You have to come." He paused. "If you don't, I'll burn it."

Her heart twisted. "Burn it?"

"I'll give you one day to decide. Only one."

"I can't leave the hospital," she pleaded.

"I won't live anymore without you."

"Severin—"

"One day, Maia. One day."

ONE DAY

Standing in the hospital parking lot, Noah called home. Pearl answered, and from the tone of her voice he instantly knew that she hadn't heard about Maia's disappearance. He asked to speak to Cat.

"She's in the shower, Noah. Is there some emergency?"

He weighed his answer carefully. "No. I just wanted to talk with her about Maia's condition. Tell her I'll call back in a little while, all right?"

He drove at a desperate speed all the way to Wisdom, dodging potholes while searching in the darkness for Maia's rented Jeep. He found it parked in a ditch and hidden beneath a thorny thatch of shrubbery near the outer edge of the estate. His headlights made out the squid-shaped brown smear on the sun-hardened clay. Tearing his eyes from the stain, he edged his way over the embankment and down to the car to check to see if the keys were in the ignition. Nothing. The hood was cool and the seats were empty. The Jeep hadn't been moved since two nights before, when Maia left his house for her ill-fated meeting with Carlson and Juan.

So where the hell was she now?

Noah climbed back up to the street, his chest wet beneath his shirt. Where could she have gone? Did she even have her wallet? And there was always the risk that she might run into Carlson or Juan somewhere on the island! Where would she go for safety?

For a long moment he looked blindly out over the crawling sea, thinking of that night, not so long before, when she had burst out of the surf, a black Venus, and come bounding up the beach and into his arms. He remembered the womanly strength in that tortured flesh and the child's willingness to trust as she gave herself to him. He heard her voice, her deep laughter, and remembered her soft cries in the sensuous dark. Something clicked in him and he had a sudden intuition. He climbed briskly into his sedan and threw it into gear, heading at full speed toward Christiansted.

Thirty-five minutes later he was parked in front of Chéz Alexander. It was nearly midnight, but he hoped against all hope that someone might still be inside. His heart sank as he saw the sign on the door announcing that the restaurant was closed on Mondays. Pressing his face against the locked grill, he listened for signs of life. He began to shout and bang on the grill when he heard faint voices coming from the kitchen.

Soon a big man in a rubber apron appeared in the main room, carrying a machete. Noah called to him and was rewarded with a grimace.

"What you want? The sign say closed, *meson!*"

Noah motioned for the man to come closer to the grill, and when he finally trundled over, he asked for Damian. The cook's eyes swept over the heavily perspiring lawyer and his face rolled itself into a sneer.

"So, you looking for a friend?" he asked sarcastically.

"Where can I find him?" Noah replied, his voice rising in frustration.

"So you want to visit the guesthouse?" the other man laughed. "They say he make it real cozy."

"Where is the guesthouse?" Noah insisted, hoping that his State-side voice might lend authority to his request.

"I know. But I no tell. You see, brother, that house belong to my employer. Not to Damian. And I have no right to send no stranger there."

Noah stared through the iron grill in silent rage. Pulling his wallet from his pocket, he held a twenty-dollar bill in the air where the other man could see it.

"I need to know," he said, swallowing his anger.

The cook came very close, looking hard at the money. Noah carefully folded the bill and slipped it through the metal bars. The man reached up, took it, then looked into the lawyer's eyes.

"Estate Inverness. Big pink house on the hill. Can't miss it."

He watched Noah jog to his car and climb in, propelling it swiftly into a narrow alley. Then, shaking his head slowly, he sucked his teeth loudly and went back to his work.

Inverness was located on the East End of the island, a fertile fist of land that was surrounded on three sides by water. Some of St. Croix's wealthiest whites lived there, and they had succeeded in getting the island government to turn it into a gated community. Noah thus had to pass through a checkpoint where his name was recorded and his driver's license inspected before he could enter. The uniformed guard, a Puerto Rican whose transistor radio was blaring an uproarious salsa, stepped out of his little white booth and looked carefully into the backseat and trunk of Noah's BMW. He then stared distastefully into the lawyer's face. Refraining from speaking, he jerked his head to indicate his permission for Noah to pass on.

Noah's cotton T-shirt was wringing wet when he trudged around the walled entrance to the candy-pink villa with the gabled roof. Three waist-tall Great Danes bounded up to inspect him through the steel fence, and one bounced up against the bars and nipped at his fingers as he rang the bell. For an eternity nothing moved inside the white-stone courtyard. Then he heard Damian's voice over the intercom.

"It's Noah," he said loudly. "Let me in, Damian."

After a deliberately extended pause, the buzzer sounded and Noah slowly opened the gate, holding out his hands so the dogs could sniff him. Hearing steps, he looked up to see a shirtless, barefoot Damian emerge from the darkness.

"Well, well. Look what the dogs dragged in." He whistled sharply and slapped his thigh. The animals turned and trotted toward him in happy unison.

Noah wiped his sticky hands on his shirt. "I'm looking for Maia."

"You've lost her again?" Damian struck a pose, rolling his eyes dramatically. "Why don't you just throw in the towel, friend? Admit it: You can't do anything for her."

"I'll keep trying until she tells me to stop."

"What you mean is that you'll keep meddling until you get her killed."

Noah took a very deep breath, using the last shreds of his willpower to remain calm. "Where is she, Damian?"

"Isn't she at the hospital?"

"You know she's not. Is she here?"

Damian shrugged extravagantly and turned to walk away. "If she turns up I'll let her know you're concerned."

"Damian—" Noah's voice broke, his anger boiling over. "I need to see her."

"Why? Have you thought up another lawsuit? Found another set of relatives? Or convinced that white scumbag to sign over what's rightfully hers?"

Noah took two steps forward and one of the Danes throttled out a growl. He straightened up, breathing hard. "If you know where she is, tell her I have to see her. Tell her I discovered something she needs to know."

"And what would that be?"

"Tell her—" Noah paused, almost choking with frustration. "Tell her I love her."

"Great," Damian snapped without looking back. "I'll tell her that she shouldn't worry about anything because Noah's in love."

When Noah got home it was nearly two in the morning. Pearl was asleep on the wicker sofa, the telephone by her side. Catherine was breathing softly in the guest room, the sheet pulled up high around her shoulders. Noah slowly climbed the stairs to the studio and sank wearily on the bed among Maia's few possessions. He was still clutching the leather satchel that the priest had given him the evening before. Reaching into the bottom of her suitcase, he pulled out Zara's little journal and placed it beside him on the mattress.

It was clear that the cover of Zara's book was tooled from the same leather as the satchel. The cover of the book bore the brand of a sailing ship masted with a cross—the sign of the Anglican diocese of the Virgin Islands—which was also imprinted on the sealing wax of Jane's letters.

So it was Jane who had made a gift of the leather-bound journal to her student, Zara Ransom. It was the vicar's wife who had encouraged her to practice her English by recording her thoughts on the homemade paper. Noah wondered whether the two young women had pressed the paper together, on a quiet afternoon in the great house of Wisdom. He wondered whether the Englishwoman, so far from her home and family on this distant Caribbean island, had traded confidences with the woman born in slavery and now in love with her former master. He wondered whether it was the friendship between the women that made Jakob encourage Zara to leave the estate and seek out a life in Christiansted. And whether, in fact, it was Jane who convinced her husband, Colin Longworth, to marry Zara and Jakob in the Anglican church on that Christmas Day.

Slowly he opened the musty satchel and pulled out the yellowing letters. He carefully unfolded the missive he'd read in John Kimball's office, letting the words take him to another time and place as he sat in the depths of the silent, ageless night.

Jane Stevens Longworth
Christiansted, St. Croix
December 25, 1854

Cherished Mother and Father,

I hope with all my heart that you are well this Christmas Day. My heart goes out to you, winging across the boundless waters to our home in Brighton. I so wish that I could see your faces and hear your voices. While it is always trying for me to be so far from you, I have found it exceedingly difficult during this, my first holiday season abroad.

Still, the Lord has given us so much to be thankful for! The weather has been complaisant, with none of the storms we were warned about despite the unwavering heat. Our rectory is stoutly constructed and the mission is beginning to prosper, despite the disapproval of the Moravian brothers who run the island schools. Colin has done much to improve relations between our two ministries, but many of the Danish inhabitants feel that we would be better placed on an English island.

Nonetheless, my many tasks keep me very occupied. Apart from my duties as the vicar's wife, I have begun to give instruction to some of the landowners and their servants. John has convinced them that most commerce is now being conducted in our language, and that it would be wise to acquire proficiency in English reading and writing. My work takes me all over the island, and often I spend several days on the estates, working with the adults and the children alike.

I have made a very good friend in a young woman on a remote plantation. She was born in bondage, but freed during the blessed liberation of the blacks six years ago. Her family has always lived on the estate, so she knows no other life. Her brothers serve as foremen, and she was being trained by her French mistress to oversee the house.

Zara (whose name means "seed" in the language of her African ancestors), possesses very natural talents in the medicinal and womanly arts. She has learned to read and write with astonishing speed, and her command of our language is proof that blacks are only doomed to inferiority for want of opportunity to rise above their stations. I believe that had she been raised in Great Britain, Zara would be the equal of any young Englishwoman.

Over the months of my teaching Zara revealed to me her lifelong love for one of her former masters, Jakob Johanssen. While I was not so perplexed by the idea of a black woman marrying a white man, it seemed to me that their differences in social position should result in dire consequences. Over time, however, I discovered that Jakob was no less enamored of his childhood friend and that, in fact, he sought to have her placed in the town of Christiansted so that her life might find a superior purpose.

I therefore undertook to train Zara as a teacher for the black children, whose needs are only partially met in the Moravian mission schools built in various locations across the island. I hope that in time Zara will become the schoolmistress of an institution specifically intended for the former slaves.

This afternoon, after many weeks of planning, I was proud to serve as the witness when Colin wed Zara Ransom to Jakob Johanssen. Their marriage represents the union of two people who love each other deeply, and it should foretell a time when the people of this island can live together without reference to distinctions in color, class, and ancestry. I am hopeful that their children will usher in a society of prosperity and goodliness for all—

Noah dropped the letter. Leaning forward slowly, he gave himself over to the tears that had burdened him for an entire night and day. He wept deeply, with great sobs climbing from deep within his soul. He wept for the slaves who had labored for endless days under the merciless sun. He wept for the freemen and women who continued to live in the poverty of their forefathers. He wept for the black immigrants who came to his island from places where the despair was even greater. He wept for his own grandfather, and his own father. And he wept for himself, knowing that he had found what he had sought his whole life—a woman who was drawn to the same struggle for justice and truth—and he had somehow already lost her.

The silvery blue dawn was crawling through the jalousies when he jerked himself awake. Stiff and sore, his palms crusted with broken blisters, he slowly began placing the letters in the satchel. As he carefully pushed them flat into the leather case, his fingers brushed a metal object tucked deep into the leather folds.

Gently he pulled the object up from the back of the satchel. It slid out into the light and bounced to his knees. He caught the object deftly with one hand and lifted it to the morning sun. It was a silver, palm-sized locket, inscribed with the initials ZRJ. Carefully, almost reverently, he turned the delicate clasp and it flipped open.

Noah looked into Maia's eyes, there on the face of her great-great-grandmother, Zara. The young woman, her dark skin illuminated by the photographer's primitive lamps, stared calmly into the future, her heavy hair braided into thick plaits around her head—not unlike his own mother. Dressed in a white blouse and wearing pearls in her ears, her face reflected the fortitude of her own African forebears.

Beside her stood a man whose strength was evident, even in the suffocating suit jacket and carefully knotted tie. His hair pulled away from his face, Noah saw the cold arrogance of the whites who had taken the land and held it as their own.

And yet. And yet. And yet: *There was something else in the gaze.* Something unexpectedly familiar. Noah looked at the lips, which were partially hidden beneath a neatly trimmed mustache. He looked at the nose, which should have borne the sharply flaired nostrils that even now distinguished the last of the Johanssens.

But the nose was oddly shaped, with wide nostrils and flat brow ridges ending along the wide cheekbones. Noah stared, reading the photograph with the eyes of the scientist he had become after so many years of struggling with the conundrums of ancestry. He looked into the man's eyes, which were darker than his Danish heritage should have allowed. He looked at the ears—smaller than those of most Europeans. He looked at the chin, which was missing the cleft that still graced Severin's, beneath the stubble.

And then Noah understood.

Marie-Paule Emilie St. Severin—the Frenchwoman who became Solomon Johanssen's wife, the first mistress of Wisdom, was black. And thus, despite his light hair and ruddy complexion, by the law of the land her son Jakob was black too.

Solomon had ignored the obvious, pressing his first-born to marry into a wealthy Danish family and become a member of upper-class Caribbean society. But Jakob chose to marry a black woman and recognize his black child. He chose a life among common people, knowing that his wealthy family would never accept his union with Zara. And he chose to give Abraham, the son he conceived with Zara, the dignity of his name.

"He loved her," Noah muttered. "He loved her and the whole world knew it. That's why the whites forced Abraham to leave the island. It wouldn't have mattered if Zara had been Jakob's lover their entire lives. Abraham became a threat to the white landowners the moment Jakob made him legitimate by marrying his mother. And that's why they sent him away."

Noah carefully closed the locket and returned it to the satchel. "No wonder Abraham never called himself Johanssen. The Johanssens banished him from his home, his family, his life." Sighing deeply, Noah picked up Zara's little book and slipped it into his pocket.

The sun had barely risen above the blue line of the sea when Noah climbed out of his car and walked blindly through the flowering courtyard to his office. He'd left without waking Catherine or his mother, for he felt as if there wasn't a moment to waste. Around him Christiansted was lurching alive, with a handful of fishing boats setting out toward the reef and several merchants throwing open their wooden shutters. A cruise ship would arrive later that day, flooding the town with another swell of sweating duty-free shoppers. The golf courses would soon be full of white-haired Americans, the beaches lined with roasting tourists.

Just another day in the American Paradise.

Vaguely hoping that Maia had left him some message, he carefully checked for a note in the stairwell, but there was nothing. The door swung open and he was struck by the odor of damp papers, warm leather, and bay rum. His odors. His lawyer's life.

Taking out all the files he'd assembled of the Johanssen papers, he spread them across his desk. The prisms at the window sent ribbons of gentle light dancing across the papers: Solomon Johannsen's banking records and the plans for the construction of Wisdom. The birth and death certificates of Jakob, his younger brother Issak, who had died while still a child. Receipts for equipment, housewares, furniture. Logbooks annotating decades of cane planting and harvesting and even the buying and selling of human beings to work the land. All were cast in the soft pastels thrown across the desk by the spectral glass prisms.

Minutes passed. Noah stared at the papers as if really seeing them for the first time. Because for the first time they were not fractals of truth bathed in splintered light, but rather the reassembled key to the puzzle of Wisdom.

The estate was created when a white man married a black

woman—only to later punish his first-born son for committing the same "sin." The seeds of destruction had begun, there, with the first Johanssens, and the end product was the soulless ambition of Paulette and the filthy degradation of Severin.

Noah Langston had finally found Maia Ransom's people. Perhaps, now, *they* would give her a reason to fight for her life. If only, he thought bitterly, he could find her! Sighing, he dropped into his desk chair and glanced at the trembling rainbows that had crept, with the ticking clock, up the walls of his office. "Maia," he whispered. "Where are you?"

He heard a light footstep on the stair and wheeled around, hoping that his desire had conjured up a woman. But when the office door opened cautiously he found himself facing a little girl of eight or nine, dressed in a plaid school uniform.

"Mr. Langston?" she asked, her eyes taking in the sweeping desk, colorful paintings, and packed bookshelves. "A lady asked me to give this to you."

She opened her book bag and removed a sealed envelope, extending it to him with a smile.

He took the letter and turned it over. The envelope bore the name of the hotel on the little island just across the bay from Christiansted. The hotel Maia had stayed in when she first arrived on St. Croix.

"Where did the lady come from?" Noah asked, reaching into his pocket for some loose change.

"Over there." The child pointed vaguely in the direction of the docks, and Noah gave her a handful of quarters. She chuckled joyfully and dashed from the office. He had the envelope open before she reached the bottom of the stairs.

Noah—

You probably know by now that I've left the hospital. Since I was supposed to return to Detroit today anyway, I decided to go home and see my own doctors. I don't mean to cause you any pain by disappearing like this. I just realized that it would be easier for everybody to simply go.

I know everything you've done was intended to help both

the people of St. Croix and me. I cannot express how much I admire you for your commitment to your community. You and Pearl have given me far more than I can ever repay. I thank you for opening your home, sharing your love, and offering me support during this difficult period. I am sorry for all the trouble I've caused in the past few weeks.

By the time you read this I'll be on my plane. I apologize for leaving before we could unearth the complete history of Wisdom, but perhaps you will solve the mystery in time.

Thank you once again for everything.

With all my love,

Maia

P.S. Tell Doctor Coleman that she was right. I can't do anything about those first symptoms.

He clutched the letter in a shaking hand, his thoughts scrambling as he tried to make some sense of this strange missive. Was it possible that after everything she'd gone through to discover the truth, she'd simply get on a plane and disappear? Had those two filthy dogs broken her spirit when they'd trapped her on that lonely road? Were her injuries worse than he realized? Or had she come to the conclusion that even finding her people wasn't worth the risk of being murdered?

Wearily he locked his office and descended the steps to the town square. He barely noticed the buses spitting out the camera-toting tourists. He missed the rolling hips of Miranda as she ran into the perfume shop to take her place behind her counter. He even ignored Juan's boat, pulled askew and left uncovered on the dock where his brother served as harbormaster. Noah silently went to his car and climbed inside.

When he passed through the gracious entrance of his arched doorway he immediately heard women's voices. He crossed the flowering atrium and entered the great room, following the sounds into his mother's kitchen. Pearl and Catherine were facing one another at the counter and there was tension in the air.

"What's happened?" he asked.

"She left," Pearl cried. "She checked herself out of the hospital—"

"I certainly didn't give anyone permission to let her leave," Catherine replied.

"But she was your patient and it was your responsibility!"

"She's a trained medical professional and she knew what she was doing!"

"Stop!" Noah raised his hands like the referee in a prizefight. "I know Maia left. I found out when I went to the hospital last night."

"Last night?" Pearl cried, her voice rising in anger. "Why didn't you wake me?"

"I looked for her all over the island. Then a child came to my office this morning with this." He placed the letter on the counter and turned away. He listened to the silence as the two women read the missive.

"I had no idea she'd try something like that when I left her yesterday," Catherine said with annoyance. "I mean, I could see that she was doing well, but I never dreamed she'd leave the hospital."

"Did she say something to you?" Noah asked.

"She claimed she couldn't remember anything about the assault. She said that she felt her situation was hopeless, and asserted that rather than seeking treatment she preferred to die on her own terms."

"You should have talked her out of it!" Pearl cried.

"I tried!" Catherine replied angrily. "I told her that we have very successful treatments in London, and I told her that she had a very good reason to live." Catherine's voice fell. "I told her she should stay alive for you, Noah." He looked up at her sharply and she shrugged. "It was a real test of the Hippocratic Oath."

Pearl straightened her back. "Her bags are still upstairs."

"She knew if she came here to get them we'd never let her leave," Noah said.

"That's true," Pearl concurred. For a few moments there was a heavy silence, as each of them thought about Maia.

"Well, since my patient's flown the coop, I guess I'd better think about going, too," Catherine said with forced cheerfulness.

"You don't have to leave," Noah began, but she raised her hands.

"If I get back home in time I can still help my mother with that monstrous wedding. It's not every day, after all, that the governor's daughter marries the richest man on the island! And—" Cat laughed lightly "—I might even be able to get in a swim or two before returning to the gray skies of England."

Without another word she turned away, moving silently toward the atrium. Noah barely noticed her departure, but Pearl's head went up and she reached across the counter and touched his hand. Their eyes met and they shared the realization that Catherine was doing everything in her power to hide her terrible hurt.

"Cat?" He caught her at the entrance to the guestroom. "I don't really know what to say," he began.

"Neither do I," she answered. "Its going to take some time for me to figure out exactly where we went wrong."

"Maybe it just wasn't meant to be," he said gently, but she winced in response.

"That's the rub, you see," she answered. "Women have been told forever and ever that if they wanted to make men happy, they should be content to just stay at home. You come from an island filled with women who'd be delighted to do that for you. But when we met, it was my intelligence and ambition that attracted you, Noah. You wanted me because I was so different. Yet inevitably it's our careers that have kept us apart. You'd never be happy in England and I'm certainly not prepared to give up my future as a surgeon to live here and stitch up foreheads after Saturday night brawls."

He was silent.

"I suppose that's why it didn't feel so bad when you asked me to help your friend," she added. "At least you and Pearl are willing to acknowledge my accomplishments as a physician. I only wish—" She broke off, then spoke more softly. "I only wish I could have done more. Her case really isn't all that hopeless, you know. If only she were willing to . . ." Cat's voice fell and she shrugged helplessly.

"I'll help you get your things together," Noah said, but Catherine laughed again. "I only had that one bag, remember? All you have to do is call the airport and find out the time of the next flight."

Noah dutifully returned to the kitchen and telephoned the airport.

He had just managed to get through to the flight-information desk when Pearl let out a cry. "Noah—check with the airline!"

"What?" he asked, his hand covering the receiver.

"How could we be so stupid?" Pearl exclaimed. "You ask them if she actually got on that plane."

"I don't under—"

"She wrote in the letter that she'd be flying out this morning. But something tells me we shouldn't be so quick to believe her. Tell them you have an emergency and need to know if a traveler named Maia Ransom left St. Croix this morning!"

Noah's face froze. "Do you really think she'd lie?"

"Of course," Pearl said softly. "She wants you to lose her trail. She thinks she's protecting you from those sick people who attacked her. She's planning to go back to that place. And she's planning to go back there alone."

Damian gently pressed the cold cloth against Maia's forehead as she lay in the shade on one of the pool chairs. The facial swelling had subsided, but she was sweating profusely and the skin around her stitches was an angry red.

"You shouldn't have left the hospital," he said for the fiftieth time, glancing down at the bandages on her hands. "What happens if those cuts get infected?"

"Fuck the cuts," Maia murmured, her eyes squeezed together. "I've got other things to worry about."

"How long do you think it will take Noah to figure out that you're still on the island?"

"The note I sent explained—"

"Absolutely nothing," Damian interrupted angrily. "He'll come straight back here to find you. Where else could you go with no money, no clothes, and with two maniacs loose on the island?"

She opened her eyes, then looked away, struggling to push her memories of the assault as far away as possible.

"They haven't arrested them," Damian said. "They're not going to arrest them, either. And that means you're not safe, Maia. I can't do a goddamn thing to help you if Juan and Carlson suddenly come over that wall—"

"All right, Damian, all right. I'll go and stay somewhere else." She began to rise but he grasped her arm to stop her.

"The only place you'll be safe is the hospital—"

"I'm not going back to the hospital."

"But they can take care of you—"

"I'm not looking for anyone to take care of me, or protect me, or rescue me, or heal me," she rasped, breaking into a ragged cough as she struggled to sit up. "I'm only looking for one thing, Damian: a way back to that mill."

"And then, what?"

"I'll find whatever's up there."

"You can't even walk."

"I'll crawl."

"You can't get to Wisdom."

"Taxis can."

"You don't have any money."

"I'll hitchhike."

"He's probably burned it by now."

"He can't burn it."

"Then he's moved it."

"No, Damian. It's still there."

"How do you know?" he cried in exasperation.

"I know because—" She paused, looking up into his eyes. "I know because he's waiting for me to come. And," she added, her voice fading to a shadow, "Zara intended it for me."

"Bullshit!"

"How do you think it survived all these years? Why wasn't it destroyed in a hurricane, or a fire, or simply by the rain? It's there because it wasn't written for a Johanssen. She was a Ransom, and she wrote it for a Ransom. I am the last of the Ransoms. It was written for me."

"Jesus! You sound just like that maniac, Severin!" Damian stared into Maia's face. Her eyes were feverish, her lips cracked. Sighing, he sat down on the chair beside her.

"What do I have to do to convince you not to go out there?"

"I'm the one, Damian. Noah can't find it. Neither can you. It has to be me."

"It doesn't have to be tonight."

"He said he'd burn it if I don't come."

Shaking his head, Damian reached up to smooth her hair away from her face. "You know, Maia, if they hurt me it won't make much difference."

"Don't talk that way," she replied quietly. "Your life matters every bit as much as mine."

"Nobody's in love with me, Maia. And even if Noah's a complete jerk, I have to admit that he's a wealthy, sexy, ambitious jerk."

"I'm not mixing business with pleasure," she replied with a weak smile. "Noah and his mother will never forgive me if they figure out that I tricked them."

"What difference does it make? You're going to get yourself killed tonight, anyway."

"I've got to find it, Damian. This is my last chance to know the truth."

"Maia," he said very softly, "there are better ways to do it."

"Don't you see?" she whispered. "I've got to go. I've got to make sure that no Johanssen ever controls a Ransom again."

An hour later Brandy's arm froze in midswing as she saw the strange duo approach, the thin man's arms wrapped protectively around the limping figure. Tossing her cloth on the countertop, she emerged from behind the bar and met them as they entered the poolside deck.

"You must be crazy!" she hissed, staring into Damian's eyes.

"I am," he agreed.

"She belongs in the hospital."

"You're right," he said, casting an angry glance at Maia.

"Then you must take her back," Brandy began as Maia cut in.

"Don't talk about me like I'm not here." She slipped away from Damian's arm and tried to balance her weight evenly on both feet.

"Don't you know how dangerous this is?" Brandy snapped, glancing quickly over her shoulder at the tables, which would soon fill with islanders.

"Those bastards are going to stay underground for a day or two," Damian snapped, "and besides, all I want is your boss's car."

"Now I know you're crazy! Are you planning to take her back out there to that place?"

"If I don't take her she's going to try to get there on her own," he said with resignation.

Brandy shot an enraged glance at Maia. "Do you realize how dangerous—" She broke off at the look in the other woman's eyes.

There was a deafening silence as the three looked from one to the other with stony expressions. Brandy was the first to look away. She turned abruptly and vanished up the narrow stone path that led to the hotel office, and returned a few moments later with a set of car keys. She motioned for them to follow her, and headed briskly out toward the parking lot.

"Where are you going?" Damian asked as he and Maia struggled to keep up.

"Where you're going," she answered without looking back. "I told my boss that my sister was taken ill and I have to go and close up her house."

"You don't have to come," Maia said as they reached the car door. Brandy glanced at her swollen face and looked away quickly.

"I don't know why you doing this," she said. "But maybe I can keep Tina, Juan, and Carlson from finishing you off."

Severin watched the sun setting from the splintered great house balcony. He was standing very still, clasping the cracked wood with quaking hands, his eyes blurred as the furious orb slipped into the silent sea. His hair had grown quickly and to his surprise the thin reedy locks were gray. The sparse stubble on his face had become a thicket and he knew his teeth were lost, forever. He chanted a child's rhyme in time to the rhythms of the gently fanning grape leaves: *"You live in peace, you die in peace, you buried in a pot of candle grease."*

Suddenly he had a wrenching desire to go on—not to simply slip away, like the blazing sun that surrendered so wordlessly to the night. He had a sudden longing, in a strangely infantile way, to go back to a time when the house was clean and whole; when women sang in the kitchens; when children ran hither and thither through the undergrowth. He wished he could smell the spicy flowers that the servants tucked into the bedding to discourage insects, and hear the birds singing ecstatically with the dawn. He could almost feel the power of a steed beneath his hips as they galloped along Wisdom's beach, hooves shattering the silvery morning foam.

But how could he do it? No one had ever given him the chance to be anything more than his brother's inferior. Their father had been so certain that Pete would grow up to inherit the estate that he had never bothered to show Severin even a single instant of love. Peter was the more beautiful, articulate, and intelligent of the brothers. Peter was kind and brave. A noble athlete, an excellent fisherman, a dedicated student, a man of faith.

Severin moved restlessly, remembering the day that he decided to spend his life celebrating the things his brother Pete ignored: black women, black culture, and the fast and furious side of island life. When the other boys—Peter, David, and even the effeminate Clay had outgrown their forbidden sexual pleasures, electing instead to form alliances with the girls of the island's white elite, Severin had remained true to his desires. When the others had purchased impressive new homes on the East End, Severin remained in the West, roaming day and night on the lush acres of Wisdom. He had spent the years swimming and riding and drinking while they accumulated fortunes in real estate and investing. They had joined the white world, had become a part of that existence, while he had never surrendered his spiritual and physical ties to his home.

And then came Maia. He ran his swollen fingers slowly along the peeling edge of the balcony, thinking about her.

Severin knew that Maia, with her blood spread so neatly across every square foot of the estate, had no choice but to return. She'd never be able to content herself with anything less than returning to her home.

"We can build a life together," Severin muttered. "I can change. I can make her happy. I'll get carpenters to rebuild the house. Paint it pink and white, like when I was a boy. We'll tile the floors and send away to Belgium for the finest lace curtains. We'll have the furniture made to order, and paper the walls with silk brocade. And we'll have children; yes, a daughter and a son. We'll teach the children to swim on Wisdom's beach. Teach them to ride Wisdom's horses, and to climb the steep hill to the tower—"

Behind him a stirring sound sent his thoughts flying to the blond filly, who was just awakening from her long afternoon siesta. She was an amusing toy. Certainly not interesting enough to hold his desire, despite her lovely body and almost wanton appetite for alcohol and sex.

But Bianca really didn't matter to him now. He knew as the flaming sun fell into the sea, the Ransom would surely come.

Paulette spilled her tumbler of Glenlivet as she read the article. Cursing, she set the glass down on the deck beside her pool chair and called out to her husband. On the other end of the deck Rose continued washing off the patio table as David sauntered through their living room and out onto the terrace overlooking the pool.

"Good lord, David—it's finally happened!" Paulette called up to him.

"What are you talking about?" he asked, leaning casually against the railing.

"Listen to this!" She stood up and walked toward him, holding the newspaper up in the late afternoon sunlight.

Tourist Attacked on Maroon Ridge

St. Croix: A tourist from Michigan was attacked on Maroon Ridge at approximately 9:50 P.M. last night. Police Chief D. P. Figueroa reports that the woman, whose rented Jeep was found near the scene, was apparently approached from behind by one or more assailants and both physically and sexually assaulted. It is unknown why the victim was at this remote location or whether she can identify her attackers. Doctors at Cummings

Hospital say that she is in serious condition, and have declined
comment on when she will be released. At present there have
been no arrests in the case.

"Do you think it's the nurse?" David asked quietly.

"Who else could it be?"

"You think Severin attacked her?"

"Of course he did. I wonder what in the hell he was thinking."

"Alcohol was probably thinking for him."

"Maybe he caught her trespassing."

"That still wouldn't give him any excuse to assault her."

"Unless . . ." Paulette's voice hissed to a stop as her mind whirred with a stunning idea. "Perhaps she found it!"

"Found what?" David asked, confused by his wife's fixed stare.

"Whatever's hidden up there in the mill." Ignoring the maid, Paulette threw the paper on a low table and crossed the deck in four long strides. Within moments she was standing beside her husband. "Hurry up and get in the car," she snapped as she scooped up her bag and keys.

"Where do you think we're going?"

"We've got to find out what's going on at Wisdom."

"Paulette, it's nearly dark and that road is dangerous enough in the daylight."

"We've driven it a thousand times, David."

"I think we should wait until the police figure this out."

"Do you think they're going to do something about it? They don't give a shit about that American woman."

"We should wait until they've completed their investigation."

"The police have no business on Johanssen property!"

"If Severin did this, then they most certainly do!"

"Severin will find some way to get out of it. But I don't want those greedy, bribe-seeking lowlifes to have an excuse to search the estate."

"The attack happened out on the road, Paulette."

"But if she identifies Severin, they'll surely go up to the house."

"You shouldn't be there if they do."

"They mustn't go anywhere near the mill. And besides, even if that woman did find something, I've got to make sure it never gets into the hands of Noah Langston."

"So what are you planning to do?"

"Whatever I have to do!"

"Paulette—" He stopped speaking at the look in her eyes.

"I've always known you were weak," she said to her husband, "but I don't think I realized until this moment how much of a coward you are."

They stared at each other for a long instant. Then David rose and silently followed his Johanssen wife out of the house while Rose picked up the phone in the kitchen.

Brandy turned off of Centerline Road before reaching the street that would connect them to Maroon Ridge, and Maia looked out from the rear seat in panic.

"Where are you going? This isn't the way to Wisdom."

"I've been thinking about that," Brandy answered in a firm voice. "I know you want to go back there. But I have a better way."

"A shortcut?" Damian asked as the car sped toward a neighborhood of small cinder-block houses built in a loose circle under a forest of ancient flamboyant trees.

"No." She turned her head, speaking to Maia over her shoulder. "No, I don't think you should go back there until you know exactly what you're looking for."

"How do you know what I'm looking for?"

Brandy pulled the car into a dusty space behind a compact, faded cement dwelling. "I don't," she said as she opened the car door and climbed out.

Damian leaped out of the front seat to follow her as Maia looked around in bewilderment. The house stood at the edge of what might have been a playing field. Shaded by the low, orange-blossomed branches of a wide flamboyant, she noted that the windows were neatly curtained, and a meticulous garden bordered the front porch. Other nearby houses were similarly modest. There was no one about, despite the cool of the early evening.

Maia emerged slowly from the car, calling out for Damian to help her. He appeared on the front porch, crossing the yard at a jog, and placed his arm around her waist. Maia took a step forward, seeing Brandy come to the corner of the house accompanied by a woman.

"Oh, my Lord!" the cry went up suddenly, and Maia instantly recognized Mimi's voice in the falling darkness. "Look what they done to you, Nurse!"

A few moments later the four sat at a small wooden table. Mimi had poured them glasses of passion fruit juice, and she couldn't seem to take her eyes off of Maia. Brandy wasn't speaking, and Damian, for once, was silent, too. Mimi seemed to be waiting for something, or someone, to make sense of it all.

And then they heard another car in the driveway. Damian started up and looked out of the window, then remained standing as another woman came to the door.

"Evening, Rose," Brandy said quietly as Paulette and David's housekeeper came into the small dwelling. She looked at Maia, nodding silently, then stepped forward to kiss Mimi's cheeks.

"We must wait for one other," Mimi said quietly to Maia's unasked question, and the entire room remained steeped in silence until they heard another car.

At last the door opened and Vashti Peterson entered the room, still wearing her nurse's uniform. Brandy stood up so she could take her seat at the table, and Damian remained standing as Rose sat down, too. The four women sat in silence, their faces illuminated by the soft glow of an oil lamp hanging above the table.

Mimi was the first to address Maia. "I am sorry for what they done to you, my cousin Carlson and Juan. I don't know where they are, but what's done in the dark will appear in the light. I'm sure they will pay for this crime."

Maia lowered her head, not bothering to pretend that she couldn't remember the attack. Vashti spoke up.

"Mimi told us that Tina hurt you on the beach. But none of us ever thought it would go so far."

The other women grunted softly in agreement. Then Mimi gestured toward Brandy. "I know Brandy since she a girl. Brandy and Tina play together every day, here, under my flamboyant. Sometimes Vashti here too, when her father busy with the cane harvest at Wisdom."

Maia looked across at the nurse's calm gaze, beginning to understand.

"You see," Vashti said, "we have always been a part of what goes on in that house. My father was the foreman of the estate."

"And my mother," Rose stated, "worked for Paulette Johanssen's parents. I grew up next door to Wisdom, and I went to live at the house on the East End when Paulette marry David."

"And I work at Wisdom for over fifty years," Mimi said with a sigh. "I watch these little girls become women. I watch Seven and his brother, Peter. I remember the mother and father when they still alive. I even remember the grandparents, who often tell me stories about the times when they were little children."

"Severin's grandparents talked to you about the past?" Maia whispered.

"They talk about the good times, just after slavery. They talk about Jakob Johanssen, who preferred to live with the blacks. And they talk about the three Ransom men who ran Estate Wisdom."

There was a silence. Maia found herself staring into Mimi's eyes.

"They was strong, the Ransoms," the old woman continued. "They work hard and make Wisdom a great and wealthy place. The Johanssens need them for everything—the horses, the fields, the millworks. There is no Wisdom without the Ransoms."

She paused an instant. "There was a woman, too. A sister. They call her Zara. The Johanssens bring her into the house because she has the Ransom power to heal. She is there to tend to the children. To help with the birthing. To nurse old Marie-Paule when she get sick. The old lady think that Zara Ransom keep death out of the house."

Damian shifted his weight nervously to his other foot. Brandy bent down and placed her hands on Mimi's shoulders.

"Tell her the rest," she said gently.

"When I was a girl, Seven's grandmother told me of the love between Jakob Johanssen and Zara Ransom. She say that Jakob love her so much that he leave the house and go to live with her in Christiansted. He no longer want to be part of the family, you see. He ask the Anglican priest to wed them, so their child would not be a bastard. He want the baby recognized as his own."

A single tear slipped from Mimi's wizened face as she looked across at Maia. "Old Solomon, he go crazy when Jakob marry Zara. He want Jakob to marry a rich white woman, you see. At first he cut Jakob from his will. But it was too late: Solomon's only other child, a boy named Issak, died when he was still a boy."

Mimi leaned forward. "Zara gave birth to a son, Abraham. She live with Jakob in Christiansted and teach at the school for black children. Then she get sick and die. The people say she dead because she leave Wisdom. And Jakob's heart is broken after her death—he has no more power against his father.

"Jakob married the white woman and they have more children. White children. Abraham grew up like a servant on his own estate, for Solomon and the others never recognized him as a Johanssen. When Jakob died the white Johanssens came together and forced Abraham to leave."

Reaching across the table, Mimi cupped Maia's face in her aged hands. "I know when you first come to the doorway that afternoon that you are the true Ransom. It's there, in your face. In your eyes. In your voice. Tina know it, too."

"And Severin?" Maia murmured.

"Seven could not stop talking about you. At first, he think you a ghost, like Peter, who lives in his dreams. He say you come up out of the past to heal him, like the Ransom who heal his ancestor."

Maia looked up at Damian. Mimi went on talking.

"Then you save his life on the beach. The doctor send you to live at Wisdom. And you keep talking about your people—"

"You heard me?"

Mimi laughed softly. "I didn't know if you was good or bad until Paulette came to the house. She hate Seven. She want to see him dead. But you stop her, cold. She can't come past you. She is banished from the house until you leave—"

"She can't get past the Ransom in you," Rose interjected.

"Yes," Maia whispered. "She came back the day I moved out."

"So Seven believe you belong there, to protect him."

Maia looked down, feeling tears gather in her own eyes.

"Now Paulette bring that blond harlot to take your place in Seven's mind," Mimi said, shaking her head. "She hope that child can change what Seven feel for you!"

"But I never intended to stay at Wisdom," Maia replied. "Why is Paulette so afraid?"

Mimi laughed quietly and exchanged glances with the others.

"She knows the family history," Vashti responded with a wry smile. "She knew that Seven would want to keep you—"

"I never wanted a relationship with Severin!"

All three women laughed. Vashti spoke first. "That doesn't matter to him, Miss Ransom. The men in Seven's world are raised to believe they can have any woman they want. It was hard for us growing up around them. You have no idea what Peter and David and Seven were like. How they hounded us."

"Just look what they done with Tina," Mimi murmured.

"And they still at it with other women," Rose confirmed.

"Paulette was afraid you'd become Seven's mistress," Vashti said.

"That he might tell you certain things about the past," Mimi added.

"And you might take her precious land," Rose declared. "She saw you at the Marienbad with Noah Langston, and she almost went crazy!"

Maia nodded slowly as the events of the past few weeks began to make more sense. She looked around the table. "What exactly does Severin know?"

For a long moment no one spoke. Then Vashti sighed. "When I was a child I often played with Peter and Seven. We ran all over the estate. They didn't touch me because my father was important to them. And because they knew I wouldn't—" She paused.

"There was a game they played in the old mill. A counting game. They would start somewhere and count the stones. The boys used to do it in French. They claimed it was a secret Johanssen code, passed down through the generations from their ancestor, Marie-Paule."

Mimi nodded. "Marie-Paule spoke French, you know. Solomon

Johanssen bring her to St. Croix from Martinique. The house was built for her. And they say the builder make a special hiding place, there in the mill, so the family papers wouldn't be lost if the rest of the house destroyed by a hurricane."

Maia's mind flashed on the ruined sugar mills that still graced hills all over the island. The plantation houses were long gone. The slave quarters were things of the past. But the stone mills still remained—

"The walls of the mill are very thick," Vashti continued. "So the builder simply hollowed out a portion and covered it with stones. You can only open it from inside the tower. But you have to know which stone to remove to get to the hiding place."

"Do you know what's in the ruin?" Maia asked, looking from one woman to the other.

"It's something from the past," Vashti said quietly.

"Something about the rights to Wisdom," Rose agreed.

"It is," Mimi said in the voice of a seer, "the deed for Wisdom that Marie-Paule's son Jakob wrote for his wife, Zara Ransom."

Maia's head suddenly began to throb so badly that she leaned forward, covering her eyes with her wounded hands. Damian was instantly by her side, and Brandy went to the sink and came back with a wet cloth.

Vashti took her pulse, then sat close beside her. "Do you want me to give you something for the pain?"

"No," Maia muttered. "I think I can handle it."

Vashti took her good hand. "I was never in the mill when they opened it, Miss Ransom. They would never let me inside. But I listened to them when they counted the stones, and I can remember at least part of the rhyme."

"So can I," Rose said proudly. "Paulette sing it all the time. At least, the line she remember. Sometimes she turn all pink with frustration, trying to get the whole thing right."

"Tell Nurse Ransom the words," Mimi urged them, and Maia strained to lift her aching head.

Staring into each other's eyes, Vashti and Rose together worked out the lines of the ancient song:

La première à gauche, deuxieme à droit,
Troisieme et quatrieme on reste etroit,
Cinquieme c'est rond, la six est noire,
Mais la septe contiene le vrai pouvoire.

"I don't understand a word," Maia said when the women completed the verses.

"And the only other language I know is German," Damian said.

"How the hell are we supposed to—"

Brandy cleared her throat. Everyone turned to look at her and she heaved a long, deep sigh. "I think I know what it means," she said softly. "My mother is from St. Lucia. I grew up speaking patois, you know. I think I can translate it for you."

"But if you can translate it now, you could have done it years ago!" Damian cried.

"No!" Mimi cried, looking back at the Americans. "She could not. You see, the papers in that mill are only meant for a Ransom. We all know that. Even Peter. Even Seven."

"It was only a few weeks before his wedding that Peter go to the mill to burn the papers," Rose explained. "But something stop him. And then he get on the airplane and he died."

"Oh, come on!" Damian exploded. "Are you trying to say that there's some kind of curse on anyone else who touches them?"

Mimi looked across the table and stared into Maia's eyes. "You are the healer. You are the last of the Ransoms. Those papers are meant only for you."

Brandy jerked the handbrake up as the car rolled to a stop in a hidden gully off the entrance to Wisdom. The dashboard lights reflected a sadness in her eyes that was matched by lips set in a firm expression of reconciliation. She knew that she had betrayed Severin—a man whom she had known since her childhood. A man who had been a longtime friend and lover.

But as she drove up Maroon Ridge, her mind traced the unwinding journey of their lives: the poverty of her childhood. Her family's vain attempts to rise above their lives as immigrant field workers on the estate. The white boys' theft of her virginity. Her lack of education. And the years of difficult labor that awaited her when she grew up.

She glanced into the rearview mirror at the woman who was leaning forward, clutching the seat in front of her, and trying hard not to surrender to the pain that wracked her body. Brandy realized that Severin and his people were responsible for the world that produced Carlson and Juan. A world that allowed Paulette to see Rose as a mindless tool. That set Mimi against Tina. That sentenced Brandy herself to stand behind the counter of a bar every night of her life.

The quest for control of Wisdom had moved beyond a question of inheritance. It was more than a battle between black and white. It had become a struggle leading to a kind of violence and cruelty that promised to destroy the most blameless—and, in fact, threatened to destroy them all.

Now she looked at her passengers. "I'll leave the car here, where I'm sure no one can see it."

"It's too damn dark to see anything!" Damian said in frustration.

"Don't worry. It will be bright enough when the moon rises," Brandy replied calmly. "You go in there, by those loose rocks. Mimi said that the men haven't finished putting up the barbed wire, yet."

"Imagine that," Damian replied sarcastically. "Maia's visits initiated the only home improvement to Estate Wisdom in at least fifty years!"

"Where are you going, Brandy?" Maia asked, closing her eyes against the pain that started to well up from her thighs.

"I go to look for Tina," the barmaid answered quietly. "I think she staying in the old boathouse near the beach. I believe Juan and Carlson might be there too."

"You can't do anything if you do find them," Damian warned her.

"I can try to keep them there long enough for you to get to the mill."

"And if you can't?" Damian asked.

Brandy was quiet for a moment. "Then we'd better hope the Ransoms are watching over you."

Damian helped Maia out of the car and they moved as quickly as possible toward the stone wall. The moon was rising, and the oily black sky was beginning to brighten. Down below the wall the sea crawled toward the shore with an incessant murmur. The air was heavy and very still, as if the night were holding its breath.

Scaling the rocks easily, Damian bent low to help an unsteady Maia over the stones. As he took her into his arms, their faces came close together.

"Are you all right?"

"I think so."

"Are you sure you want to go through with this?"

She nodded, biting down hard on her lip as pain streaked up her bruised hip. He stared at her for a few moments, then began to guide her carefully along the somber path.

"Damian?" Her voice was a ghost in the darkness. "Why are you here with me?"

Turning, he looked into her eyes. "Sometimes I think we really did dance together in another life," he whispered with a fleeting smile.

"You getting good and high," Severin rasped as Bianca slid toward him, her hips rocking to a make-believe rhythm. Through the thin sarong she had knotted at her hips he could see the full imprint of her thighs and the soft thatch of hair in between. She threw back her head and the shadows whipped weirdly in the room's low light. Her bottle of rum was already half-emptied, but she tipped it carefully against her full lips, giggling as it splashed off her bare breasts to his dusty medications on the bedstand.

"My little baby from Brazil," he murmured, gazing at her through half-closed eyes. She swept closer, then danced away, holding the bottle aloft like a torch. He leaned back on the bed, scratching at his matted chest, then raised one leg to the mattress, leaving the other stretched out on the floor. Bianca turned toward him.

"Don't you like my samba, baby?"

He grunted, watching the light dance on the arcs of her pear-shaped breasts.

"Come and dance with me," she intoned, slipping one hand into the knotted cloth so that it slipped off her hips and swished down her legs to the floor.

Severin slowly drew in his breath. He wondered if she'd come through the front door, like a true Ransom, and claim the house through her heritage. But then, he thought, after the events on the road she was unlikely to take such a chance. She was no fool, and with her people to guide her, she'd arrive at Wisdom safely. If she'd only been inside the estate the other night, Carlson and Juan could never have touched her.

Severin's head dipped slowly, his lids heavy. He hadn't drunk much, but the pain in his gut, which had been swelling steadily since Maia left Wisdom, was nearly overwhelming. Covered in clammy sweat, he struggled to smile through the grotesque sound of his own labored breathing. "I'm used to the hurting," he whispered stubbornly, imagining his brother by his side. "I won't let them know that I'm finally dying. I won't give them that pleasure. And besides," he throttled softly, "she's not here, yet."

He'd said the last words aloud, but Bianca was no longer paying attention to him. She had begun to spin, slowly at first, her hair fanning out in a golden mass. Whirling like a child, she threw out her arms and began to laugh and laugh and laugh, the sound growing warped and shrill in the molten night.

Neither one of them heard the doors slowly opening, as feet unaccustomed to the plan of the house entered the foyer. Neither heard the hastily whispered comments as the intruders passed the kitchen and approached the doors to the great room. Severin had just closed his eyes as the hysterical dervish threw herself drunkenly on the bed, her intoxicated squeals turning to soft moans as she leaned dizzily forward to kiss him.

Severin's arms came up to hold her at bay, but it was too late. The door to the great room opened. Instead of his longed-for guest, his destiny had arrived.

Catherine leaned back in the BMW, wondering what Noah hoped to do when they arrived at the estate. She had never seen him so tense; never seen anything like the expression in his eyes. Silently he'd slid a sharpened machete under his seat as they got into the car, and she saw something black shoved into his hip pocket.

"Perhaps we should call the authorities," she remarked calmly as they left civilization behind and began the steep rise toward the isolated, cliffside road.

He didn't answer.

"We might need an ambulance, you know."

He shifted gears without speaking, the German sedan neatly hugging the treacherous dirt road.

"You really should have someone else with you, Noah."

"I have you, Cat," he said in a low tone.

The sun had fallen into the sea a few moments before, and the sky was flecked with vibrant orange and purple clouds. In the distance the water shimmered with a silvery light edged with deep, calming blue.

"What happens if we run into her attackers?" Catherine asked.

"I'm praying that we do."

"I don't want to be involved in any violence."

"Then you can close your eyes."

"So I'm just here to pick up the pieces?"

"You took an oath to care for the sick," Noah replied sarcastically. "You have nothing to do with how they got that way."

She looked across at him in anger. "You have no right to do this."

"Did they have a right to rape her and try to kill her?"

"No, but you can't become one of them, Noah."

He met her gaze. "I'm just going to make sure," he said, "that they never, ever do anything like this again."

"I thought our primary purpose was to find Maia."

"I'll find her," Noah answered. "And I'll find them, too."

"Noah," she said desperately, "in all the years I've known you I've never seen you do anything this stupid."

"In all those years you've never really known me, Cat."

"Are you trying to pretend that all the time we've spent together means nothing?"

He twisted the steering wheel to avoid a huge pit in the road. "If you really knew me," he answered when they were moving forward again, "we wouldn't be having this argument."

Noah pulled his sedan up behind Maia's abandoned Jeep and turned off the engine. His hands clasped the steering wheel and he stared straight ahead, as if searching for the strength to handle his emotions. Beside him Catherine stirred restlessly.

"I suppose you've got a plan."

"No, Cat, I don't."

"Well, I'm sure that gun in your pocket does."

He turned his head slowly, his eyes very cold in the darkness. When he spoke, his voice flattened out to a dead tone. "I'll do whatever it takes to protect her."

"You mean you'll risk everything for a woman who may very well choose to die."

"Nothing else matters."

A car hurtled past, leaving a cloud of dust in its wake.

"She only cares about this land."

"She's got to find herself before she can give herself to anyone else."

"This is too dangerous, Noah."

"I'm partially responsible, Cat."

"I think you should call the police."

"And I think you should listen." He loosened his grip on the steering wheel. "I've been trying to understand it," he said in a muted voice. "Trying to understand what went wrong between you and me. Why we could never really make it work."

"This really isn't the time," she began, but he shook his head.

"You're strong and brilliant, Cat. God knows you're beautiful. You've worked hard and I admire you for that. The thing is—" He glanced out as the moon rose eerily over the horizon. "You've always believed that playing by the rules means you'll win the game. But life's not like that for some of us. Sometimes we have to break the rules, or make new rules in order to survive."

"You're wrong, Noah. And I see the results of your thinking in the emergency room every day."

"The difference between the two of us," he said, "is that pain and suffering only convince you that the world needs more rules. But it's the rules that cause the suffering. Maia's ancestor was forced away from his home and this island by rules. Rules about race and class and property and wealth. It's rules that stopped her from rediscovering her heritage. And those same rules are still keeping her from property that's legally hers. I'm sorry, Cat," he said with finality. "But I'm going to help her break them."

"You're an attorney, Noah!"

"I'm a black man, Cat. My race comes first. It has to. The rules made it that way."

Catherine looked angrily into Noah's eyes. "Somebody's going to get hurt with that gun, Noah."

"Guns are the only language some people speak."

"Then I'll wait here until you need me to mop up the blood."

"Yes," he said softly as he climbed out of the car. "You do just that."

Paulette might have seen the BMW parked just off the road, but the moon had not risen high enough to cast a reflection on its silvery finish. She was driving at the speed of someone who knew Maroon Ridge very well. So well, in fact, that her husband was bending down to light a cigarette as they passed the couple arguing in the car parked in the darkness.

"I think you're overreacting," David commented with feigned composure as they roared around a curve.

"That's because you never react to anything."

"It's because Severin's not our business."

"Everything that happens to my family is my business."

David clenched his jaw and glanced at his wife, almost admiring her steeliness. In some ways it was a shame that so much power was trapped in a woman. "Look, Paulette," he said, "all you're going to find is Severin, dead drunk, busily banging the hell out of your little friend Bianca."

"You just wish you could bang her yourself." They reached the entrance to the overgrown drive and, slowing down, Paulette maneuvered the car into the narrow opening.

"We should have brought Clay," David muttered as the smothering night closed in.

"Why? Clay is even less a man than you are."

"What's that supposed to mean?"

"He didn't even have enough guts to screw the black girls when you were kids!"

David laughed viciously. "Come on, Paulette. We both know that you chose me when you saw me in the bushes with Tina. It must infuriate you that a white man finds black women more desirable than you."

"Fuck you, David—"

"It's not hard to understand, really. Those black women don't have the bitchy pretensions of the white Danish royalty on this godforsaken rock! All of you act like this is the most valuable, important place in the world. You think it's worth lying and cheating and even dying for! And you think that the rest of us are weak simply because we don't buy into your bullshit!"

Paulette turned her head briefly toward her husband. "You don't have to buy into anything," she said coldly. "But as long as you're swimming in a pool, sleeping in a villa, and playing golf in a club paid for by Johanssen money, you need to shut the hell up."

Suddenly the silhouette of the decaying house began to emerge from the grape vines, and Paulette pounded on the horn loudly, deliberately announcing her grand arrival.

"This is really stupid," David began, but Paulette was already out of the car and leading the way up the circular drive. She managed to get halfway up the weedy slates when something stopped her in her tracks. Picking his way carefully behind her, David collided heavily with his wife. "Goddammit, Paulette! Why don't you—"

"Shut up!"

The door to the house was thrown open, and despite the feverish darkness, David Fairchild and his Johanssen wife could already see that death was waiting for them inside.

Paulette would always remember the blood in those wild, golden waves. The blood that had splattered from the bed sheets to the wall. The blood already soaking through the floorboards to the deep earth below. The room was in chaos, the chairs turned over, mattress torn from the bed, and Severin's many bottles of medication strewn wildly across the floor. The doors to the balcony were thrown open, one leaning woefully off its hinges. The silence was deafening.

David pushed Paulette aside and ran into the great room, impervious to the fact that the killers might still be there, hiding in some rotting corner of the dwelling. He knelt beside the young woman and slowly turned her over, finding that she was still grasping the neck of a bottle in her slippery red palm, while the long cracked shards of glass remained imbedded in her naked belly and breasts. One shining chunk was still lodged in her cheek.

Paulette turned away, her knees buckling beneath her. Grasping the door frame, she coughed and coughed, until her mouth filled with the bitter remnants of her dinner. She leaned against the wall and waited until her stomach calmed. Then steeling herself, she looked over her shoulder at David.

He had closed Bianca's eyes, and with a trembling hand he smoothed the locks of hair away from her parted lips. His fingers came away scarlet, and the sight of the blood galvanized his wife.

"Go wash your hands."

He remained crouched beside the body, murmuring softly.

"You're bloody, David. Go wash your hands!"

When he didn't move Paulette began to shout, overcome by a violent, uncontrollable rage. "Don't you understand? She's dead! You can't do a fucking thing for her now!"

David looked up, tears in his eyes. "What kind of woman are you? You're standing over her like a vulture, and all you can talk about is washing our hands?"

"We've got to get out of here—"

"We can't leave her like this!"

"What difference does it make? It's done! It's over! She's dead!"

"But she's a human being!" David shouted. "What the hell is wrong with you?"

Paulette looked around wildly. "Whoever did this might come back."

"Whoever did this?" he repeated. "What do you mean by that? Severin obviously did this!"

"That's impossible!"

"You were perfectly willing to believe that he attacked the American—"

"But this is different, David!"

"Why? Because Bianca's white? Because you brought her here and gave her to him? Because you can't allow a murder to be attached to the Johanssen name?"

Paulette backed up into the doorway. "I won't have anything to do with this. And if you're stupid enough to get involved—"

"We're already involved!" he screamed. "This young woman dated your brother before you introduced her to Severin! She was murdered in his house—no, in his *bedroom*. And we discovered the body! How can we pretend not to have anything to do with this?"

"Fuck you, David," Paulette stammered. "You can stay here and feel sorry for her if you want to, but I'm leaving."

"I'm calling the police," he declared, pulling a phone from his pocket.

She came to a standstill in the doorway without looking back. "I don't care what you do. But I will not be a part of this."

"God help you," David Fairchild said as Paulette Johanssen crossed the threshold and staggered out into the night.

B randy almost thanked God that there was moonlight. The rocks seemed to leap up out of nowhere, and despite a childhood spent playing along the beach of Estate Wisdom, without the cool etchings of the moon, she would never have found her way to the boathouse.

She could see faint candlelight through the thicket of grape leaves. According to legend, the boathouse had once been inhabited by the Ransom ancestors. But for many years its only inhabitants were lizards. Severin had allowed Tina to clean it out, and now the two rooms were stocked with broken furniture from Wisdom. There was a gas stove, but no running water. Brandy reasoned that after attacking Maia, Carlson and Juan really had nowhere else to go.

She hoped that they'd be there, and that they weren't too drunk. She hoped that she could convince them to take the money she had hidden in her bra and to leave the island. She hoped that they would see the folly of trying to complete what they'd begun.

As Brandy came closer to the house, however, she found herself more and more afraid. She had seen the two men in their drunken frustration, and she knew what they were capable of. If they'd already decided to finish the business they'd started with Maia, there'd be little that Brandy could do to stop them. Still, she approached the boathouse with the same calm confidence that she showed her customers, even on very difficult nights. It made men respect her. Made even the drunkest customer leave her absolutely alone.

Edging carefully forward, she finally got close enough to look in through the windows. Ropes and chains and old sail fabric lay piled inside. A crude table held a carton of cigarettes and several empty bottles. In the faint light she could see Tina's shoulder and her unclasped hand. She appeared to be alone. And whether from alcohol or fatigue, she was sleeping deeply. Brandy softly called out her friend's name.

Nothing stirred, so Brandy pushed open the door and went inside. The smell of rum and cigarette smoke thickened the air. A brown-stained T-shirt and jeans were visible beneath a plastic tarp, and the remains of half-eaten carambolas lay at Tina's feet. Brandy knelt down beside her.

"Hey! Come on, Tina! Wake up!"

The heavy woman stirred, a throaty snort escaping from her lips.

"Tina. Wake up now, *meson*! I need to know where Carlson and Juan gone!"

Brandy continued to shake her shoulders and call out her name until Tina's yellow eyes opened. Grunting malevolently, she lifted her head to peer at the other woman.

"Brandy? What you want out here?"

"Where they go, Tina? You got to tell me, now!"

Tina heaved herself up slowly on one arm, looking past Brandy into the night. She exhaled a noxious perfume of smoke and alcohol, then spat on the floor.

"I don't know nothing about what they do."

"Tina. Did they go up to the house?" Brandy insisted, taking Tina by the arm.

"Why I tell you?"

"You must tell me before they do something terrible," Brandy insisted. The other woman choked out a mean laugh, then lay back down and closed her eyes.

"You don't have nothing to worry about. When they finish, Seven belong to me again."

"What you mean, Tina?"

"I mean it's better if you stay down here with me," she muttered, staring at her childhood companion through hollow, bloodshot eyes.

Panting with exertion, Maia had to stop halfway up the moon-sculpted hill. Each step sent a knife into her battered hip, and her injured hand had begun to throb, too. Her head was pounding in the thick, humid air, and she had to blink to keep tears out of her eyes.

"Why didn't you let that nurse give you something?" Damian whispered.

"I need to stay focused," she muttered. "And anything strong enough to stop this pain would knock me out."

She looked up toward the mill, standing like a phantom lighthouse at the top of the hill. Thankfully, Brandy was right—it was almost as bright as day, and that fact alone made the climb much easier. Her eyes took in the supernatural clarity of each pebble at her feet. The night was so still that she could hear the fretting of the waves against the rocks below. No locusts sang and no crickets called. The silver-edged grape leaves hung in perfect stillness.

"We'd better keep moving," Damian said softly, and he took her hand, bracing his palm against her lower back to support her. Maia moved slowly, drawn upward as if an invisible hand were guiding her. Deep inside she repeated the English words to Marie-Paule's poem, praying that she'd gotten them right:

> The first stone on the left, the second to the right,
> The third and fourth remain straight in your sight,
> The fifth stone is round, the sixth is black,
> The seventh stone will hand the power back.

Steadily they made their way up the embankment. Maia could see the enormous boulder that looked out over the sea—the rock where, she was sure, Zara Ransom had searched the horizons of her life and dreamed about her future. The boulder where Maia herself had hidden, only two nights before, when Severin tried to destroy her past. The place where, she thought as they drew painfully nearer, she might finally be safe. And whole. And free.

A few moments later Maia lay against the boulder, feeling the stone reign cool and smooth against her aching limbs. The moon had risen higher and a shaft of light fell into the opening of the mill, just a few feet away. "Come on, Maia," Damian whispered, urging her to move faster. "We can't waste any more time."

Exhausted and aching in every muscle in her body, Maia was afraid she'd be unable to take the last few steps. She'd spent her whole life, from the time she was just a child, dreaming of the moment when she'd set foot on her island. Her land. Her home. But now, when she was so close to touching the last proof that she was walking in the footsteps of her people, she was suddenly afraid.

Grasping Damian's arm, she looked desperately into his face. "What if this isn't right?"

"This land is yours," he answered, already moving toward the entrance.

"No—wait!" She lowered her voice. "What if the papers are evil?"

Damian turned and stared at her. "The people who used these papers to hurt your ancestors were evil."

"Won't I become one of them if I take them?"

"What do you mean?"

"Won't I be just like Severin and Paulette and all the masters who enslaved us?"

"No, Maia," he said softly. "You'll be ending one hundred years of deceit. There's nothing evil in that." With these words he led her forward, pausing at the entrance of the mill so that she could precede him.

The circular room was cool and dark, the only light a sharp rectangle that peered in through the open doorway. Maia looked around her helplessly, lost in a checkerboard maze of stones that vanished skyward into the black cone of the mill.

"How in the hell are we supposed to do this?" She knelt down painfully and began to brush the dirt away from the lower stones. "It's too dark to see anything."

Damian grunted and slipped down beside her. "What did it sound like when Severin was in here?"

"What do you mean?"

"Did he move around a lot? Did he seem to be dragging something heavy?"

Maia tried to focus on the scene—just two nights before—when she had listened to Severin as he tried to destroy the deed. She remembered that he had moved around almost frantically in the mill, but that the papers were very quickly hidden from view.

"It can't be too heavy or too high," she remarked, climbing slowly to her feet.

"Of course not! Your ancestor wouldn't have been able to use an inaccessible space."

"But it wasn't created for Zara! Marie-Paule Johanssen had it built when Wisdom was first constructed."

"Oh come on!" Damian snapped. "She was a woman, too! And I seriously doubt that she was as tall or strong as you. After all," he added sarcastically, "she had the Ransoms doing everything for her."

Maia leaned back against the inner wall, feeling herself break out in a cold sweat. Her injured hand had stiffened to a dead limb, and she was finding it extremely difficult to think clearly.

"All right," Damian whispered, sensing her discouragement. "Let's stop thinking like seekers and start thinking like the keepers." He glanced around the hundreds of stones that formed the interior of the mill. "I wish I had some decent light—"

His voice broke off. Then suddenly he began to pat his pockets, beginning with his button-down shirt and working his way downward toward his thighs. Maia watched in exhausted curiosity as he drew his wallet out of his hip pocket and flipped it open.

"Let there be light," he beamed.

Maia stepped closer and looked down at the small mirror tucked inside Damian's wallet. He angled it back and forth until the moonlight began to bounce nervously off the mill's interior walls, like a flashlight.

"Slow down," Maia complained as the beam flew from side to side.

"We don't have time for sightseeing. Let's just try to find the first stone."

They knelt side-by-side and Damian turned the mirror so that the reflected moonlight moved systematically along the lowest stones. It was impossible to decide where to begin, because the base of the mill was carved into the sandy hill, and the lowest level of stones varied in depth from the front to the rear.

"We'll never find it," Maia said desperately.

"We'll find it."

"How? The reflections don't even reach the complete interior."

"They wouldn't have to. Tell me, Maia: What time was it when Severin was here?"

"What difference does that make?"

"It will give us some idea which corners of the mill might have been visible by moonlight."

"He's been here a thousand times! He doesn't need light."

"Was he drunk?"

"Yes."

"Very drunk?"

"He was talking to himself."

"But he managed to get it open and shut again in a hurry?"

Maia looked around in dismay. "Drunk is Severin's natural state—" The words caught in her throat as she realized something: Severin had been standing up when he reached into the hiding place. She'd seen him stagger both into the mill and out. The hiding place had to be at waist-level! Severin hadn't been crawling around near the ground!

"Look higher, Damian! Severin didn't have to bend down to—"

She felt her friend's hand as he gripped her arm. The reflected moonlight glanced off of a small stone that shone like a crystal in the darkness. Compared to the other sandstone blocks, this smooth rock resembled a chunk of cool ice, stuck strangely into the rugged mosaic of the wall.

"That's it," Maia throttled. "Look where it was placed—just parallel to the door. That means it reflects both sunlight and moonlight."

"All right," Damian said very softly. "What were the words of the rhyme?"

"First stone to the left, second to the right."

He carefully lifted the mirror, searching all the rocks around the small, shining crystal. "There it is," he purred as a rusty-veined crystal appeared.

"The third and forth remain in our sight," Maia intoned, praying that Brandy had translated the verse correctly. Damian simply raised the mirror. Two more stones appeared, both granite speckled with silver and gray chips.

"The fifth should be round and the sixth black—"

Damian searched the rough interior wall, his mirror casting its light on the stones just at his waist level. A perfectly spherical stone, several inches above the others, could be seen, and he moved on silently, looking for their black landmark.

"Onyx," he whispered as the mirror found an oil-colored stone. "Now we only need one more . . ."

They both raised their heads at that instant. There were voices approaching outside. Damian put a hand on Maia's arm to steady her. "Don't be afraid," he whispered.

"But Damian—"

"Remember," he said firmly, "you're here because this is what Zara wanted."

Noah hacked down the newly installed barbed wire with his machete, and crossed into the estate by the path he knew best. He counted on needing only a few minutes to reach the mill, for the full moon had risen above the hilly landscape and the world was aglow in a ghostly haze. He moved quietly, using his tool to cut the low-growing bushes away in case he needed to make a hasty retreat. Certainly, he reasoned, Maia wouldn't go anywhere near the house now that she knew where Severin had hidden the papers. And certainly—he turned the thought carefully over in his mind as he paused to catch his breath—Juan and Carlson weren't stupid enough to be anywhere near the estate.

He tried not to think about Cat, whose bitterness weighed on him. It wasn't that he needed her approval. No, he was absolutely sure that what he was doing was right. But after knowing her for so long, and caring about her so much that he'd even considered marrying her, it just felt wrong that they should be divided. After all, this night would, whether they liked it or not, determine the direction of the rest of his life.

Noah was so focused on following the fastest path to the top of the hill that he almost missed the strains of voices wafting through the supernatural stillness from the beach far below. He froze, leaning back into a cusp of thick grape leaves, and listened as the tones grew louder.

They were male. They were Cruzian. They were coming closer.

Noah tried not to breathe as the voices stopped and started. He could make out threats, curses, and enraged shouts. He could tell that the men were engaged in a struggle that went far beyond a brawl induced by rum or ganja. He knew this was something serious, perhaps even deadly, and he melted into the shadows, willing himself into invisibility with every fiber of his being.

"Why you take up with that bitch?" he heard someone say. "Why you send my sister off to live like a slave after all the years she care for you?"

Fucking shit, Noah thought, his hand tightening on the machete handle. *Carlson.*

"I don't send her nowhere," someone rasped. "She come and she go as she please!"

There was a hard, muffled sound, followed by a long groan. Then the other man spoke.

"First you with the nurse. Then you have that blond bitch. How long you think Tina take that shit from you?"

Yes, Noah thought, *oh yes. It was Juan!*

The question was underscored by the sound of a swift, hard kick. The answer was a low-pitched, animal moan. The two men laughed. "You not looking so good, now," Carlson remarked. "You used to having all the pussy, eh Seven? Well, now you scared that we take care of them both. We got one and we going to find the other. You must be wondering who left to sleep with you now?"

They got one? Noah felt the sweat burning in his eyes and his fist tightened on the machete until it ached. He sensed the weight of the gun, shoved tight into the hip pocket of his jeans. It was hard to tell exactly where the men were standing, for the humid air was carrying sound with an uncanny clarity. But he wished that they would come into the range of his hatred. Into the range of the bullets. Or the curve of his razor-sharp blade.

"So why don't we just finish this asshole off right now?" Carlson asked. "Might as well make sure the job gets done."

"Tina will get over him soon enough," Juan agreed. "And to be honest, she will not want to live in the house now that it's so messed up."

"True, that," Carlson remarked coolly. "Now the house is sure to be haunted."

Their laughter rang out in brutal fraternity, like schoolyard bullies grown into vicious beasts. They struck their victim again, then again and again, the sounds ranging from slaps, to punches, to inhuman kicks. They beat him in payment for their lives of impoverished misery.

Then a panting silence fell as the assailants paused to catch their breath. Severin's soundlessness might have been the quiet of death, but then his voice pierced his own agony.

"Stop," he begged. "I give it to you."

"What you give us?" Juan asked.

"Wisdom. You can have Wisdom."

"What? You mean you marry Tina?" Carlson asked in mock outrage. "She too good for you, motherfucker." He followed this pronouncement with another hard kick.

Severin moaned, his voice breaking. "No. I give you house, land, everything."

"Right," Juan said sarcastically. "We call a lawyer and you can sell it to me!"

"We call up Noah Langston," Carlson agreed. They burst into sarcastic laughter.

"No," the dying man moaned. "I give you papers."

"What papers?" Juan demanded.

"The deed. You take papers. Wisdom yours."

There was a weighted silence. The men didn't believe him. They knew, after lifetimes of thralldom, that their master would never willingly set them free. But they also knew the stories about Wisdom. About the banished son and the secret deeds. About the Ransoms.

"Where the papers?" Juan demanded.

"I tell you and you let me go," Severin muttered.

"You tell us and we think about it," Carlson said.

"No. I free if I give you papers," Severin muttered. Listening from his hiding place, Noah was amazed at the fallen man's cunning. Or was it simply his desperation?

For a moment no one spoke. Noah could well imagine Carlson and Juan looking at each other, considering whether or not the deeds to the estate would be enough to give them true ownership of Wisdom.

Then they decided.

"Give us papers and we might let you go," Juan said softly.

"I tell you where to get them and—"

"You come with us," Juan interrupted. "When we have the papers, we decide if we let you live."

"I hope you not lying," Carlson remarked, "because to tell you the truth, Seven, I really want to watch you die."

Juan laughed as he shoved the stumbling, panting Severin through the bushes, just a few feet from the crouching Noah. Carlson had taken up the rear, looking around nervously as they reached the top of the sharp slope pitching down to the sea. Juan leaned easily on the large boulder that faced the mill and looked around calmly, as if enjoying the view.

"Shit," he remarked as his gaze fell on the distant horizon. "Pretty nice up here. Why you keep it a secret, Sev?" He glanced across at Carlson, who had suddenly gone silent. "What's wrong with you?" he barked, seeing the strange tension in his companion's manner.

"This place spooky," was the response.

"Going to get spookier in a few minutes," Juan replied. He flicked his head toward their captive. "All right, Mr. Johanssen. Where those papers you so eager to give me?"

Severin raised his head unsteadily, as if finding it hard to believe where he was. His lips were split wide open and he was nearly blinded by his swollen cheeks. Matted with blood, his naked chest was a mass of black shadows. He was trembling, his legs visibly shaking in his blood-flecked drawstring pants.

"Paper in mill," he scratched out, and pitching forward to his knees, he managed to remain upright by bracing his arms on his thighs. He coughed up a throat full of thick red mucus and managed to spit it at his filthy feet.

"We waiting," Juan said.

Severin dropped his head as if searching in the depths of his wretched lungs for enough strength to take another breath. Wavering dizzily on the steep path, his legs buckled and he leaned forward dizzily.

"Oh, shit," Carlson muttered.

"I need a whip," Juan commented. "Like the Johanssens used on their slaves. Might help him move a little faster." He stepped forward and planted a kick on Severin's lower back and the man fell forward with a whimper. He vomited more blood.

"This a pathetic sight," Juan said. "And I getting tired of waiting. Where the papers, Seven? You tell me now and maybe you don't die in the next sixty seconds."

Severin lifted his tear-filled face to the moon. He lay broken on the hill, his chest barely rising and falling. He lifted a shaking hand and pointed to the mill entrance.

"Go, Carlson," Juan barked.

The other man hesitated, looking from Juan to the blackened doorway. "I said, go!" Juan repeated, and Carlson took a reluctant step forward.

At that moment the entire world seemed to freeze, then move forward in slow motion. For just as Carlson turned his frightened eyes to the secret chamber, a skeletal figure appeared in the black opening, as gaunt and emaciated as Death itself.

Carlson cried out and fell back, stumbling over the prostrate Severin. He went down heavily and scrambled crablike toward the shadows.

"What the fuck—" Juan began, turning to gaze up at the mill. But before he could begin to understand what he was seeing, Noah leaped from the thicket of grape leaves and struck him hard in the temple with the butt of his pistol.

Juan flew forward to his knees, but years of sailing small crafts on the open, sometimes storm-driven waters had made him lithe and strong. His quick hands found a rock and he was up in an instant, whipping around to slam his opponent with his powerful arms.

Noah stumbled backward, losing his footing on the steep, rocky slope. He fell against the boulder where Maia sang her ageless songs and raised his machete to ward off Juan's blow. The sailor lurched forward, ignoring the blade that slashed the moonlight in a whistling arc. Juan's chest erupted in a scarlet fountain and he let out a furious howl.

Carlson exploded from the shadows and slammed Noah with the full weight of his body. The gun flew from Noah's hand and skidded toward the bushes and both men fell on top of the lawyer, seeking to pitch him down the steep incline.

The struggle was a quiet dance of life meeting death. Juan's clothes were suddenly soaking and he peered down, his eyes bulging in wonder. Releasing the lawyer, he lifted a curious hand to the moonlight and sat back heavily, staring at the hot sticky liquid. Noah rolled to the side, carrying the writhing Carlson with him, and instantly the force of gravity sent them both hurtling down the rocky slope, a tangle of grappling limbs. There was a sickening snap as Carlson's lower arm was crushed between a sharp stone and Noah's weight and he screamed in agony, reaching desperately toward his shattered bone.

Noah slid farther down the slope, his shirt ripped by rocks and bushes, his fist still closed over the handle of the bloody machete. Scrambling to his hands and knees, he used the blade as a pike to regain his balance, and began a desperate climb toward the mill.

By the time he reached the boulder, Noah was panting too hard to call Maia's name. Rising shakily to his feet, he rubbed the dirt from his eyes. What he discovered was a vision of hell.

Severin lay in his vomit, his legs drawn up in a fetal position. Juan was crouched in a stupor, his hands clutching his chest as if his fingers alone could stem the gushing flow of blood. The earth was painted with thick, scarlet sand. Carlson had disappeared into the darkness and the gun was nowhere to be found.

Dripping with sweat, the lawyer lifted his eyes to the waiting tower. It was only then that he saw a woman's shadow, clearly illuminated in the moonlight, approaching him swiftly from behind. Her arms were raised high above her head and he knew that she was carrying the largest rock that she could manage. He began to turn, staggering defenselessly against the boulder, when a voice pierced the night with otherworldly clarity.

The sound was sharp and cold and strong. It wasn't a scream, exactly, yet all the terror and pain and confusion of that night were in the sound. He looked up in wonder as Paulette halted in midstride, the rock still balanced above her head. He saw her stare up at the yawning mill in fear. He saw her recoil, the rock thudding heavily at her feet. And only then, when she stepped back with a whimpering sound, did he dare to follow her gaze.

Maia was standing at the threshold of the stone mill, with Damian barely visible behind her. Her loose garments were torn and soiled, but she was standing straight and tall. In the pure, silvery light her eyes were dark hollows, the thick lashes like paint around her gaze. Her lips were parted and tears washed the cheeks of another woman, from another time.

She looked down on the slaughter, her gaze moving steadily from Paulette to Juan, then coming to rest on Severin. He stirred, giving a rumbling cough, as if conceding his defeat. Then Maia's eyes found Noah, and her arm moved slowly as she lifted her hands toward the night. A sheath of yellowing papers sealed with red wax caught the moonlight and seemed to glow a luminous white.

Noah took a halting step forward. He didn't understand the loud noise or scorching thrust of pain that entered and exited his body. His eyes still trained on Maia, he was surprised when his balance failed, and he lurched forward into a heap, not far from Severin's bloody, broken body.

Everything became a swirl of movement then. Maia hobbled from the mill, supported by Damian as Carlson emerged from the bushes, the gun swaying crazily in his good hand. He aimed recklessly at Paulette, then turned the barrel back on Noah, then wheeled around as if trying to vise Damian and Maia.

"You goddamn demons," he spat as his eyes settled on Maia's haunting face. "*Mwe kay-tsue*! I kill you both for this! You and Seven Johanssen, too—"

A strangled cry exploded from the grape leaves as Tina hurtled desperately toward her brother. She grasped the gun from his shaking hand and threw it behind her, shoving him hard against the boulder. Carlson went down, cursing as he curled himself around his broken limb.

Tina crawled through the dirt and knelt beside Severin, just as Maia and Damian reached Noah. The lawyer groaned and pulled himself to his elbow, staring blankly toward his wound. Maia leaned over him and pulled away his shredded shirt. Her fingers found the hole where the bullet had entered his flesh, just beneath his ribs.

"Cat's in the car. On road," he whispered as his head rolled loosely to the side. Damian climbed to his feet and looked down at Maia. Their eyes held for an instant.

"Go," she whispered. "I'll be fine."

As soon as Damian vanished into the moonlight, Paulette moved stealthily forward. She took in the fallen men and the women who crouched unsteadily beside them. She saw the yellow papers, still bearing the Johanssen seal, lying beside the boulder in the bloody sand. She saw the nurse's hands as they worked to slow Noah's bleeding. She saw Tina weeping over the prostrate Severin.

In a matter of seconds she could reach the hated papers. In even less time she could crush the brittle pages and hurl them downward, toward the sea. Before any of the broken and bleeding witnesses could stop her, she could destroy the past forever.

She took one cautious step, and then another, ignoring the suffering of her dying cousin, the last of the Johanssens. Her heart beating wildly, she was only inches away from becoming the mistress of Estate Wisdom. She reached out, the tips of her fingers scraping the rough parchment.

"Don't touch that," a calm voice said, and Paulette whipped around, coming eye to eye with Brandy, who carefully leveled the gun at her face.

A burst of thick, chortling laughter caused them all to look over at Severin. Tina had taken him in her arms, and now his head lay in her lap. "They beat you, cousin," he rasped. "They win the game."

"This will always be Johanssen land!" she spat, but Severin shook his head.

"It belong to the Ransom. To Maia Ransom," he replied, his eyes wandering toward the nurse. His voice tumbled to a fading whisper. "You find your people, at last. Look at me, Maia: I am one of them. Now you know us all. You have a reason to live." He choked, his mouth filling with blood. "I told you Wisdom protect you," he rattled. "I only wish Wisdom protect me, too—"

The silence was like a knell. Noah's eyes were locked on Maia's face and she turned back to him, tears in her eyes. Picking up the papers, she pressed them into Noah's hand.

"I love you, Noah."

"And I love you, Maia Ransom," he said as she wrapped her fingers over his.

Damian hadn't gone far when he encountered Catherine working her way along the path Noah had cut with his machete. Hearing the gunshot in the heavy stillness, she'd set out alone, intent on helping whomever she could.

Despite the gruesome scene at the mill, the violence was finished. Juan had passed out beside Carlson, whose badly broken arm prevented his flight. Severin was unconscious, but Maia already knew that he was bleeding internally from his terrible beating. Her own pain forgotten, she'd torn her blouse into strips and bound up Noah's flesh wounds. Tina was weeping silently beside her lover, and Brandy was holding her shoulders, trying to calm her. Paulette had vanished into the night, certainly seeking the fastest way back to her safe and comfortable life.

Sirens and flashing lights soon descended upon the scene, alerted by David Fairchild's frantic call. Attendants began treating the hurt and wounded, and a procession of gurneys made its way along the rocky, moonlit path. Maia insisted on walking, and with Damian's help she made her way back to the road. Noah was carried on a stretcher and lifted inside an ambulance. Catherine climbed in beside him and silently inserted an IV-drip into his arm.

"Thank you, Cat." His voice was strong, despite his pain and loss of blood.

"It's the least I can do for you." She began adjusting the monitors, then tore open a bag of sterile wipes. "There is one thing you could do for me, however," she said as she cleaned a scrape on his forehead. "Convince Maia to give me a chance to help her."

Noah's breath caught in his throat. "I'll try," he whispered.

Catherine looked away as if trying to control her own emotions. "You were right, Noah. I sat in your car, telling myself that what you were doing was wrong. I sat there, even though I knew that you and Maia were in danger. I couldn't bring myself to move until I heard the shot." She cleared her throat. "I know that what you're doing here is right. But I also know that I'm not quite brave enough to do it with you."

"Cat—"

"No, Noah. They did everything they could to break her. But she wouldn't give up." Catherine laughed quietly. "That's the kind of woman you need. So I'm going to do everything in my power to see that she survives."

A few steps away Maia listened in silence while Damian described the events at the mill to a police officer. She was still holding the papers, which now were blood-smeared and sandy. Running a trembling hand through her short hair, she relived what she'd felt when she finally touched the seventh stone, now smooth from the many Johanssen hands that had moved it. Damian lifted the stone away, and she reached into the sudden coolness of the empty space, her fingers brushing something brittle: the deed left by Jakob for Abraham, his beloved son.

How could she ever describe the surge of strength that passed from that document to her desperate fingers? Or to express to her own children what it had meant to press those papers into the hand of their father, Noah Langston?

Damian touched her face as the policeman walked away. He managed to smile. "Well, Maia. Was that enough dancing for you?"

"No," she whispered. "If you go away, I'll have to dance alone."

"You've got Noah."

"He hates Club Pan."

"To be honest with you, so do I." They laughed, and she put her arm around him.

"Do you remember when I told you that I loved you? Well, I wasn't lying."

He sighed. "I know, Maia. But this place is crazy. Too beautiful. Too dangerous." His twinkling eyes met hers. "How could I even think about leaving?"

They looked up as Catherine climbed out of the ambulance. She smiled, gestured to Maia, and walked away.

"Looks like the coast is clear," Damian said. "Go take care of business."

Maia stood up painfully and turned toward the ambulance. Something made her stop and glance over her shoulder. A curl of smoke rose over the treetops in the distance.

Wisdom.

She stood in silence, watching as the smoke thickened into fire. And she knew that before anyone could stop it, the white-hot flames would swallow the dry-rotted planks, sweeping down the once-gracious corridors into the suites of Marie-Paule Emilie St. Severin and Solomon Johanssen. She knew the tongues would lick wildly at the traces of wallpaper imported from Paris to match the canopy of the now amputated bed. She imagined the inferno sending a lava of ash over the lush grape leaves to the hidden beach below.

And Maia knew that the mill would soon be cast in the bloodred glow of every man and woman who had labored, lived, and died on the estate. She understood that the house had survived long enough to give Wisdom back to its people. Now Wisdom wanted her to know that true wisdom is not in bricks or beams or land.

True wisdom is the love of those who came before. And the love of those who are yet to come.

ABOUT THE AUTHOR

A professor of English at Eastern Michigan University, **Heather Neff** attended the University of Paris (Sorbonne) and received her Ph.D. at the University of Zurich. Fluent in German and French, she also worked as a translator and as a language coach for film productions. Before returning to the United States, she spent two years teaching at the University of the Virgin Islands. She is also the author of *Blackgammon*.